HARD PLACES

KIRSTYN McDERMOTT

TREPIDATIO PUBLISHING

ISBN: 978-1-68510-057-5 (sc)
ISBN: 978-1-68510-058-2 (ebook)
Library of Congress Catalog Number: 2022942642

First printing edition: July 22, 2022
Printed by Trepidatio Publishing in the United States of America.
Cover Design: Mikio Murakami
Edited by Sean Leonard
Proofreading and Cover/Interior Layout by Scarlett R. Algee

Trepidatio Publishing, an imprint of JournalStone Publishing
3205 Sassafras Trail
Carbondale, Illinois 62901

Trepidatio Publishing books may be ordered through booksellers or by contacting:

JournalStone | www.journalstone.com

for Ellen and Deb
witches always and forever

CONTENTS

ONCE UPON A DARKNESS...

Kirstyn McDermott is an award-winning author and with good reason. If you're not familiar with her work, then I suggest you remedy that post-haste. Then again, you're here, aren't you? So, I guess that's taken care of.

She's a horror maven through and through, often to be found weaving together tales of fear and woe, warning and want. She's like a three-in-one Norn, an unholy trinity of observer, documenter, and editor of truths and lies and everything in between. Her tales draw in art, destruction, abuse, sex, birth, death. Love, hate and whatever the thing in the middle is that's neither one nor the other, but just as powerful. The supernatural and the mundane, and monstrosities that feel very real. And there is a red price to pay for everything: every favour or transgression, boon or ill deed.

Her work conjures all the hallmark emotions drawn from the reader by a horror story: dread, disgust, fright, awe. However, we're not talking mere shock value, hack'n'slash horror—anyone can wield a pickaxe. Not every writer can make you cry at the end. Each one of McDermott's stories contains something unexpected; something extraordinary.

She excavates the very bones of the darkness, unflinchingly knits nightmares, creates monstrous humans and inhuman monsters. Yet she's not just trying to scare you: she's making you witness our very inhumanity towards each other. She's mapping the hard places of life and heart, the paths of desire and agony. She's creating tales of vengeance and loss and, surprisingly often, hope. Redemption.

Hard Places brings together fourteen stories (thirteen reprints and one brand new tale). Stories as black as night, white as bone, red as blood. Stories that are confronting, and aching, and oddly comforting.

From the sinister notes of "She Said" to the gothic cautionary tones of "Monsters Among Us". From the surprising sorrow of "Caution: Contains Small Parts" to the body horror of "Painlessness". From the forgetful mourning of "We All Fall Down" to the bloody fairytale plaint of "Triquetra". From the unexpected liberation of "Self, Contained" to the panic of "Smile for Me". From the rime of "Frostbitten" to the heartbreaking "The Home for Broken Dolls". From the agonising love of "Cold" to the syllables of a dark future in "Mary, Mary". From the domestic violence of "Accidents Happen" to the promise of "Hard Places". You can see why McDermott is a frequent award-winner.

These stories are dark gems gleaming from the shadows; the collection is bitter and bracing as coffee and chocolate and the bite of first blood. Beware: the path is rocky and laced with thorns, but the experience is well worth the price of admission—just a tiny drop of red, after all.

Angela Slatter
Brisbane, Australia
30 September 2020
The Year of the Plague

HARD PLACES

SHE SAID

FINALLY, THE SOUND of weeping stopped and Mallory hobbled out of the bedroom on legs that seemed to grow both thinner and whiter with each new day. She clutched an empty baby food jar in one hand and stared at me through the shards of her uneven, grease-black fringe.

"You'll need this," she said. "For the clouds." And she coughed, harsh and hacking, skinny ribs hitching high with each hard-drawn breath, and spat something dark and clotted into the jar. She held it out to me with trembling, blood-scabbed fingers and I took it, trying not to look too closely at the contents.

"Mix it with indigo," she said, as she wiped a smear from her chin.

"Mal?"

"For the clouds."

"Mal, come sit with me a bit." My invitation was less than half-hearted and I hoped the relief didn't show on my face when she shook her head.

"I'm going back to bed, Josh. I'm tired." She paused at the bedroom door, scratched her thigh through the ratty black slip she'd been wearing for longer than I cared to think about. "Do some fucking good with that, yeah?"

The bedroom door closed almost soundlessly behind her. I retrieved a tube of indigo blue from the mess scattered over the floor, squeezed about half of it into the jar Mallory had given me. I started to stir, slowly, carefully, blending colour and consistency to something new, something no one had ever quite seen before, and as I did, the skin on the nape of my neck crawled. I could already see the paint moving over the canvas, wet and violent and alive, could feel it sliding beneath my brush with a purpose all its own.

I turned to the half-finished cityscape that loomed from the easel by the window: my abandoned, nameless city with its buildings left to rust and rot and ruin, left to cower and hope beneath the threat of an oncoming storm which must surely mean its end. Massive thunderheads little more than charcoal sketches because I'd been uncertain how to render them.

Until now.

As I lifted my brush to the canvas, as I felt the paint flow thick and eager from the bristles, I could see the end, how it needed to be finished. I could see the promise that glimmered beneath the threat, the mercy inherent in destruction. My hand steadied, and worked.

Hours later, I pushed my face into Mallory's neck while we fucked. Her sickly, sweat-stale smell filled my nostrils, seeped down the back of my throat; even then it was better than looking at her. Better than having to meet that weepy, red-rimmed gaze and pretend. But she knew. Turned away as soon as we were done, her fragile fetal curl on the edge of the mattress familiar as breathing now, and I knew better than to try and touch her again. Even if I'd wanted to.

Instead: "I think the painting's done, Mal. I think you'll like it."

She whispered something into her pillow.

I swallowed. "You'll see it in the morning anyway."

Minutes dragged by unanswered, the dry scrape of sandpaper on skin, and just as I was beginning to hope she'd drifted off to sleep, Mallory sighed and rolled back over to face me.

"I know about her, Josh," she said.

***

Fiona. Fee. My dirty little secret, not so much it seemed.

I'd bumped into her on the street, literally, *crashed* into her as I'd come out of the art supplies place on Greville, head down, suspiciously counting the change the emo kid behind the counter had dumped into my hand. I didn't see the girl till I'd almost knocked her over, knocked the breath from her lungs with a small, startled *oh!*, knocked the cardboard carton she'd been carrying from her hands.

Then suddenly, magically, the air was full of feathers.

Thick and white and swirling all around us as though someone had exploded an angel, or a pillow factory, and *oh!* the girl said again, softer this time, and grinned. I was grinning too, trying to apologise as I brushed the feathers from my shirt. A handful had come to rest in her hair and, without thinking, I reached out to pluck them from her ash-blonde curls.

"Sorry," I said again. "I didn't see you."

"Don't worry about it," she told me. "This was so much better than whatever he had planned for them."

She'd been dropping off the box for an artist friend who was working on some kind of an installation to do with animal liberation or sleep deprivation, she couldn't remember which. Shrugging, the girl shook a few more feathers from the hem of her brightly coloured skirt. I was fixated on her arms, so smooth and tanned, jangling with a dozen or more gaudy plastic bracelets.

"Are you an artist too?" I asked.

"Me?" A coy, sideways tilt of her head. "More an artist's assistant. Admiration and inspiration, that sort of thing."

"And plumage procurement."

"Yes, sometimes that as well." She held out a hand. "Fiona."

"Josh." Her skin was warm, her grip purposeful. She looked about ten years younger than me, maybe in her early twenties, twenty-five tops.

"Well, Josh, my fine new friend, I think you owe me a coffee." She slipped around to my side, hooked her arm through mine and flashed me another brilliant, straight-toothed smile. "At the very *least*."

I could have said no. I *should* have said no, should have gone straight back home with my tubes of paint and the new size 4 sable brush I couldn't really afford. Back home where Mallory would have been waiting with her nails gnawed down to the bloody quick and her eyes full of thunder and hurt.

Instead, I followed Fiona to her favourite café and then, later, back to her flat in St. Kilda. We sat on her sixth-floor balcony with a bottle of wine, looking out over the bay and arguing, good-naturedly, about whether or not we could discern a curve in the horizon from that height.

"So, you're a painter," she said at some stage. "Any good?"

"Sometimes yes, sometimes definitely not."

"We might have to see about that."

Evening had crept up on us; I could barely make out her features in the growing darkness. But I leaned forward anyway, and kissed her. Slowly at first and then, with her lips moving against mine, more urgently. I caught her hair in my fists, tangled those soft, pale curls around my fingers.

Finally, she pulled away. "It's not going to happen tonight, Josh."

But her smile was wolfish, and more than a little regretful, as she pulled me to my feet and sent me off, alone, into the dusk.

***

Sunk deep into the sagging centre cushion of our couch, Mallory pulled the blanket tighter around her shoulders. A scab on her left knee was flaking and she scratched at it absently.

"I don't know, Josh. There's something...missing?"

She was right, she was always right. The painting was done, done as I felt I could make it, but it wasn't finished. The abandoned city, the brooding storm-laden sky; it wasn't enough, it didn't sing, or even mutter. More and more, I felt trapped by the canvas, caught within the very oppression I'd been attempting to create.

And I couldn't help but think of the other canvas I'd been working on over the past few weeks, the one Mallory didn't know about, could never know about. The painting that currently resided high up in a certain sixth-floor St. Kilda flat. My huge, half-finished portrait of a girl with ash-gold curls and a grin coaxed straight from a fairy tale.

"I'm done, Mal." I rubbed at my forehead. "It's done."

"No, you're not, and no, it's not either."

I shook my head, refused to meet her eye. The buildings I'd painted reminded me of her somehow. Those empty, abandoned facades agape with broken windows like the teeth she'd lost just the other day. A sharp-pointed incisor and its less interesting neighbour, offered on a shaky, flattened palm for my inspection. *They just fell out, Josh. They fell right out of my mouth.* A childish wonderment in her voice, but also, unmistakably, fear.

"You'll find it," Mallory said from the couch, and sniffed.

"Find what?"

"The way through. You always do, in the end."

"Mal—" I turned, and whatever I was about to tell her slid away as I saw the runnel of blood edging sluggishly from her left nostril. Revulsion kicked at my guts. Revulsion, and something else besides. "Mal, your nose."

She frowned and sniffed again, extended the tip of her tongue above her lip to catch a smear of scarlet. "Oh." Her hands disappeared beneath the blanket for a few seconds before resurfacing with one of her empty little jars, and she leaned forward, one hand pushing her hair out of her face, the other holding the jar carefully beneath her nose. Blood seeped down the clear glass sides as I watched, pooling toxic-thick at the bottom.

And I could see the buildings in my painting bleeding like that. Just like that. Weeping bitter streams of rust and corrosion from every crack and windowless crevice. Not simply waiting for the storm, but falling before it, flowing apart at the edges. Forsaken, even by each other. *Forsaken.* The word tasted swollen and hollow and cold as I whispered it beneath my breath.

It tasted of surrender. It tasted *right*.

"Josh?" Mallory was sitting up again, the jar resting on her thigh. It held an alarming amount of blood. "Yes?" she whispered.

"I think so," I replied. "Yes."

Her lips parted in a faltering, gap-toothed smile, and as she lifted the jar up to me, its contents glinting dark and crimson in the failing afternoon light, I leaned over and kissed her, my fingers closing over hers and over the jar, and I tasted the blood still smeared beneath her nose.

And, just for now, that tasted right as well.

* * *

"Let me see." Fiona rose from the wicker chair and retrieved her robe from the floor. It was bright blue and patterned with huge orange flowers, one of which sat over her left breast like a mutant, six-fingered hand as she tied the belt loosely around her waist. I could make out the dark circle of her nipple through the flimsy, semi-sheer fabric.

"Who said the man couldn't paint?" Fiona nudged me with her elbow. "It's beautiful, Josh. Seriously, it's amazing, and I'm not just saying that cause it's me. The way you've made it so it almost *glows*, that's... Wow."

"It's not quite finished yet, I don't think."

"Really? It looks finished."

The truth was, I didn't *want* it to be finished. I didn't want to give up these mornings in Fiona's lounge room, watching the sun as it spilled through window glass and over her naked curves, watching the rise and fall of her chest deepen whenever she slipped into a doze. But the portrait was too finely balanced now, and I knew if I added so much as a single brushstroke, it could fail.

Fiona was right, it was finished.

"Hey, Josh?" She looked at me sideways and smiled. "You didn't actually need me to sit for you today, did you?"

I reached out and squeezed the back of her neck. "Not technically, no." My hand moved around to her throat; her pulse beat hard beneath my fingers. "But a little extra inspiration never hurts."

She returned my kisses at first, her tongue giving playful chase to mine. Only when my hands moved down to her hips, sliding through the folds of her robe to grasp at her soft, sunwarm flesh, did she push me away. "It's not that I don't want to," she whispered, her hand trembling on my chest. "But you know if anything were to happen, it would just get too messy. And I try to avoid mess."

"You don't think something has already happened?"

"Josh, you have...complications."

"Let me guess," I snapped. "You try to avoid those as well."

Her eyes widened. Her hand fell to her side.

"Ah, Fee." I looked at her portrait again, so full of light and grace and joy I could barely believe it had been born from my brush. And I thought of the dark, decaying cityscape I'd been working on back home, and the cycle of taut, claustrophobic abstracts before it, and before *those* the grisly series of canvases I'd started within days of meeting Mallory. The ones she'd dubbed *abattoir nouveau* without even the slightest trace of irony.

"I don't love her." I was half-surprised to have spoken the words aloud. "I did once, I think. But not now, not for a long time."

"But you need her," Fiona said. "Or you want her. Same difference."

I shook my head. "I want you."

Fiona sighed. "It's a beautiful painting, Josh. But what if that's all there is?"

"I don't believe that." My hand found hers and squeezed, gently. "There's something here, right? It's not just in my mind?"

She moved closer, rested her head on my shoulder.

"Yes," she said. "There is something."

***

Mallory made a face and dumped the half-eaten jar of baby food onto the kitchen table, pushed it towards the centre. *Apple and Banana Custard*, the label read, though it all looked like the same puréed muck to me.

"I thought that was your favourite," I mumbled around a mouthful of peanut butter sandwich.

"It tastes off," she said. "I'm not hungry anyway." She sat back and crossed her arms over her chest. The veins on her hands bulged blue against her chalk-dry skin as she clenched and unclenched her fists. Her flesh so wasted away now, I half-expected to hear the grate of bone against bone.

"You should eat," I told her.

She glared at me. "It would be easier if I just left, wouldn't it?"

"Mal—"

"It's not me you want here anymore." Her bottom lip was chapped and tattered and as she spoke the skin split a little and beaded red. "It's her."

"This is your home too, Mal. I'm not just going to throw you out."

"You can stop being so fucking noble, it doesn't suit you."

Her voice broke on the last words and I couldn't look at her. Instead, I stared at the tabletop, tracing a fingernail over the motley collection of scratches and cuts that crosshatched its surface, some made by me, others by who knows how many previous owners in kitchens past. In the corner was a little heart pierced by two arrows, complete with fletching and tiny droplets of blood suspended from the tips. Mallory had etched that with a compass point one pissed-up night, back when we still got drunk together.

"Mal, this isn't working. We can't keep pretending that it is."

A scrape of chair against lino and then she was sitting at my feet, her fingers picking along the seam of my jeans. "This is what you wanted, Josh."

"No." I swallowed, rested my hand on her head. "Not like this."

"Then it's up to you to change it," she said. "Because I can't do it for you, it's not my choice to make. It's never been my choice."

"I'm so sorry, Mal. I never meant...any of this."

Fingers digging into my thigh, she pulled herself shakily to her feet. "Stupid boy," she whispered, moving around behind me. Her arms draped over my shoulders and she pressed her lips against my neck. "You think she's gonna give you what you need? You think she's all fire and light and fucking glory be?" Her breath smelled of copper and of sour, discarded things. "You need to take into account the common fucking denominator here, my love."

I turned my head away. "Mal, don't. Please."

Mallory straightened, dragging her hands up over my cheeks and across my scalp. She was breathing heavily through her nose, like she always did when trying not to cry. "Go to her then, Josh," she said. "Just fucking go."

***

Fiona answered the door in her robe and for a single, green-tinged moment I wondered if there was someone else in the flat with her. Another painter she was sitting for, or just some guy waiting impatiently in her bed with his dick in his hands, and I couldn't for the life of me have said which possibility cut the deepest.

"What happened to you?" she asked. "There's blood on your neck."

"It's nothing." I rubbed at the place where Mallory's mouth had been less than an hour before. "It's not mine."

"Come inside." She took my hand and I followed her into the lounge room where my painting—*our* painting—still leaned upon its easel, bold and golden and luminous. And I knew I'd made the right decision.

"It's over," I said. "She hasn't left yet, but she will. It's over, Fee, it really is."

My vision blurred and something I hadn't even realised was there uncoiled itself from around my chest and slunk away, defeated. And then Fiona was kissing me, her robe falling to the floor and us falling close behind it, and for a while there was nothing in my head but light.

***

The sun was well into its daily arc by the time I got back home the next morning, but the flat was dim, all the blinds still drawn, and silent.

"Mal?" I called. "Mal, it's me."

The bedroom door was shut. I eased it open a crack and peered through to find her curled up beneath the blankets, tight little Mallory-ball so small it almost hurt to see. Almost. Still no response when I called her name again, little more than a whisper this time, so I closed the door quietly behind me.

I lifted my dead city painting from the easel and leaned it against the wall, face down. Driving home, I'd pictured myself taking to it with a Stanley knife, shredding the paint-stiff canvas to harmless strips, but now something stayed my hand. There was a certain fatalistic grandeur to its darkness that demanded further consideration. So I left it to itself for now and cleaned up all the half-curled tubes of paint and near-empty jars from the floor. I scrubbed my hands with turpentine, digging out the last stubborn dregs of black and indigo and cobalt blue which had taken up near-permanent residence beneath my nails.

Then I made toast and ate it thickly buttered over the sink and thought about the look that loosened Fiona's face when she came.

Afterwards, I went to the bedroom again and knocked on the door. "Mal, you awake yet?" No answer, not even the slightest sound of movement in the room beyond, and suddenly everything felt wrong. *Leave, just leave now and don't ever come back.* But instead, I turned the handle and pushed open the door.

Mallory was still in bed, still tightly cocooned in the blankets, and I placed a hand on the bump I guessed to be her shoulder. "Mal, baby, you okay?" She felt odd, sort of *spongy*, and then, as I shook her, she just...wasn't there.

"Fuck!" I stumbled backwards, tripping on some stray bit of crap on the floor, and coming down hard on one knee. Bolts of pain shot up my leg, and I swore again through gritted teeth, but never once took my eyes from the bed, from the newly flat and barren place where Mallory had been. Ignoring the persistent voice in my head that was telling me again to leave, *leave now, and whatever you do, don't look don't look don't look*, I reached out and grasped a corner of the blanket. Lifted, then swallowed hard, and pulled it all the way back.

Thick and viscous, like treacle or honey left too long in the fridge, the sludge that quivered and spread across the bottom sheet in a shape that too painfully resembled the form of a girl lying on her side. Mallory, the way I'd seen her all too often: curled with knees pressed against her chest, skinny arms hugging her shoulders, and her head tucked chin to breastbone like a Bronze Age sacrifice awaiting the slow mummification of peat. I didn't even realise I'd touched the stuff until my fingers were at my mouth, glistening dark and smelling of salt and iron and loss.

She tasted like nothing I could begin to describe.

I crawled to the toilet and vomited until my guts were sore and only hot strings of bile were coming up.

Back in the bedroom, I spotted the little jar I'd stumbled over before and bent to pick it up. And saw under the bed a battalion of them, tiny glass soldiers guarding a tomb. My breath caught in my throat. Mallory had been eating nothing but that shit for weeks, maybe months, but still I couldn't believe the sheer number of empties she'd managed to accumulate. I stared at the mess on the bed, then at the jar in my hand, and slowly unscrewed the lid.

It took less than half of them to contain her.

The rest of the jars I collected into two plastic shopping bags and took straight down to the bins on the street. I stripped the bed and threw the sheets away as well. Contemplated burning them, consigning the last of the stains they harboured to fire and ash, but it was hardly a practical solution and I didn't want them in the flat a second longer.

I didn't know what to do with the jars I'd filled.

Briefly I considered taking them out to the bay and throwing them into the water, or burying them somewhere up in the Dandenong ranges, deep in the earth where they'd never be found. But something inside me balked at the idea of taking them anywhere, of taking *her* anywhere, so instead I simply stowed them under the bed again. Lined them up against the wall beneath where my head would lie, making sure all the lids were screwed on tight.

I had no idea whether or not she would spoil.

* * *

It wasn't the light. My flat was dim, sure, the new compact fluorescents overly harsh, but the painting could have been standing beneath the brightest of summer suns and it wouldn't have made the slightest difference.

It wasn't the light; it was what the light exposed.

I rubbed hard at my forehead, wondering how the fuck I could've ever believed Fiona's portrait to hold any real worth at all. Simplistic and garish, it had nothing to say beyond the most clichéd commentary on beauty and the female form, nothing that hadn't already been said by the likes of Klimt and Modigliani—decades earlier and with infinitely greater eloquence. I could imagine prints being sold by the truckload out of suburban shopping malls, disconnected housewives only too delighted to find something pretty and cheerful and just a little bit risqué. Something that didn't clash with their new designer lounge suite.

At best, the painting was vacuous; at worst, utterly mute.

I felt sick.

"Josh?" Fiona called from the bedroom. "You're sure she doesn't want any of this stuff? She's not coming back for it?"

"Just bag it all," I told her. "She's not coming back."

My ruined city reproached me from its place against the wall, and rightfully so. For all its flaws, it at least possessed a tongue.

"How weird would it be if I hung onto this?" Fiona asked from behind me. "Most of her things are kind of dire, but this suits me, don't you reckon?"

I turned, and my throat tightened. I remembered that dress. The bright red fabric dotted with tiny white flowers, the deeply scooped neckline and that row of buttons which ran all the way up the front and were damn near impossible to undo in a hurry. How long had it been since I'd seen that dress, seen Mallory in it?

"Where'd you get that?" I asked.

"In the wardrobe, shoved behind everything else." Fiona twirled and the skirt flounced around her bare thighs. It fitted her curves perfectly and I seemed to remember it sitting the exact same way on Mallory once. I tried to picture how she looked when we'd first got together, before she lost all the weight, back when there was something beneath her skin beyond the bitter jut of bone.

I couldn't.

"So, too weird?" Fiona asked.

"It's a bit weird," I told her. "But keep it, if you want."

She crossed the room, put her arms around my waist, and pressed her cheek against my shoulder. "I don't have to move right in," she said. "You know, if it's too soon. I can find another place." The lease was up on her apartment and her arsehole landlord had decided to double the rent. It'd been my suggestion that she come live with me; anything else just seemed like delaying the inevitable.

"I want you to be here, Fee." I ruffled her hair. Dark roots were starting to push up through the pale blonde, and I tried to imagine how Fiona would look if she ever quit the peroxide habit.

The skin on the back of my neck prickled. I could see how the painting could be saved; moreover, I could *feel* it deep in my guts, the *rightness* of it. The undercurrent of darkness that needed to sit just beneath the surface, the hint of sordid truth behind the beautiful lie that we all want so desperately to believe. But I had to be subtle with it, sound a barely discernible note of unease, just enough to knock the portrait off kilter. Shadows and hollows and the sly insinuation of decay.

Of defilement.

"Ow, Josh, that hurts!" Fiona was struggling in my hands, my fingers digging deep into the soft flesh of her upper arms. I released my grip, watched its ghosts bloom angry and scarlet on her skin.

"Shit, Fee, I'm sorry. I didn't even realise."

"It's okay." She rubbed at the places I'd been holding her. "Where'd you go just now?"

"Nowhere, just thinking." I kissed the top of her head, still thinking. About how to fix the painting, and about the jars that waited beneath my bed. I could see how that dark opalescence would mix with the airy golden tones of Fiona's portrait, how it would give them texture and weight. How it would make them real.

My fingers flexed, ached for a paintbrush.

"I'm going to make chai," Fiona said. "You want some?"

"Hmm? Yeah, sure." My eyes followed the sway of her hips as she strolled towards the kitchen. Just as she reached the doorway, I called her name and she half-turned, her face bright and open and expectant.

"You look good in that dress," I told her.

Fiona smiled. "Thanks," she said.

I listened to the safe, domestic sounds of tea-making and wondered how long the jars would last, how many more canvases Mallory could permeate before she was finally gone. Already, my brain was beginning to clutter and swarm with new visions, new ideas, and I got down on my knees to retrieve my sketchbook from where it had slid beneath the couch, a stub of charcoal marking a new page. But my hand was too cautious, too careful, its first little sketch so timid and needy. Frustrated, I flipped the page.

You'll find it, Josh. You always do, in the end.

I nodded. Closed my eyes and tried to recall the sharp, pinched lines of Mallory's body, the lost and broken expression on her face. I'd never drawn her, not once, which seemed a strange thing. And now she was too scattered, too faded, and I couldn't get the pieces to stay together.

Josh?

"I'm sorry, baby," I whispered.

Josh.

"I'm so sorry."

"Josh!"

My eyes snapped open. "Fee?" I lurched to my feet and half-ran, half-stumbled into the kitchen where Fiona was standing over the sink, both hands pressed to her face. "Fee, what's wrong?"

"My nose." She sniffed, loud and wet and awful, as blood started to seep through her fingers. "I need a tissue."

There was more chance of finding a silk handkerchief in this place, so I snatched up a tea towel instead. She waved it away, protesting about stains, but I shook my head—"It doesn't matter, Fee"—and held it gently to her nose. Blood soaked through the cloth.

"Fuck. Here, sit down." I guided her to a chair. "Keep your head back."

It took almost five minutes for the bleeding to stop completely. Half a roll of toilet paper littered the table and floor, all of it bright with crimson blotches. Kitchen as surgical ward, triage tent, autopsy room, with Fiona hunched pale and shaky in the centre, one hand clutched sweaty in mine.

"It must be the dry weather," she said at last.

I nodded, unable to look away from the patterns made by the blood.

"I think I need to lie down," she said.

"Good idea."

I helped her into bed, and she asked me to sit with her for a while, so I did. Stroking her hair and contemplating the mess in the kitchen, all that blood-soaked paper, and how wrong it seemed to simply throw it away.

Just when I thought she had fallen asleep, Fiona slid a hand from beneath the sheet and squeezed my thigh. "You still want me here, don't you, Josh?"

"Of course." A dry crust of blood stained her upper lip, and I licked my thumb, rubbed most of it away. "I need you, Fee." And she smiled, or nearly did. Weary little shadow of a smile that barely creased the corners of her mouth, and I didn't think I'd ever seen anyone look so fragile. Not even Mallory.

"That's good," she said. "That's perfect."

MONSTERS AMONG US

"HEY, YOU LITTLE cockatrice, what are *you* doing?"

The tallest girl in the group, eyes lined immaculate and plum-dark lips pouting and glossy and smooth, staring across at Fledge who shadows the wall on the opposite side of the train station foyer, trying to be noticed with being too noticeable. Fledge shrugs off the question, eyes flicking shy to her book, precious Poppy Z. Brite paperback with at least one crease on each corner from being jostled around in her schoolbag all week. Unable to focus on the print any longer, breath held dizzy-anxious in her throat as, "Hey, babygoth," one of the others calls out, "come over here, why don't you?"

So she does, deliberate slow to pick up her bag, sling it over her shoulder, hoping her make-up hasn't smudged overly much in the heat. Melbourne summer, not anywhere near as sticky as Brisbane but still not the kind of weather to favour a goth. Runnel of perspiration down her spine as she moves away from the wall, one hand still holding her book and the other sweat-clenched in the black lace of her skirt, bought just yesterday at Gown of Thorns, forty-three dollars of her own money and the rest appropriated from her father's wallet. Seven circles of hell to pay if it's missed, but she'd needed it, needs the skirt to catch their attention, this night-clad flock of punks and goths and slinky-skinned hybrids who clutter the entrance to Flinders Street Station of an early evening, all cynical laughter and preening, pretending indifference to the gaze of all who pass them by.

Their own gaze fastened now upon her as she shuffles across the foyer, collective inscrutable smirk which could mean anything, and Fledge swallows hard, gnaws at the waxy-tattered skin of her lip until one of the group steps forward half a pace and grins: "Salutations." A girl with bottle-black hair creeping back to auburn at the roots, torn fishnet gloves and an impressive collection of rings, moving aside just enough to admit Fledge into the circle. "You're new."

Not really a question, but Fledge answers it anyway, and one of the boys snorts loudly when he finds out where she's from—

"BrisVegas! No one actually *lives* in BrisVegas!"—but the tall girl, the one who'd first called out to her, just smiles, asks if she has a name. *Fledge*, managing not to stutter as she gives it, and even so that same boy begins to laugh, acne-riddled cheeks blooming bright through the greasepaint, his clumsy Crow mask melting at the edges. Nasty-rude laugh, wanting to know what sort of shit her parents were on when they came up with *that*, and could he please get some of the same, and the tall girl turns to him, mouth pressed to a taut black line.

"You need to learn when to keep it closed." Shiver of winter in her teal-green eyes, almost as chill as the tone in her voice. "*Evelyn.*"

The entire tribe laughing in response, brassy faux-shocked guffaws as though they've not heard *that* before, and maybe some of them haven't. The boy himself burning crimson and Fledge sees that there are two ways this can go, mean or jovial, and he chooses mean. "It's fucking *Byron*, okay? I've fucking told you to call me that a thousand fucking times."

The tall girl blinks at him. "Okay, Fucking Byron. We'll all try really, truly hard to remember that from now on."

More laughter from the others, loud and pretty much good-natured—*we're-laughing-with-you-not-at-you* kind of giggles, and Fledge has known enough of both to tell the difference. But the boy just pulls up the hood on his cloak, his soft-muttered reply lost in black velvet, and the tall girl rolls her eyes at Fledge, extends a slim and pale hand.

"Welcome to Melbourne, girly-girl. I'm Elise."

* * *

"Is his name really Evelyn?"

Elise smiles, shakes up the bottle of nail polish before unscrewing the lid.

"Absolutely," she says. "Now hold these little piggies still for me." And she begins to paint Fledge's toenails with the scummy green polish, dull rancid colour like bathroom mould that flashes a brilliant purple in just the right light, at just the right angle. Pretty as an oil slick, Fledge thinks, waving her still-wet fingernails before her face and humming along to the Nick Cave CD that plays on Elise's stereo.

"Weird name for a guy."

"What can I tell you? His olds are probably literature freaks."

Fledge says nothing, not understanding, not wanting the other girl to know she doesn't understand, but Elise just nods her head towards the bookshelf beside them. "Third shelf from the bottom, over to the right." Fledge's hand wavering uncertain over the volumes and *back a bit,* Elise directs, *a little more, little more,* and *there you go:* slim grey spine with *The Loved One* stamped bold in black but the author's name so faded she has to squint to make it out: Evelyn Waugh.

"Oh." Fledge pulls the little book free from the shelf. Four wooden coffins on the cover, three of them standing upright and the third bent in two places as though its intended occupant were to be buried sitting down, and she grins at the thought of that, traces a fingernail over the green iron railing in the foreground. "Weird picture."

Elise smiles. "It's pretty famous, that painting. René Magritte."

She has a book about him as well. So many books, in fact, more than Fledge has seen anywhere outside a public library, twin rosewood bookcases double-stacked to overflowing and more volumes heaped precariously on the floor, the desk, every flat and available surface. And when she finally leaves, it's with a pile of them cradled in her arms, precious-heavy papoose wrapped in a black plastic bag that Elise rummaged out from under the bed. Paperback novels for the most part, expensive US imports that Fledge could never have hoped to find here, but also some poetry—Milton and Blake and Baudelaire—and *The Complete Books of Charles Fort,* and "Take as long as you want," Elise tells her at the door, "I know you'll be careful with them."

Green eyes smiling bright as her neat white teeth, so white they're almost blue, and Fledge is grinning too, stupid puppy-dog grin, but she can't seem to help it, Lou Reed crooning soft in the background now

shiny shiny shiny boots of leather
whiplash girl-child in the dark

and for one gut-fluttery moment she thinks Elise might be about to lean over and kiss her, thinks that maybe she wouldn't mind so very much if she did.

But no, just that smile for Fledge to take away with her into the night, stark retina afterburn sweeter than the tears spilled later, much later in the dark and silence long after her parents had retreated to bed. Tears and girl-sweat and teeth biting hard on her pillow, spit-slicked fingers moving to their own urgent rhythms, and it's not Sean who floats behind her eyes this time, pretty-boy Sean who won't have spared her a second thought once she left Brisbane, brutal truth be told. Not him, nor any of the other boys around whom her fantasies have spun till now.

Not any *boy* at all.

* * *

"*We therefore never find in any true story that any man ever became a woman, because Nature tends always toward what is most perfect and not, on the contrary, to perform in such a way that what is perfect should become imperfect.* What a twat." Elise, laughing as she reads aloud from her new-bought prize, slim grey paperback, $63.95 at Borders and that's more money than Fledge could ever think of spending on a single book, but Elise is pretty rich, she's beginning to see. Rich and with parents who don't seem to care how she spends her money, or her time, and that makes her doubly so.

"How old is that thing again?" Sasha J, not looking up from the *Marie Claire* she'd swiped from the coffee table downstairs, thin black felt-tip in her hand and half the male models now sporting elaborate gothic eyeliner and ink-fat lips.

Sixteenth century, Elise tells her, barely a pause for breath before flipping forward to relate how some woman in 1494 still-birthed a child with a live snake growing from its back and—"Listen, it gets better"—the snake was actually *eating the dead baby* when it came out. There's a picture too, old-fashioned hand-drawn sketch with the child looking more like a full-grown man, and everyone *eeews* and *ohhhs* and makes gleeful retching sounds except for Byron who just rolls his kohl-lined eyes and tells them all to grow up, as if that could have ever happened. *As if.*

Byron, pissed because it was Fledge who'd found the book that afternoon, a recent translation of some obscure French medical treatise: *On Monsters and Marvels*, goat-faced mermaid on the front cover, complete with horns and sag-soft breasts, and instantly she'd known Elise would love it. Freak-obsessed Elise, accepting the offering with enormous delight: "Ambroise Paré! Oh, I have to have *this*." But the glitter-gloss press of her lips so brief, fake cherry taste the simple flavour of gratitude, and Fledge knew better than to hope for anything much from this; girls kiss girls all the time.

Now, shy corner slump with a strand of hair wound tight around her index finger, purple-cold tip so numb she can't even feel her thumbnail digging in. Listening to Elise read and watching the others: Sasha J working on a moustache and sleek little goatee for Milla

Jovovich who scrubs up surprisingly well in drag; Nikki and Aaron, coupling Siamese on the end of the bed, heads bowed over a Tarot spread and fish-pale hands turning card after card as they smile and nod, fingers touching fingers in a secret silent language all their own; and, of course, Byron.

Byron, pretending not to watch her pretending not to watch him, and both of them pretending their eyes aren't drawn again and again to Elise.

Elise, who abruptly closes her book and drops it to the floor. "Children, do you believe in fairies?" Tongue darting pink and wet between her teeth and now she has everyone's attention; even Sasha J has put down her pen, and Byron grins and says, "Only if they're green."

A ritual, obvious and oft-repeated, with Fledge left to shiver on the outer.

Nikki, wriggling belly-wise beneath the bed, "Are you out of sugar cubes?" before a muffled sneeze. "No, wait. Got them." It wouldn't hurt Elise to vacuum under there once in a while, she says, coming back out with a cardboard box in one hand and a ziplock bag of small white lumps in the other. Dustbunnies in her fringe for Aaron to pluck away, blow away—"Make a wish, Nik-Nak"—the two of them giggling like pre-schoolers flush with dandelion seeds.

Fledge shuffles closer. "What's in the box?"

"Gwyneth Paltrow's pretty head," Byron sneers, mock punch to her shoulder too hard for friendly, and Elise seems to notice this, frowns but says not a word, just takes the box from Nikki and reaches inside.

"*La Fée Verte*," she says. "The Green Fairy." Tall, slender-necked bottle in her hands, flip-top lid and maybe a quarter filled with glassy emerald liquid. No label, but some kind of alcohol, Fledge guesses, and she's right: absinthe, Elise informs her with a slanted smile; special homemade blend distilled right here in Melbourne and unquestionably superior to anything found this side of Paris.

"You make it yourself?" Fledge asks, and Elise shakes her head, no, but she's on terms with someone who does. *On terms*. Strange turn of phrase, heavy with implications Fledge doesn't really want to think about, and so she doesn't, just sits wordless and watchful as Elise retrieves six cut-crystal glasses from the box, lines them up on the floor at her feet. An inch or so of absinthe in each followed by a sugar cube and then Sasha J—sock-clad feet so silent, Fledge hadn't even noticed she'd been gone—is back with a large bottle of spring water from the kitchen fridge.

"You're not meant to do it this way," Elise says. Lifts her eyes to the ceiling and explains that what you're *meant* to do, if you want to get all French and authentic about it, is sit the cube on a special sort of slotted spoon and drip the water slowly over it so that sugar melts and mixes on the way down—but that takes a minute short of forever and it never dissolves properly anyway and besides, this way, *her* way, you get to suck on what's left of the sugar cube later, sweet absinthe-drenched candy better than anything Willy Wonka could have come up with.

"Better than a tequila worm," Aaron chips in, and, "As if you'd even know," snaps Byron back at him, and Elise just snorts, begins to pour the water slowly, drop by drop at first, then a thin dawdling stream, into the first glass. Where it clouds to a murky yellowish green, stormwater green steeped in black liquorice to judge by the smell, and "See that," Elise says. "If it doesn't do that, there's no wormwood and all you have is a pretty expensive bottle of drain cleaner."

Fledge nods as though this is something she already knows.

Absinthe. The word only barely familiar to her—scant throwaway references in the novels she likes to read, decadent Gothic horror tales for which she'd trolled insatiably among the shelves of second-hand bookshops until meeting Elise, and Elise's library—and what she does know muddled together from hint and insinuation: she'd thought the drink was illegal now; thought the wormwood made it poison.

And maybe this is true. Sniffing tentative at her glass before lifting it to meet the others, harsh crystal *chink* and some of the absinthe sloshing onto her hand, its sharp liquorice breath twisting nauseous in her guts and she hasn't had so much as a sip, not sure that she even wants to, and if it were just her and Elise she might have begged off. But Byron staring straight at her, half-drunk glass cradled smug in his hand, as he licks his lips, "What's the matter, babygoth? Forget your permission slip?"

Middle finger at half-mast, half-hearted *fuck you* because he deserves little better, as Fledge sucks a small and hesitant mouthful through her teeth, tries to take another but already her throat is closing up, going for the gag reflex, and it's all she can do to keep the first swallow down. Ghastly stuff, awful; liquorice never a favourite and this is liquorice gone rabid, liquorice that has danced with the salamander and learnt to breathe its fire.

"I don't think I can drink this," she tells Elise, "I—I don't really like it."

Mock-horror gasp from Nikki, palms slapping flat to her flushwarm cheeks, and Aaron wide-eyed beside her, shaking his head. "Don't say that! Every time you say that a green fairy *dies!*" But Elise just smiles, wicked-soft smile that reaches low down into Fledge's belly and tugs, then crawls across the floor towards her. Awkward three-limbed shuffle with glass held aloft and unspilled, some weird kind of grace in each and every movement and Fledge can't look away.

"*La Fée Verte* can be difficult to get along with at first," Elise says. "Maybe if the two of you were properly introduced..." Small sip of her drink before drawing Fledge close, hands so smooth and cold but her lips warm as they press against Fledge's own, their gentle insistence useless to deny. and is it possible that this time the absinthe *is* different? Warmer of course, warm from Elise, from being inside Elise, but also the taste: spicier somehow, more forgiving of her virgin palate, and this time she swallows easily.

And Elise keeps kissing her.

She's only vaguely aware of the whistles and whooping noises that Nikki and Aaron are making in the background, of Sasha J telling them to either get a room or share it around, for crying out loud. Because this is *Elise's* tongue so slippery-eager in her mouth, *Elise's* fingers that flutter and scratch like hungry birds at her throat, and now this is *Elise's* breath tickling her ear, *Elise's* absinthe-edged whisper: "Can you stay over tonight, do you think? After the others go?"

Fledge nods, too dizzy to hunt down words of her own, just nods and grins like an idiot as Elise squeezes her hand. And it doesn't matter that Byron is glaring daggers at her from the other side of the room, knuckles flexed psychotic-white around his glass as though dreaming it were her neck.

Because when girls kiss girls like *that*, it's never just to say thank you.

* * *

Between the six of them, the absinthe had been easily finished off. Not really enough for each to have a third glass, even after Sasha J demurred, curling foetal round a pillow with fists tucked beneath her chin, muttery fitful doze lasting until Aaron's older brother had finally rocked up to take everyone home. "Christ up a duck," leather boot nudging the girl's hip hard enough to bruise, and, "You kids better brush your teeth or something," he'd said. "Your folks'll fucking freak, they get a whiff of that shit."

Now, flat on her back on the bed, Fledge stares at the ceiling, her eyes following patterns in the ornate plaster mouldings. Flowers and vines and fat-bellied fruit, bony dead-white shapes, and if this was her bedroom she would paint them all in luscious colour, living colour; decides to mention this idea to Elise who's taking a piss across the hall, who's been doing that for quite some time now, it seems.

"You fallen in, or what?" No answer to that, so maybe she didn't say it out loud after all, maybe just thought it and maybe Elise heard anyway; she'll find out soon enough. There's been no absinthe-spun visions for Fledge, no fay visitations; just an incredible heat seeping through her entire body, honey-thick and equally lethargic, a tingly sensation in her fingertips and the hard-fought urge to kiss everybody in the room, even Byron.

To find out if they knew what she knew.

"What do you know?" Elise kneeling beside her now, arms twisted awkward behind her own back, and Fledge grins, "I forget," and reaches out, suddenly starved for the warm, damp hollows of the other girl's neck.

But Elise flinches away. "Wait," she says, "I need to show you something." And then she's undoing her dress, black lace peeling down over shoulders so pale they might never have known sunlight, black satin slip underneath, and after the slightest hesitation this comes off as well. Naked now apart from briefs that might as well not be there for all the coverage they fail to offer, and Fledge's breath catches hard in her throat, and she wonders if she mightn't be hallucinating after all.

Not the marble-smooth skin anticipated for so long, but a complication of whorls and deep-etched grooves that cover most of Elise's torso, flowing across ribs and the soft curve of her belly, over her left hip and partway down her thigh. Curling round her back as well, and now Fledge knows why she's never seen Elise in the cutaway tops so beloved by Nikki and Sasha J, no low-slung skirts or anything which might have exposed this scarred and fractured flesh to the scrutinising world, and, "I want to touch it," she whispers, and Elise slowly nods.

Hot living skin that shifts over the bones beneath, moves with each breath its owner draws, and how ridiculous that Fledge could have expected otherwise, but still: a surprise, her sharp involuntary gasp causing Elise to flinch again, and, "Sorry," she says, fingers tracing over fissures and flesh-forged spirals, eyelids fluttering shut—*all the better to feel you with, my dear*—hyperaware of the blood that pulses beneath her touch, of her own blood burning potent as lava in her veins.

Before Elise grasps her gently by the wrists, pulls her away, and, "It's not too bad, is it?" she asks, voice trembly hoarse. "Not too hideous?"

Fledge wants to laugh, the very idea so utterly absurd. Instead, she bends to kiss one of the more intricate whorls, one that spirals outwards from navel to hip, her tongue daring to flick at its sharp-raised edges, before lifting her face to meet Elise's uncertain emerald gaze.

"I think it's the most beautiful thing I've ever seen."

Then immediately thinks: *No, I lied.* Because the fat teary smile that breaks sudden and strong over Elise's face, the smile that only Fledge will ever get to see, *that* leaves all else for dead.

* * *

Her mind almost made up to buy the ring, delicate silver bird skull so precise it might have been cast from life, or rather from death, when a movement in the glass catches her eye. Reflected black beetle scuttle too familiar to ignore, and she turns from the shop window to see Elise pacing swiftly along the footpath opposite, heading towards Flinders Street. Hours early but then so is Fledge, ditching school in favour of a day alone in the city and the hope of finding a birthday gift for Elise, something special, unique, like this ring which will look so cool on those slim pale fingers.

And for which she can always come back.

Dodging between trams as she crosses the street, Elise already half a block ahead, and Fledge would have called out—*Hey, Lise, wait up*—but the words die in her throat. Odd, the way the other girl moves: shoulders hunched beneath a backpack and hands stuffed deep in coat pockets; her gaze fixed stolid to the ground, to the hurried march of her black-booted feet. Furtive. Stealthy. Clandestine. All those things amounting simply to this: Elise does not wish to be seen.

So, of course, Fledge follows her.

Not to the station where they'd arranged to meet with the others later, but through the mess of alleys and dodgy arcades that cut between and across the main city grid, and twice Fledge almost loses sight of her quarry in the pressing lunchtime crowd, twice has to run to catch up, heart beating hard against her ribs, only hoping that Elise won't pick this moment to glance over her shoulder. Until finally: rounding one last corner to spot her slipping into a doorway not twenty metres down the lane, dim little shopfront with a sign that Fledge can't make out from this angle, and she pauses a moment for breath, and to marshal her thoughts.

Hey, Lise, what are you doing here?

Must be fate, running into each other like this.

Just happened to be going by, freaky coincidence or what?

Shaking her head, nothing in there that wouldn't come off like the most desperate Hollywood drivel, and why was she so nervous anyway? Just walk on past, girlie-girl, look in the window and smile. It's only Elise in there.

Except that it isn't.

Isn't anyone, just an empty shop. Humbug Wine & Spirits, all the lights switched off and a handwritten note clinging to the inside of the plate glass door—*Sorry, back in 15 minutes*—faded tattery note that's been used several times before, to judge by the strips of old yellowed tape stuck to its edges. Fledge with her nose pressed against the window, nothing to see beyond shelves and shelves of bottles and a well-illuminated fridge hugging the back wall. No movement whatsoever, and the door handle merely rattling in her grasp, refusing to turn.

But she'd seen Elise go in there. She *had.*

Fledge squints through the glass, thinks that she can make out another opening at the rear of shop, thick dark curtain hanging down in place of a door and okay, so that's where they've gone, Elise and whoever else was here when she came in. A back room of some sort, storeroom maybe, and okay, fine: they'll have to come out some time. Fifteen minutes, if handwritten notes can be believed, and she slumps down in the doorway of the shopfront opposite. *Tobacconist,* its faded sign says, and *Keys Cut While You Wait,* but not anymore: the premises now vacant, home only to broken fittings and a sizeable accumulation of mail that's been shoved resolutely beneath the door. Like most of the shops here, she realises. One-way alley leading to nothing but a grey metal door in a brick wall, fire exit or service access to whichever office building it might be that provides the dead end to this place, and in the corner a big yellow industrial skip, graffiti-proud squat and the smell of rancid, rotting food.

"Gross," Fledge mutters, checking her watch. Fifteen minutes will give them till half past one, give or take, and she folds her arms across her chest, glares at the note on the bottle shop door as though daring it to argue.

Fifteen minutes.

* * *

Except it's more like fifty by the time the curtain shifts and Elise comes shuffling out of the dark towards the front of the shop. Head down as she unlocks the front door and steps through, careful to close it behind her, and she doesn't notice Fledge until the girl stands up right in front of her, hands angry on hips but her face significantly less so, and she knows it. Anger long since seeped away, and for the last twenty minutes there's only been nail-bitten worry and fear.

"Elise..." No words, just harsh held-back tears to burn away the worst offerings of her imagination—scenes of Elise lying naked and broken, bleeding onto a dust-layered floor; vile thoughts of what might have been done to her, of what in all this time Fledge had *allowed* to be done to her—and all she wants to do is hug her, hold her, assure herself that none of it is true.

But Elise stumbles back a pace, mascara-smudged eyes wide with shock. "What the fuck are you doing here? Spying?" Venomous *sotto voce* only a serpent could match, and Fledge shrinks away, tries to explain how she'd seen her before up on Swanston Street, had followed but wasn't able to catch up in time, and that was all. "I wasn't *spying* on you," she says, and must be making some kind of sense because Elise doesn't seem upset anymore, just very, very tired.

"Hey, are you okay?" Fledge asks. "You don't look so good."

Elise rubs at her forehead with the back of one hand and, "Yeah," she agrees, "I think I'll go home and crash for a bit. Tell the guys for me?" And of course she will, of course, if that's what Elise wants, but maybe Fledge should go home with her first, make sure she gets there all right and doesn't end up collapsed in a gutter somewhere because, in all seriousness, that looks like a distinct possibility right now.

Elise already shaking her head, thanks but no thanks, and, "Come on," she says, "we shouldn't be hanging around out here." Black oversized backpack hitching high on her shoulders, heavy clank of glass on glass sounding from within, and she winks at Fledge, grabs her by the elbow. "I'm not exactly legal at the moment." Alcohol for her party this weekend, not-so-sweet sixteen at last, and Fledge *is* coming, isn't she?

"Of course, wild horses and all that."

"Cool." And if she appears to be moving more stiffly now, favouring her right side a little perhaps, then who is Fledge to notice, much less pass comment on it? So, silent as she follows Elise from the alley, one final glance back over her shoulder towards Humbug Wine & Spirits, and surely it's just some tricksy reflection, a subtle warp in the glass and her imagination still stuck on hyperdrive; surely that's all it is.

Not a face that stirs in the window: impossible ash-white face too long, too thin for human, withdrawing assassin-smug into the dark.

* * *

He has her trapped beside the fridge, lanky-tall boy with Adam's apple big as a golf-ball, excitable flesh-pink lump that travels the entire length of his throat as he speaks, and for some daft reason Fledge can't take her eyes off it. Maybe cause it's the least offensive thing going for him, a point of morbid fascination more palatable than the acne sprouting angry-red across his cheeks and forehead, the dandruff riding the spikes of his greasy goth-punk hair. Or maybe she's just too fucked-up already—cheap yellow chartreuse, an even nastier red wine—and it's easier simply to stand here and listen to him babble on endlessly about Funeral for a Friend and My Chemical Romance than try to figure out a means of escape.

Until: "Piss off, dickbreath." Sasha J, all of five foot in platform boots, slipping between them with her middle finger thrust straight and narrow in his face. "You haven't got a prayer in pandemonium." Waiting until the boy has retreated, sullen scowl and something that sounds like *fucking dykes* muttered beneath his breath, then turning to take Fledge's hand. Elise is upstairs, she whispers. The Green Fairy too, and neither lady likes to be kept waiting for long.

Yet another hateful glare from Byron who's been stagging it across the room all night, impossible for him to have overheard, but still he knows, knows enough to tell when his presence is no longer welcome at court. Fledge tosses him a smile, victorious little smirk sweeter than absinthe-soaked sugar and just as vicious.

Suffer, Evelyn. She chose me.

Urgent, impatient tug on her hand: "Come on, girl. Her majesty awaits." There's been a private audience already for Sasha J, to judge by the bright manic glitter in her eyes, and Fledge nods, follows her through the hall and up the cream carpeted stairs. Cigarette butts and wet-dark stains to point the way, Hansel and Gretel gone squalid suburban, and behind them the sound of breaking glass.

"I think your house is being trashed," she tells Elise when they reach the bedroom. Elise, who moves not an inch from her position on the bed—cross-legged, a chill glass of absinthe in each upraised hand—just shrugs and says that her parents will see to it when they get back tomorrow night.

"Won't they be pissed?"

Another shrug, then: "Come here, beautiful girl. Drink with me."

Blood rushing hot to her face, Fledge turns to find Sasha J already gone, door closed silent and shrewd in her wake, and it's just herself and Elise left in the room. She grins, wobbles to the bed and sinks down, eyes closed against the sudden spin of the ceiling. Something cold splashing on her cheek, liquorice smell and the taste of it in her half-open mouth and, "Hey, you're spilling it," Elise laughs, and bends to kiss her.

Liquorice lips, liquorice tongue sliding insistent against her own.

Until: "I don't think I can drink anymore," Fledge says at last. "I'm already pretty wasted."

Elise pretends to pout, but only for the briefest moment before placing the glasses down on the bedside table and reaching out her arms: "Come here then; kiss me some more." And to this command Fledge happily acquiesces, more than happily, presses herself hungry-lithe to the other girl's body, so close she can feel their hearts beating against one another, two rib-caged creatures turned frantic in expectation of release. Her hands move slower, as always, seeking out the small smooth buttons hidden within the fabric of Elise's dress, vintage Victorian mourning gown all silk and stiffened black lace.

Finding the buttons, undoing them. One by one by one.

Until, as always, those glorious scars are revealed, laid bare to the eager ministrations of her fingers and her tongue. Their origin a mystery still—*Had she been burnt? By fire maybe? Hot oil left careless on the stove for childish fingers to grasp? Or was acid the culprit, spilled by accident or with a slit-eyed malice too deliberate and awful to think about?*—all these questions asked and answered with non-committal shrugs and nods, sure, whatever you want to think, babygirl, and so, no more. Elise will tell her when she is ready or else never, though

Fledge finds she no longer cares very much. The disfigured flesh seeming so intrinsic now, she wouldn't be surprised to find that Elise had been born that way; would perhaps be disappointed to learn otherwise.

Feathersoft, her fingertips chase patterns through the whorls and intricate skin-spun spirals that span Elise's hip, her belly, her thigh. Patterns that, as always, seem to have shifted in configuration from the last time, seem to have spread outwards, intent on the colonisation of newer, blander flesh. An alteration too subtle for absolute certainty, especially in this booze-addled frame of mind, and, "Do they move?" she asks. "I think they move."

Elise just sighs, wispy-happy little sigh that catches right at the centre of Fledge's chest. "Silly girl. You say that every time."

Her answer, not anything of the sort. As always.

***

The dregs of cappuccino number three mud-cold in the cup and Fledge sorting through what's left of her change to see if she has enough for a fourth, because they won't let her sit here *gratis* for much longer, book open in hand and gaze flicking constantly to the window, to the footpath beyond and the alley yawning opposite, the way she has been all morning. Lunchtime fast approaching and the waitress already tossing pointed, hard-eyed glances in her direction: someone else could be at that table she's hogging, someone willing to pay for more than just coffee.

And then Elise walks past.

Those familiar harried steps, head down and shoulders hunched, furtive glance about her as she turns down the alley, another before she slips into a shop halfway along. *The* shop. Humbug Wine & Spirits.

Fledge sits motionless, forces herself to count to one hundred before moving. She knew it, had known it ever since the phone call last night, Elise all evasive and unwilling to make plans for day or night: *Too much stuff to do, babygirl* and *You'd just be bored if you came with* and *I'll call you Sunday, yeah?*

Yeah, right. Fledge knowing exactly where she would be going, wanting to know far more besides. Her late-night thoughts too obsessive of late, dreams foul with absinthe, with questions unasked and unanswered. What does Elise offer in exchange for all those pretty emerald bottles so greedily emptied, so faithfully replenished? What favours are bestowed, what liberties permitted? Does he touch her, the Humbug Man? Place his hands on her scars? Kiss them with lean, reptilian lips as he crushes her to his chest, invades her body in ways that Fledge never can?

Does she sigh for him and stroke his thinning hair?

Does she like it?

Messy-warm swill in her guts as Fledge leaves the café, jealousy and caffeine and nauseous anticipation, one hand fishing about in her bag for the ball-peen hammer she'd filched from the kitchen drawer that morning. Smart and shiny little tool used by her mother for the driving of picture hooks into walls, to be used now by Fledge for the smashing of glass. One small hole in the door, just enough to thrust through her hand and flick the lock, and she'd have to be quick about it.

Smash. Flick. Open. Run.

Between the shelves. To the back room. Gotcha!

Twenty steps from the shop, now ten, heart pounding so loud the whole world can guess her intention, and is she really going to do this? Is she—

No. Not necessary, not with all the lights still on and the door swinging open beneath her sweat-damp palm, not with a skinny, blonde-haired woman perched imposingly behind the counter, cheap ballpoint pen in hand and newspaper spread open to the crosswords. A woman who spares but the merest glance for Fledge, snorts and shakes her head: "Sorry, love. Not if the devil himself has faked your ID."

But at the rear of the shop, the curtain hangs dark as clotted blood, heavy dust-worn velvet rippling like the flanks of some shallow-breathed beast until Fledge closes the door behind her, cutting off the breeze. "I don't want to buy anything," she improvises. "Elise asked me to come here, to meet her here."

The woman looks up, grey eyes drawn scalpel-sharp. "Elise?"

Fledge nods, trying not to swallow or drop her gaze, just a single dip of her head, righteous-smug with teeth clenched tight against the anxious babble of words that threatens to spill uselessly, ruinously forth.

"Mouth bigger than her brain, that girl," the woman says at last, points to a wooden stepladder squatting in the far corner of the shop: Fledge can sit herself down on that, can wait right there for Elise to finish up, and there had better not be another peep out of her until then.

And Fledge nods again, turns and drags her feet so very slow across the floor until she hears it, the faint newsprint scratch of a crossword puzzle resumed which means it's now or never, and she breaks, bag slipping to the floor as she makes a dash for the back of the shop. Hitting the velvet curtain with arms outstretched and the woman's outraged roar in her ears, the darkness beyond almost palpable, but she pauses for less than a second, half a breath, before running towards the dim sliver of light only metres away. Floor level light, bleeding from beneath a closed and solid door, and dragging with it the strained, muffled cries of someone in pain.

Elise. Blood thrumming murderous in her fingers as they scrabble for the door handle, find it, turn it. Whatever's happening in there, Fledge is going to kill him, the Humbug Man, she is going to rip his filthy fucking dick off and—

(oh. oh god.)

—it's all she can do to keep her knees from buckling as she braces herself against the doorjamb, mute slackjaw gape and the taste of rising terror iron-flat on her tongue, mind barely able to register the footfalls clattering up behind her, the fingers that dig furious-sharp into her shoulders and the vicious hiss of the woman telling her to move, to let go of the fucking door, you little bitch, let go right fucking now. Aware only of what she cannot possibly be seeing: Elise bent white and naked, spine angled so extreme it hurts just to witness, but one arm flung wide, fingers clutching ecstatic at empty air, and the other circled possessive around the thing that holds her, folds her over its lap and presses its pallid, elongated snout to her belly.

Into her belly, *into* her scars.

Elise, head lolled back and those cool green eyes fluttering open, rolling round to fix their dilated, bliss-burned pupils on Fledge. *Babygirl*, the word little more than a whisper, sliding from Elise's mouth on a thin stream of saliva that stretches and puddles to the floor. *Babygirl*, the last thing Fledge hears before the woman pulls her away, drags her back down the dark little corridor and into the shop, back to the bright lights and the dusty sneer of bottled wine.

"Impatient little slut!" Unexpected, the brutal backhanded slap across her jaw, loud toothy *chink* and the taste of blood in her mouth enough to spark a rush of tears, but the woman just snorts, pushes her face right up to Fledge's: "Couldn't wait to be asked, huh? Think this is a fucking freakshow, you can just stick your nosy little beak anywhere you damn well please?"

But Fledge cannot think, can only stare at the open collar of the woman's blouse, topmost button recently popped and the creamy fabric flapping loose to reveal the barest glimpse of malformed flesh. Scar tissue patterns too chaotic for coincidence, the deep-etched whorls too, too familiar.

Then: "Out!" the woman growls, and Fledge stumbles through the door, stumbles or is pushed, the concrete footpath shaving several layers of skin from her palms, and she doesn't even bother trying to get up. Just crawls deeper into the alley, shaky hand and knee skitter right to the end where she crouches beside the big yellow bin and vomits. Bile and coffee and not much else, empty-gut convulsions and if only her mind could do likewise, could spit its new and toxic knowledge into the gutter.

Because now she has all the answers.

Afterimages of Elise burning so bright Fledge fears she'll never be rid them: Elise and that *thing* so invidiously entwined, greasy long tongue secreting some sort of fluid, brilliant green and thick as rancid milk, sliding serpentine over her scars, changing them, shaping them to its own monstrous design. The smell of anise heavy in the air, heavy still in Fledge's nostrils even over the stink of garbage, and she retches again, not wanting to think about all those empty absinthe bottles or what they might have contained.

A special homemade blend, Elise had told her once.

But the precise ingredients, never.

A door slams shut behind her and Fledge looks to see her bag arcing through the air, graceless tumble-turns and all her stuff spilling with a clatter to the ground. Pens, books, the weighty jangle of her keys; even the little ball-peen hammer comes skidding across the concrete towards her, and how badly she wants to take up *that* invitation. Longs to march back into the shop with weapon in fist and smash the Humbug-thing right through its blind and eyeless skull, smash it to lifeless bits of bone and brains, except—

Except for the sounds Elise had been making, the little moans and choking cries that until now Fledge had imagined were hers alone to elicit. Desirous, desiring sounds of pleasures granted and received, their echoes scraping hollow-raw at her heart, and she starts to cry again, wanting nothing more than to take it all back, take everything back, everything she has seen and heard and smelt.

A useless, impossible wish, and she knows it.

Knows that nothing, not the slightest thing, can ever be the same again.

***

"Felicity, phone!" Her mother, never one to knock, opening Fledge's bedroom door just enough to poke her head through and frown at the Nine Inch Nails track blaring from the stereo. How many times does Fledge have to be told not to play her music so loud, she wants to know. Especially *that* music, nose wrinkling as though it's found something dead, and dead for a long time too. "It's that girl again," her mother says, *that girl* in the same disgusted tone, *that girl* as though Fledge has never once mentioned Elise's name, and, "I'm not going to lie for you anymore. If you don't want to talk to her, get off your lazy butt and tell her yourself."

Down the hall to the kitchen, dreaded gallows-bound path avoided for over a week. Her mobile switched off for almost as long, dead plastic stone at the bottom of her bag collecting god knows how many texts and voicemails; she'd killed it after the first dozen *where r u?s* from Sasha J and Nikki. But only Elise had called the house. Had kept calling.

So now: the kitchen phone cradled cautious to her ear: "Hello?"

"Fledge? It's me." Elise, distraught, begging her please not to hang up, please just listen a minute, just hear her out, please. Please?

Fledge swallows. "Okay."

And then Elise is crying, anxious-hasty words tripping over one another to explain how sorry she is, how she hadn't meant for Fledge to find out like that, not ever like that. How she'd planned to introduce her properly, when the time was right, would have brought her to him and let her see for herself what it was all about, how amazing it was. "You would have understood," she says, and, "Why didn't you wait, Fledge? Why couldn't you have waited?" Because now it's too late. Because the jealous old bitch Judith has taken him away, her exquisite monster, her beautiful freak, has closed up shop and left for fuck knows where. Another city, another country, it hardly matters; Elise hasn't the first clue where to start looking.

And if she did, Fledge wants to know. If she did, what then?

Elise sighs. "You have no idea what it's like to have that stuff running through your system. It's like flying, like being outside your body, outside the whole world. And the things you feel, the things you *know...*"

But Fledge doesn't want to hear any more about hallucinogenic spit or whatever it is the Humbug-thing secretes, or how it must contain a natural anaesthetic of some sort because the act itself is utterly painless and afterwards there's only the dullest ache beneath fresh-healed scars. She doesn't want to know that Elise is certain the better part of the deal is her own, as all the Humbug-thing gets is some of her blood—but maybe not, because it does seem overly grateful for it. And she really doesn't want to listen to the other girl crying again, snuffling into the phone and weeping over the loss of it, her creature, the Humbug-thing.

All Fledge wants is amnesia.

And so: "I have to go, Elise."

"Please don't. I can't lose you as well."

Fledge closes her eyes, sees Elise bent ever backwards, that long serrated tongue carving spirals into her flesh, her mouth a round eternal O—*Babygirl*—and she knows that it will always be this way, that she will never be able to forget if Elise is still around. Will never be able to rest her lips upon those pale, pale scars. Not without horror. Not without revulsion.

And not with love, not ever again.

So, once more: "I have to go, don't call me back. Please."

But three more times the phone rings, and three more times Fledge lifts the handset then gently, oh so gently, returns it to the cradle. Another ten minutes waited out in the kitchen, in the silence, ten minutes according to the clock above the stove, ten full turns of the littlest red hand to count down upon her fingers, before she finally slips back to her bedroom. Precarious stack of books on her desk, volumes borrowed from Elise and now never to be returned, for Fledge can't face her again, can't face the gaze of those wounded, wounding green eyes, even if she wanted to.

Which she doesn't. Does not. Will not.

Packing the books into a plastic bag instead, pausing only at the last: the Paré book with its butt-ugly mermaid, arcane little text through which she has thumbed over and over this past week, desperate quest for something, anything which might yield a clue about what she had seen in that dank little back room. Nothing, of course nothing, and yet Fledge opens the book once more, flips to a page with its corner turned down, tatty little dog ear she herself has left behind.

Wanting to read one last time a sentence underlined by Elise, the single solitary mark in the whole volume, this sharp-scored pen mark drawn with such force it all but pierces through to the other side. Perhaps the words had hurt Elise, touched too raw a nerve, or maybe she'd merely highlighted it out of scorn, as something to show Fledge or the others later. Something at which to snicker and scoff.

It is not good that monsters should live among us.

Fledge shivers. Not good, no. And yet they do.

She puts the book in with the others, wrapping the end of the bag mummy-tight around the lot of them before getting down on her hands and knees to shove the package beneath the bed. All the way under, leaving it to brood alone and hopefully forgotten amid the dust and the monsterless dark.

CAUTION: CONTAINS SMALL PARTS

TIM PLACES THE small wooden dog on the coffee table and checks inside the box a second time. No card, no note, nothing besides the dozen or so crumpled sheets of week-old *Herald Sun* that cushioned the toy during its journey through the postal system. Nothing to explain what it's for or why it's been sent to him.

"Maybe it's a joke," Linda suggests.

Grabbing the twine that's strung like a garrote through the dog's neck, she pulls the toy along the tabletop. It has smooth wooden wheels in place of legs, painted a bright and glossy shade of red, and a brass bell on the end of its tail that tinkles with each movement of its multi-coloured, segmented body. The head bobs back and forward in a strange, jerky way that gives Tim the creeps. More like a mutant pigeon than a puppy. What sort of parent would buy their kid a toy like this anyway? What sort of kid would want one?

"There's no return address?" Linda asks.

"No, just mine." Printed in thick black capitals, and Tim can't decide whether or not the handwriting looks familiar.

"It's sad."

"You think?"

"Yeah." She drops the twine and the dog creaks to a standstill. "Look at its sad little eyes, and its sad little mouth. Poor thing, I feel sorry for it."

Tim shrugs. It doesn't look sad to him; it looks...wrong.

"Maybe it got sent to you by mistake," Linda says. She turns back to her trashy gossip mag, to the photospread of *Stars! Caught Without Makeup!* and shakes her head. "You should hang onto it, in case you have to return it. Might be some child's favourite toy got sent here by mistake, you never know."

"Yeah, maybe."

As Tim picks the dog up, meaning to put it back into the box, a patch of chipped paint on one of the wheels catches his eye. Not really chipped, now that he looks closely, more like bitten or chewed.

A toddler with serious teething issues, with serious *teeth*, to gnaw away so much wood. He dumps the dog into its nest of expired newsprint, then closes the flaps on the box and kicks it beneath the coffee table. Stupid toy.

Later, after Linda's gone home, he'll take the whole thing out to the bin.

***

Four minutes past three in the morning according to the red glow of his alarm clock, and Tim lies perfectly still in bed, his ears straining for a repeat of whatever sound it was that woke him. Nothing. He rolls over, reaches for the glass of water on the bedside table. Empty. He must have forgotten to fill it before turning in; never mind, he'll do without. But his tongue catches on the roof of his mouth and the more he thinks about not needing a drink, the thirstier he feels. At sixteen minutes past three, he swears and swings his legs over the side of the bed.

In the kitchen, light from a near-full moon washes through the window so Tim doesn't bother flicking the switch. Just fills his glass with tap water and stands in front of the sink, looking out into the back yard as he drinks. The lawn needs to be mown, but he can still see dozens of lemons nestling amid the grass like overripe hand grenades. Linda usually picks a few to share with the girls at her gym, but even they can't keep up with the prodigious output. Lemons. The most useless fruit in the world and he scores a yard with two trees full of the bloody things.

Not for the first time, Tim wishes he'd rented a townhouse or unit instead. Some modern, low maintenance prefab with concrete and pavers to keep Mother Nature at bay.

Behind him, a bell tinkles.

Tim jerks around. Water splashes over his hand and across the front of his shirt, and he swears again. Then he sees the thing sitting just inside the kitchen doorway and further words desert him.

Impossible—*impossible*—that the small wooden dog should be there, *right there*, where he would have had to walk past it, step over it maybe, as he came into the room. Not when he threw the toy into the outside wheelie bin just that afternoon, not when he lugged the very same bin out onto the side of the street, where the garbos will be coming to empty it in a few short hours.

Impossible.

Without taking his eyes from the dog, Tim reaches around and lowers his glass into the sink, wipes his hands on his pyjama pants. Unless...unless he only threw out the box itself. Linda might have rescued the toy without him realising, maybe hid it somewhere as a joke. Tim frowns, tries to remember the feel of the box in his hands, the weight of it. Tries to remember if he heard the bell ring as he tossed it into the half-empty bin. He shakes his head. It doesn't matter what he remembers—the dog clearly couldn't have been in the box because right now he's staring at the damn thing with his own two eyes. Okay, so Linda took it. Put it...under the kitchen table? Where the vibrations of his own footsteps caused it to roll out? Sure, why not? Witching hour logic, but it's good enough for Tim, or nearly so.

He takes a step towards the dog but finds himself loath to touch it—not with his bare hands anyway—and he doesn't want to think too hard about why that might be so. It's just so creepy, all painted eyes and flat black stare, sitting there now not so much motionless as...coiled.

Ridiculous, but still. Tim throws a tea towel over the toy before picking the bundle up with both hands, and finds himself almost relieved when it doesn't begin to wriggle within his grasp. His jaw clenches, anger seeping into his blood now as fear beats a shameful retreat. Damn Linda and her childish bloody jokes. He's not going to give her the satisfaction of even mentioning it.

Outside, his breath frosts the air. Tim jogs down the driveway to where his bin now stands beside those of his neighbours, a trio of patient old soldiers huddled shoulder to shoulder against the darkness. He lifts the lid and drops the wooden dog inside, tea towel and all. The muffled tinkle of a bell sounds from the depths.

"Good dog," he mutters. "Play dead."

*　*　*

The phone rings as soon as Tim arrives home from work the next evening. Groaning, he hurries into the kitchen, juggling keys, work satchel, rain-soaked umbrella, and a thin plastic bag of takeaway Thai which has been threatening to snap a handle ever since he picked it up. Only two people ever call him on the landline: his mother, who doesn't trust mobile phones; and persistent offshore telemarketers. He dumps everything onto the bench and reaches for the handset. The caller has a private number, which does nothing to narrow the field—his mother doesn't trust phone directories either; she hasn't been listed for years—and he considers just letting it ring out. But if it is his mother, she'll only call back in five minutes, and five minutes after that, and five minutes after that. Better to get it over with.

He presses the answer button. "Hello?"

"Is this Tim Jennings?" The voice belongs to a woman. She sounds young and weary and possibly, vaguely familiar.

"That's me," he replies. "Who's this?"

"It's Anna Vidicci." A pause. "Melanie's sister, you remember."

It's almost instinctive, the way his guts tighten. *The Crane?* Why is the Crane calling him? It's been almost four years since he broke up with Mellie; what can her bitch of an older sister want from him now?

"Anna, hi. It's been a while." Tucking the phone between his cheek and his shoulder, he pulls the containers of Thai from their bag. The red chicken curry has leaked through the edges of its lid; coconut sauce drips across the bench, pools around his keys.

"Do you have a few minutes to speak?"

"Um, I'm kind of in the middle of something here." He rinses his keys beneath the tap, leaves them in the dishrack to dry. Grabs a handful of paper towels to take care of the mess on the bench.

"I have some bad news." Her voice is thin, its edges sheet-metal sharp.

Tim licks his fingers. "Look, can I call you back? What's your number?"

"Melanie's dead."

"What?" He couldn't have heard her right, she couldn't have just said—

"Last Thursday," the Crane tells him. "I thought you should hear it from me. The funeral's on Wednesday, if you want to come. Sorry about the short notice, there were a lot of people I needed to call."

You were the last name on my list, are the words she leaves unspoken.

Tim closes his eyes, allows himself to slide down the front of the cupboard to slump onto the tiled floor. A handle digs into his back; he doesn't move. Today is Monday—four days ago, Mellie was still breathing somewhere. Still scribbling in those notebooks of hers as well, most probably, and talking to people who weren't there, and sniffing her food for traces of poison—but still breathing. Still alive.

"What happened?" It's a question he's not sure he wants answered.

"Melanie wasn't well, you know that. There were a lot of bad days, especially after you left. Thursday was one bad day too many."

He swallows, tries to ignore the accusation in her tone. "I'm sorry, Anna."

The way she speaks, the Crane always seems to be accusing somebody of something. He can picture her now, those pale lips pursed to a thin line, the furrows in her brow deepening to troughs as she pecks pecks pecks at the phone, determined to find fault, eager to apportion blame.

"Do you want to know about the funeral?" she asks.

Tim pretends to write down the details, repeating them back to her even though he already knows he won't be going. He can't see the point. It's been over with Mellie for longer than they were ever together and it's not like they bothered to stay in touch, not even on Facebook. Before tonight, he can't recall the last time he even thought about her. No, it would be stupid to go to the funeral. Mellie's family wouldn't want him there; the invitation is merely protocol.

"Thanks for calling, Anna. I'm sorry about Mellie, I really am." He pauses, tries to conceive a suitable condolence. "She was a special kind of person."

"Yes," the Crane says, and, "Well."

They exchange awkward goodbyes and Tim stands to return the phone to its cradle. Left lidless on the bench, the Thai curry has started to separate and congeal. Orange pools of oil glisten on its surface. He picks up a plastic fork, stabs half-heartedly at a large chunk of chicken. Pale and tender, the meat splits easily apart, dripping red as he lifts it from the sauce. The smell is thick and rich and close to nauseating. Tim puts the lid back on the curry and returns it to its bag along with the rice and the little parcel of deep-fried spring rolls, then shoves the whole lot into the fridge. He can nuke it in the microwave later, or maybe tomorrow.

Maybe tomorrow, he'll feel hungry again.

* * *

Friday nights, Linda comes over to eat pizza and watch movies. Sometimes she brings her overnight bag and stays the weekend, but not tonight. Tonight the only things in her hands when Tim answers the door are a couple of new release DVDs, a six-pack of Mexican beer, and a small wooden dog.

"Starting a collection?" She grins, brandishing the toy like it's some kind of weapon. The bell on its tail jangles fiercely.

Tim takes a backward step. "Where the fuck did you get that?" It's the same damn dog—it can't be, but it is. He can see the scratch marks—the *bite* marks—on the front wheel.

"Hi, *Linda*," she says, and pushes past him. "How *lovely* to see you."

"Sorry," he mutters, not really meaning it. He closes the door then follows her deceitful arse into the kitchen, tries not to look at the dog that sure as hell better not be looking at him from where it now sits on the kitchen table. "Just, seriously, where did the toy come from?"

"It was on the front steps when I got here."

"When you got here."

"That's what I said." She grabs a bottle opener from the top drawer, flips the caps on two of the beers. "You have any lemons inside?"

Tim shakes his head. "You didn't bring it?"

"How could *I* bring it?"

"Come on, Linda, a joke's a joke. What, because I never said anything about Sunday night, you thought you'd have another go? Okay, fine—you scared me a little. Happy? Wanna tell me how you did it now?"

She glares at him. "Whatever. I'm getting a lemon."

"No." Tim grabs her arm as she moves towards the back door, wrenches her back around to face him. Ignoring her startled yelp, the shock that flares bright and sudden in her eyes, he pulls her face close to his own. "First you tell me."

"Ow— Let me go!" Her nails dig into the skin of his wrist. "I don't even know what you're talking about!"

Beneath the pain and the anger that contort her features, Tim glimpses a real and genuine bewilderment. She isn't lying, she really doesn't know anything about the stupid dog, and here he is manhandling her like some kind of Neanderthal, one hand squeezing her arm hard enough to bruise, the other flexing to an eager fist at his side. Horrified, he releases his hold.

"God, Linda. I'm so sorry." Meaning it this time, for what little he knows it's worth. "I didn't—I've had the worst week."

She snorts. "Oh right, you've had a *bad week*. No problem, feel free to take that shit out on me whenever you need to." There's a slight tremor in her voice, and she's looking at him now like it's the very first time she's really seen him. Like it might be the very last.

"I'm sorry," he says again. Her expression remains unchanged and so he tries to explain—about the stupid dog, about the Crane and Mellie—but it doesn't make much difference. He's cold, she implies, for not going to the funeral; colder still for not mentioning his ex-girlfriend's suicide until now. *Disconnected* is the word she uses, but he knows what she means. Cold. Heartless. Maybe she's right. Should he have called her after talking to the Crane, asked for her shoulder to cry on? Is that what the protocol is?

They order pizza, though he has to force himself to eat even two slices of his usual meat lovers special. Beer helps the doughy, clotted mess to go down, but it still sits like a lump in his stomach. Linda doesn't eat much of her Hawaiian either, and as the credits roll on the first movie, she gets up from the couch and slings her handbag over her shoulder.

"You're going?" Tim asks.

"Tonight's not really working out." She ejects the DVD from the player and returns it to its case. "Did you want me to leave the other one for you? It's due back tomorrow."

He shakes his head. Some American comedy about a Las Vegas bucks night gone wrong which Linda probably rented with him in mind—an attempt to balance out the dire vampire romance they'd just sat through—but he couldn't care less. "Take them both," he tells her. "I think I'll hit the sack early."

Her face stiffens. "I'll get going then."

Tim follows her to the front door. Is he supposed to ask her to stay, is that the game they are playing now? And is that because she wants to say *yes*, or because she needs to tell him *no* one last time? Doubt curdles anxious in his guts, a sensation old and familiar and decidedly unwelcome. This was how he felt around Mellie a lot of the time near the end—uncertain, apprehensive, forever trying to avoid countless unseen fractures in the ground beneath his feet, and all the while suspecting that this was exactly the way she wanted him to feel. No, he won't go back to that place, not with Linda. Not with anyone.

"Sorry about before," Tim says. "The thing with the dog. I shouldn't have taken it out on you."

"No," she replies. "You shouldn't have."

"I'll give you a call next week then?"

"If you like."

Linda stands there, head tilted slightly to the side like she's waiting for him to make the next move, but Tim simply leans forward and kisses her on the cheek. If there's something to be said, *she* can damn well do the talking. He's done playing the psychic boyfriend game. Instead, he tells her to drive safe, then waits dutifully at the door until the taillights of her Mazda disappear down the street. She doesn't beep the horn like she usually does; he doesn't bother to wave.

Back inside, he wishes the house felt as empty and hollow as he does.

* * *

What Tim doesn't do is take the dog out to the bin with the cold, stale pizza the next morning. Because what doesn't get thrown away can't come back to surprise him. For *surprise*, he absolutely doesn't tell himself, read *haunt*.

And when Tim invites himself around to his brother's place to watch the AFL match that afternoon, it's not because he can't stand to be alone in his own house for any longer than necessary. No, it's just that he hasn't hung out with Rick in a while, Rick and Sally, who's pregnant again—a girl this time, she tells him, a little sister for Liam who's going to be two this August, can he believe it?—and half a dozen of their football-mad friends who crowd around the massive plasma screen television, eating corn chips dipped in Sally's homemade guacamole and exploding into raucous cheers every time Hawthorn scores a goal.

Afterwards, when he drinks so much during the impromptu victory barbeque on his brother's deck that Sally confiscates his car keys and insists he spend the night on the sofa bed in the games room, it's not because he's leery about going home. That's also not the reason he tags along on their Sunday shopping expedition to the kiddie supercentre, holding onto Liam's hand while his parents bicker mildly about whether the colour of the Sports Deluxe twin stroller they're looking to purchase should be charcoal or champagne or a combination of both. And when Rick takes him aside after dinner to suggest that, while the weekend's been great and it's brilliant for Liam to spend time with his uncle, maybe Tim should think about heading off soon—just so Rick and Sally can have an evening to themselves, right, little bro?—Tim certainly doesn't think of asking if he can maybe just crash for another night or two.

No, he doesn't think about that, not even for a second.

In the same way, he doesn't think about the fact that the wooden dog is no longer on the kitchen table when he gets home, or that it's inexplicably removed itself to the living room and is now perched on the end of the couch where Tim himself usually sits to watch television.

Tim doesn't think about the toy at all over the next week or so. He especially doesn't think about it while lying in bed in the dark, trying to sleep with his iPod speaker-docked and cycling on random, the volume turned up loud enough to cover any noise that might otherwise seep in from beyond his bedroom door. Which means that he doesn't hear the wooden scrape of wheels along an uncarpeted hall floor. Or the discordant jangle of a tinny, brass bell.

Tim doesn't hear these sounds every single night.

And he's fine with that. He's absolutely fine.

* * *

Until one sleep-starved morning, he shuffles into the kitchen for coffee and toast—not looking for the dog, never looking for the dog—and sees the boy.

Around the same age as his nephew, maybe a little older, but with dark brown hair instead of Liam's straw-coloured curls. Sitting cross-legged with his back half-turned, red-and-orange-striped pyjamas too baggy for his too-skinny body, shoulders hitching up and down like he's playing with something on the floor in front of him, so real Tim can hear him breathe.

Tim sags against the doorjamb, a strangled gasp caught in his throat.

The boy pauses. That small, dark head lifts. Begins to turn.

Tim slides around the doorway, presses himself against the adjoining living room wall. Behind him, he doesn't—he definitely *doesn't*—hear the pad of bare feet on kitchen tiles. Not what he expected, not a *boy*, not a *child*. Maybe—not that he ever thought about it, because he doesn't think about it—but if he did—maybe it's Mellie, he might have thought, maybe it's something to do with Mellie. Not that she is—because that's impossible—as impossible as the toy dog which absolutely does *not* roll through the house in the middle of the night, which absolutely does *not* toll its fucking bell at all hours of the fucking night.

Breathing. Behind him. Beside him.

Any moment, he feels certain, any moment now it will touch him. Tiny cold fingers, tiny cold hands, reaching up to clasp his own, and a tiny cold face with a tiny cold mouth opening wide—

"Enough!" The strength of his own voice surprises him, propels him back around and through the door and into the kitchen.

The *empty* kitchen, or very nearly. Because in front of the sink, in the space where an impossible child absolutely could not have been sitting, are scattered a jumble of brightly coloured wooden shapes. Tim picks up a red disc, runs his finger along the rim where jagged gouges catch at his skin. Most of the wooden pieces now bear similar marks. A piece of green dowel as thick as his finger has been snapped—*bitten*—in half. Torn from its body, the dog's head now lies on its side, one painted eye staring up in dumb accusation. Tim swallows hard. A trickle of sweat runs down the side of his face.

He wonders what else the boy might be capable of disassembling.

***

"How did you get this number?" the Crane wants to know when he calls.

"I remembered you were in real estate," Tim says. "Your mobile's listed on the company website, you know."

The Crane sighs. "What do you want?"

"Can we meet somewhere? I need to talk about a few things."

"We're talking now."

"Not like this, not over the phone." He wants to do this in person; he wants to see her face. "It's about Mellie. There's, ah—I have some questions."

"We didn't see you at the funeral."

"No, I—I couldn't get time off work."

"Really? Not even for a funeral?"

"I'm sorry, I know I should have been there."

The Crane makes a sound somewhere between laughter and a snort.

"Please, Anna. It's important."

Silence, stretching crisp and brittle-thin between them.

"Anna?"

"I have half an hour between open houses this afternoon," she says at last. "You can talk to me while I grab a coffee."

This time he does write down the address she gives him, some café way out in the northern suburbs. He'll have to leave work right after lunch, claim sudden illness or some kind of family emergency. Tim grimaces. Family emergency, right. That might only be halfway to a lie.

"This doesn't make us friends," the Crane is saying.

"I know that," Tim tells her.

"We've never been friends."

* * *

She hasn't changed. Tall and excruciatingly thin, the same beaky nose and stoop-shouldered way of moving that earned her the nickname in the first place—a snide sisterly baptism he eagerly picked up and ran with long after Mellie herself let it drop. Because it fit, because it was perfect. Anna the Crane, perpetually hovering around her younger sister as though Mellie was the last chick in the nest, fragile and still to fledge, the need for constant vigilance a given.

Turns out, maybe she wasn't so wrong about that.

Tim lifts his hand to wave at the exact moment the Crane spots him. She nods and marches over to the table where he's been sitting for the past fifteen minutes, an obligatory coffee growing cold by his elbow.

"I wasn't sure you were coming," he says.

"The open house ran late," she tells him. "There's a lot of interest in this area right now. I won't have as much time as I thought." A waitress materialises and she orders a large skinny latte with no sugar to go, hands over a five-dollar note.

Her attitude pisses him off. She doesn't have time to talk about her sister, barely a week in the ground? Fine, he'll cut to the damn chase then. "Why didn't you say the funeral wasn't just for Mellie? Hoping to surprise me?"

"What?"

"You know."

"Tim, I really don't." The Crane reaches into her bag, pulls out a folded sheet of paper, and slides it across the table. "Here. We had spares."

It's a memorial pamphlet, obviously homemade on a computer and printed off somewhere like Officeworks or Kinkos. There's a photo of Mellie on the front, skin too orange and smile too fake, listless brown curls falling half across her face.

"It's the best we could find," the Crane says. "You know how much she hated being photographed."

Beloved daughter of Rocco and Yvette, and sister of Anna.

No other names are mentioned anywhere. Tim frowns, bites his lip. The words he's been rehearsing all afternoon lodge stubborn in his throat; he can't bring himself to loosen them. Mellie stares out at him through tangles of hair, silent now, and forever. *What happened*, he wants to ask her, *what did you do?*

"You said you wanted to talk," the Crane prompts, her tone edged with impatience. "You said you had questions."

"Yeah." Tim takes a sip of his coffee, lukewarm and sugarless, but at least it moistens his mouth. "See, this *thing* has happened, this weird thing, and I thought it was to do with Mellie, that she maybe—I mean, did she ever, was there—you're her sister, you'd have to know, right?"

"What?" Lacquered fingernails tap briskly on the tabletop. "What would I have to know?"

He takes a breath, then plunges straight in. "Look, did Mellie have a kid? And did she—did the kid die as well?"

The Crane's eyes widen. "Don't be ridiculous."

But her gaze flickers, darting briefly away from his own before returning with twice the chill of winter. That's more than enough for Tim. "What aren't you telling me, Anna? Was there a kid, a little boy maybe?"

"This is insane." She pushes back her chair.

"Wait," he says. "I want to show you something." Reaches for the plastic bag at his feet, hauls it up and drops it on the table in front of her. "Look."

She doesn't move. "What's in it?"

"*Look.*" Tim turns the bag upside down, allows the pieces of wooden dog to fall with a clatter from its mouth. A red disc describes a lazy arc, then settles by the Crane's hand. She flinches as though it might bite.

"Where did you get that?"

"You know what it is? What it used to be?"

"*Where did you get it?*" she hisses.

"I think Mellie must have sent it to me," Tim says. "Before she, you know."

"Keep it then. I don't want the damn thing."

Their waitress returns with a takeaway cup and a fading smile, finds a space on the table for the former then quickly leaves. Tim waits until she's out of earshot. "It's a kid's toy, Anna. Who did it belong to?"

"No one," she says. "Melanie bought it, years ago."

"But why?"

"Who knows why my sister did anything?" She's leaning back in her chair now, arms crossed over her chest. "Put it away. Please."

He doesn't move. "What was his name?"

"For God's sake!" The Crane rises swiftly to her feet, scooping up her bag and the takeaway coffee in a single angry motion. "I'm not listening to any more of this. You're worse than Melanie ever was."

"I've seen him," Tim says. "Little boy, kind of skinny, dark brown hair."

She pauses. An uncertain expression, some strange twist of fury and fear, flashes across her face. But it's too quick to catch hold, and she shakes her head, squares her jaw. "I don't know what you think you've seen, Tim, but Melanie never had a child." Her hand holding the coffee cup is shaking just a little. "You know, sometimes I really wish…"

"What?"

"Beggars and horses." The smile that twitches her lips could not be more broken. "I'm done with this, okay? Don't call me again. I'm *done.*"

Tim says nothing, just watches her walk, shoulders more hunched than ever, out of the café and across the road to where a silver Honda coupe is parked. She sits in the driver's seat for maybe three or four minutes, head bowed over her coffee, motionless. He wonders if she's crying, if she's even capable of crying. He's never once seen the Crane with tears in her eyes. Finally, she starts the car and drives off to her next appointment.

He gathers up the pieces of dog and returns them to the plastic bag. The rattle of wood on wood is somehow comforting.

It sounds solid. It sounds real.

Mellie gazes up at him, orange and flat and far beyond reach. Only four years, and there's not much he can remember of her with any degree of clarity. He can't decide if that's wrong. "I'm sorry," he whispers, digging into his pocket for enough change to pay for the coffee.

Tim leaves the pamphlet behind on the table. He doesn't need any more baggage.

* * *

"I'm not really up for anything," Linda tells him. "I've got work tomorrow."

This phone call is the first time they've spoken since their last abortive movie night, and Tim isn't even sure why he's rung her now. He doesn't want to go home alone—or *unalone*, or however the hell the situation back at the house could best be described—but neither does he have the headspace for being social. Linda seems the best compromise.

"We don't have to go out," he tells her. "I'll bring something over. You feel like Chinese or pizza?"

Linda sighs. "Let's not, okay?"

"If you're still mad at me about the other night—"

"Tim, just stop."

"What?"

She remains silent for a few seconds, and he can picture her rubbing at her forehead, at the twin creases that form between her eyebrows whenever she gets irritated or perplexed, or both. "Maybe we should just let things rest for a while," she says at last.

"Rest? What do you mean, rest?"

Another sigh. "This isn't really going anywhere, is it?"

"What isn't?"

"Look, you're a fun guy and you're easy to be with most of the time, but I think it's all starting to get a bit...*complicated*, and right now I'm really not looking for complicated. Sorry if that sounds harsh."

"You're dumping me?"

"Oh, Tim, please don't pretend like we ever had anything serious going."

He swallows. "No, I guess we didn't."

"Because that was kind of the idea, right? Nothing serious?"

"Yeah, it was."

Then she reminds him what a nice guy he is, really, and how he'll make some equally nice girl very happy one day if he ever decides to come out of his shell, lower the barricades, take down the walls—just not Linda, because Linda isn't looking right now—and her tone echoes the Crane's parting words.

Don't call me again. I'm done.

"You sound tired," Linda says. "Are you getting much sleep?"

Even after he hangs up on her, Tim can't stop laughing.

* * *

He keeps the bag of dog parts beneath his bed, right beneath the spot where he lays his head on the pillow.

On the pillow, and sometimes under it, those nights he definitely doesn't hear the pad of small, bare feet on the hallway boards outside his door, or the high-pitched keening that might be the cry of a child waking in darkness, or delight. Those nights when he absolutely does not feel the subtle shift of the mattress at his back, or the tickle of breath over his cheek.

Those nights especially, Tim's eyes remain resolutely closed.

Because there is definitely, absolutely nothing to see.

* * *

Walking home from the train station after Friday night drinks with the guys from sales, Tim's half-blinded by a sudden flash of headlights, twice in quick succession. The car is parked out front of his house, its paintwork pale and gleaming beneath the glare of the streetlight. He can make out the vague shape of a driver, but nothing else.

Tim pauses. The headlights flash again. Just once.

Cautiously, he keeps walking. As he approaches the vehicle, its passenger side window slides down with a low, mechanical hum and the interior light switches on. "Tim?" the Crane asks. "Do you have a few minutes?"

A mild sense of relief shivers through him. "I thought you were done," he says, annoyed. "Isn't that what you told me?"

"Please." She reaches over and opens the door, pushes it outward.

"Uh, it might be more comfortable inside."

The Crane shakes her head. "I'd rather stay out here. No offence."

"Whatever." Tim slides into the passenger seat, pulling the door closed behind him. The heater is running on full; sweat beads along his hairline almost immediately. "How long have you been waiting here?"

"Long enough." Her lips press so tight together they turn white. "What you brought to the café the other day. My sister really sent it?"

"I think so. The box is long gone but the handwriting—what I can remember about the handwriting—I'm pretty sure it was Mellie's."

She sighs. "I suppose it's the only logical explanation. I turned our flat upside this past week, you know, in case she had hidden it somewhere. Nothing, so it must be the same one."

"She was still living with you?"

"It was easier. Melanie was...problematic."

Tim isn't dumb enough to take that sort of bait. He simply nods and waits.

"She called him Jacob," the Crane says.

"The dog?"

"No." She glares at him, pointedly. "Not the dog."

Tim lets out a breath he didn't know he was holding. "There *was* a kid."

"No," she repeats. "I told you, she never had a child."

"I don't understand—"

"Here." The Crane reaches around to the backseat and retrieves a green canvas shopping bag, thrusts it towards him. It's full of toys—rattles, stuffed animals, oversized plastic Lego blocks—padded out with neatly folded baby clothes. "Melanie bought all of that, and more. I kept sending it off to charity shops, but she replaced it quicker than I could keep up with. That wooden dog you have, that was the very first thing. She was hysterical when I donated it along with a load of other stuff. I had to go down to Vinnies the next day and buy the bloody thing back."

Tim takes a bright blue teddy bear from the top of the bag. "Why would she do that?" The bear stares back at him with eyes of empty glass.

"I used to hear her talking aloud in her bedroom," the Crane says. "Sometimes I even thought I heard someone talking back."

"Someone?"

"She called him Jacob."

Tim drops the bear back into the bag. "Why?" he asks again.

"Melanie wanted that child so badly," she whispers. "Sometimes I worry that maybe it would have been the best thing after all."

"Anna, you have to tell me what's going on."

"Why do you think I'm here?" She smiles at him then, that same broken smile he remembers from the café. "I'm so tired of keeping it all to myself. Maybe if I tell you, maybe I can start to let her go."

* * *

Tim closes the front door behind him, lets the green shopper fall to the floor. He can't summon any hatred for the Crane, no matter how much he would dearly like to, no matter how much easier that would make everything. Because she's probably right. She was probably always right.

After you broke up with her, Melanie found out she was pregnant.

Why didn't she say something?

She didn't want you to come back just because of a baby.

You mean, you didn't *want me to come back.*

I did agree with her, yes.

You never thought Mellie and me should be together.

It's a moot point, Tim. You wouldn't have come back anyway.

Leaving the lights off, he feels his way into the bedroom, gets down on his hands and knees and reaches into the darkness beneath the bed. His fingers brush plastic, and he pulls the bag towards him. Wood rattles against wood; the sound is as close to comfort as he deserves.

Melanie wanted to have the baby on her own. She thought being a mother would be fun; she thought it would be fulfilling.

I bet you didn't agree with her about that.

Melanie could barely cope with being Melanie most of the time. How could she possibly bring up a child?

His toolbox is in the laundry. Nothing flash—he's never been much for DIY—but Tim finds a proper screwdriver among the assortment of Allen keys, along with an adjustable wrench and probably enough orphaned bolts and screws of various sizes to get the job done. Satisfied, he snaps the lid shut and takes the toolbox with him.

You should have told me, Anna.

Melanie didn't want me to.

I could have helped.

I'm sure you could *have. But the question is, would* you *have?*

Sitting cross-legged in the middle of the kitchen floor, Tim empties the plastic bag out in front of him. Dog parts scatter over the tiles. The little brass bell tinkles to a stop beneath the fridge. He uses the screwdriver to fish it back out, blows away the dust bunnies with a couple of forceful breaths. Holding the bell between finger and thumb, he shakes it, gently. "Are you there, Jacob?" he whispers, and shakes the bell again.

What happened to him? How did he die?

I've told you already, Tim. She didn't have the baby.

But you just said she wanted him.

I convinced her otherwise. It wasn't easy.

You convinced her to…

She could always have had a child later. With someone who cared, someone who was serious about her and actually wanted a family.

You made Mellie get an abortion? You made her get rid of her baby—our baby—is that what you're saying?

Be honest, Tim. What would you have made her do?

The house is silent and still. Tim arranges all the pieces carefully on the floor, putting them in some sort of dog-shaped order so he can see how they're meant to go together. Most of the bits of dowel are broken. He uses electrical tape where he can, decides to substitute a couple of bolts where he can't. It's not like the toy needs to be kiddie-safe.

She called him Jacob.

He thinks about Mellie, whose face he can now only picture in the cast of that awful memorial photograph. She was always so anxious, so clingy, constantly needing to be touched, to be reassured that, yes, he loved her, yes, he thought she was beautiful. A need so hungry, not even the ghost of a child, summoned from frantic desperation and the smallest scraps of half-formed flesh, could begin to quell it. Maybe a real child could have. Maybe the Crane was right about that too.

Neither of them would ever know.

"I'm sorry, Jacob." Tim fits the dog's head onto its neck, makes sure the joint is loose enough to bob. "See, I'm fixing it for you, mate. I'm guessing it's your favourite, right, your very first toy?"

There's no sound, no change in temperature from one heartbeat to the next, nothing at all to indicate that the boy now stands behind him. Merely the calm, absolute certainty that he's there.

"Your mum loved you a lot, Jacob, she really did." Tim spins a wheel around on his finger. He should buy some sandpaper to smooth out the gouges, some red paint to touch up the damage. "But she was sick, you know, so sick she had to go away. And I think maybe that's why she sent you to me. She wanted to make sure there would be someone to take care of you."

Bare feet shuffle against the tiles. Closer, closer.

"It must have been scary, being in a strange place all of a sudden, without your mum." Tim tries to laugh. "Guess we scared each other pretty good, hey?"

A small face presses its cheek against his back. It's a curious sensation, the presence of a weight he doesn't so much feel as believe in. A tiny hand flutters by his ribs. Tim closes his eyes. He wonders if the boy will keep growing, keep getting older. If one day he'll be demanding Wiis and iPhones, or whatever will have taken their place in another ten years or so. If there ever will be one day.

daddy

Less whisper than vibration, this word he hasn't even dreamed of wanting to hear before now. It runs through him, beating a rhythm along with the blood in his veins, a yearning inexpressible and sudden and vast.

daddy

He can sense the boy standing right in front of him now, that unseen face leaning in towards his own, those tiny teeth bared in the sharpest of smiles. "I'm sorry, Jacob." A tear slips warm down his cheek. "I didn't realise, I didn't know who you were."

daddy

"I'm so sorry," Tim says, and opens his eyes.

PAINLESSNESS

CHRIST, NOT AGAIN. Hard enough to sleep with the afternoon sun sleazing through the Venetian blinds, the dull ache in each and every joint of her sweatsick body, and Faith groans as she rolls over to grab the bottle of water beside her bed. Blister pack of tablets beside that, antibiotics of some kind, and RelaxaTabs as well because the doctor refused to prescribe her any sort of decent sleeping pill; she takes two of each.

Natural rest, my arse.

Hard enough to sleep with the near constant vertigo and the quilt pulled right up to her chin, sweating and itching beneath it because otherwise she'll only wake up with chattering teeth and her fingernails a disturbing shade of blue.

Hard enough without *this:* the sobs and muffled shouts pressing through the shoddy townhouse wall, the nameless thumps and yesterday even the sound of smashing glass.

Faith pulls the pillow over her head but it's too hot, too close; she can't breathe properly even when she's *not* trying to smother herself. Stretches her legs instead, trying to kick the cramps from her knees, and when the shouting from next door starts up again she raises a fist for the umpteenth time to pound against the wall.

And, for the umpteenth time, stops herself at the very last second.

It might only make things worse.

No idea who her neighbours are, after all. *A single woman*, the agent's assurance during inspection, *quiet and tidy, you'll have no trouble there*—and with that now so obviously a lie, who the hell knows *what* she's moved in next door to on a fucking twelve-month lease?

The shouting ceases, gives way to sobbing. Soft, feminine cries that Faith almost can't hear, and somehow that only makes it worse. So: two more RelaxaTabs before curling tight beneath the blanket with her chin tucked close to her chest and no matter that it's harder to breathe through her congestion like that.

Harder still to sleep with what she can hear—and imagine—beyond that wall.

* * *

Between the opening screech of her neighbour's security door and the brash metallic clatter as it slams shut again, Faith shrugs into her dressing gown. Cinches the faded terrycloth belt around her waist and hop-foots it down the hall wearing just the single Ugg boot slipper because god only knows where the other one's hiding and there sure isn't any time to mount a search party. White-trash Cinderella half tripping out her own front door and, "Hey," she calls to the woman already turning away from the letterboxes. "Hey, wait up."

Whatever she might have expected, it isn't this. Tall, much taller than Faith herself but certainly not much older, early thirties at most and even that would be pushing it. A sundress of faded sky-blue clothing the sort of slim-hipped androgyny Faith might once have killed to possess, and something so...solid in the way she pauses, tiger-in-the-grass motionless with her face half turned away and hidden beneath a wave of blood-bright hair.

"Can I help you?" the woman asks, blade-sharp voice with an accent too vague to place.

Faith blinks in the morning glare, one hand raised to shield her eyes. "Sorry, just wanted a word. About the...um, the... Look, I'm feeling pretty crap right now and I really need to get some sleep, so..."

"I'm making too much noise."

"Well, yeah. I mean, normally—"

"Normally you wouldn't be here." The woman looks up then, looks right at her with dark eyes surrounded by even darker flesh, fist-sized bruises and a scabby-swollen cut on her lower lip, and Faith swallows, tries to find some words, any words, but the woman waves them away. "My apologies. I assumed you worked during the day. I didn't realise you were ill."

Forget about it, Faith wants to tell her, wants to ask if there is anything *she* needs like maybe a hospital or several shots of morphine maybe, but all at once it's so damn hot out here and the sunlight really is too bright, searing-white-bright like the unmarred skin on the woman's face, what little there is of it, and, *how rude, when she doesn't even know me from Adam.*

So: "I'm Faith." Right hand stuck out and trembling, and the woman regards it like a dead thing for a moment, dead or near enough. Looks at her that way too with oil-slick eyes impossibly black and shot with colours like Faith has never seen before, colours she can't even name. "Mara," the woman says.

Mara, a bassline thrumming through the sparks that jump and scratch behind her eyelids and Faith holds onto it, clutches it tighter than she clutches the frost-cold hand now closed around her own. *Do you hear that?* she says or maybe she doesn't after all.

The birds, do you hear their wings?

* * *

If ice could boil, and still stay frozen, this is how it might burn:

The seething shiver of skin on skin, on cloth, on the bare bathroom floor as she lies spreadeagled in an effort to touch absolutely nothing, or as much of it as she can. The water that ebbs around her chattering teeth, slips into her mouth despite the cool strong hands that hold up her head, long fingers curved firm around her chin when all she wants to do is slip beneath the surface and sink, sink, sink. The light that swells her skull, her bones, her guts; seeking to split her wide and spill itself into the world.

blood-fever

Barely a whisper from no one she cares to know.

* * *

Here, drink this.

Can't, I'll throw up.

You won't. Drink it.

The taste too strange, ginger and chamomile and something else that just doesn't belong, and—*oh god, oh christ*—the red plastic bucket still smelling of vomit from last time and this only makes her puke more, spasms so violent it hurts, until finally she rolls back onto the couch with a groan.

Told you I'd throw up.

The woman's smile so subtle it's almost not there at all.

Yes, and don't you feel much better for it?

* * *

Three days, Mara tells her, perched stray-cat cautious on the edge of the bed. Three days since that morning when she'd passed out by the mailbox, and Faith feels nauseous all over again. Three days, which would make today what then, Saturday?

"Sunday," Mara says. "Your work called on Friday. I told them it was highly doubtful you'd be in next week but you would let them know once you were conscious again. Frankly, they didn't sound too concerned."

Unsurprising. Newbie telemarketers being more dispensable than used Kleenex, especially newbie telemarketers who were barely scratching at the lowest rung of their daily quota levels; if EzyEzcape bothered to even keep her shifts alive it would be no minor miracle. Never mind that, after almost a week without pay, if she manages to scrape together next month's rent in time, it will be the loaves and fucking fishes all over again.

"Shit." Faith tries to sit up, fails. There isn't a part of her that doesn't ache.

"I don't think you're ready for vertical," Mara observes.

"I have to go back to work tomorrow. I can't afford to be sick anymore."

Mara shrugs, a do-what-you-have-to-do sort of shrug, and rises to her feet in a motion that is at once elegant and utterly final. Jaundice-faint shadow of a bruise on her cheekbone as she tucks her hair behind her ear, and only now does Faith remember.

"Hey, you said three days? That's how long I was out of it?" Frowning as the other woman nods because that can't be right, can it? Faith has had coffee table bumps take longer to fade than that and, sorry, she insists, but that *can't* that be right.

Not three days, not *only* three.

"Why would I lie?" Mara seems amused, as though this is all some elaborate game, a prank, or maybe some sick-day surprise. Like maybe everyone Faith knows is huddled out in the loungeroom with party hats and sparklers and a huge handpainted banner strung across the window: *welcome back to the world.*

"But your face..."

Words failing as Mara lifts a hand to her own cheek, fingers falling across model-smooth lips that look as though they've never even been chapped let alone left split and bleeding. "I heal fast. It has been three days." Said as though that were an eternity in itself, and her eyes are equally desolate.

Leave it alone, girl; you have no business with it.

Faith swallows, throat too dry for more than a muttered apology, and the smile Mara returns is only tooth-deep. "You seem *compos mentis* now. I'll be home all day if you need something." The square set of her jaw an unspoken challenge—*but you won't need anything*—holding Faith's gaze for a full three seconds before walking away, three long paces to the bedroom door.

Only three days.

"Wait." The woman pauses but doesn't turn round, only angles her head a little, and Faith takes this acknowledgement as all she's going to get. "Thanks, okay? Thanks for taking care of me."

"There's multivitamin juice in the fridge," Mara says. "You're dehydrated and you're probably ravenous, but I wouldn't recommend solid food until tomorrow. Otherwise, you know."

A curt nod toward the red bucket in the corner, then the bedroom door closes and Mara is gone.

***

Friday night, and Faith sits at the kitchen table with a bottle of red wine, unopened. The same kind she left on Mara's front step a few days ago with a thank you note scribbled in haste after her knocks went unheeded, the kind she'd once again planned to present in person, with more thanks, tonight. She'd hoped her neighbour would invite her in, that they'd crack open the bottle and drown whatever collective sorrows they managed to scrape together—which had to be quite a few—and maybe lay the foundations of something that might one day be called a friendship.

New city, new job, and Faith is lonely. Not that she would ever admit as much with a clear head, a clean bloodstream; hence the wine.

That had been the plan anyway.

But mice and men and smothered, broken blondes, Mara isn't alone.

Faith can't hear the sounds all the way out here in the kitchen. Those same whimpers and thumps she remembers from when she was ill, sounds she'd later decided—hoped?—had been amplified by delirium, fever-swollen and exaggerated beyond all measure of reality. Until now. She picks up the cordless phone for the second time that night, index finger hovering above the 0 on the keypad.

What if Mara hates her for calling the police?

What if the boyfriend? lover? (rapist?) takes it out on Mara herself?

What if the police don't arrive in time, or even at all?

Damn it. She places the undialled phone on the table, creeps instead down the hall to the bedroom and listens by the door. Nothing, no sound at all from beyond the wall, and is that a good thing or does it mean that something much worse is happening next door? Or has happened?

Bitch!

The jagged masculine snarl so loud it might be in the next room and Faith near jumps out of her skin, hands quickly at her mouth to stop the cry that rises in her throat.

But it's what comes after that finally kicks her indecisive arse into gear. The muffled sobs for him to stop, to *please just stop*, echoing in her head as she races back through the townhouse. Grabbing the wine bottle on her way—weapon? appeasement? excuse?—and then straight outside, bare feet smarting on the gravel path that joins her place with Mara's, running so fast that by the time she's pounding on the woman's front door, Faith is breathless.

A small eternity until, just as she thinks no one is ever going to answer and she's going to need that phone after all, there's a flicker of shadow over the peephole and the door opens a couple guarded inches.

"What do you want, Faith?"

Mara's eye is near-shut swollen, she's bleeding from two nasty cuts on her cheek that seem in dire need of stitches, and that's just the side of her face that Faith can see. "Are you...are you okay?"

Only the most stupid question she could have possibly asked, but Mara actually smiles, thin icicle smirk accompanied by a shake of her head, that glossy red hair rippling over her face, and Faith wonders how much of that colour tastes like iron right now. "I'm fine. Go home."

"You don't look fine. You look like you need help."

Mara closes her eyes and sighs, a blood-smeared hand rubbing hard against her forehead. "Faith," she says, and, "listen," and then there is some scuffling behind her and the door is jerked all the way open.

He's shorter than Mara, shorter even than Faith whose eye he refuses to meet as he pushes narrow-shouldered between them, shrugging into a grey suit jacket with a peacock blue tie hanging from its pocket. Faith can see the red wedged beneath his manicured nails, the flecks of crimson on his creased white shirt.

"Phillip, wait," Mara calls out, but the man doesn't even pause. Just half turns his head to mutter something which might have been *forget it* or *fuck it* or something else entirely before scuttling through the little front gate like a cockroach surprised at midnight. The hazard lights on a silver Audi flash twice as he crosses the road towards it, and within seconds the man is inside and speeding away.

"Great," Mara says. "That's just great." Sounding more resigned than angry, even though she's standing there with both hands on her hips and eyebrows drawn together in a frown that just about freezes Faith's heart. As does the blood runnelling down both her cheeks, and the sticky-wet way that black satin robe wrinkles against her ribs.

Faith swallows. "He won't be back tonight, will he?"

"God no," Mara snorts. "*He* won't be back." Then her gaze drops to the bottle of wine hanging uselessly at Faith's side and she sighs once again. Bitterdeep breath that holds all the cares of the world and then some.

"Come inside," she says, stepping back from the door. "You and me, we need to talk."

* * *

Of course she's going to look around. Mara having excused herself for a quick shower, leaving Faith to open the wine and wander through to the loungeroom, glasses in hand and bottle tucked awkward beneath her arm, and surely it doesn't hurt to look. Not that there's much to see; Spartans lived larger than this.

Big navy blue sofa along the far wall, bare-topped coffee table and two mismatched chairs—one with a grey pinstripe fabric, and the other the kind of patchy brownish velvet you only find in the most desperate op shops or the trendiest of retro-funk café bars. Small television in one corner and a lamp standing sentry opposite, its shade almost—but not quite—the same deep blue as the sofa. But no DVDs, no CDs, no books. No little knick-knacks or photos in frames, no junk mail or shoes or shopping lists left lying around.

The only remotely personal touch, the only hint that a human being might actually inhabit this space, is the large unframed canvas hanging adjacent to the window. A stemless, scarlet rose blooming against a near-black background, petals open and weeping viscous red tears onto the once-white feather floating below it. Blood tears, bloodflowers; how did that song go again, that Cure song she'd left behind in Sydney along with her night-cast wardrobe and the rest of her angst-ridden trappings? Bittersad lyrics about trust, about never really knowing who you can. The feather is soaked, bedraggled, but still curves resiliently upwards, its tip pure and unsullied, so bright against the darkness that it almost glows.

Faith runs a finger across one of the glistening droplets, and is almost surprised to find the canvas rough and dry, her skin unstained.

"A friend painted that for me. Do you like it?"

The question quietly asked, but Faith still jumps, fights the urge to hide her hand behind her back like a schoolgirl caught with cigarettes or something much worse. *Yeah*, she tells Mara, who has reappeared with showerdamp hair and a flock of bright white butterfly stitches on both cheeks, black satin robe swapped for jeans and a sleek grey jumper. "Yeah, I like it a lot. Might have wanted to arm wrestle you for it once upon a time."

Once upon a time, not so long ago.

"Not now?" Mara smiles, or almost smiles, as she crosses the room to claim her glass of wine from the coffee table. She sits down carefully, right in the middle of the sofa, one leg curled beneath her.

"I'm sort of starting over. You know, leaving the past behind me."

"Hmm, mysterious."

"It really isn't," Faith explains. "It's just that the people I used to hang with, my *friends* or whatever you want to call them, the whole *goth* scene"—bobbing air quotes with both hands around *that* word— "they got to be a little...poisonous."

"Goth scene?" Mara arches an exquisitely plucked eyebrow.

"You know: black clothes, eyeliner, swanning around like they *invented* depression. Like it's fucking *profound* or something."

"I know. There are goths in Melbourne too, you realise."

"Yeah, but it's not my scene down here. And anyway, I'm..."

"Over it?"

"I'm over *me*." Faith slumps into the brown velvet chair, licks the resulting splash of wine from her wrist. "I'm over who I was back there. I'm over feeling shitty every damn day, and *liking* the fact that I'm feeling shitty, and then really hating the fact that I *like* it, if any of that makes any fucking sense at all."

"Perfect sense."

Mara is good, Faith will give her that. Sitting there sipping wine and encouraging Faith to babble on about nothing like this is just some cozy girls' night in after all, like she hasn't been cut to pieces by her arsehole boyfriend or whatever variety of pondscum he happens to be.

"Listen, Mara, are you okay? Really?"

"I'm fine."

"Maybe I should drive you to hospital. Get someone to check you over, just to make sure there isn't—"

"I'm *fine.*"

Her tone icier now, a note of warning clearly sounded, but Faith plunges ahead nevertheless. "You don't have to put up with that shit, Mara. You don't have to be scared of getting help either, and if you need someone to be here with you when that arsehole comes back—"

"He won't be coming back," Mara snaps. "Believe me."

"How can you be so sure? Guys like that—"

"Do you take me for an imbecile? A victim?"

Faith swallows, searching for the right words. "I'm just...concerned. I can hear stuff through the walls, you know. Stuff that doesn't sound too good."

"What you do think is happening here? Do you think that man is my *lover?* That I need to be *rescued* from him?"

The sneer in her voice unmistakable despite the peculiar accent, perhaps even because of it, and all at once Faith has had enough, has had more than enough. Feels a little like she's being kicked in the guts herself one too many times tonight and, "Oh, fuck *off.* I'm not the one sitting there with my face looking like it got pushed through a plate-glass window."

Incredibly, Mara laughs.

"This is funny? Some sad prick beats you up a couple times a week, and it's meant to be funny?"

"He's not a prick," Mara says, still smiling. "Well, he may be that, but he's also a client. Or at least he *was*—tonight was his first visit and I doubt he left with a good impression. Lasting perhaps, but not good."

"What sort of a client?" Asking even as the pennies start to tumble.

"The kind who pays for *services rendered.*"

It's not like Mara is the first prostitute Faith has ever encountered. Hell, half her former friends could be considered whores in kind, blow jobs and sleights of hand casually swapped for half a tab of speedspun bliss almost any night of the week, a gram or two of pot any given morning after.

Faith takes another mouthful of wine, its flavour grown acidic and sharp.

"Look," she says. "That doesn't matter. Just because a guy pays you, doesn't mean he gets to hurt you."

Mara shakes her head. "Sweet girl, that's what they pay me *for*."

* * *

Except that they don't.

Pay her, definitely. Pay her enough to mean she only has to work when she wants, and can afford to be choosy about who she sees, and how often.

But they never actually *hurt* her.

The disorder has a complicated name and an even more complicated diagnosis, but what it boils down to is her nervous system is defective, has been all her life. What it boils down to is she can't feel any kind of pain, can't feel extremes of hot or cold either for that matter, can't feel much more than pressure and touch.

What it boils down to is this:

Mara can be slapped and bruised and cut and burned and left broken in more ways than any human being should ever have cause to know, and none of it will hurt. All of it will heal, and most of it will heal very fast.

This makes her special.

This makes her *expensive*.

* * *

Faith hasn't bothered setting up an internet connection at home yet—no one she cares to email and too many who'll be wanting to email her—so she's McSurfing through her thirty-minute lunchbreak instead. Greasy hamburger in one hand, fritzy trackball mouse in the other, and nothing but frustration on the screen in front of her. Loads of words, masses of infocrap—googling *can't feel pain* gets her more than sixteen million results just to start with—but nothing really useful. *Sensory neuropathy* and *congenital insensitivity* and *Riley-Day syndrome* and every time a piece seems to fit, it turns out she's just been holding it upside down.

Mara doesn't fit anywhere. Not precisely.

Unless it's on one of the forbidden pages, the family-friendly blockerbots insisting she maintain a minimum safe distance.

Yet another click to bring up *congenital analgia* and maybe this is it at last: *a syndrome characterized by a global insensitivity to physical pain.* Following the links to find not a perfect fit but the best one so far, even with the short life expectancy, the high rates of undiagnosed infection, the frequency of scratched corneas, amputated fingers, and tongue-tips bitten clean off in infancy. List after list of predictable injuries, obliviously accidental wounds without pain to give notice, but so what?

Maybe Mara just knows how to take care of herself.

Rattle of ice from the boy behind her who's slurping the dregs of his drink right in her ear, and Faith takes the hint. Five minutes late already and they'll dock her for that, dock her but still demand that she make up the sales, push her quota of crappy holiday deposits onto pensioners who only leave their homes every second Thursday to punch the pokies and dream of rolling over those three magic bars.

* * *

Mara has brought fruitcake. A large, moist lump of a thing that crumbles when Faith tries to cut too thin a wedge, her butter knife clearly not up to the job.

"Don't feel obliged to eat it. I didn't."

The cake left by one of Mara's clients last Christmas and Faith wonders at the type of men who take pleasure in first reducing a woman to tears and bruises and bloody wounds, and then in bringing her gifts.

"It's good, I like fruitcake. You sure you don't want a piece?"

Mara wrinkles her nose. "Thank you, no." She's only come to say there'll be company at her place tonight, from eight until ten give or take half an hour depending on how things develop. In case Faith would rather not be here.

"Thanks for the warning."

"I don't mind if you play loud music. That's what Matthew used to do."

"Who?"

"The tenant who lived here before." That midnight gaze sliding over the kitchen where the two of them sit at the wonky little table Faith picked up for twenty dollars at St. Vinnies, along with three matching wooden chairs. "Not as neat as you, but better furniture."

"Right." Faith wonders just what sort of man he had really been. The bury-your-head-in-the-stereo kind, or the kind who angled for a free sample. She breaks off a sizeable corner of cake and pops it into her mouth, chews very slowly and tries to ignore the thought that emerges yet again from some sick little hollow of her mind.

Sneaking up on Mara with a needle, just to see what would happen.

Just to see if she could make her flinch.

"Come on then," Mara says, and Faith almost chokes on a chunk of maraschino cherry. "You obviously have questions. Ask away."

The cake now dry as unbuttered toast on her tongue, too much of it to swallow quickly so Faith chews and chews, but Mara is already flicking a dismissive hand in the air. Never mind the questions, those cautious-curious inquiries posed by so many others in not so many ways. She knows them all by rote anyway, so how about they just skip straight to the answers?

The clients, these men who come to see her, they each have their reasons: sadistic power trip or erotic wish fulfillment, extreme role playing or morbid curiosity plain and unadorned. In some, the reason dwells deep below the surface, inscrutable even to themselves, and there is only the *need*, a desire pure and compulsive and absolute, that draws them to her. Some she only sees the once before they retreat ashen-faced from her door, the experience not quite what they'd expected, or else, too much more. Some are regular as the new moon. *All* of them want to hurt her; an uncommon few wish the favour returned. The clients, they're complicated.

As for Mara, it's simple. She does it for the money. And for the record, there is no sex involved; she's not that kind of whore. On occasion, for a certain kind of client, she'll use her hands to finish things off. But that service costs extra, quite a bit extra, and in any case, most of those who need it prefer to relieve themselves.

What she does, it's not about *sex.*

And never mind the soundtrack; every good girl knows how to fake it.

"So you don't get hurt?" No matter how many websites she looks at, Faith can't really get her head around this. Pain doesn't *cause* damage, it heralds it, and if someone can't feel pain, then how can they judge if they're hurt, or how badly?

"I see a specialist," Mara says. "Regular checkups."

"Does he know? How they happen, I mean, all your...injuries?"

That greyhound smile again, swift and lean and borderline dangerous. "He should do. He causes his fair share."

"Okay." Faith swallows, hard. Pushes the rest of her fruitcake away. "I'm not even gonna pretend that I understand—"

"I don't *need* you to understand," Mara cuts in sharply. "I don't even need you to care. I'm not a puzzle, I'm not something you need to solve. Or rescue. I've told you this so you know what's happening and you won't come hammering at my door again in the middle of a session and cost me a client."

"I already said I was sorry—"

"I don't need *that* either."

The two of them glaring at each other until at last Mara pushes back her chair and gets to her feet. "I realise you're lonely, Faith. But I don't do friendship."

"Even if I paid you for it?"

A cheap shot instantly regretted, but Mara only laughs. "Even then, Faith. Especially then."

***

She doesn't leave. Doesn't turn on any music or even the lights. Just sits on her bed in the dark with her cheek pressed against the wall, and listens.

To nothing very much, in the end. Random sounds of movement and the occasional murmur of voices, low-key and indecipherable. Not every psycho likes his girl to scream, apparently, and Faith wonders why she doesn't feel more relieved.

(Or less disappointed?)

Awkwardly crossed, her left leg has fallen so deeply asleep that she needs both hands to straighten it out. Heavy-numb lump of flesh below her knee, and only the vaguest sensation of pressure as she digs a fingernail into the muscle of her calf, digs hard enough to leave a little red smiley behind.

Is that what Mara feels or, rather, what she doesn't? Ever?

Faith tries to imagine what it would be like to have your whole body cocooned in this way, to have never known even the incidental pain of stubbed toes, torn fingernails, and paper cuts, never mind anything more profound. Might it be so bad, if you were careful? Thinking of the reasons she left Sydney, left the people *in* Sydney, what was left of them, Faith grimaces.

Painlessness, on both sides of her skin: she could wish for worse.

***

Sometimes, Mara leaves a note. Little scraps of powder blue paper wedged into the screen door at eye level with a handwritten date and time, three or four days' notice for Faith to make other plans if she feels the need.

(Mostly she doesn't.)

But more often lately, it's a personal appearance, a handful of words or perhaps a whole cryptic, fractured conversation about spoiled milk, lost languages, or the tribe of magpies that wander along the street each morning, spotting grubs in the nature strip and marking each passerby with a polished-marble glare.

"Friend of the crows," Faith murmurs.

"Pardon me?"

"I used to know someone who said that whenever she saw a magpie: *friend of the crows*, and she'd point two fingers at it and then back at herself. So they wouldn't dive-bomb her come spring."

"And was she?"

"What?"

"A friend of the crows."

Mara sounding so serious that Faith has to laugh. "Geez, I don't know, maybe. Never did get swooped on, not that I remember." And Mara nods, once, and turns on her heel, and that's the end of that yet again. Two steps forward, three steps back, like someone braving herself to jump from the high-dive board, and Faith wonders what it is that Mara is after. Why she can't come out and say straight up that maybe she is just as lonely as Faith, that a friend might actually be what she needs.

And yet.

There is definitely something not quite right about the woman. Not drugs or drink or any other kind of mundane madness—and Faith has known enough of these in recent times to tell—but something else she can't quite identify.

Mara is just...not right.

* * *

Middle of the night phone calls never a good thing and Faith swears loudly as she lurches from her bed, tripping on a boot and bumping her knee on the corner of the dresser on her way to the door. Three months in the townhouse and she still can't find her way in the dark, so it's a speedy zombie shuffle down the hall with arms outstretched to fumble for the loungeroom lightswitch while she tries to pinpoint the handset's location from its shrill, persistent ring.

Who the fuck could be calling at this hour?

No one has this number except work and her mum, and she's sworn, she's *sworn*, that no matter who turns up on her doorstep or what they say or plead or promise, she won't let them know where Faith has gone.

Of all people, she *knows* the importance of this.

The phone is under a couch cushion. Faith's stomach tightens as she presses the talk button, lifts the thing cautiously to her ear. "Hello?"

Someone breathing, or just static on a crappy line? *Hey, babygirl, when you gonna come back to us?* She can almost hear Livia crooning those words, and she swallows hard. Please not her, not Liv—the one person in the whole damn world she can refuse nothing, even when those brilliant green eyes are cracked and scattered and ice-locked, or perhaps especially then—and *hello*, she says again. "Hello?"

"Faith? Faith, it's me."

"Mara?" The voice so scratchy-faint that for a second she thinks she's guessed wrong. Thinks she should hang up right now before it's too late, because she really doesn't have the strength to do this all over again, but *please* the voice whispers, *please come get me*, and her heart falls back from her mouth just a little.

"Mara, what's wrong? Where are you?"

* * *

She must have misheard, or miswritten, because Grafton Avenue only goes up to number 119 and then it's nothing but parkland. Close-huddled shrubs and knee-high grasses, with a wan yellow streetlight illuminating the sign that tries to pass this place off as *Urban Forest*. Yeah right, and Faith checks the envelope where she scribbled down the address. Definitely 141, but maybe it should be 114? Or perhaps not Grafton *Avenue*, but Street or Crescent or Road, if such a beast exists?

Unclipping her seatbelt, she reaches across for the Melways on the passenger seat and flips to the index. The interior light in the old Toyota hasn't worked for two years, so she's squinting her way through the G's when something taps at the driver side window. Little scared-mouse tap still sudden enough to startle: Mara standing out there in the night with a half-curled fist and a face bleached whiter than Faith has ever seen on someone still living, pointing at the locked rear door with her other hand, her mouth moving soundlessly beyond the glass.

Three frozen seconds before Faith finally gets her arse up and out of the car. Mara is wrapped in something that looks like a sheet, low-budget toga costume hanging in thick folds from her shoulders, the dull-dark fabric even darker in patches, and Faith doesn't want to think too much about those just yet. More concerned with getting Mara into the car, Mara who shakes her head when Faith tries to lead her around to the passenger side, who wants to lie down instead, who says she *needs* to lie down, and so Faith opens the back door and helps her crawl inside.

Even with legs loosely curled, Mara takes up almost the whole length of the seat. This tall, lean woman not so solid now, and the way she shivers in her goosepimpled skin almost breaks Faith's heart. One bare foot sticks out from beneath the sheet with toes clenched tight, pallid little piggies turning their backs to the world, and Faith tugs a corner of the fabric over them.

"Mara, don't go to sleep on me, okay?" Leaning in and over the woman, pushing damp-matted hair from her face. "Listen, I don't know this area. Where do I go, where's the nearest hospital?"

A cobra could not have struck as quickly.

"No hospitals!" Hand closing rat-trap tight around Faith's wrist, pupils so dilated they make her whole eyes glow black, and no, she hisses again. *No hospitals.*

"Fuck that, Mara. You need—"

"No! If you even *drive past* a hospital, I swear to—" Turning her head aside as she starts to cough, brutal as broken glass, and when it's over her chin is smeared with blood. "I swear I will get out of this car. I'll get out right now, if that's what you're planning." And she almost does, pushing herself up off the seat and sliding towards the door until Faith wrestles her back down, or tries to, tells her not to be so fucking stupid, but she already knows the battle is lost. No way she can take this woman anywhere against her will, and she'd bet both tits that Mara really would throw herself from a moving vehicle if she so much as *smelled* an Emergency Room sign.

"All right. All *right*, fuck!"

A long, tense moment before Mara nods and finally releases her grip. "Just get me out of here. Please."

"Where to?" Faith asks bitterly. Fresh handprint of blood on her arm and she wipes it on her shirt, navy blue fabric none the worse for such a stain. "Home to warm milk and jim-jams?"

"No, not home." Mara closes her eyes, sinks back against the cheap vinyl upholstery. "Get us onto the highway and drive south. There's a motel about twenty minutes from here."

Faith is done arguing. So when she spots the bright-lit storefront of a twenty-four hour pharmacy—*Because Your Health Shouldn't Have To Wait!*—after only a few kilometres, she doesn't even ask. Just flicks on the indicator and pulls into the near-deserted carpark. "Don't even start," she tells the rearview mirror, Mara's instantly suspicious gaze catching her own within the glass. "Unless you reckon you can put yourself back together with whatever this cruddy motel of yours has in its minibar, then I'm picking up some stuff here. That okay with you?"

Not really a question, and Mara doesn't answer it, doesn't say another word until Faith returns to the car. Two small plastic bags rustling with bandages and Dettol and surgical tape and anything else she thought might come in handy. Paracetamol too, for the headache that looms at her temples, and she presses a couple of these into her palm straight away. Dry swallows and turns to flash the box at the woman in the back seat, "Don't suppose *you* want some..."

Mara's laughter splinters to a wet and ragged cough.

"Rainbows End."

"What?"

"The motel, it's called Rainbows End. Keep driving, you'll see it."

***

She almost didn't. Almost sped right past the place, with its tall pine trees half hiding the vacancy sign out front, and now that she's standing in the cramped reception area, she wishes she'd done just that. The night manager pushes a form across the counter and Faith hesitates for a second, pen in hand. She doesn't know Mara's last name and is reluctant to use her own because...well, just *because*, and so: *Courtney Love*, the first words that pop into her head and now nothing else will, but the man doesn't even blink when she slides the form back.

Made up name, made up address, the tariff paid with cash. Two nights in advance because otherwise they'll have to be out by ten this morning and it's already almost four, and Faith feels sick.

Sick and scared and royally pissed off.

Their twin-share room right at the end of the complex, no neighbours if the absence of cars is any indication, so thank fuck for small mercies. Faith parks at the front and gets out to open the car door for Mara, chauffeur duties never grimmer than this as her passenger extends an arm for support, stares up at her with eyes deeply shadowed but still burning bright. Tiger eyes, savage and regal, and how it must sting for Mara to have to lean against Faith like this.

Beneath the pine-sharp patina of disinfectant, the room smells of strangers and stale cigarettes. Faith helps Mara over to one of the beds, dumps the pharmacy bags beside her, and then goes back to sling the *Shhh! Guest Sleeping!* sign onto the doorknob. Flimsy chain latch on the inside and she pulls that across too.

"I want some water," Mara says.

"Let's have a look at you first."

Mara shakes her head, clutches her toga-sheet with both hands. "I can look after myself." Weighty blue-green cotton like you'd find in an operating theatre, far too much of it soaked magenta by now, and Faith has well and truly had enough of this shit.

"Fuck you then."

Four long strides to the door of the room, fishing the car keys from her pocket with one hand while the other reaches for the security chain, because this isn't her problem and never was and—

"Wait," Mara whispers. "Please." Little-girl-lost voice Faith has never heard before, little girl lost *forever*, and somehow that's more frightening than all the blood. A voice to stop her dead, and she turns to see Mara rising carefully to her feet. "Look then," Mara says. "Look if it matters so much to you." And she lets the sheet fall.

Bride of Fucking Frankenstein the first thing that comes to mind, but it's so much worse than that.

Black-bristled sutures winding their jagged way from clavicles to pelvis, vaguely Y-shaped like an autopsy incision and crowded by an ugly patchwork of cuts that could only in these circumstances be thought lesser wounds. Ribs and belly and the almost non-existent swell of her breasts all bearing the mark of knife or scalpel, some stitches torn apart and bleeding fresh crimson rivulets to join the dark and clotted mess that cakes her body from the waist down.

"Christ."

The word little more than appalled, astonished breath, but Mara just grins. "Nothing to do with *him*," she says, as a thin trickle of blood slides down her calf and around her ankle, pools on grotty grey carpet that has seen better days—though surely not worse ones.

For an entire precarious minute, Faith just stares, car keys digging sharply into her palm. She can still leave, can still turn her back on this whole fucked-up mess and just walk away, drive away and try very hard to pretend that she never even heard the phone ring tonight, *because this is not her problem.* This is Mara's nightmare but if Faith doesn't leave right now, if she doesn't open the motel door right this second, then it will become her nightmare as well and god only knows when—or if—either of them will wake up.

Mara wobbles a little, unsteady on her feet, then half-sinks, half-falls back onto the bed. "Can I have that water now?"

And even as Faith closes her eyes, even before she takes her first resigned step towards the ensuite, a shored-up space within her cracks and splits and breaks wide open, and something far too familiar worms its way out, uncurls its long and greedy limbs, and laughs.

***

The scant, thin hour before dawn and Mara seems to have fallen asleep at last. Her shallow breathing has deepened, become more regular, and there's not the slightest response when Faith calls her name. No movement, no murmur, not even the semi-conscious flutter of an eyelid, but Faith thinks she'll wait a little while longer just to be sure.

Wet, bloody-pink wads of cotton wool litter the floor, and a stained towel huddles at the end of the bed where Faith left it once Mara finally pushed her away. *Enough, enough for now,* after Faith finished washing the dried and crusted blood from her chest, her stomach, her ribs. Pale fists bunched in the sheet around her hips, clenching tighter when Faith tried to pull that down as well, tried to see the damage lurking below but *There's nothing,* Mara said. *Just blood from everything else,* and clean or dirty, what she really needed was rest.

The smell of antiseptic fills the room and Faith worries what Mara might look like beneath her sutured skin.

Or even just beneath the sheet.

Finally, careful to make not the smallest telltale sound, Faith slips from her bed and pads over to Mara's. She takes hold of the stained and crumpled fabric and peels it slowly back, wincing at the whispersoft crackle of dried blood as she draws it all the way to Mara's parted knees, morbid magician flourish to reveal—

Just what, it takes Faith a second or two to fathom.

Nothing left of what should be found between a woman's legs. Only several deep cuts cleaving flesh right down to the glisten of bone, vicious wounds like someone put a fucking *axe* to work, and filled with so much dried and crusted blood that Faith tastes bile rising fresh to her throat. So much blood that maybe it seems worse than it is—nothing band-aids are gonna fix, sure, but still maybe not as horrendous as she thinks either—and she forces herself to lean forward, to look closer.

Too close: not enough time to withdraw as Mara suddenly twists sideways and draws up her legs. Kicks out and catches Faith full in the chest with enough force to send her spinning across the room, winded and gasping like she's been kicked by a frightened horse. Tacky carpet beneath her hands as she lands and scuttles backwards on her arse, more than a little frightened herself now with Mara getting up from the bed and stalking naked towards her. Amazon tall and stitched together like a broken doll, a piece of her too large—too *chunky*—to be simply skin flapping open between her legs, slapping against her thigh with each determined step.

Faith barely makes it to the toilet before she throws up.

"Hey." Hands on her back, her shoulders, reaching around to pull the hair from her face. "You shouldn't have seen that, you should have trusted me. You should have listened when I said I was fine."

"You're not *fine*." Turning to find Mara with a motel towel wrapped close around her waist, greyish-white and already spotted scarlet. "Can you even see yourself, can you see what he's...*done* to you? What he's..." The image of torn, bloodied flesh still stark behind her eyes, blinding, and Faith stuffs a fist into her mouth. *Mara*, she whispers, and *oh christ*, and then *Mara* again.

They're all the words she can summon.

Mara sighs and sinks heavily to the floor, knees pressed tight together. "You don't understand, Faith. You don't even know the half of it."

* * *

The story is, last night was a game of Doctors & Nurses. More precisely, Doctors & Doctors—Mara's *specialist* friend with some friends of his own along for the ride, medical degrees decidedly optional. A room in a house done up as an operating theatre, and Mara the star attraction.

A patient who would remain fully conscious while you sliced and prodded and poked around inside her. A patient who would speak on command, who would weep or gasp or not speak at all if that's what you preferred. Eyes wide and bright and completely aware, even as you curved a hand around her heart to feel its rhythms against your awestruck palm.

Even as you stitched her closed again, your fingers sweating, trembling, inside their surgical gloves.

The story is, even this was not enough. Sex never in the contract but one of them had pulled down her bikini briefs anyway, the others circling close like leering wolves with the scent of blood thick in their nostrils. Until they forced apart her legs and saw what wasn't there.

As for what *was*, well. Nothing any of them could ever have seen before.

Simply, *nothing*.

Mara thinks they used a cleaver. They'd brought all sorts of tools, all kinds of implements to play with. A cleaver, or some other heavy-bladed knife.

But the story is: Mara gave far better than she ever might have gotten and by the end, not all of the blood spilled had been hers.

Not even most of it.

* * *

Faith doesn't want to know exactly what that means. What any of it means. Is only too grateful to be sent in search of the small combination-locked suitcase Mara has left in care of the management for precisely such an occasion.

"Should have told us you was with her, love." A different man from the previous night, tall and hollow-cheeked, leaning towards Faith with both forearms flat on the counter. "She stays as long she needs, tell her. No charge."

Then, with genuine concern, "She okay, you reckon?"

And Faith, who knows nothing about anything anymore and is trying very hard to feel just the same, merely nods. "I think so. She says so."

Back in the room, Mara thanks her for the suitcase and disappears with it into the ensuite. There is the sound of the door locking and, after a few minutes, the rhythmic patter of the shower. Faith flops onto the bed—*her* bed, not the other one—and throws an elbow over her eyes to block out the morning sun now squeezing slantways through the not-so-vertical blinds.

Thoughts of Sydney crowd forward and, for the first time in a long time, she doesn't push them automatically away. Livia and Ben and all the others she left behind, one thousand kilometres worth of behind, because who knew how wide that particular vortex yawned. *We're, like, exploring Antarctica here*, someone had mused late one night. Russ, or maybe Corin, she can't recall. Wedged in her memory instead, the wired exultation in Liv's reply: *Baby, no, there's dirt and rocks and shit under there. This is the fucking Arctic Circle: nothing but ice all the way down.*

Livia, raccoon eyes now perpetually smudged with day-old eyeliner, her dyed black hair overgrown with greasy blonde.

Livia, finding veins in her ankles so she can still go sleeveless in summer.

Livia, scratching herself to ruin in the search for subcutaneous life.

Faith had fled. No dramatic watershed moment, no death or overdose or even accidental injury to propel her into the harsh light of day, just waking up one winter morning with frozen toes and the even colder realisation that if she dragged herself off to Livia's that night she might never, ever find her way back home.

Four weeks at her mum's instead. Best mother in the whole damn world to keep her under lock and key like that, self-imposed house arrest in suburbia while she cleaned up, thawed out, thankful that she hadn't really even begun to plumb the sort of depths that Livia and the rest had so eagerly dived to. Surfacing from that level might have—almost certainly *would* have—been impossible. Would have been impossible regardless if she hadn't then picked up and moved to Melbourne with barely a pause for breath or the burning of all her address books. Faith had proved herself stronger than she'd thought, but no way would she ever be strong enough to close a door in Livia's face if that girl decided to come knocking.

Only now there's Mara, and Faith wonders if she doesn't have some sort of subconscious freak-compass guiding her every movement.

The ensuite door swings open, spilling forth steam, fluorescent light and someone Faith almost doesn't recognise. Mara has cut her hair, close-cropped schoolboy style slicked back from her forehead with gel or maybe just water from the shower. Dressed in black jeans and a baggy black t-shirt, she even seems to move differently. Loose-hipped, almost a swagger, with pale arms swinging by her sides as though buffeted by a careless breeze.

"Still here?" The surprise in her voice, no matter how mild, is just too much. This is impossible, *Mara* is impossible. Pain or no pain, no one gets cut open like that and walks around so effortlessly the very next day; no one gets *butchered* the way this woman has been and walks around *at all*, never mind in fucking *jeans*. Faith realises that if she wasn't so furious, so well and truly *fed up*, then she'd most likely be terrified out of her wits right now.

"What are you, Mara?" Anger definitely the preferred option, and she lets it all the way loose. "What the *fuck* are you?" Launching herself from the bed, reaching for Mara with no clear intention beyond doing some sort of violence of her own, but it hardly matters. Mara catches her wrists in hands too strong to be human, crosses them over and then pushes her away. Hard.

Faith lands on the corner of the mattress and topples straight to the floor, terror now sliding into prominence as she rubs her wrists together, so sore the bones themselves seem bruised.

Mara regards her in silence for a few seconds, then nods, as though arriving at some kind of decision. She sits down on the bed opposite, legs apart and elbows resting on her knees. "I'm not sure what I am," she says quietly, staring at a point between her bare, blue-veined feet. "You have so many stories, it becomes difficult—confusing—to hold onto the truth."

Faith swallows, not daring to move.

"I did not fall." Mara glances up, her tear-glazed eyes still sharply focused. "But neither did I choose a side. And more than that, I can't remember."

She winces, hand moving swiftly to her waist where it rubs in smooth, slow circles just below her ribs. "Not all of them doctors then." And to Faith's wordless, uncomprehending shake of the head, "The liver, I think. Re-arranging itself to the proper position."

"But you... It looked like that hurt. *Did* that hurt?"

Mara shrugs.

"You told me you didn't...that you couldn't..." Not finishing, not wanting to finish. Not wanting to say the words to make it real, so Mara says them for her.

"I feel pain, Faith. I feel everything that's ever been done to me, while it lasts." Half a smile, half a grimace curving her thin, pale lips. "But think, would you really feel a mosquito bite if your leg had just been severed? Or would you want to feel it even more? Would you long for that bite, that almost insignificant sting, because the other pain—the loss, the *absence*—was just too unbearable?"

Faith gets to her knees, gets oh so slowly to her feet. "Mara..."

"No." Even with half a room between them, the raised hand snaps her frozen to the spot. "It's too late for *Mara* now. Whatever she had, you can have. Or not. I won't be returning to that place."

Run. Run. Run. Each beat of her heart imploring escape, but Faith can't seem to move. Finds her mouth opening instead, asking if there is something she can do, because if there is anything at all that might help—

"What can you do?" the woman that was Mara snaps. "You and your kind who know nothing but selfishness and cruelty." Rising from the bed, one hand lifting her shirt as if to illustrate the point. Jagged central incision that actually does look markedly better, even after these few brief hours—until two long fingers dig their way beneath the stitches and tug, pulling out half a dozen with a sickening wet *pop*. Gaping, bleeding wound in her belly big enough for a hand to slip into, and it does, emerging again scarlet and dripping and offered to Faith like a promise. "Tell me, what can any of you do?"

Faith feels the motel room door against her shoulder blades, even though she can't recall backing into it.

And the woman, the *creature* that was Mara stalks towards her, taller than ever with bitter-black eyes darker than the despair of stolen souls. "Cruel. Selfish. Arrogant beyond sufferance." But that hand, those blood-soaked fingers, are unexpectedly gentle as they caress Faith's cheek, slide down to cup her chin.

"Yet you are loved," the creature that was Mara whispers. "You are *all loved.*"

Faith can only hope the taste of salt on her lips comes from her own tears.

"Leave." The hand loosens, those terrible eyes close. "Leave now."

And for once, Faith does not need to be told a second time.

* * *

The door to Mara's townhouse stands slightly ajar, slightly crooked.

Half off its hinges, Faith sees when she approaches, and inside the place the damage is worse. Furniture broken, upholstery torn. Smashed crockery and glassware turning the kitchen into a glittering minefield, and the bedroom reeking from the dozens of bottles of perfume that have been spilled onto the stripped and blood-stained mattress. In the wreck of a home still devoid of intimate possessions and personal touches, the saddest thing is the painting of the floating red rose. The canvas now cut to pieces, palm-sized scraps scattered over the loungeroom floor, and the wooden frame upon which it had been stretched cowering in a corner like some skeletal, broken-backed beast.

By her foot, a bit of canvas lies face down. *arest Mar* scrawled on its back in a small but confident hand, and Faith gets down on her knees to find the rest of the inscription. Oversized, paint-stiff jigsaw with too many blank pieces, but finally she has all the ones she needs.

For My Timeless Love, My Dearest Marguerette, who waits for no man. Arthur. New Orleans, July 1928.

And Marguerette may not be Mara. And Mara may have lied about the artwork being done for her by a friend. And Arthur, whoever he was, may have painted this canvas for a woman who did decide to wait for him after all, a woman with whom he grew old and lined, a woman who was mortal and human and who did not look up at the stars at night and remember what it was like to walk above them.

But Faith doesn't think so.

Especially when she turns the pieces of canvas over to see they show the curved, blood-draggled feather. Long and thin and silverwhite, the feather of eagle or albatross or some other creature equally glorious and skybound and doomed.

Arthur, whoever he was, he had known.

Faiths curls up on the carpet, knees drawn close to her chest, and wonders when she'll stop crying. *Don't you ever forget how strong you are, sweetheart,* her mum had said. *You got yourself through this, you can get yourself through anything.*

But right now, all she wants is to feel Livia's arms around her, Livia murmuring meaningless shit into her ear. All she wants is not to feel the weight of a new day, the weight of new knowledge too frightening to consider except from the most oblique of angles. Never mind how she gets there.

Never mind if she never, ever finds her way out again.

You are loved, it had said, blood running down its slender wrist.

Right now, the scraps of canvas clutched in her desperate, desolate fists, Faith thinks love never burned colder than this.

WE ALL FALL DOWN

"NO WAY, NOT again you're not," Holly snaps, leaning forward to switch off the radio before Wham even gets past their second jitterbug. "What's that, the hundredth time they've played that piece of crap song today?"

Emma shrugs. "It's been in the charts for weeks, I guess they have to play it."

"Yeah, well I don't have to listen to it." Pissy little voice getting pissier by the minute, and Emma keeps her eyes on the road. Cyclone Holly brewing ever since the cassette player chewed up her mix tape an hour ago, but Emma doesn't want to fight. Not this weekend. Not *their* weekend.

"Check the glovebox," she suggests. "There should be a couple tapes in there. Velvet Underground maybe, and—"

Holly snorts. "Fuck Lou Reed."

"Or we can just talk." Another snort, served with extra derision, and Emma leaves it alone. Less than an hour and they'll be at Buchan anyway, though with the sun already an hour past setting it'll be too late to go up to the caves tonight. They hadn't even left Melbourne until after four—Holly not being able to find first her boots, then her keys—and it's ended up being a longer drive than either of them predicted while studying maps on the kitchen bench. Somehow, this is Emma's fault, along with the Corolla's dodgy cassette player and the fact that Holly has left her camera back at the flat. She only hopes the motel is as good as it looks in the tourist guide. Hell, clean sheets and high-pressure hot water will do. With Holly coaxed into the shower, few are the wonders a pair of soap-slicked hands cannot work.

"What are you grinning about?"

"Huh?" Emma shakes her head. "Nothing much, just thinking how good a hot shower's gonna feel tonight."

"If they even *have* hot water out here. Fricken Hicksville."

"Hol, come on. Stop looking for problems."

"Don't have to look very far, do I?"

Emma sighs and sneaks a sideways glance at the girl in the passenger seat. Even in the post-twilight haze she can see the crease drawn deep at the corner of her mouth, the strand of long brown hair winding, unwinding, and winding again round her index finger, tight enough to stop blood. Fair warnings for foul weather, and Emma feels the angry spark of tears behind her eyes. God damn it to hell, nothing ever seems to go right these days; the rift widening between them for weeks and every attempt to bridge it proving futile. Holly is falling away, faster than Emma can run to catch her, and she hasn't the faintest idea why.

What has she done? What hasn't she done?

And if the girl is planning to leave her, why doesn't she just bloody well get it over and done with instead of scattering this daily minefield of eggshells for Emma to tiptoe over. Damn it, why doesn't—

"Em! Fuck!"

She's already seen the animal by the time Holly screams, but it's still a fraction of a second too late and her stomach rolls as she wrenches the wheel to the left, riding the brakes as the car skids off the road and onto the shoulder. Gravel crunches, sliding sharp beneath the wheels, and the kangaroo seems to almost turn in mid-air, a balletic turbo-charged leap to clear the bonnet, and in its place a looming, shadow-thick shape that Emma barely registers as a telegraph pole before the car slams into it. Sickening metallic crunch louder than the blood beating in her ears, the seatbelt jerking tight against her collarbone, throwing her back against the seat with a sharp whiplash jolt, and throughout it all the flow of time slower than honey poured out on a cold winter morning.

Beside her, Holly starts to cry.

"Holly? Baby, are you okay?" The girl has her face in her hands, breathworn sobs hitching her shoulders in sharp, spastic rhythms, and when Emma touches her thigh she whimpers. Soft, kicked-puppy whimper and then she's fumbling with the door handle, half-climbing, half-falling onto the road, with a wet-dark shadow on her cheek that makes Emma sick to see. Calling for the girl to wait, to please just *wait*, as her own seatbelt refuses to unbuckle and her masochistic brain flashes up every Hollywood post-crash explosion she's ever witnessed. *Damn it, Holly, help me.* Then the belt slips loose at last and she clambers out, panting in the chill night air.

Fresh night air. No stink of leaking petrol, no greasy smell of smoke.

Holly is standing in front of the car, what's left of the front of the car, skinny arms crossed over her chest. The headlights are still shining, albeit askew, and Emma can see the blood on the girl's face. Dark red smear like the worst kind of raspberry birthmark, and she swallows the panic that threatens to rise. "Holly, are you hurt? How badly are you hurt?"

The girl shakes her head. "I'm fine."

"But you're..." Emma limps around the car, a dull pain throbbing in her right knee. "You're bleeding, baby. A lot."

Holly pushes Emma's hand away. Sniffs and wipes at her face with the back of her wrist. "Just a bloody nose, I must have bashed it."

"You sure, cause it looks—"

"What the fuck *was* that, Em?"

"A kangaroo, I think."

"I *know* it was a kangaroo, I mean what the fuck were you doing? Why weren't you paying attention to the road instead of...of...of whatever it was you were doing? You could have *killed* me, Em. Don't you fucking realise that?"

Emma bites her lip, reaches out, but the girl pushes her away. Hard. Pushes her away and lands a series of savage kicks on the crumpled radiator grill, as though she could hope to outdo the telegraph pole in the damage stakes. "Look. At. This. Shit."

"Holly, calm down."

"*You* calm down." Crying again, her voice hoarse and broken.

Emma says nothing, because nothing will help, just grabs the girl and pulls her close. Holly such a tiny thing, little more than skin and bone and sharp, furious elbows, and Emma holds her until she stops struggling, holds her tighter than she ever has, than she ever might again, and makes soft, soothing noises into her hair. *It's okay*, she whispers when the girl finally gives up, burns out, and sags exhausted against her. *It's okay, we're okay, we're okay, we're okay.* Over and over and over again, until she's no longer talking about the accident.

Until it no longer feels like so much of a lie.

***

There isn't a clear path up the hill, not one that is lighted at least, and Emma swears loudly as she trips for the third time. Her knee is really hurting now, little darts of pain marking every step, but she isn't about to beg for a rest break.

"Em?" Holly's voice falls down through the darkness. "You all right?"

"Yeah," she grunts. "Just tripped on something."

A sigh, short and sharp, edged with frustration. "Come on, almost there."

Which seems about right, looking up. Close enough to the house to make out the striped curtains hanging on each side of the lighted window, the shapes of furniture within. No movement inside though, and Emma lets out a breath she hadn't realised she'd been holding. If no one is home after all, if they've walked up this damn hill for nothing...

"Em?"

"Coming." One foot in front of the other, never mind the pain, never mind the fact that they probably would have been picked up by a passing motorist by now if they'd just waited by the car. Once Holly noticed the light on the hill—*Come on, Em, we can use their phone*—that was that. The girl refuses to wait for anything if she can help it, if there is something she can be *doing* instead. Even if the alternative ends up costing more in time and effort, for Holly anything is always better than standing still.

It's one of the things Emma loves about her. Most of the time.

There's a yellowish porch light shining by the time they reach the house, so maybe someone's heard them coming and rolled out the welcome, or maybe she just didn't notice it before. No bell or knocker, so Holly thumps three times on the front door with the flat of her fist. Loud enough to raise the dead but there's no response from inside the house, no footsteps or floorboard creak, and Emma opens her mouth to say something she probably shouldn't, how Holly better be prepared to *carry* her back down that fucking hill now but—

"Shhh," Holly says, tilting her head. "Listen."

So Emma does. Closes her eyes and even holds her breath for a couple seconds, trying to pluck a sound from beyond the ratchety, rhythmic buzz of the cicadas which seem to have colonised the surrounding trees in near plague proportions, but there's nothing. Nothing whatsoever until she opens her eyes again to see Holly with her cheek pressed close against the front door, her lips slightly parted, and even then it's not something that she *hears* exactly. More like feels, or senses.

Something standing motionless on the other side of that door, its lean-long face turned in precisely the same manner as Holly's, with two slim inches of hardwood the only thing between them.

Emma doesn't think, just grabs the girl's arm and jerks her backwards. Away from the door, away from whatever it is that's waiting on the other side—"Let's *go*, Holly!"—and she's still tugging on her when the door swings abruptly open, and both of them shriek in sudden fright.

All *three* of them, actually: Emma, Holly and the plump, middle-aged woman who stands before them with one hand on the doorjamb and the other fluttering at her throat like a pale, panic-struck bird.

Holly is the first to recover. "Sorry, we didn't mean to scare you."

"That's all right." The woman forces a dry, cracked chuckle which says otherwise. "Seems I scared the two of you just as badly."

Emma doubts that as well. The woman has lowered her hand, but her fingers still tremble at her side, and her face is ashen. It's the face of a woman who lives alone, who has no one to come running from the back of the house should she cry out again. A woman who is already regretting the decision to open her door that night, and who might just slam it shut again at any second.

"I'm Emma Vargus," she says quickly. "This is my friend, Holly Davidson." Nudging Holly with her elbow to ward off the scowl that's already forming at her use of that word—that *friend* word—cause now is damn sure not the time for flag-waving, and for once the girl steps into line, switches gears and produces a smile that would put the sun to shame. When the woman makes no attempt to offer her own name, Emma presses on, rushing to explain about the accident and the long walk up the hill and how bloody glad, excuse her language, they are that someone was home and how much gladder they'll be if they could just make a quick phone call to the RACV and get a tow-truck organised.

"Or you could call for us," she finishes. "If that's easier."

"Are you hurt?" the woman asks.

"No, I don't think so, not really. My knee's a bit sore and Holly had a nosebleed for a while, but I think we're okay." Emma grins, hopes it looks less psychotic than it feels. "I mean, we managed to walk up your hill without keeling over."

The woman nods—satisfied, decisive—and steps back from the doorway. "The mozzies will eat you alive if you stand out there all night." A strange half-smile shadows her lips. "There's no getting rid of them, once they have a taste."

* * *

Holly is scowling as she stalks back into the living room where Emma has been studying an unframed painting of two little girls sitting on a merry-go-round. It's the old-fashioned kind, with prancing horses and gold-spiralled posts, and one of the children seems to be half-climbing, half-falling from her saddle as she reaches for something off-camera. The other girl clutches the hem of her friend's bright red sundress, her mouth a round splotch of paint the colour of maraschino cherries. The execution is clumsy, the expression on the young faces ambiguous, and the rolling white eye of the closest horse gives Emma the creeps.

"Useless!" Holly says.

Emma turns to face her. "What did they say?"

"Nothing, I was disconnected three times."

"You didn't get through at all?"

"Yeah, I think I just said that," Holly snaps.

As though it's Emma's fault the damn RACV have a dodgy phone line. But then, everything seems to be Emma's fault these days.

Behind them, the woman who finally introduced herself as Mrs. Jacoby clears her throat. "If I can make a suggestion?" She is less nervous now, obviously no longer afraid that her unexpected guests might be about to slit her throat and make off with the family silver. "Why don't you both stay the night and try again in the morning? If you still can't reach anyone then, I can drive you into town myself."

Emma looks at Holly, who shrugs, noncommittal. Those two vertical frown-lines between her eyebrows have deepened, and her lips are drawn tight. It's obvious she's going to leave all the decision making to Emma from this point on—all the better for apportioning blame later—and anger flares hot and sudden in her guts. Fine, what-the-fuck-ever. "That'd be great, Mrs. Jacoby," she says, forcing a smile. "I mean, if it's not putting you to too much trouble."

"Not at all. I always keep the spare room made up." The woman's gaze flicks between them as she runs a hand through her short, silvery-grey hair. "It's a double bed; I hope you girls won't mind sharing?"

Emma, this time refusing Holly even the briefest of glances, barely skips a beat. "I'm sure we'll manage."

Mrs. Jacoby smiles—that queer, slim twist of the lips—and Emma wonders if perhaps she isn't in on the joke after all.

***

Rubbing her shower-damp hair with one of Mrs. Jacoby's fluffy green towels, Emma closes the bedroom door quietly behind her. "All yours," she says, and then, "Jesus, Hol, you *still* mucking about with that thing?"

The dollhouse is huge. A massive Victorian, its base covering almost the entire surface of the table upon which it has been set up, easily a metre square and maybe more, and inside there are three separate storeys, plus some extra little rooms in the attic. Holly is poking about inside these now, standing on tiptoes to lift out and examine pieces of scale replica furniture from the very back corners.

"It's amazing, Em. You need to come look at this." She holds up what appears to be a tiny steamer trunk, then slips a fingernail beneath the lid and pops it open. Inside is a small square of tartan cloth, about the size of a matchbox, folded into quarters like an old woollen blanket packed away for the winter. "Fricken details, huh?"

"Yeah, but I don't think you should be playing with it."

"Why not?"

"Cause it's probably worth more than my car." Emma pictures her Corolla's intimate new friend, the telegraph pole, and grimaces. "Definitely, now."

"She wouldn't have it here if she didn't want people to touch it."

"Hol, this is her *spare room*. How many houseguests do you think that lady actually gets? Just be careful, okay?"

Holly's eyes narrow, the frown lines returning to furrow her brow. "I'm not five years old, you know."

Sometimes I fucking wonder. But Emma bites her tongue. She's tired—more than tired, damn near *exhausted*, caught deep in a post-adrenaline crash—and she doesn't want to fight. Not now, not here in this house with Mrs. Jacoby right down the hall, blankets pulled up to her chin as she wonders just what it is that two young l-e-s-b-i-a-n-s get up to when the lights go out. Emma steps out of her jeans, modestly donned for the brief trip from bathroom to here, and slips an arm around Holly's waist.

"Have a shower and come to bed, baby." She squeezes the girl's hip. "Please?"

"I don't feel like doing anything." Holly doesn't look up from the little red chaise longue she's turning over and over in her hands.

Emma sighs. "Neither do I." Her arm drops to her side. "To be honest, I don't think the bed does either. Creaky old thing sounds worse than the one at your gran's. Remember when we stayed over that time?"

"Yeah," Holly says with a smile. "She couldn't even look at me at breakfast."

"Baby, things we did, *I* couldn't look at you at breakfast!"

Grinning now, Holly returns the little chaise to the doll house. "There's a secret room or something under the staircase, I think. See those seams in the wall?"

"Come on, let's just get some sleep."

"Help me find the catch first. Don't you want to know what's in there?"

"Just leave the stupid house alone and come to bed!" Not meaning to raise her voice, but the sound of Holly's fingernails scrabbling around in the stairwell sparked a tight, queasy feeling in her guts which needed to be quelled.

Holly isn't smiling anymore, and that feels even worse.

"I'm sorry, Hol. It's been a real shitty day and I'm tired."

The girl says nothing, merely turns her shoulder and retrieves a small wooden cabinet from the dollhouse. It has a glass-fronted door that opens and closes on tiny brass hinges, and Holly spends a second or two doing just that.

"Okay, fine." One pissy little straw too many and Emma stalks over to the bed, pulls back the musty, seldom-used sheets. "Do whatever you want, as always."

"Fuck you, Em," Holly hisses. "I wish I could!"

"Fuck you right back, baby." Emma curls her bare legs to her chest and pulls a pillow over her head to block out the overhead light. Faintly, she thinks she hears Holly starting to cry. Soft, muffled sounds that tear at her heart, tear at her resolve, and *Fuck you, Holly,* she says to herself, for herself. *Fucking crybaby.*

You know where to find me once you're done.

* * *

It's dark, new moon dark, and the grass is slippery-wet beneath her feet, even though she doesn't think it has rained for a long time. Up ahead, Holly calls out again, calls out her name and something else that Emma can't make out above the cicada song that rises and falls like slow-drawn breath. *Holly? Hol, wait up,* she shouts, but her voice is lost to the night and to the insects, and so she just starts running again.

She doesn't want to open the door, doesn't want to even touch that tar-black wood, but her hand is already on the knob, fingers grasping, wrist turning, and she holds her breath as it swings away from her. *Look at this*, Holly is saying, *you need to look at this*. Kneeling by the dollhouse which seems bigger now, or maybe Holly is smaller, Holly in a pretty red sundress that Emma has never seen before—*never? never ever?*—Holly kneeling with her palm outstretched and on it, something small and yellow and crumpled. A toy car, matchbox size, and, *That's not right*, Emma says, *it's doesn't fit, it's too small. See, Holly, it's only as big as the steamer trunk.* But the girl just smiles. *You need to look harder.*

Because it *is* the steamer trunk and Holly pops the lid again, pulls out that little scrap of tartan and unfolds it. Unfolds it again and again and again, that shonky old magician's trick, the blanket growing bigger, heavier, and Emma has to grab one end to keep it off the floor. The wool so rough against her cheek, dry as old dust, as she pulls it up over her shoulders, tucks herself in like a good little girl sitting here in the corner beneath the sloping attic ceiling, and watches Holly play with the dollhouse on the other side of the room. *Do you know where you are? Em, do you know?*

Running, still running, breath painful as broken glass in her lungs, and all around her the damn cicadas continue to fill the air with their manic, buzzing chorus. It can't be more than a dozen steps away, that huge Victorian house with its porchlight shining the way home, not more than half a dozen now and there's Holly waiting for her at the front door, bare arms outstretched and waving. Waving her *away*, warding her off, and, *Leave me alone*, the girl shrieks, tears streaming dark as blood down her face.

It's not right, Holly says, and turns her back. *You don't fit.* She's right, the dollhouse is too small, way too small for Emma to get more than an arm and a leg inside and only then if she starts smashing down walls. Holly is crying, and Emma reaches out to touch her, to pull her close, because that might quell the ache in her arms, the ache in her heart, only it's not Holly she's holding onto now. *Let me go*, Mrs. Jacoby whispers, not even the ghost of a smile left on those thin, pale lips. And Emma begins to scream.

* * *

Light, the harsh light of early morning streaming through the curtainless window, and for a few dream-dazzled moments Emma has absolutely no idea where she is. Only when she reaches out a sleepy arm to find the bed empty beside her, empty and cold, does she remember.

"Holly? Baby?"

No answer, no indication that the other side of the bed has been slept in or even sat upon, no trace of Holly at all. Okay, fine, so the girl stayed pissed with her and crashed somewhere else. Downstairs maybe, sprawled on Mrs. Jacoby's red chaise longue like some absinthe-soaked poetess and—

No, that's wrong. The red chaise isn't downstairs, it's in the dollhouse. But even that thought is wrong, because there *is* no downstairs. Not in *this* house, not in the *real* house.

Emma shakes her head, rubs at her eyes until stars begin to spark behind her lids. Too many damned dreams, too much time spent chasing her own frightened tail; no wonder she's still exhausted. At least her jeans are where she left them. And as she pulls them up over her hips, Emma finds herself staring at the dollhouse, wondering if it's just the daylight that makes it look different this morning.

Because it really does seem smaller, more crowded somehow.

Then she sees the dolls and her breath catches hard in her throat.

There are two of them, about half the length of her hand in height, their tiny porcelain faces painted with such exquisite attention to detail that Emma can even see the familiar smatter of freckles across the nose of the one with the long, brown hair. The one dressed in purple shorts and a white peasant-style blouse far too similar to what Holly was wearing yesterday for coincidence to lay any claim. Definitely not if you count the second doll, the one wearing blue denim jeans and a t-shirt that might once have been black before too many rides round the washing machine rendered it a dirty, charcoal grey.

The doll with short-cropped hair grown back long enough to curl. Frizzy blonde ringlets like those Holly once begged her to leave alone, to let grow out, just to see what they would look like.

Lil' Orphan Annie with a serious peroxide problem, Emma joked.

The dolls stare at her, their unblinking gaze the most frightening thing she has ever seen, and Emma has to force herself to snatch each one up in a trembling, white-knuckled fist before she flees the bedroom, expecting all the while to feel the frost-sharp bite of tiny porcelain teeth.

* * *

Calling Holly's name as she runs down the hall, bare feet slapping on old floorboards, ridiculously thankful that there still *is* a hall—long and empty and leading straight to the front door—and not a winding Victorian staircase. But no answer, no sign of anyone in the house at all until she reaches the living room and there's Mrs. Jacoby standing by the window in a lilac terry-cloth robe, hands wrapped tightly around a steaming mug. Mrs. Jacoby who turns now to regard her with a look that Emma doesn't like one bit: disappointment blended with resignation, the look of a parent whose daughter has failed yet another important exam.

"I thought you might be gone," the woman says, and sighs. "I thought, maybe, if I didn't check the room, if I waited..."

"Where's Holly?"

"Oh, *she's* gone."

"Gone where?" Emma crosses the room and holds out her fists, opens them without looking because if she sees those frozen little faces one more time she might start screaming. "What the fuck are these?"

Mrs. Jacoby doesn't flinch, merely takes a sip from her mug as she glances at Emma's flattened palms. "Where did you get those things?"

"From the dollhouse."

"Odd," the woman says. "That one's almost certainly a Greengrocer. The other might have been a Black Prince, perhaps a Black Friday. Hard to tell."

Confused, Emma looks down to see not dolls in her hands but two smaller, stranger shapes, desiccated and almost weightless, their spike-stiff legs sickle-curved to scratch at her skin.

"I think a Prince," says Mrs. Jacoby. "We're too far south for Fridays."

Emma cries out, shakes the empty cicada husks to the floor and very nearly stomps them to pieces, has one foot already raised before she stops herself. No desire to feel the crack and split of those things against her bare sole, no desire to touch them again *at all*, and only realises that she's actually backing away from them when her hip bumps against the open door. "What *is* this?" Raising her voice against the imminent threat of tears. "What the fuck is going on?"

But Mrs, Jacoby only shakes her head. "You need to ask your

friend."

"Holly? Where is she?" Nails digging into her palms—*deeper deeper deeper*—because this has to be another of those whacked-out dreams, right? And she just needs to wake herself up, right? *Right?* "Where's Holly?"

"She went to wait by the car."

"Bullshit, why would she do that? Why wouldn't she tell me?"

"Perhaps she'll tell you now." And with that Mrs. Jacoby turns away from her, turns to stare out the window once more, and when she speaks again her voice sounds weary and old. "Just go, Emma. For once, just go."

***

Amazingly, Holly *is* there. Sitting in the dirt by the rear wheel of the wrecked Corolla, knees drawn up to her chest and head bowed, and Emma almost sobs to see her.

"Holly!"

At the sound of her name, the girl looks up. Shades her eyes with one hand to watch Emma crab-hobble the rest of the way down the dew-slick hill, but doesn't smile or call back a greeting, just sits and waits as though she's been doing it her whole life and doesn't expect to have to stop anytime soon.

"What are you doing here?" Emma asks when she reaches the road. "Why didn't you wake me?"

A shrug, and Holly looks away, looks back down the road from where they'd come the night before. Emma follows her gaze but there's nothing, just empty black-top already starting to simmer in the morning heat, barren brown fields on either side, and above them the sky sprawling vast and cloudless as a faded sheet.

"Get up, Hol. We have to go."

But the girl just shakes her head. "Where? Where are we going, Em?" A grim, razor-thin smile splits her mouth as she whacks the side of the car. "And how we gonna get there?"

She's right, they're pretty much stranded out here. No one and nothing within even the most ambitious of walking distances, just that crazy old woman with her crazy old house, and ten seasons in hell won't get Emma to trek back up there. So they, what, just sit on their butts in the dirt until a car comes by and picks them up? Might as well get moving anyway then, two feet and a heartbeat all that's needed to get them up and away and out of sight of that damn spooky house. Two feet that Emma now remembers are *bare*, her Docs still in the bedroom where she kicked them off last night before her shower, and she swears, punches the car roof, and swears again as pain shoots up her wrist.

Holly is muttering at her feet and for one blood-seared second Emma wants to kick her, takes a deep breath instead. "What did you say, Hol?"

"Look in the front seat," the girl says flatly. "You need to see it."

No, she really doesn't *need* to see anything, certainly not anything that has Holly so cowed, but she's already moving around to the front of the car, wincing because in this light she can see how bad—write-off bad—the damage is to the front end, and it's a damn wonder that—

That—

It flickers, the thing that is—that isn't—that is—in the front seat.

Impossible blacklight flicker that gives Emma a headache, turns her spit to dust, and she blinks, and she squints, and she tries to look at it from the corner of her eye, and still the damn thing isn't there. And is there, still.

"You need to look harder," Holly whispers in her ear, and Emma yelps, tries to take a step backwards, several of them, but Holly is behind her, pushing her closer to the crumpled yellow car with its windscreen that isn't shattered so much as caved in, the safety glass cracked and streaked with blood and shit and matted fur from the animal that lies half-in, half-out of the driver's seat. The flickering over and done with now, but Emma would give anything to have it back, to have what is in front of her returned to the realm of what isn't.

The young woman slumps in the passenger seat, bloodied face and bloodied throat and bloodied God knows what else beneath the tartan blanket someone has pulled up over her shoulders. Tucked in like a child on a long drive home, eyes closed and blonde hair smoothed back from her face, as much as unruly curls can be smoothed, but it's wrong. *It's all wrong*, and Emma wants to pull the blanket higher, up and over that waxy, bruise-blemished face because that's what you *do* for dead people, that's what would be *right*, because that woman is—

Is—

Then Holly is tugging at her sleeve, steering her away from the car and over to the side of the road, where Emma stumbles on something sharp and hidden in the long scraggly grass that grows there, and doesn't even try to stop herself from falling.

"Are we?" she whispers. "Did we?"

Holly sinks down beside her. "No," she says, squeezing Emma's shoulder. "No, Em, we didn't." Intensely sweet, the feeling of relief, but it lasts for less than a second before Emma gets her meaning.

We didn't.

"I'm so sorry," Holly says. "I tried, I really tried, but there was so much blood and no one drove past, not one fricken car the whole time." Weeping softly as she describes dragging Emma across to the passenger seat, admitting that maybe she shouldn't have moved her at all but the kangaroo was impossible to shift, so heavy, and she couldn't just leave Emma entangled like that. Thick and black, the claws which did all the damage, those powerful hind legs thrashing about in panic and pain after the animal came through the windscreen, and Emma's throat right in their path. Emma's face and arms and chest as well, more blood than Holly had ever seen in her life, and she couldn't stop the spill of it.

She just couldn't stop it.

"The blanket," Emma whispers. "It's from the dollhouse."

Holly shakes her head. "It's from the boot. My picnic blanket, remember, from when we went up to Mount Dandenong? I left it in your car." She rubs at her bare arms. "You were cold, you kept saying how cold you were, so I went to find a jumper or something and the blanket was right there, too easy, but when I got back..."

Emma swallows.

"I didn't know what to do, Em. I just covered you up and waited, and finally this truckie came by in a semi and called the cops on his CB." Holly sniffs and wipes her nose. "He waited with me too. Pretty nice guy, gave me half his sandwich and some coffee from his thermos. Didn't have to do that, didn't have to wait either, but he did. Nice guy, you know."

"I don't understand, Hol."

Holly sighs. "What?"

"You didn't die?"

"I didn't die."

"So what are you doing here? It doesn't make sense, if you're still alive." Emma thinks about that, and frowns. "Are you still alive?"

"Oh, I'm still alive." Holly rises to her feet, brushes dust and grass from her backside and shades her eyes again as she looks up towards the hill opposite them. "I bought that house almost ten years ago now.

Ten years come October."

Emma shakes her head. "Ten years ago you were fourteen."

"Then," Holly says. "Well, *now* I guess. *Here.*"

"Hol, please. Try making some sense."

Holly swings around to face her. "What year is it, Em?"

"Stop fucking around."

"1984, right? The year you died. But up there?"—waving her hand in the direction of the hill and the house that perches upon its crest like a weather-beaten vulture, a house Emma doesn't even want to so much as glimpse again, so she keeps her eyes firmly locked on Holly's and finds that vista only marginally less terrifying—"Up there, it's *years* later. Decades. And it's where I live."

"What, with that Jacoby woman?"

Holly smiles, and that's worse than what Emma saw in the front seat of the Corolla. Possibly worse than anything she has seen anywhere, ever.

"Every time I think you'll realise," the girl tells her. "Every time I think you'll finally catch on, but you never do. Add a good twenty-five years to my age, Em—no, make it a *bad* twenty-five years—cut my hair and turn it grey, throw in some wrinkles, *lots* of wrinkles, plus an extra twenty kilos or so. What do you see then?"

Emma shakes her head. "You can't be her. You can't be her and you *both*. How is that even possible?"

Holly runs her hands through her hair, a gesture of exasperation Emma knows only too well, and she wants to grab those hands, squeeze them tight and never, ever let go. But Holly has already turned her back again, is kicking at the grass with one white-sneakered foot, and Emma is afraid to move because the world now feels so unstable, so insubstantial, that even a misdrawn breath might send it spinning off its axis and into the hungry dark.

"You won't let me leave," Holly says in a small, thin voice. "All these years, I've tried so many things but nothing works. I can be doing the dishes, or watching a movie, or trying to enjoy my honeymoon for godsake, and you just...call me back. And I'm here, in that car, and there's nothing I can do. I've tried explaining things to you over and over, showing you, but you never listen. Or you listen, but mustn't remember, because you..."

Her voice breaks on that last heavy syllable.

"Holly, baby, I—"

"Shut up!" Turning on Emma with flashbright eyes, furious eyes, one skinny finger stabbing right in her face, and Emma obeys instantly. "I bought that damn house because of you. I thought if I was closer to this place, maybe I'd be stronger as well, stronger than you. But it didn't work, and now all I can do is set stupid little traps and tripwires and hope that maybe the truth will slip in sideways and wake you the fuck up, or send you on your way, wherever the hell *that* might be. But it never does, every time we end up back here..."

Traps and tripwires.

Emma closes her eyes. Mrs. Jacoby, the carousel painting, the damn dollhouse she had refused to examine—did she always refuse? always?—and who knew what other subtle hints and whispers Holly kept hidden in plain view up in that house. Because she's right, clever girl: truth wields a razor blade with more finesse than a sledgehammer, and now Emma knows (remembers? relives?) what happened

—glass and claws and pain and blood and cold—

what always happens. Every time. How every time she pushes it away, aside, asunder, because she doesn't want to believe, doesn't want

—blood and cold and dark and fear—

to die. Doesn't want to die.

And doesn't *ever* want to be alone.

"You know what the worst part is?" Holly is crouching in front of her now, gloss-damp eyes red round the edges. Emma shakes her head mutely, not sure she wants to know, but sure she always has. "We were *over*, Em. That stupid cave trip was *my* idea, you didn't even want to go. You didn't love me anymore, you'd told me that, but I thought if maybe we just went away, just the two of us... And now you've swapped it all around inside your head somehow. As if that will fix everything."

Holly picks up Emma's hand, presses it against her cheek. "You don't *love* me, Em. You don't love me, but you *still* won't let me go."

And Emma swallows hard, and nods, and feels the thin cold blade slide between her ribs. "I'm sorry, baby. I'm so sorry."

"You always say that."

"I know, I remember." She studies Holly's face, those gentle curves that she really did love once, those pale blue eyes that could break her heart a million times over and still be able to put it back together. "And I *will* remember, I promise. Next time, okay? Next time it'll be different."

Holly smiles, empty-sad twist of her lips that Emma can't stand to look at. "You always say that, as well."

No answer she can make which won't taste like a lie, salt and ashes and bitter-cold dirt, so she says nothing. Just sits there with Holly's fingers entwined in her own, watching the slow roll of tears dampen the girl's face as, behind them, the darkness seeps ever closer, ever colder.

"Please," Holly whispers. "Just let go this time. Please, Em?"

And Emma nods, and squeezes Holly's hand, and tries not to think about all the sweet and terrifying ways a person can fall.

TRIQUETRA

I shall drown you in the river where the willows grow. Their branches will reach for you and in desperation you will grasp for them but they will break between your fingers like the bones of small birds. As the water fills your throat, the last thing you shall know will be my two hands holding you down.

I ONLY VISIT my stepmother during the time of the new moon. Although she hasn't been given access to so much as an herb garden since she came to stay in my husband's castle, I don't trust the magic to lie completely fallow in her breast, and would not dare step foot in her rooms when the moon rides full and high in the sky. But now it's noon and I balance the round silver tray on one hand as I rap three times on her door with the other. This is a courtesy only; the door is kept locked and the key, when not borrowed by our housekeeper at mealtimes, dangles from a blood-red ribbon on my belt.

A voice bids me enter and I do so, closing the door gently behind me. For a moment, I hesitate, struck to find the woman standing by the window, staring out at the snow-covered trees.

"Stepmother?"

She turns to face me, hobbling on her birchwood canes. My stepmother is a vain woman still; normally she likes to be seated when I arrive, skirts neatly arranged to hide her feet. "Sit down, Fairest." She gestures towards the small, round table where we customarily take our wine.

Setting down the tray, I inquire as to her well-being and she replies, as she usually does, that she is no better, no worse, before plonking herself down with all the grace of a mill-woman. "They're no better either," she says, catching me looking at her feet.

I avert my eyes and pour the wine into our goblets. Thick and sweet, my husband has it brought in barrels from the south, and I've developed quite a fondness for it of late. Lastly, I take up the apple along with the sharp little paring knife and begin to slice it down the middle. The flesh is whiter, crisper, than it has any natural right to be this deep into winter. But the tree behind the stables has borne such fruit, month after month, since my wedding night. One single apple each time, ripening to a bright and glossy red, and no one can pluck it but myself. Which I do, each new moon — pluck it and place it upon my silver tray, and bring it to my stepmother to share.

She takes a slice now, holds it to her nose a moment as she always does, then pops it whole into her mouth. I can hear the crunch as she bites down and my own mouth waters. She always takes the first taste of the fruit. We eat in silence, my stepmother and I, until the apple is gone. She spits the seeds into her hand, arranges them in a circle on the tray, then moves her hand over them in a quick, sharp sweep. Does she think I do not notice? Later, I will burn them in the fire. Whatever pitiful magic she attempts, it will be reduced to nothing but ash.

I do this every month.

We do this every month.

"What are your intentions, Fairest?" My stepmother sits back in her chair, fixing me with her gaze. Her eyes are brown and glossy as apple seeds.

"My intentions?"

"Regarding your daughter." She leans forward. "And your husband."

Some wine splashes onto my wrist as I return my goblet to the table, and I wipe it hastily on my skirts. "My daughter is happy and healthy," I tell her. "And my husband is travelling on matters of business. You have no need to ask after either of them."

"But that is *why* I ask, Fairest. The time to close the barn door is now, before the horse is stolen away."

"Bolted. Before the horse has *bolted*."

"I know precisely what I said."

I gather the goblets onto the tray, still half-full the both of them, and make to rise. The woman grabs my wrist, quicker than a hare before hounds. "Do not close your eyes to this, Fairest. You of all people know his proclivities. You know his *heart*."

I wrench myself free. It's not her place to speak to me so, I stammer. If it were not for me, she would have no visitors at all. If it were not for me, she would likely be dead, long dead and rotted in the ground. If it were not for me—

"I would still walk with ease," she says, sticking out a foot from beneath her skirts. Although she wears her customary fur slippers, the scars are still visible around her ankles — red and ropy welts where the skin melted as candle wax does. I don't need to see more than that. I know her feet too well. All those months tending to her horrendous wounds, cleaning away the foul-smelling pus and infection as she screamed her agony into my ears, forcing tonics down her throat to break her fevers, allowing her to clutch my hand so tightly that her nails left crescents that did not heal for days. We both bear the scars from those times; she has no cause to remind me.

"I was a child," I whispered.

"And that child chose my punishment."

"He asked me—"

"Make her dance in iron shoes, you said. Make her dance until she falls down dead."

"A child's wish. I—I had no idea of what it meant. I was only *seven!*"

"Seven," she echoes. "The age he made you his bride."

"The age *your* mirror condemned me."

"The age your daughter is now."

My lips ache, I'm pressing them so hard together. Standing, I pick up the tray. It's all I can do not to throw it into her face, goblets and all.

"He thought you were the most beautiful creature in the world when he saw you in that coffin," my stepmother continues. "When you were seven."

"Be quiet."

"What does he think of you now, I wonder? Those broad hips of yours, that bosom which has nursed a babe? Not much *girl* left to you, is there? Not much to catch his wandering eye."

I am half out the door before she calls out again. "Fairest?" The edge has been shaved from her voice; she sounds almost plaintive now, and I pause, tilt my ear in her direction.

"How?" she asks. "How will it be?"

Without turning around, I tell my stepmother how I will kill her the next time we meet. My tone is clipped; there's no joy in it for me now, despite the many nights I spent concocting my method, choosing just the right words—and the many more nights I lay awake in anticipation of delivering them. It was particularly vicious this month. My stepmother waits until I am done before telling me of my own murder. I can hear the smile in her voice, the satisfaction, and in any other month I would have been pleased by her inventiveness.

But not now, not after what she has already said to me.

"Next moon then," I say, and step through the door. As I lock it behind me, her voice seeps through the wood.

"Sooner than that, Fairest. For your daughter's sake."

I make no reply. I have no reply to make. But I will send word to the kitchen about her supper. My stepmother shall have boiled liver tonight, taken from an old sow. I count my footsteps as I return to my parlour, hoping to distract myself from their cold and empty echoes. The sound reminds me too well of a clock, counting down its minutes until midnight. There are two hundred and forty-eight steps in all, though admittedly, I made my final three small and tidy to avoid crossing the threshold on two hundred and forty-six.

I dislike figures with sixes in them; they do little to comfort me.

I will lay you naked upon the snow, stretched between four iron stakes. Before your skin can chap too badly, I will take a keen-edged blade and peel it from you as someone might peel an apple. Blood will pool rich and red around your body. I will leave your fingernails until last and spit them into the snow when I am done.

My daughter's hair is like fine-spun gold. She has her father's hair, and his envy-green eyes. But she has my lips, plump and red as blood, and my fine, snow-white skin.

I watch through the window for a minute or two, not wishing to disturb whatever game she's playing in the little courtyard outside the stables. The building is empty now that my husband is away with his horses and the others—including my daughter's beloved pony—have all been sold to repay some debt or another. He has assured me that he'll replace them when this current venture reaches fruition, but such words would be no comfort to my daughter. It won't be her pony that comes trotting back to the stables, if indeed any pony comes at all. These days, my husband's promises run thin as melt-water. She cried herself to sleep the night I had to tell her little Klaus was gone, and for days afterwards, when she remembered his absence, her lips would tremble.

Yet here she is, building a snowman outside his very stable, her small face tight with concentration, her nose nipped red by the cold. Children can be so resilient. How astonishing that they are able to bear the very worst of losses and still step forth into each new day as though some fresh delight awaits them there. If I could spare my daughter anything worse than the loss of a favourite animal, I should count myself among the best of mothers.

We must find a match for her soon, my husband told me the evening before he left.

When I protested that she was still a child, he merely glared at me and shook his head. His eyes these days are red-veined and yellowing from the amount of wine he consumes. I couldn't bring myself to meet them, and instead bowed my head over my supper. I loved him more than I feared him once, thought him brave and wondrous and strong. How naive I was: a child with no knowledge of the world.

She is the granddaughter of the king, he reminded me. *There will be a wealth of eager suitors, eager enough to plump the coffers of this pauper province I've been saddled with.*

It's a complaint I've heard so often, I could recite it word for bitter word. His two older brothers were given the best lands in the kingdom to govern, my husband insists, while he is forced to preside over lazy peasants and all manner of useless men. Though I've heard it said that these lands where we make our home were prosperous before he took governance of them, that it has been his taxes and sporadic, unannounced levies that have brought poverty among its people and made them fear what each new season might bring. What value is there in the daughter of such a man? Short of a plague running through the rest of the royal line, she will never wear the crown of a queen—I should not even think such things, though I am certain my husband would rejoice in such a tragedy.

She's too young to be married, I told him. *She's too young to leave us.*

He laughed. *I would only see her pledged, not handed over. She is unripe fruit; it would not do to have her plucked too early in her season.* He smiled, more to himself than to me, before stuffing a whole rasher of bacon into his mouth. I could see the soft meat being rent between his teeth as he spoke. *Worry not, dear wife. Our daughter will remain under my protection for some years yet. But this is how the world works—not all brides are stumbled upon as fortuitously as you were, arrayed so prettily under glass.*

How I wish it were so. I would rather see my daughter sleeping safe in a glass coffin for a thousand years than have her hurt by the waking world and those who walk within it.

Five times I tap on the window, although my daughter looks up at the first knock, grinning to see me standing there. "Mama!" she cries, and pushes herself to her feet. As she runs over to the courtyard door, I can better see the creature she has been building. Not a snowman, but some lumpish thing, hunched over and seeming ready to collapse at a breath. It makes my skin prickle with gooseflesh to look upon it.

"What have you been making, my pet?" I ask as she comes charging through the door to hug me. I crouch and fold her gloved hands within my own. Her cheeks are pink. Her teeth chatter.

"Mama, it is Klaus!"

"Klaus?" I stare again at the poor, misshapen thing outside. It could be thought a pony, I suppose, if one squinted hard enough, or viewed it with a mother's eye.

"The fairy told me to make him out of snow and he would come alive and I could ride him again."

"What fairy, my pet?"

"The fairy who came last night."

Sighing, I smooth her hair back from her eyes. "That was only a dream."

"No, Mama, look!" She points beyond the window and I follow the angle of her finger to spy a large black bird perched in one of the leafless trees overlooking the courtyard. Its silhouette, dark against the wintry grey sky, is distinctive. "See, the fairy!"

"That's only a raven, my pet, a feckless bird come to see if we have kitchen scraps to scavenge." I've never liked those birds, with their ink-black plumage and cryptic, guttural croaks. There's often one flitting about the castle grounds, and I never count it as a good day when I happen to spy it. Softly, I kiss my daughter's brow. "Now, remember what I told you? Little Klaus has grown up and gone away to be with all the big horses."

She swallows and her eyes glisten. "When I grow up, will I go away too? Will I get to see him again, when I grow up?"

"I don't know, my pet. Klaus has very many important things to do now. As will you, when you grow up." She doesn't say anything to that, merely hugs me tight and presses her face into my shoulder. I know that she is crying and doesn't want me to see. I rub her back until her small frame ceases to shake. Outside, the tree where the raven perched is empty. Foolish as such feelings might be, I'm relieved to see it gone.

Unbidden, my husband's face swims into my mind. His golden hair, once so glorious, now lank and greasy against his neck. The burst veins in his cheeks spreading like the webs of tiny spiders. Is it memory or imagination, the way his tongue darted across his lips as he spoke of auctioning my daughter to the highest bidder? As he spoke of how young she was, and how fair?

You know his heart, my stepmother said, and she is right.

His heart, and every other dark part of him.

I will keep my daughter safe. I must, I must. But I need to know what threatens her, and there is one thing in this castle that will tell me the truth of it.

> *I shall feed you honey, spoon after golden spoonful of it. I shall pour it down your throat until you can swallow no more, until it soaks every organ and your veins are stopped with the cloying thickness of it. Then I shall cleave open your breast and catch the gleaming nectar as it drips from your ribs onto my outstretched tongue.*

I've never once spoken to the mirror. My stepmother brought it with her when she came to my wedding, so little could she bear being apart from the monstrosity even for the span of a week, and it's been kept in a small, windowless chamber ever since. I know the sly deeds of which it's capable, how it sniffs out a crack in a person's heart and prises it open. Until now, I've never wanted to seek its counsel—or, at least, not enough to risk its manipulations. But I need to know about my husband. I need to be certain.

The mirror never lies, my stepmother told me once, when I pressed her on the subject. *The trick is to know whose truth it is speaking.*

There's a woman standing outside the mirror's chamber as I approach. Tall and thin and wrapped in dove grey, I recognise the arrogant set of her shoulders even before she turns to greet me.

"Lady Heron!"

The woman sniffs, her lips a taut line. "I have been waiting for one half hour. More!"

"I—I'm sorry. I had—I was unavoidably detained." In truth, I'd forgotten utterly about her appointment, a fact she has no doubt surmised.

She smiles with all the grace of a blade and nods towards the narrow wooden door behind which the mirror awaits. "Shall we?"

I would like to ask her to leave, to return at a later hour or even another day, but there is the matter of the small linen bag that she clutches. I need the coins it contains; they will pay for good meat for our table and perhaps a warm winter cloak for my daughter. After all, the women come more seldom these days; the mirror seems to have exhausted them.

"Of course, Lady Heron." I hold out my hand and she deposits the bag in my palm. It feels lighter than I'd hoped, but perhaps the coins inside are silver. After unlocking the door, I step aside and gesture for the woman to enter. She hesitates a moment, visibly steeling herself, before sniffing once more and marching past me.

Quietly, I close the door and move to the other side of the hall to wait.

She won't be very long. They never are.

Scarce six minutes pass by my reckoning before she emerges once more, shaken and trembling, a handkerchief pressed to her mouth.

"Lady Heron?"

The woman waves me away. "I shall see myself from the castle." Her eyes are red-rimmed and she refuses to meet my gaze. As she walks, her skirts rustle on the tiles in whispered accusation. But how is it my fault? I don't make them come here, these women with their coins and haggard hearts. I don't even know how they learn of the mirror's existence—a network of gossip and half-truth, I suspect. Whatever they expect, whatever they are told, most do not visit more than once.

This has been Lady Heron's fourth visit. Is her heart that ravenous?

I hesitate with my hand on the doorknob. One turn and I can be in the room with it. Three steps to place me before its glassy face. A handful of words in return for...what? I scarce know what I need to ask, let alone how to phrase it.

(Don't I know? Oh, don't I?)

Another day, then. When I have had more time to ponder my question.

Carefully, I insert the key into the lock and turn it. The weighty clatter of the tumblers brings me more comfort, I am sure, than the words of the mirror ever would. But do I imagine it? That barely heard sigh from the chamber beyond, so heavy with disappointment and with desire? Before leaving, I tap my toe three times and brush the tip of my nose.

Am I mad to have even considered such a diabolic audience? My stepmother has twisted my thoughts, most like for her sport. My husband is not a good man but he is not—

(a monster)

He is her father. He would not—

(you know his heart)

I need to occupy myself with practical matters and stop this foolishness. The snow has stopped and I have coins that need to be spent before my husband's return, lest he find a more worthwhile cause for their use. I will take my daughter down to the village and buy her that winter cloak. Already I can picture her wearing it, a scarlet weave folding soft and billowy around her slight frame, all that golden hair kept safe beneath the hood.

Oh, I know that I won't be able to find such a thing as that. It will be lucky enough if the village seamstress has one of sparrow-egg blue or the bright green of ferns, anything other than muddy hues of brown or grey. If it be trimmed with rabbit fur, then we shall be luckier still. For red, I would have to place an order, and all of that would take too long.

My husband returns in a fortnight. The coins will need to be spent by then.

> *I will hunt you down with dogs. Hungry, vicious hounds that have been starved for days before being given your scent. You will beg for your life when finally they bail you up, circle you with their jaws snapping and slavering, but I will let them have you. I will let them tear you to pieces. I will let them take their fill of your flesh. All that will be forbidden them is your heart. That I shall bring home with me, safe in a locked, lightless box.*

The gatekeep steps into our path as we approach, my daughter's mittened hand clutched tight in my own. It takes four more steps to reach him. I do not like four as a number—it is slippery and too easily split in twain—but I dare not take a fifth.

"Weather's closing in, Your Highness," the gatekeep says, his shoulders squared.

My daughter squeezes my hand. *Mama*, she starts to say, but I shush her quickly. The sky above us is a weak blue and utterly clear of clouds.

"We are only going down to the village," I tell the man. "We will not tarry long."

"The little one will catch a chill." He does not move, though his fingers tighten their grip about his staff. "Best get her back inside."

"Thank you for concern, but we—we are warmly dressed, the both of us." As I tug my daughter forward, the gatekeep too takes a step closer. So close that his broad, leather-clad chest almost bumps my own. His breath fogs as he speaks and I can smell the warmth of it.

"You may go to the village if you wish it," he says. "But the little one should go back inside."

For a moment, I'm too flustered for words. Then I picture my stepmother and the manner in which she used to conduct herself when I was a child. How imperiously she would speak to everyone, even my father himself. I draw myself upright. "Do you propose to tell your mistress what she might do with her day?"

The words taste flat as failed bread in my mouth and the gatekeep doesn't so much as flinch. "On instructions from His Grace, your master and mine both. He did not wish the princess away from the castle in his absence. The winter is foul and the woods are wild and he would not have his only daughter come to any harm."

He smiles now, a genuine smile, yet my daughter hides her face in my skirts. Part of me wishes to push past him regardless, to see if he will truly dare to lay a hand on his royal mistress. But another, more certain part burns with the humiliating knowledge that he would not hesitate to do so. My jaw begins to ache, so hard are my teeth clenched together.

"Mama? Are we not going to the village today?"

I force a smile to my lips. "No, my pet. This kind gentleman thinks that it will storm, so we had best stay warm and dry by the fire."

She kicks at the dirty snow that lies piled at the side of the path. "I wanted to see Klaus."

"Silly poppet, Klaus is not in the village. I told you, he's with all the big horses now."

The gatekeep laughs, a far from pleasant sound. "You'd be best served looking for that old nag in the knackery."

My daughter stares up at me, confused. I glare at the gatekeep but the man merely winks. "That's—that's a place where the big horses live," I tell her quickly. "Come, my pet. We shall go down to the kitchen and have Cook warm you a mug of honey-milk."

"I'm not cold, Mama," she replies, her words frosting in the air. "I want to see the knackery. Please can we visit the knackery?"

The gatekeep's rough laughter follows us up the path as I drag my protesting daughter back to the castle, and I curse him beneath my breath. High in the sky above, a raven flies in a slow circle. I curse it as well, wishing for its feathers to turn to stone, for its abruptly heavy body to fall to the ground and shatter like so many thwarted dreams.

It takes one hundred and nineteen steps before we are inside once more. I don't care for that number either. It has sharp edges and seems keen to draw blood.

> *I shall bind you with silken threads, wrapping them around and around your body until every inch of skin is cocooned. Only your eyes shall remain uncovered, so that I might peer into them over the days and weeks it will take for you to wither and waste and starve, stoically, silently, to your death.*

My husband doesn't care for the stories of my childhood, of the times before he jolted me from my poisoned sleep and lifted me boldly from the coffin, but my daughter loves to hear them. Each night, I sit by her bedside and tell her tales of the kindly little men who took me into their mountain home when I was lost, and for whom I kept house for several months. I tell her how I would make their beds and darn their socks and prepare their dinner the way they taught me. I do not tell her about poisoned combs or apples, nor about coffins made from glass; she is too young for such horrors.

Neither do I mention my stepmother. My daughter will have too many questions that I'm still unready to answer.

Instead, I relay happier stories of happier days—for there were many happy days betwixt the huntsman and the coffin—as well as the stories that the dwarves used to tell me. Tales of crafty foxes and wise, well-born hares; dancing princesses and frogs with jewels hidden deep in their bellies; mighty frost giants who once lumbered through the mountains, and mischievous pixies with a taste for stolen sweets.

"Can we leave a cake out for the pixies?" my daughter asks me tonight.

"There are no pixies in our part of the world, my pet. It would only be a family of rats who come to nibble on your cake."

"Talking rats?" she asks hopefully. "Magic rats?"

Smiling, I set aside the nightgown I'm hemming. My daughter grows so fast; this is the second time I've let it down and there won't be fabric left for a third. "No," I say. "Fierce and hungry rats who will gobble up their cake and then creep under the blankets to nibble on your toes!" I grab her foot and tickle it until she shrieks.

"Stop it, Mama! Stop it!" She's almost breathless as she struggles to pull away.

Laughing, I release her and begin to straighten the bedclothes. "Come now, fidget. It's past time you were asleep."

She wriggles beneath the quilt. "Can we visit the pixies, Mama?"

"One day, perhaps."

"When? When?"

"They live very far away from here."

"But we can use magic and fly to see them, quick as blinking."

"Hush now." I pull the covers up to her chin.

"But, Mama, we can—"

"Hush!" Though her talk is fanciful, I don't like to hear my daughter speak of magic. "It's no small thing, my pet, to use magic. There is always a cost." I kiss her three times, once on the forehead and again on each cheek, before gathering my sewing together. The candle flickers as I pick it up, casting moving shadows on the walls. My daughter cringes to see them.

"Surely you're not still afraid of the dark?" When much younger, she cried whenever her candle was taken away, but many years have passed since then.

"No, Mama," she whispers, her gaze flitting to the corner of the room. "But sometimes he is there when I wake up."

"Who? Who is there?"

"The Night Man. He watches me in the shadows. I don't like him, Mama. I don't like his watching."

"Is he here now?"

"No, Mama. You have the candle. He does not like the light."

"It is a dream, my pet. A nightmare and nothing to fear."

She frowns, doubtful, and I lean over to kiss her again. Forehead, cheek, cheek. "I shall leave the candle then, shall I? Just for tonight?"

I find my way back to my own bedroom by moonlight and memory, keeping one hand on the wall as I creep along the corridors. It's a luxury to leave a whole candle to burn while my daughter sleeps, but the way she spoke of the Night Man chilled me.

I don't like his watching.

Has he visited her, this Night Man, while her father has been away? I hadn't thought to ask it and, surely, it is a foolish question. It's only a nightmare. It must be a nightmare.

You know his heart.

I do. I do know his heart.

I will come upon you in darkness, my breath burning hot on your cheek. My ungloved hands will close around your neck and my fingers will squeeze, unrelenting, throttling your startled cries. You will die with your last words lodged, unspoken, in your throat.

I knock my customary three times but do not wait for an answer before unlocking the door to my stepmother's room and swinging it open. The woman is sitting on the edge of her bed, jerking a robe over her bony shoulders. She wears nothing underneath; I glimpse the sag of a breast, the wrinkle and fold of belly skin pale as fresh cream. Her long, grey hair is dishevelled, hanging in tangles about her face, and her feet are bare. Quickly, I turn away, an apology stammering to my lips.

I've never sought such intimacy; my skin burns with it.

"What did you expect?" my stepmother asks. "I've scarce had warning of your visit."

"But it's past noon!"

"Do you suppose me unduly burdened with morning chores, Fairest? Or blessed with a surfeit of company for whom I should make myself presentable?" She waves a hand at the corners of the ceiling. "The spiders here care not a whit for appearances, I can assure you."

I'm ashamed to admit I've not spared much thought for how she spends her days. She is fed; she is clothed. I keep her moderately stocked in embroidery thread, albeit often coarse and dull of colour, and have even brought the occasional book from my husband's ever-shrinking library, as she once expressed a yearning for words. Royal histories mostly, but also some volumes of verse. If I've ever had cause to think on my stepmother all alone in this room, it has likely been to imagine her daydreaming by the window with book or embroidery hoop in her lap, still elegant despite her fading finery, with all that wild hair swept into its usual immaculate coiffure.

It is a shock to witness her so... diminished.

"I—I have come to ask— That is, I wish to know—"

"You might meet my eye when you speak to me, Fairest. It would be polite."

I turn around to find my stepmother now risen from the bed, robe tied close around her body, fingers working her hair into a rough braid. I'm careful not to look at her feet, though I glimpse her two canes leaning nearby. "I wish to ask about your—your mirror."

Her eyes narrow. "You told me that you have never gazed upon it."

"I've not had need...until now."

The woman takes up her canes and hobbles across to the small table where the two of us normally sit. With a soft groan, she lowers herself into a chair, then gestures to the one remaining. "I have nothing useful left to tell about that *thing*."

"I've come to ask your aid in...crafting a question. One that it must answer clearly, without trickery or guile. One that is...is..."

"Unambiguous? Fairest, there is no such question. The mirror will know your purpose as soon as the words part your lips. It will twist its own words accordingly."

"If it may only answer 'yea' or 'nay'? How can that be twisted?"

"You cannot impose such restrictions; it will answer as it will, with as many words as it chooses, or as few." She leans forward. "Heed me well, Fairest. When you stand before that thing, when you peer into its depths, you also allow it to peer into you. It will see the very darkest of your fears; it will sup on them and find them delicious. And it will use them against you in terrible ways."

"But I need to know!"

"You already know."

"No, I *suspect*, I *worry*, I *dread*—that's not the same."

"It is enough for you to take your daughter and leave."

The laughter bursts from me like a startled bird. Leave? How simply she puts it, I scoff, as though I might just pack a trunk, snatch my daughter by the hand, and waltz out into the world. As though there are carriages and fine horses to carry us wherever our whims direct. As though no burly gatekeep would stand in our path, no armed men hunt us down should we persist.

As though, even if we can find a way to leave, we have a place to go.

"There are always ways, Fairest, if you have the knowing of them. And places."

"This is a waste of my time."

As I stand up, my stepmother reaches forward and grasps my hands. She moves more quickly than I would have thought her capable and this, along with the warm, dry press of her skin against mine, shocks me into place. I can't remember how long it's been since we've touched. The woman pulls herself to her feet, pulls me closer, her face inches from my own.

"I can help you," she whispers, "but first I have need of some things." Her breath is oddly sweet. It smells of spring blossoms, and of apples. My knees threaten to buckle and I find myself clinging to her as much as she does me. Her eyes locked with mine, she gives me a list, then asks me to repeat it back to her. "Again," she says, and I do, twice more, as her thumbs move in slow circles over my wrists. At last, seemingly satisfied, she releases me.

My arms drop to my sides. I feel muzzy-headed, woolly, as though I've just woken from a troubled sleep. My mouth is dry. "You—" I cough, backing away from the table, away from the woman now supporting herself by its edge. "You spelled me!"

"Only your memory, Fairest. My needs are precise."

"You—you wretched creature! I wish you *had* died on my wedding day!"

Smiling, she sinks back down into her chair. "No, you don't. There is too much kindness in your heart, even now, even for such a *wretched creature* as myself."

I am too furious to speak another word. I want to throw something, break something, break *everything* —but the only thing to hand is a pewter goblet which makes a hollow, unsatisfying clatter as I hurl it against the wall. How dare she? I will leave her to starve. I will tell the kitchen to send her nothing but spoiled milk and rotted meat. I will—I will—

"I can help you," my stepmother says again. "Please—for your daughter's sake."

Jaw clenched to aching, I glare at the woman for one long, cold moment before marching from the room. My hands shake so badly, I drop the key twice as I try to lock the door behind me. As I stalk down the corridor, my stepmother's list rolls unbidden, unwanted, through my mind, each word a barb that catches and throbs. It so distracts me that I completely forget to count my steps.

> *I shall simmer you slowly, until your skin sloughs away and your flesh becomes soup. Your bones will be boiled for stock so that I might dine with special delight on the consommé drawn from your marrow.*

The mirror chamber is cold, windowless, and dark. For several moments, all I know is my own breathing, shallow and fast, as I stand in the centre of the room with the door closed firm behind me. Then the glow begins. Faint at first, then brighter and brighter until I might be surrounded by a dozen candles, so forceful is the light that shines from the glass oval on the wall opposite me.

I haven't seen the thing for years.

I'd forgotten how plain it is, had in my memory conjured an ornate, overwrought frame around its edge in place of the thin band of wood that actually bounds it. It's smaller than I remember as well. I could have sworn the glass to be longer than the span of my arms, and near as wide, but in actual fact I could likely carry the thing in two hands without much effort.

Not that I would touch it in a million moons. My skin crawls at the very idea.

Well met, child.

The voice doesn't seem to come from the mirror. It doesn't seem to come from anywhere in particular, yet it fills my whole head, louder than any thought of my own, almost to the point of bursting. I can't imagine a worse sensation than this.

What would you ask of me?

"I—I want... My daughter— Is she...under threat?"

Only so long as she draws breath in this world.

"But here, in this castle, is she in danger?"

She will always be in danger, child. You cannot protect her from all the ills that may befall her.

My thoughts are thick and slow. I can't summon the right questions to ask, the right words to pull the answers I need from the glass before me. There's a sudden tightness in my chest and my breath comes too fast to catch. "My husband..."

He loves your daughter. More than he loves you.

Closing my eyes, I press fingertips to my temples, press so hard into those soft and pliant hollows that stars shatter behind my lids. The pain is an anchor. A compass. "And does he...does he *desire* her also?" For a heartbeat, I wish I could unsay those words, so solid do they sit in the air, so blunt and inescapable is the echo of them. But it is done. It is said.

It is said.

More than he desires you. The voice of the mirror swells and gloats. *Beware, child, and tread carefully; your position in this household grows precarious.*

With that it departs, leaving me as empty as a pumpkin shell scraped for seeds—or nearly so. My stepmother's list drifts from my memory like smoke from a snuffed candle, her words wispy and thin but persistent nevertheless. I shake my head. Will my mind ever be my own again? The glow from the mirror is gone; the chamber is pitch black. "Come back," I call out. "I have more to ask of you."

There's no reply, no sense that the mirror is even listening. The chill in the room deepens; beneath my sleeves, gooseflesh shivers across my skin. The audience is over. I have been dismissed.

I turn and retrace my steps to the door. But my outstretched hands find nothing more than bare, unbroken stone. No smooth, polished wood or jutting handle of brass, nor any crack or join that might suggest an exit. Frantic, I pace the short length of the wall, palms slapping against stone, as the gorge rises in my throat and the taste of spoiled milk coats my mouth. By what devilry has the mirror trapped me here? For what purpose, and for how long? I thump at the wall with balled hands, demanding to be released, for the door to be restored. I will not rot in this wretched chamber, in darkness and silence behind this newly solid facade, while my husband and my daughter—

Behind me: the creak of a hinge, a shard of yellow light, and a timid voice calling, "Mama? Mama, are you there?"

For a strange, disorienting moment, I can't make sense of it. Then my daughter's head pokes around the edge of the door she has opened—the door! on the wall adjacent! so ridiculously close!—and my cheeks burn with foolishness. I stalk over and, snatching her by the arm, jerk her into the hall beyond. She cries out, the thin, high-pitched squeal of a snared rabbit that sets my teeth to grating, and I give her a rough shake as I pull the door shut behind us.

"You don't ever go into that room! Not ever!"

The girl is starting to snivel, her green eyes wet and bright with shock, and there's a part of me whose heart breaks to see it—but that part feels so very far away, so very small and distant and powerless in the face of the fury that boils in my breast, and I shake her again. "Stop it! You're not an infant anymore. You need to start acting like a lady."

She tries to swallow her tears, she does, but her thin shoulders hitch and her mouth contorts with the effort and my fingers dig deeper into her flesh. I want to—I want to—

Nearby, a throat is cleared. "Your Grace?"

Startled, I look up to see Lady Heron standing but a few paces away, hands clasped at her waist. She stares at me in an odd manner, an expression shaded somewhere between pity and fear, before nodding towards my daughter. "Do not berate the lass too harshly, Your Grace. I asked her to bring me here, after you were not to be found." The woman taps the linen bag that hangs from her belt. "I wished another visit."

Releasing my daughter, I straighten. "Go to your room," I tell the girl. "Stay there." She obeys, walking as fast as she possibly can without breaking into a run, and I wait until she has turned the corner at the end of the hall before informing Lady Heron that she can expect no visit today. Not today and possibly not ever again. For which she should be grateful.

"Have you stood before the mirror, Your Grace?"

"You have no right to question me."

"Shall I instead advise? Do not accept the counsel of the glass. Do not stand before it again."

The laughter that bursts from my throat is coarse and ugly. "Shall I rather take the counsel of a hypocrite? Why do you not heed your own words, Lady Heron, be they so wise?"

The woman bows her head. "I am weak. I wish I were not."

I open my mouth to tell her to go but the words that trip forth are my stepmother's—the wretched list with which she spelled me.

Lady Heron tilts her head. "Your Grace?"

I repeat the list and she echoes me, her grey eyes flat and glazed. There's a curious satisfaction in speaking the words aloud, the feeling of tumblers falling into place, a sense of being *unlocked*—and yet I cannot find any pleasure in it. The manipulations of my stepmother and her mirror have left me drained and shaken, my stomach subjected to sour swells of nausea the results of which I have no desire for Lady Heron to witness.

"Leave," I snap, once my tongue feels again my own. "You're not welcome here." Without waiting to see that she obeys, I turn and march off down the corridor. Bile prickles at the back of my throat and I swallow, hard and hot, with one hand pressed close against my lips.

one-two-three, one-two-three, one-two-three

I cannot keep more count than that, but it doesn't matter. Three is the safest number, after all, and it's a simple thing to match my steps to its calm, protective rhythm. The parlour is closer than my bedchamber; I'll draw the drapes and sit awhile in my favourite chair.

one-two-three, one-two-three, one-two-three

I pass my daughter's room without pause. Pass, almost, without notice. The door is closed. All is quiet beyond. I'll speak with her once I am rested. I love my daughter, with her green eyes and golden hair. My position is not precarious. I love my daughter.

one-two-three, one-two-three, one-two-three

I will bring you before the mirror; let it tell the hard and glassy truth of your death.

When there comes a gentle rapping at the parlour door, I expect it to be the housekeeper with a fresh bottle of wine. Wine and, perhaps, a plate of cured meats or a bowl of stew, along with yet more earnest supplications for me to eat, eat, eat. But I've had no appetite for food these past two days, not since speaking with the mirror; the mere thought of eating anything, of *chewing* and *swallowing* anything, makes me feel ill. But the wine—oh!—so red and sweet on my tongue. It helps me to sleep, it helps me not to think.

My head is heavy with all that I do not wish to think upon.

But it's not the housekeeper who marches into the room at my summons, stern of face and bearing nought but a small calico sack. Sketching a curtsy so shallow it might nearly be an insult, Lady Heron at least keeps her gaze averted until I have risen from the chair by the window where I have been sitting. My embroidery hoop, forgotten, falls with a clatter to the floor. Neither of us acknowledges it.

"H-how dare you intrude upon me here!" My cheeks feel hot, my knees unsteady.

The woman curtsies once again. "Forgiveness, Your Grace—I have your price."

Frowning, I stare at the lumpy, cream-coloured sack in her outstretched hand.

"It is everything you requested," she says. "May I visit now?"

Even as I back away from her, Lady Heron steps forward, pressing her *price* into my grasp and bidding me to look. I don't wish to touch the sack, let alone peer inside of it. I can no longer remember the specifics of my stepmother's list and have no desire to invite it into my mind once more. Hastily, I drop the thing onto the little table where my sewing basket sits, then wipe my hands on my skirts. My mouth is dry; I wish my wine goblet were not so empty.

"Why—why do you keep returning here?" I demand of Lady Heron.

She smiles, thin and sharp. "You have stood before it, Your Grace. Do you not hear its whisper? Do you not feel its pull?"

No, I want to retort. *No, I am stronger than that. I am stronger than you.* But the woman is not a fool; she would see the lie in my face as quick as blinking. Last night I woke to find myself huddled against the door to the mirror's chamber, fingernails scratching at the wood. I didn't recognise the sounds that came from my own throat—pathetic mewlings like those a starving kitten might make before its head is pushed beneath the water—and it took all my will to force myself back down the hall.

I remember stopping at my daughter's bedroom, easing open the door and slipping inside to stand in the shadows. Like the Night Man. (Like my husband?) I watched her sleep, the swelling moon lighting her face through the window, all those golden curls turned to frost. Her mouth lolled open, a gentle snore easing between her lips. Did she dream of Klaus and of fairies? Or did she dream of becoming queen?

Your position in this household grows precarious.

I remember taking a step towards my daughter's bed. I remember the surge of malice in my breast. And I remember running, horror rising with the bile in my throat as my daughter's confused, sleep-bleared voice called out in my wake—*Mama? Mama, is that you?*

This morning, I found my fingernails broken and split, with a narrow splinter of wood lodged beneath my left thumb. I still haven't spoken to my daughter—I'm frightened to look upon her face. Frightened of what I might feel when I do.

He loves your daughter. More than he loves you.

"What does it say?" I asked Lady Heron. "What does the mirror tell you?"

"Words that are mine alone to hear, Your Grace." She straightens her spine. "As, having received your own private counsel, you must surely understand."

I hold her gaze for one long, difficult moment before reaching for the keys on my belt. "One final visit then, Lady Heron, after which you may never return. If you have any sense left in your head, you will thank me for it."

"And who shall keep the key from *you*, Your Grace?" Her smile twists nearer to a smirk. "Who shall protect *you* when the mirror whispers in the night?"

Making no reply, I stride past the woman and out of the parlour. My footsteps echo in the empty halls; Lady Heron's come half a beat behind, her skirts rustling as she hurries after me. Once this visit is done, no one will come near the chamber again—she can spread the word among all the sorry women who scuttle up to the castle, coin in hand, eyes brimming with hopeful despair.

Whatever words the mirror chooses to speak, they will be mine alone to hear.

I shall grind glass so fine that it glitters like drifts of moonlit sand and then I will use it to salt your supper. The grains will grind through your innards, scouring your tender, secret parts until each movement is torture and you beg to be released from the agony that is breathing.

Lady Heron has been in the chamber for less time than it takes me to pace the length of the hall and back—fifty-nine steps all told—and my palms are sweaty and warm from rubbing too vigorously against one another. I should not have allowed the woman this visit. I should not have left her alone with the mirror. For what if the choice is not mine to make? What if the mirror decides that *she* will be its favoured confidante? What if—

Enough. *Enough.*

I fling open the door, demanding that Lady Heron take her leave right this instant, but my voice falters and I stop barely two steps inside the chamber, unable to properly comprehend the scene before me. The woman is hunched like an old fishwife, mouth contorting in fierce silence as the glow from the mirror grooves deep shadows into her face. In her right hand she wields a small hammer—though *wields* is perhaps too strong a term for the shaken, struggling manner in which she lifts it, lowers it, lifts it again.

"Lady Heron, what—"

Child, leave us.

The mirror's voice slides into me, fills me, and I stagger forward with arms outstretched. "No," I whisper. "No, please. I must stay. I have questions."

They will not spoil for waiting.

Sensing its imminent withdrawal, I pounce on the first words to trip across my tongue. "Am I safe here in this castle? Am I safe from my—my husband?"

You are safe from nothing, child. And if you do not leave now, you will never again call this castle your home.

The voice burns with fury; the pain is so great that I sink to my knees, hands pressed uselessly to my ears. Before I can beg forgiveness, there comes a great bellowing and a crash so loud it might be cannon fire exploding in my skull, and then

all the world

is dizzy

and dark.

Gradually, I become aware of two things: the cold, hard stone of the floor beneath my shoulderblades, and a strange sputtering noise from nearby. Opening my eyes, I roll over. Something cracks beneath my hip and, in the dim light filtering in from the hall, I can see shards of broken glass littering the chamber floor. On the wall, the mirror frame hangs barren. A few feet away, Lady Heron sits propped in a corner, breathing heavily. She sees me staring and grins with gleaming, dark-stained teeth before sputtering again. Mindful of the wreckage, I crawl over to the woman. Her grey dress is stained and wet, and a pool of blood has formed beneath her. She has a hand pressed to her side, pressed to the place where a sharp and glittering edge protrudes.

"What have—what have you done?"

"It is over," Lady Heron croaks. "She'll rest now."

"Here, let me help." Carefully, I take hold of the shard in her side and pull it loose. More blood bubbles up through the wound and she groans, catching my free hand in hers. Squeezes hard. Coughs. I wad up some of her skirt and hold it against her side, but it soaks red in a heartbeat and Lady Heron is making that sputtering sound—laughing. She is laughing! Though her life now must surely be measured in breaths.

"Thank you," she says, shaking her head when I try to hush her. "Tried so many times. Each time, it held me. But couldn't hold us both. Not together. Couldn't hold me. With you there." She's lifting her right hand, curled in an empty fist. Bringing it down, lifting it again. "Couldn't hold me."

Taking her hand, I press it between my own. The hammer is over on the far side of the chamber, I see now, most likely flung from her grasp once she struck the mirror. My stomach clenches; my cheeks flush with anger.

"No more whispers," Lady Heron says. Though her voice is weak, her speech slick with blood, her eyes are clear. "No more whispers, Your Grace."

"You had no right," I snap. "It was not your place."

She smiles. "You would not remember her."

"Remember who?"

"My niece, my darling. Stood before the mirror." Another cough, harsher this time, and the woman's smile fades. "Drowned herself, my darling." Her shoulders stiffen, then relax. "But it couldn't hold me. Tell my sister. Couldn't hold me."

Her gaze is locked with mine when she dies.

Shakily, I push myself to my feet. I try to wipe my hands on my skirts but they are no cleaner, no drier. Everywhere is blood and broken glass. I wouldn't have thought the mirror so large as to produce so many glittering shards—nor Lady Heron capable of containing all that red mess. Have I as much in my own small body? If my throat were slit, would such an ocean surge forth?

You will take the blame for this, child.

No, it was—it was an accident.

The wife of Lord Heron lies slaughtered in a room to which you hold the only key.

No, I—

You are soaked to the skin with her blood.

But—

And a sack of witchcraft left in your parlour for any passing housekeeper to find.

I—

See how well you have furnished your husband with your own death warrant.

"Stop! Please, stop!" The voice falls silent but doesn't depart; my head might burst from the pressure of it. I stamp down on the nearest shard, a strange satisfaction rippling along my spine at the sound of cracking glass. I break another piece beneath my heel, and another. But even as I do, a sick terror begins to curdle in my belly. Damn Lady Heron to all the unknown hells for her treachery! Damn Lady Heron and—and—

Is there another, child? One who might wear the noose destined for your pretty neck?

Dizzy, I lean my back against the wall. All at once, everything draws together. It has been her from the beginning, marking out the pattern, tying off the threads, and how doltish I have been not to see it. "Stepmother," I whisper.

Oh yes, child. Oh yes and at last. Stepmother.

> *I will bury you alive. Not in a coffin or wooden box. Not even wrapped in a shroud. Bound, on your knees, you will feel the dirt scrape against your skin as I shovel it upon you. And when you are buried, I will salt the earth where you lie so that you might be shunned by each and every living thing.*

The old crone looks up, aghast, as I storm into the room.

Fumbling with her canes, she starts to rise from her chair but I'm upon her too quickly, grasping her bony shoulders and shoving her back down. She gives a soft, startled gasp and, for the first time I can remember, those brown eyes kindle with fear. "Fairest, whose blood is this?"

"None of it mine," I snap. "As much as you wish it were."

She pushes her face closer, nostrils flaring as she sniffs the air. "I would not be so sure. You are cut—"

I slap her hand away as it reaches for my cheek. "Never touch me again!"

"What has happened?" She touches her chest, hand hovering over the place where her heart would dwell, had she ever possessed such a fine organ. "I felt...I felt..."

Do not listen, child. This wretch would have you banished from this place. From your home.

"I see you, witch. I see you now for what you are. For what you have always been."

Her gaze sharpens. "You have spoken to the mirror."

It would have been better to have let her die.

"You failed to destroy me once before. You will fail again."

It would be better to kill her now.

"Fairest, I beg you. You must not listen—"

No more, no more of her evil, insidious words, fighting even now to free themselves, even as my hands clutch her pale, wizened throat and squeeze. Eyes wide, she struggles against me, fingers scratching at mine in an effort to loosen my grip. But her nails are as old and brittle as her soul, snapping before they can hope to break the skin, and the pitiful manner in which she writhes only serves to stoke my wrath. I will end this. Now. I will end her—

My hands close around air.

Unbalanced, I tip forward, bracing myself against the abruptly, impossibly empty chair. A raucous, rasping chorus fills the room, goblin laughter bold and burbling, and I whirl around, shielding myself from the sudden mass of black feathers that swoops upon me. The bird caws again, flapping vengeful at my face as it pecks and claws, and I try to move away, turn away, but it is everywhere, dogged and inescapable as death. Covering my eyes—for surely it is those soft and vulnerable globes it seeks to pluck from me!—I stumble blindly for the door, only to step on my own skirts and fall. My knee cracks on the stone and the pain robs me of breath. I cry out, rolling and reaching for my aching knee, and the bird is there, all feathers and fury, its black wings beating a gale as its beak latches onto my cheek.

And then, emptiness.

Warily, I prop myself up on one elbow. The bird, a raven as large as a cat, is on the floor nearby. Catching my gaze, it hops well beyond my grasp. The movement is awkward, ungainly; there is something wrong with the creature's talons, an unnatural curl that twists them back upon themselves, and even as I peer closer—

—the raven vanishes. Or, doesn't vanish precisely, but is simply *gone*—with my stepmother now crouched, naked and breathing harder than I am, in its place. Reaching into her mouth, she pulls out a shard of mirrored glass the size of my thumbnail. "You will feel more yourself, Fairest," she says, her voice hoarse and broken, "now this foul thing is removed."

I touch my cheek, feel the blood running fresh from the wound. I remember Lady Heron, and the glass I pulled from her side. The dauntless scarlet flow that leeched all warmth from her flesh. *Tell my sister.* My hands begin to tremble. *Couldn't hold me.* My stomach convulses and I lurch onto my side, vomiting a thin burgundy gruel onto the stones.

"Fetch my robe," my stepmother says. "And my canes. Please, Fairest."

Her neck is red, marred with deep crescents that will likely bruise. Shaking, I wipe my chin with the back of my hand. "I—I don't... I'm sorry..."

"Hush now." She smiles. "After all these years, what use have the two of us for apologies?"

I fetch my stepmother's robe. And her canes. We sit at the round wooden table, the small shard of glass between us. I fuss at my fingers, trying to scrape away the dried blood crusted around my nails. What a fright I must look. "How—how... The raven, I mean..."

"I was a witch long before you were born, before I even laid eyes upon your father. Did you think I had forgotten all my clever tricks?" She pauses, prods the shard with her index finger. Gingerly, as if it might bite. "Though, for a while, I could do nought but mend. It swallows no small part of you, Fairest. I think you have had a taste of that."

I look away. From the shard, from my stepmother. "But how long?"

"Several years now." Her chuckle is raspy, dry as the last leaves of autumn. "Blessed three, I should have gone mad locked in this room without my wings."

"But you could have fled at any time!"

"Is that what you think? That I could leave you to the fate I myself had wrought? You, and then your daughter? The mirror held me for so long, so sweetly and so ruthlessly—but the fault was mine. I stood before it. I asked my foolish question. I opened my heart to its hooks."

"Has this been your penance?" The words taste as bitter as they sound.

"No, Fairest, it has been my justice. And it is not yet done." My stepmother stands and hobbles across to her nightstand. Moving with care, she retrieves the jug of water left for her bathing and returns to the table. Gently, she takes my hand in hers. I flinch but stop short of pulling away. My stepmother works patiently, rubbing at my fingers with an old linen napkin. "So much blood," she murmurs. "And so little of it yours."

I tell her everything, words spilling from my lips like stolen jewels.

My stepmother listens in silence as she cleans, pausing now and then to dip her napkin in the water. Soon the cloth is pink as my daughter's cheeks—and oh, my daughter, my darling one! How could I have spoken to her with such fury? How could my heart have been so quickly hardened against its sole delight that almost I wished her—

"Yet you did not," my stepmother says, wiping at my tears. "And she is not."

"Oh, but what have I done? My husband returns in a matter of days."

"Lord Heron will miss his poor wife sooner than that." Leaning back in her chair, she nods at the mirrored shard between us. "Take that thing and throw it from the window. Its song is faint, but still I hear it keenly."

The sky outside is a cold, wintry blue and I fling the shard as hard as I can, the mirrored side glinting in the sunlight as it sails its final arc. My thumb smarts; blood beads from a fresh-made cut. "Good riddance to you," I mutter. Despite the chill, I linger by the window a moment more, staring out at the pine forests that border this side of the castle grounds and at the mountains beyond, their crowns hidden in low cloud.

She could have fled at any time. Fled and flown and been free.

"Fairest," my stepmother calls. "There isn't much time."

Squaring my shoulders, I take a deep breath and turn to face her.

"Tell me then. What must I do?"

> *I shall leave you alone. Without light. Without song. Without the skin of another soul to warm you in the night. You will pass in absolute solitude, knowing only the unsteady beat of your failing, fragile heart.*

My daughter is wholly unafraid of the old woman who sits before her, smearing a clear but strange-smelling ointment onto her face. She giggles, wrinkling her nose, and reaches out to run eager fingers through my stepmother's hair. "Are you a fairy?"

My stepmother smiles. "Some might say so." There's a kindness in her voice and in her eyes. Gently, she untangles her hair from my daughter's grasp and sweeps it over her shoulder. "Now stop wriggling, little one."

"Mama says magic is dangerous."

The woman flicks me a glance. "Your mother is right. You should mind her words."

Beneath its ointment, my face itches and my mouth is dry with doubt. She could have fled at any time, I tell myself, fled and flown and been free. Fear is a stubborn habit; it must be broken again and again. Though my stepmother was well pleased with what Lady Heron had brought to the castle, she refused to let me watch as she mixed her ingredients. *It is not for you to know, Fairest. One day, perhaps, if you choose such a path, but not this day.* I was sent instead to fetch my daughter, whom I found curled up on her bed, speaking in whispers to the yellow-haired doll my husband brought back from his travels last spring. Her eyes widened as I entered the room, and she shrank back when I sat down beside her.

I'm sorry, my pet. Please forgive me.

Are you still cross with me, Mama?

Oh no, my pet. I pulled her into my arms, held her and rocked her as I did when she was a babe. *No and never again.* Pressing my face into her hair, I soaked in the sweet, familiar scent of her scalp until she started to twist against me, protesting the tickling of my breath. *Tickling, am I? Tickling?* My fingers found her ribs, and the soft hollows of her knees, wiggled in beneath her arms until she was shrieking with laughter. *Come,* I said at last, smoothing the tangled curls from her eyes. *There's someone who wishes to meet you.*

The doll she left discarded on the bed, its glass-eyed gaze fixed on the ceiling.

"Fairest?" My stepmother holds my daughter by the hand. "We are ready."

"Where—where is your ointment?"

"My enchantment was wrought to last. I have no need of unguents, nor any quills save what fledge from my own skin." She nods at the two feathers lying side by side on the table, sleek and black with promise. Muttering beneath her breath, my stepmother selects the smaller of the two and twirls it between her fingers.

"Will it hurt, Lady Fairy?" my daughter asks, voice faltering.

"No, little one. Quite the opposite."

Quick as a serpent striking, the woman stabs the feather into my daughter's chest and I gasp, rushing forward even as the nightdress she was wearing puddles to the floor. Puddles, then begins to flop and bounce. Chuckling, my stepmother pokes at the linen with her cane until from beneath a fold there flies—a raven, smaller than my stepmother when she takes the form, but so beautiful. As the bird circles the room, swooping and soaring, my fear dissolves into pride. Such mighty wings, such grace! My daughter flies as though she has spent all of her days in the air!

"It might be simpler if you disrobe," my stepmother says. She's holding the second feather in one hand, beckoning me close with the other.

"What if we become lost? What if—"

"Do you suppose I have frittered away all these years without making preparations? Without securing us a haven? You need to trust me, Fairest, one last time."

I shed my blood-stiff garments and take a deep, steadying breath. She could have fled at any time, fled and flown and been free.

"Three days, Fairest, before this magic weakens. We have much ground to cover."

I close my eyes. Already I can smell the mountains, can taste the snow-crisp air. Then a flash quiets my mind, and I feel myself flexing and folding, stretching and sharpening and—flying, flying, oh! Flying so fast, too fast for this too-small space, with giddying swoops, and banking as a wall rises before me, and another wall, and another, and there—the window and through it to the open air. From behind me, a black arrow shoots. She wheels and caws, and there at her tail is the smaller bird, the beloved bird—oh, my beloved bird!

I follow them both, our wings beating us through the clear and boundless sky.

When death comes at last, your hair will be silvered and your bones grown thin with years. I will stay by your side, spinning sweet tales of fairies and goblins, of soft-hearted dwarves and maidens bold and fearful and true. The birds, too, will come to honour your passing, ravens and crows and all the souls of the air. Do you see them, stepmother? Do you see them flying, so fast and so free?

SELF, CONTAINED

MEREDITH HOLDS THE dead bird in both hands. Last week, it was a sparrow, small enough to nestle in the cup of one palm. This morning, it's a wattlebird. She brushes the dirt from its feathers and smooths its wings to its sides. The lifeless head lolls against her fingers. There are two clear puncture wounds on its breast; spatters of blood stain the brown stripes.

Meredith scans the houses on her court with narrowed eyes. Across the road at Number Five, the fat tortoiseshell is sunning herself on the concrete driveway. The ginger tom from Number Three is perched in his favoured spot on the sill of the large bay window. This means nothing; Meredith has seen him outside often enough. She has spotted another cat from time to time as well, a lean streak of tabby whose home, like its current whereabouts, remains unknown to her.

She doesn't know which one is responsible for the birds.

Nor which owners are *ir*responsible enough to let their pet stay out at night, despite the council curfew.

She has letter-dropped before, pleading with her neighbours to keep their cats indoors after dark, explaining the vulnerability of roosting birds and how easily they might be plucked from branch or nest by a night-stalking predator, all furry and fanged.

It is clear that letters will no longer suffice.

***

The man at the store said that fresh mince makes the best bait. Raw and bloody and impossible for any carnivore to resist, no matter how well fed it might be. Meredith has chosen prime beef. She leaves a bowl of it in the back of the cage trap, behind the pressure plate that will trigger the door once her quarry is safely inside. She has no inclination to harm the animal, only to capture it, to be able to brandish irrefutable evidence of its nocturnal expeditions in the face of its owner.

Meredith has no particular quarrel with cats, so long as their natural hunting instincts are kept firmly in check by human hand. Though, largely, she does prefer dogs. (Unconditional love is a hard trait to beat.)

She pushes at the plate with a stick. The door falls instantly, snaps shut with a metallic rattle and clang.

Smiling, Meredith re-sets the trap.

* * *

That night, she finds herself merely dozing, slipping but briefly into the shallowest of slumbers before startling awake again. (And again. And again.) Only after she hears the unmistakeable snap of the trap being sprung, followed by a thin, low-pitched yowl, does she nestle into her pillows and sleep.

* * *

The animal she has caught is huge, its fur black and bristling through the wire mesh. Meredith isn't even certain that it *is* a cat, the shape of it is so confined, so compressed. It seems to fill the entire trap and she wonders at how it managed to squash itself so completely inside that the door was still able to latch closed behind it.

She doesn't know what to do next. She has never seen the cat—if it *is* a cat—around the neighbourhood and so hasn't the foggiest idea to whom her captive should be presented. Nor, if it is the bird-killer, does she want to release it. If she surrenders the beast to the council pound, they might simply euthanise it as a stray without even bothering to find its home. (She has heard stories, read them in the letters section of the local paper.)

Meredith wishes the cat no harm—it should not be faulted for merely following its nature.

She lifts the cage by its handle; it weighs surprisingly little. Inside, the cat begins to growl. A yellow eye glares amid the gloss of black fur.

* * *

The bathroom is the best place. Small, no furniture to hide beneath, its neat white tiles easily cleaned should the animal, from fear or fury, make a mess.

Meredith sets the trap down. As she unlatches the door and lifts it free, her fingers brush against that midnight pelt. The fur is soft, silken as the hair on a newborn baby. She dares another stroke, elicits another growl from the cage's occupant.

You can come out now, she says, stepping back. *No need to be scared.*

A moment passes, or several, while Meredith holds her breath. Then that mass of black fur begins to ripple, begins to wriggle, begins to push itself from the trap until it swells livid and yowling and wrathful into the room. It's a cat by form, certainly, but seems more akin to a small dog in size, something like a Kelpie, or perhaps a border collie. The yellow of its eyes has been all but eclipsed by twin saucers of furious black. It arches its spine and hisses, pink tongue curling between inch-long fangs.

The cat takes a step toward her. Claws make a *tac-tac* noise on the floor. Another step.

Meredith flees the room, slamming the door behind her. A heartbeat later, the wood reverberates with the impact of a solid, furry body. Meredith presses her ear to the door. She can hear the cat growling. She can hear its claws on the tiles.

And beneath it all, she can hear her own blood pulsing hot through her veins.

* * *

The phone is a mute plastic puzzle in her hand. If her husband were still here, such an escalation would be his to deal with. And although he did come back that first winter to repair the leaky garage roof, and again to prune the crown of the lemon tree, Meredith can hardly call upon him to remove a feral cat from her bathroom. They have agreed—they have *both* agreed; haven't they?—to keep their lives, along with their problems, separate and apart. Right now, her husband is probably sitting down to breakfast with his new wife. (Not his younger, or thinner, or even much prettier wife. Just new.)

Meredith cannot call him.

Briefly, she considers Mark. But her son is always so busy, always *just heading out* or *behind the wheel* or *expecting an important call* whenever she rings. (She can't remember the last time he rang her.)

Besides, she suspects he sides with his father—or would, if pushed. She doesn't want to push him. Things are fine the way they are. He always remembers her birthday.

Instead, she calls her daughter, Kim, who immediately wants to know how the cat got into the bathroom, and then what the hell Meredith was doing mucking around with animal traps, for Godsake, and lastly, why she cared so much about the bloody birds in the first place. It's just nature, right? Red in tooth and claw, wasn't that what Coleridge said?

Tennyson, Meredith corrects her. *It's from a Tennyson poem.* She can almost hear Kim rolling her eyes. Her daughter says that she's already running late to drop Liam off at daycare, but since it's her half-day at work she can maybe zip on over afterwards to help with the cat. She has to pick up some dry-cleaning on the way, and needs to collect Liam again by four, but if the thing with the cat won't take long, then she supposes she can zip on over.

You could leave Liam with me today, Meredith suggests. *I could pick up the dry-cleaning.*

I'm not leaving my kid in a house with a feral animal, Kim says. There's a pause, before she laughs. *I didn't mean you, Mum.*

Meredith laughs as well. *Of course you didn't.*

***

After two cups of peppermint tea and one hour of feigning nonchalance, Meredith can no longer wait for anyone to zip on over.

There is no sound from the bathroom. No yowling or growling, no *tac-tac-tac* of stalking claws. She smiles, relieved. The cat has calmed down, is probably crouched in a far corner, sulking. Carefully, she opens the door, or tries to.

Something presses against it from the other side. The door yields but a handspan and then, as Meredith pushes harder, a shock of black fur fills the entire gap, top to bottom. She jumps aside as a huge paw whips out. A paw the size of a Kelpie, or perhaps a Border Collie, and never mind the rest of the cat. The very tip of one claw snags across the skin of her wrist. Blood beads, then wells.

Meredith stumbles down the hall. Risks a glance over her shoulder.

That great paw is pulling the door inward, as fur bristles through the gradually widening space. Bristles and swells and spills itself beyond the tiled confines of the bathroom. (Cats are, in essence, a fluid; everyone knows this.)

Her blood is dripping onto the wooden floor. The cat is slowly filling the hall.

Meredith runs from the house. Slams the front door in her wake. Her slippered feet smear little crimson crescents across the porch.

* * *

She sits in the yard, beneath the Japanese elm, watching the windows. Though the scratch has long since clotted over, her wrist is sore. She should put Savlon on the wound. She should fetch a warm coat. She should do many things. Her phone is in the pocket of her trackpants, but who might she call? Not her husband or Mark; they would find the situation preposterous. Or they would find *her* preposterous. (Or they already do.)

Kim might already be zipping on over. Meredith is of two minds about whether she wants to see her daughter. (She is of two minds about many things.)

Her wrist itches. Meredith scratches at the dried blood. It flakes to the grass, leaving behind a line of soft black hairs that quiver beneath her touch.

She looks up at the windows again. The cat has grown so large now, its pelt is pressed tight against the glass; she can see the fur rippling as the animal curls through the neat and homely rooms that confine it. A massive yellow eye regards her from the top corner of the living room window. Rage locked in amber, for far too long. The eye blinks once, then disappears. (It isn't gone; it will never be gone.)

Meredith brushes a finger over the hair growing from her wrist. She shudders. Deep in her belly, she feels the flex of newly sharpened claws.

And as Meredith sits, she stares at the seething mass that fills her house, and she smiles at the possibilities that might be unfurled when at last she opens the front door and lets that bristling black cat loose into the vast and boundless world.

SMILE FOR ME

IT WAS THE model who answered his knock, smileless, opening the door those few suspicious inches. No, not a model, or at least not *just* one; not that she wasn't beautiful enough (god, she was gorgeous, and Justin kind of hoped she was doing some sets for the guy, just to see her out of those jeans), but her green eyes were too sharp and he'd known too many models, too many vacuous flesh mannequins, and so knew better. This girl just stood there, backhandedly pushing short dark hair from her face (all the better to see you with, my dear), pale lips motionless, pinning him down with that cutting emerald gaze.

Justin coughed, Doc Martens scraping the doormat in an anxious schoolboy shuffle. Since when had he been nervous around women?

"Yes?" The word so clipped it seemed less than a syllable but he snatched at it anyway, grateful for the opening. He needed to speak to an M. J. Harris and had been given this address. Was Mr. Harris at home?

A twinge of a smile now, the corner of her mouth lifting slightly, so slightly, and involuntarily too—he would stake his life on it.

"You're looking at him."

"Oh, I...er...oh."

She nodded slowly, mockingly. "Oh."

Slipping the porno mag from its plain yellow envelope, he flicked past the bound and gagged cover bimbo to the bookmarked photoset, pointed an awkward finger: he'd come about these. Instantly her eyes narrowed, glittered with strange feline warning—*Don't fuck with me, arsehole*—and the door slammed viciously shut. A chain rattled.

Shit. Not expecting a girl, not with this sort of work, she had taken him off guard, his carefully rehearsed gambit shredded by those eyes.

Two deep breaths to clear his head before knocking again, ignoring the sharp ache in his knuckles.

"I'll call the cops if you don't piss off." The threat pushing faintly through the heavy wood, though none the less forceful for it. She *would* call the police, no doubt about that; perhaps they were already on the way.

"Hey, look, I'm not here to harass you." His voice was too pleading, too whiny; the upper hand well and truly lost. "My name is Justin Thorpe, okay? I work at Zoom and I was just wondering..."

The door eased cautiously open, security chain stretched taut. "Zoom?"

An art gallery, he rushed to explain, in Brunswick; surely she'd heard of it? They exhibited photography mostly, a lot of local artists, some really good stuff actually—

"Oh, I've *heard* of Zoom," she interjected. "Pretentious load of crap is what you exhibit. Did Dante send you?"

She knew Dante? "Uh, no. I came on my own."

The woman frowned. "Why?"

Brandishing the magazine once more, mumbling about how he'd seen this spread and thought, wondered, if maybe she did anything else, any other work that was a little more, that is to say, a little more...

"Arty?" Bitterly sarcastic, her eyes rolling. "Do you know who I am?"

"M. J. Harris?" The wrong answer, obviously, but the only one within reach.

"Try Morgan Hartley."

Impossible. *This* was Morgan Hartley, the egotistic pseudo-artist about whom Dante was constantly sniggering; the witch-bitch who would gladly whore her way into galleries if only there was anyone willing to screw her, and god knows not even William down at Project-X was that desperate; the bimbo wannabe who probably considered Anne Geddes the epitome of cutting-edge photography; *this* was Morgan Hartley? Impossible.

"You really had no idea, did you?" she asked. "This *is* amusing."

Apologising, trying to explain that he'd never seen any of her work before, didn't know she used a pseudonym; he'd only heard Dante say...things.

"Dante is a weaselly little prick."

Justin smiled; there was certainly no love lost between himself and his boss either. That was why he was here, wasn't it? Because he was sick of Dante taking credit for everything? The *Fallen Angels* exhibition had been only the last straw of many to sting his shoulders; Justin had come up with the concept, organised the whole damn thing, alternatively cajoled and bullied the artists involved, and still

Dante had managed to step into the limelight at the last minute, to slip his pallid palm into the handshake of gallery owner Susan Keyes, a woman whose influence in contemporary art circles bordered on the legendary.

Yes, "weaselly little prick" summed Dante up just fine.

"Don't worry about him," Justin said adamantly. "I'll clear the show with Zoom's owner directly; Dante doesn't have to even know until the last minute." Shrugging, eyes cast half-shamefully to the ground. "That's sort of how I wanted it anyway."

"Out to steal his thunder?"

"Actually, he's been stealing mine."

Morgan laughed, then shut the door without another word. A slight swell of fear rose in his stomach (he'd said the wrong thing again; what the hell was the *right* thing to say to her anyway?); but no, she'd only been releasing the chain. Now, standing back from the doorway, skinny scarecrow arm waving him in, "So long as you're a fan of Dante's..."

***

Sitting knees together on her couch, steaming coffee in a chipped Far Side mug, strong and acrid black (not his preference, but she'd been out of milk for two days, no inclination for shopping), portfolio of loose photographs spilling over his lap. Nude studies, most of them, though "study's" too dismal a term for what she'd managed to capture: brutal curves carved pale as though from granite, the cool jut of elbow, hip, or clavicle, angles that remained closed to casual penetration, to indifferent scrutiny; *oh but you'll have to do better than that, my dear, so much better; you'll have to know me, to* want *to know me, and then and only then may I allow you in.* In others the flesh rendered soft and pliable as though inviting the most intimate of touches; the full curve of a belly or thigh consuming the entire shot; you could touch it, sink fingers or tongue deep into that pressing, embracing heat, defying skin and muscle, checked only perhaps by a stubborn nub of bone. And more: studies that propelled a cacophony of limb and glossy shadow from the paper, body parts almost unidentifiable, all purpose forgotten in a mad rush to combine and recombine, to twist serpentine and angular, deviant from humanity, from any semblance of servitude to the whole, choosing instead the simpler laws of the flesh; a monstrous tumult devoid of order and yet somehow orderly, a chaos of pattern and form unknowable to the accidental glance.

Yet knowable. If only you could conceive of how.

"I like these. A lot." Justin frowned, traced a fingertip along the shallow curve of a...calf? a forearm? or something else altogether? Damn, but the photographs were so unusual, so bloody—

"Confusing? Disorienting?" Morgan was smiling, lips closed and drawn tight.

"Yes, but more than that. It's like they want to..." *Speak to you.* Stupid, but he'd almost said exactly that. *It's like they want to speak to you, ask questions, demand answers.* What would she have thought if he'd uttered something so inane?

Maybe she would have liked it.

"Trickery."

Justin blinked. "What?"

"You heard me." She flapped a hand sharply, dismissively, and began to gather up the photographs from his lap.

"Yes, I did. I just wasn't sure what, ah..." No, it hadn't been deliberate, the sudden bumping of her fingers against his crotch, merely a careless peripheral movement; she hadn't even noticed.

But he did. All at once he noticed everything: the close and sudden proximity of her beside him on the couch; the all-but-faded scar that curved above her left eyebrow and puckered when, as now, she frowned, appraising one particular photograph with a slight shake of her head before sliding it back into the black vinyl folder; and how, beneath the pungent stink of developing fluid that clung to her like an aura spoiled, she smelled faintly of sweet, green apples.

Stupidly, his cock began to stir, and the old uneasy blend of arousal and pre-pubescent shame slyly unfurled its banners: *remember me, little boy?* Flushing, snatching the last of the prints from her fingers, he tugged it back to his lap, stabbed at a tangle of pale, emaciated bodies, faceless, every head obscured somehow or else severed by a clean, straight edge.

"This one though, this is very, uh, very surreal."

Don't think of pink elephants. No, do think of pink elephants; think of anything you want, just don't think of green apples. Don't think of her.

Morgan wrinkled her nose. "My Holocaust phase." Not that long ago but best forgotten really, weeks eaten up by anorexics and wannabe fashion models, chosen for their bodies which were already halfway there, already distorted and challenging to the perceptions;

her inspiration drawn from old Nazi atrocity photographs, the death camps and mass graves with their clutter of wasted, stark-ribbed corpses, so terrible and petty in the very humanness of it all, yet still horribly intriguing; can you really do that to a person, can you really reduce them to that? And, green irises almost glowing as she spoke, could you do *more?*

Wordless, Justin handed her the photo. His erection had retreated with due decorum as soon as she'd mentioned the camps, her words summoning long-buried images from the recesses of memory: a history documentary he'd been forced to watch in high school, the liberation of Auschwitz or Sobibor or Treblinka, Jews shuffling in the rain like stilted, spastic dolls, skin-stretched skeletons with lank hair and dull hollows for cheeks, no longer even caring to hide their shrunken penises, their shrivelled breasts. For him, *this* was the horror. That which had been merely abstract before, dry words on paper, brought screaming and crazy home: that this *could* happen, that you *could* be reduced to this, the lowest common denominator of flesh and bitter consciousness, and that through it all you could still be forced to endure, to breathe, to *live.*

What more was there?

"You tried to turn the Holocaust into art?" He felt as though he should be offended, or at the very least disgusted, but such emotions eluded him.

Besides, she was already shaking her head. "I'm not interested in that sort of bullshit. It's more Dante's line. Remember the AIDS installation?"

Oh, did he. On the walls: nude, lifesize self-portraits of a little-known Melbourne photographer coolly documenting various stages of the disease, bruises and lesions digitally enhanced, pinned there by dripping scarlet handprints splayed across each corner. And in the centre of the room, spot-lit and pedestalled: six one-litre beakers of blood, supposedly all that the human body contained, coaxed over a period of three months from the scrawny arm of the artist himself, the glass containers permanently sealed and inscribed with the warning symbol for Biohazard, razor-thin savagery rendered deliberately crude and childlike.

And, for an immodest sum, you could purchase your own small, sealed vial of infection (complete with miniature Biohazard insignia of course), a sanguine memento to be carried in your pocket or placed fearfully by your bed.

Lest we forget.

Lest it be you.

The goth chicks had loved it.

"Did you know it was Dante's idea?" Morgan asked. "All of it?"

Justin shook his head. "I thought he only came up with the, ah...the 'souvenir' aspect of things."

"No." She was furious now, but calmly so—and all the more dangerous for it. "It was all Dante's work, every step of the way. Brian came to Zoom with pictures of sunsets and lovers, for fuck's sake. It was Dante who told him to use AIDS, to embrace it and exploit it as though it were some bold new artistic statement. It was Dante who stole his blood."

"I didn't know."

"Brian's dead now, but I'll bet you didn't know that either."

He lowered his eyes, said nothing.

"And I wonder how much longer he would have lived if it hadn't been for Dante. Brian couldn't afford to lose that blood, he couldn't afford to make himself so weak, so often." She smiled bitterly, a slow rictus grin. "How much of his life do those trendy little fucks have sitting on their mantelpieces right this minute?"

Again, there was simply nothing to say to that, no words of either defence or commiseration to utter, and so he merely sat in uncomfortable silence as she rose from the couch, allowing the folio to slide forgotten from her lap.

"I have to work now."

Panic: no, not yet, not without giving him *something*. But she was already at the front door, fingertips tapping impatiently against her thigh.

"That means you have to leave."

Reluctantly, he retrieved his magazine from the coffee table and stood up, folding a page corner absently between finger and thumb, nervous little dog-ear, back and forth, back and forth. "About the exhibition..."

"I already told you—"

"I know, but just listen a minute, okay?" Perhaps it had been a mistake to cut her off like that, but he pressed on regardless, trying to ignore the sudden glint in her eyes, the way her mouth compressed to a thin white line. "So Dante is a fuck; we both know that. But he won't have anything to do with this, I promise. It can all be done—"

"I don't care about Dante."

"Then what?" Justin raked stiff, exasperated fingers through his hair. Finding the right buttons and giving them a good hard twist was usually not a problem, but with this woman he was fumbling blind.

"Didn't you see?" Morgan snapped. "I have nothing *good* enough to exhibit."

And never in a million years would he have pegged her as one of those pouting primadonnas, smug in the knowledge of their own genius, yet inexhaustibly seeking out praise and reassurance from others, eggshell egos too fragile to withstand even one second of existence without the gentle stroke of an approving hand. Well, he was utterly sick of them, and if Morgan was like that, then she could just go fuck herself—he wasn't about to pamper her. Nor leave without a fight.

"Who are you trying to kid?" he demanded. "That stuff you showed me is brilliant and you bloody well know it."

"Trickery."

That word again, but what did she mean by it? Her eyes flashed when he asked, and she snorted derisively: what did he think she meant? There was no magic in those damn photographs, no real art, just pretty little tricks with light and shadow; she was merely messing with perception and perspective, cutting and pasting within the crimson glare of the darkroom to get those effects; a slight error in scale here, a subtle misalignment of form there, that was all it took. Subverting natural rhythms, distorting shapes: trickery.

Justin frowned, confused. "But that's what photography is about, isn't it?"

"No!" Furious now, all of her frustrations set savagely loose upon him. That *wasn't* what it was about at all, didn't he see? What would be the point in the end? Playing tricks on people wasn't art, it was goddamn David Copperfield.

"I'm not sure I understand."

No, of course he didn't, why would he? But the purity of art was all to do with *seeing* things, seeing what no one else could or would, and then showing it to the world; it wasn't about fooling people with shoddy illusions, making their minds spin with optical deceits and subconscious trip-ropes. Truth not trappings, that's what she was after, and she was so close to it now, so close to something really huge, if only she could just figure out the machinations, if only she could put on film what she saw in her fucking head!

"Don't you see?" Her words half plea, half derision, as she snatched the magazine from his hands, flipped it impatiently to the images she herself had shot. "There, it's almost there. Look!"

And he turned his eyes once more to the pictures upon which he'd already gazed for so many hours, time after time compelled to return to those same pages: by candlelight in his bedroom, flour-and-bleach smell of his own semen still crisp in the air as he stared at the nude, bound figures, trying desperately to discover the secret of their profound impact on him. Outwardly no different to the hundreds of similar photosets that his extensive bondage collection had to offer, yet so inexplicably superior in terms of quality, of sheer potency.

But why, when these girls were no more or less beautiful than any others, when their poses were cut from the same brutal cloth as previous spreads, when the lighting, the angles, the entire setup, while handled with perhaps somewhat more delicacy and taste, fell nonetheless neatly within the generic demands of pornography. This was a skinrag after all, not *Black & White*; there was no messing with perception here, no oblique use of pattern and shadow, no *trickery*. So why did he just *know* that photographs such as these would be greeted with murmurs of awed approval at Zoom (or any other gallery, for that matter), whilst ones lifted from another page would be laughed off the walls? He'd put it down in the end to a sensitive, highly personal artistic vision, to some skill that defied easy definition, and had set about tracking down the photographer.

Who was standing here now, thrusting the magazine in his face, telling him to *look* for fuck's sake, couldn't he see what she was talking about? Well, couldn't he?

And of course he could *see* it, just as clearly as he could see anything else in the photograph (the way the skin on the blonde girl's wrists buckled and creased around the steel bite of the cuffs, for instance; or the callous gleam in the brunette's eye as she brought the leather switch down hard on her captive's thighs, hard enough to leave yet another grinning red slash on the pale curves); oh yes, he could he see it, the elusive *sheen*—for want of a better word—that caused the entire image to quiver and glow.

Seeing wasn't the problem; it was the why's and the how's of the thing that refused to make themselves known.

Subtle, defeated shrug. "I don't understand it."

"Neither do I," Morgan responded. "Yet."

***

His next visit was by invitation, the phone ringing during his lunch break at Zoom, Dante reaching it first and handing him the receiver with a frown. "For you, Justice, some chick." (*Justice*, how he hated that, but Dante was big on twisting names—except for his own precious appellation of course; no one could touch that). Her voice, low and faint in his ear: "Can you come? I need to talk."

On the couch again, milk in his coffee this time (the carton bought from a petrol station on the way over), Morgan chewing on a dark strand of hair that only just reached to her mouth. There would be an exhibition, but not until she was ready, not until she'd worked everything out and had something genuinely amazing to show them.

And she *would* show them, all of them, even Dante.

Especially Dante.

But not until she was quite, quite ready.

"Which will be when, do you think?" Justin asked, careful with his words.

"Never, at this rate." Piqued, she flopped cross-legged to the floor. It was all to do with energy, she explained, that much was obvious now, but there was more to it than simply that; there had to be. The magazine he'd brought with him last time, that bondage shoot had been the start of it—oh, not that she hadn't done dozens of similar sets before (surprising how *easy* freelance porn was to sell, so long as it was vaguely erotic, and anything with kinks brought in more than enough to pay the bills, thank you *very* much), but this had been the first one where she'd noticed the difference.

No, not just noticed; *felt.*

"Those two were so into it, so incredibly into it." Morgan closed her eyes, her tongue constantly darting out to moisten her lips as she spoke. The entire studio had been so charged, not like the usual sessions, with their constant pauses for posing and direction and all the fussy little adjustments of light and makeup and costume; this time she'd felt cast more than ever into the role of spectator, documenter.

And yet she'd been an integral part, the closing link in a circuit; without her it wouldn't have, couldn't have, been possible.

Justin placed his empty mug on the floor beside his feet. "Pity you can't figure out how you did it."

She looked at him then in a curious, open-faced way that made him wonder how many masks she usually wore. "The thing is, maybe I don't have to."

***

Instinct.

That was what she'd meant. After all, wasn't the best art—the stuff that gives you gooseflesh and makes your breath catch—wasn't all that conceived in the heart and not in the head? Felt, rather than thought out?

Wasn't it?

He hadn't an answer to that; apparently, she no longer needed one.

***

The redhead in the sleeveless floral dress opened the door before he'd even had a chance to knock. Plum-coloured lipstick smudged askew on her mouth, right eye swollen and bruised from an obviously recent blow, almost walking straight into him as she tried to leave the house.

"Hey." Reaching for the bare flesh of her upper arm, the muscle repellently soft and flabby beneath his touch. "Are you okay?"

Preoccupied? No, her gaze was altogether too vacant to be called that.

"I have to go home now," the woman murmured.

"Where's Morgan?"

No reply.

"Morgan Hartley," he prompted. "She lives here."

Again the soft, childish whisper: "I have to go home."

But she didn't move away, and Justin realised (with a certain amount of distaste) that he was still gripping her arm, his fingers perhaps digging a little too deeply into the sallow, too-spongy skin.

Muttering an apology, he released the woman and took a step back, surreptitiously wiping his hand on his jeans; greasy, so damn greasy.

"I'm going home," she was saying, drawing the words out a bare fraction slower than normal. "Now."

"Fine, whatever." Into the house now, slamming the front door behind him; weird, just too weird, that one, even for Morgan who had been getting a little freaky herself recently, raving on and on about how she almost had it, just a few more sessions, a few more models, but never the same one twice because that spoiled it somehow, shattered the energy rhythms; but just a few more now, surely Justin knew where to find them?

And how could he tell her that it was getting harder and harder, that word had circulated around the art colleges and freelance circles about Mad Morgan Hartley; how she made you sit for hours and hours without even touching the camera, talking about stuff that you never thought you'd mention to anyone, not even your best friend (especially not your best friend); how she goaded you to tears and screams and near-ballistic rages before finally, *finally*, picking up that goddamn black box and whispering: *smile.*

There simply wasn't enough money in the world to make you put up with that sort of shit, the models sneered.

And the artists, and the critics, and everyone who was anyone (and some who were not and never would be) listened eagerly, filing their claws to razor-sharp points as they waited, waited for her to finally, *finally*, show her face.

Mad Morgan, they laughed snidely. The witch-bitch wannabe from hell.

Dante was having a ball.

But where was she? Calling her name, Justin marched through the house, knocking three times on the studio door before nudging it shyly open (she hated to be disturbed in here, even if she wasn't working), only to find the room empty and cold, windows wide open to admit the chilling breath of winter.

So: down the hall to the darkroom, door firmly closed, Salvador Dali print staring enigmatically at him; melting clocks, a reminder of how time ceased to function when she was in there.

Like now.

Screeching in answer to his hesitant taps. "Don't you come in here, Justin! Don't you fucking dare, you hear me?"

Of course he did, and of course he wouldn't, what did she think?

"Go away, just— Look, there's some old croissants or something in the kitchen; help yourself? I'll be out soon."

And the addendum, the coarse excited whisper so soft that he almost couldn't hear it through the wood: "This is it. This is fucking it!"

***

Not croissants but bagels, one of them already flecked with mould round the edges and he'd thrown it away immediately, then changed the bag in the bin. Morgan would have simply allowed the garbage to build up and up until the whole house stank of rot; she hardly bothered herself with such trivialities at the best of times, and lately—

"Look."

How long had she been standing there, still-dripping print pinched between finger and thumb, absurd, almost alien expression on her face; a child just come home with her first ever drawing from kindergarten: pride, anxiety...and joy.

Daddy, look what I've made.

Justin took the sheet carefully, squinted at the dozen or so black-and-white images collected there; a contact print the first time as always, tiny proofs arranged in near-perfect parallel rows. Honestly, she could be so anal about developing; he imagined her hunched over in the darkroom, meticulously ensuring that each strip of negatives lay in just the right place, before carefully, so very carefully, lowering the glass that would pin them down during their brief period of exposure.

A trembling finger, nail gnawed ragged and bloody to the quick, stabbed impatiently at the paper. "That one, there. Look at *that* one."

But they were all so similar, head-and-shoulders shots of the woman in the flower-print dress, her tangle of red hair drained almost to black by the monochrome film, the bruises on her face rendered even more ghastly in their newly acquired hues of grey. Dutifully, he peered closer at the particular frame Morgan had singled out, not really understanding how it could be all that—

Different.

Utterly, shockingly different.

The same wave of revulsion he'd experienced upon colliding with the woman at the front door spilled over him again; those slack, smudged lips stretched too thin over teeth crooked and narrow, the flat fish-eyed vacancy of her gaze, the utter laxity of her pose, all of it conspiring to propel him from the image in disgust.

And something more than that.

Violence: an intimate, impulsive desire to batter anew her already battered features; to savour the pulpy crush of her mouth beneath his fist, the shred of lip against tooth; to know the base gratification of broken bones and bruised, bleeding flesh. All that from a tiny photograph, from a mere thumbnail of a face?

"You feel it, don't you?"

Her question startling him, shaming him into admission: yes, yes, of course he felt it, whatever *it* was.

"You want to hit her." Grinning as she took the sheet from his fingers, subjected it to her own close scrutinisation. "Yes, you really do. You just want to hit the stupid old cow so fucking hard. You want to make her *cry*."

And the way her eyes gleamed as she spoke those words—too horrible a thought, but still he had to ask. "Morgan, those bruises. You didn't..."

"Beat her up?" Laughing now, genuinely delighted by the apprehension in his words. Of course she hadn't touched the woman, hadn't so much as smoothed her hair or straightened the loathsome rag she called a dress; such an action would have been criminal, completely defeating the purpose of her art. No, it had all been wonderfully serendipitous: Morgan out walking to clear her head, to reason through her failures, and the woman weeping still and silent on a bench in Lygon Street, the torrid bloom of fist-fresh wounds pushing out from behind cheap plastic sunglasses, smugly purple pansies torn and tattered by a not-so-gentle breeze. But oh the energy, that was the really special thing. Raw and livid, it surrounded her like, well, like an *aura,* for want of a better word, emanating from her, feeding from her even; the precious, elusive charge of emotion that Morgan had been trying so goddamn hard to conjure or cajole from every dumb model who'd walked through her studio door in the last five weeks; there it was, right there in front of her, and at that moment Morgan would have gladly surrendered her soul for access to a camera.

"I mean that, Justin." That happy-anxious grin again. "My *soul.*"

Such a sacrifice had hardly been necessary, however, with the woman willing to be led back to the studio on the promise of a modest sitting fee, a fee that was never paid in the end—perhaps she was too shy, too embarrassed to accept it, who knew?—all that mattered was that Morgan had at last been given an opportunity and she had seized it with both hands eager and able, snapping frame after frame after frame until, midway through the third roll of film, she'd felt it.

At the very instant the shutter closed, she'd known.

Click. The shot was hers.

"Click!" Morgan repeated, snapping her fingers bluntly. "Simple as that. And can you guess what the most brilliant thing is, Justin?"

He shook his head.

She smiled. "I know I can do it again."

* * *

Less than an hour later, cross-legged on the fraying loungeroom, skinny arms supporting the weight of her head as though her neck had wearied of the task, Morgan sat and wept.

Loudly at first: chafing, jagged shrieks that approached the hysterical and frightened Justin more than he cared to admit; then softer sobs, bony shoulders hitching with each hard-fought breath, snot edging thickly on the crest of her upper lip; and now this, silent tears slipping from eyes rubbed red-raw, her entire form perfectly, terribly still.

Gingerly, he touched her knee, nudged a finger across the spot where the denim had worn white. "You're sure it's the right one?"

"What do you think?" she snapped, glaring sideways at him through a sullen swish of hair. Her face was puffy and blotched. "I only did it three fucking times."

They lay there now in front of them, dull testament to her ineptitude as she saw it, as she'd bloody well *screamed* it from the darkroom, her anguished cry sending him in a panic to the locked door, pathetically bleating her name and demanding that she open up right this minute, did she hear him, right this goddamn minute. She'd ignored him, of course, finally emerging a full five minutes later with her skin even paler than usual and her fingers icy and trembling as she thrust the photographs dumbly towards his chest, the still-wet sheets flat and smooth and slippery like baby stingrays in his hands.

Eyes slitted, Justin scrutinised the three A3 prints he'd arranged so carefully on the floor, each an exact reproduction of the small image on the sheet he held in his hand, the frame she'd circled with a fat red felt-tip. Yes, it was definitely the right one, with every line and shadow matching precisely, down to the single twist of hair that fell across the woman's right cheekbone, neatly bisecting the bruises stamped into her flesh.

Perfect A3 enlargements, exact replicas down to the finest detail, and yet you would swear on your own grave if need be that these three copies displayed a strikingly different image to that of the original contact print.

Because they *weren't* the same.

Because the energy, the emotional gut-punch simply wasn't there.

And be damned if you could figure out why.

"Maybe," Justin mused aloud, "maybe it's the size. The enlargements could show up too many details, make you just see too much."

"Dilution of the image." But her tone was bitter-sharp, and if he'd been paying close attention he would have shut his mouth then and there.

Instead, he pounced eagerly upon her words. "Well, it has to be something like that, doesn't it? You could try a little smaller, like A4 size, and maybe—"

"Stupid."

"What is?"

"You," Morgan hissed. "You're such a stupid little fuck, Justin. You and your idiotic fucking theories. You don't understand any of this. Not one fucking thing!"

This time he did shut up, averting his gaze as she raged on and on in venomous *sotto voce*, insisting that he didn't see what she was trying to do, that he had never understood her, that he was just another weaselly little hanger-on, most likely snickering with the others behind her back, and he shouldn't presume for one second that she didn't know just what people were saying, the jealous cunts, because she wasn't the stupid one around here, oh no, Justin had certainly proved himself the rightful claimant to that title, providing of course that King Shit Dante was willing to surrender it...

And it wasn't until she began to tear up the bland, two-dimensional faces of the woman, all three prints one after the other, that he rose and walked calmly to the front door, thinking that maybe he really didn't get it, but if you had to be crazy to understand then Morgan was welcome to the privilege.

She followed him onto the verandah, tossing dull-edged shards of paper into his face as he turned to tell her he was nobody's whipping boy, not even hers, but the phrase sounded hollow in his mouth and he wished he hadn't spoken, wished he'd simply left without a word.

Morgan laughed and pressed a torn scrap into his hand. "Come back when you know what I know."

The original tiny image of the woman stared up at him from his palm as the front door slammed shut, security chain rattling coldly. Swallowing the familiar feeling of revulsion, pushing down the sudden swell of violence in his guts, Justin tucked the photo deep into his jeans pocket.

Mad Morgan Hartley.

Maybe they were right.

And maybe it just wasn't healthy to know what she knew.

* * *

But still he couldn't banish her from his thoughts, or his dreams. Surreal visions, cluttered with twisting, pressing forms, impressions obviously spun from her photographs and overlain, for reasons he failed to fathom, with the cloying reek of putrefaction. Warm, living flesh, the sweet breath of decay; finer details than these deserted his mind soon upon waking and would not be summoned into consciousness no matter how hastily he snatched at their fast-fleeing shadows.

Only one clear image lingered through each day, lurching forward from behind his lids whenever he closed his eyes, unbidden and certainly unwanted: Morgan with pale limbs impossibly elongated, reaching down to where he crouched, abject and insignificant between her ankles; Morgan crooning softly—*smile for me, oh do smile for me*—and there, at the juncture of her naked thighs, a subtle flash and wink of light from what he feared upon reflection (for in the throes of the dream he thought nothing, was nothing, was simply looking up at her, up and up and into her) could only be the tiny shutter of a tiny lens snapping suddenly closed.

Come back when you know what I know.

Impossible.

And too proud, far too stubborn to call her, although he sat with fingers hovering above the phone-pad more often than he cared to acknowledge, dial tone purring encouragingly into his ear: *Hi there, just wanted to see how you were doing?*

Ridiculous. Out of the question.

But still he wondered.

Which was why, when the girl came bouncing into Zoom early one morning, scarlet-dyed hair a mess of plaits and dreadlocks and brightly coloured elastic bands, grinning wide around the ring she wore through the centre of her lower lip and asking if he knew Morgan Hartley's address (a friend of a friend of a model having directed her to him), Justin was only too eager to scribble it down for her.

"I'll put the phone number here too." Transcribing each digit from his address book onto the back of a Zoom business card with undue care and precision, as though he didn't already know it by heart. "You might want to ring her first; she doesn't...ah, she doesn't like being barged in on."

But the girl shook her head as soon as he'd finished. "I've already got that one; it doesn't work."

"Doesn't work?"

"Nup. Disconnected."

Frowning, Justin slid the card across the desk. Disconnected? Surely this signalled no disaster greater than the neglection of an unpaid phone bill.

"Ta for this." The girl had picked up the card and was flicking it lightly between finger and thumb. "I'm Cynthia, by the way."

He nodded, forced a smile. (What if something were actually wrong?) "Are you interested in Morgan's work?"

Cynthia lifted her left eyebrow and winked. "I'm interested in *Morgan.* Period."

A sudden stab of jealousy twisted his stomach. Was she a rival then, this motley scarecrow-cum-clown, with her neo-hippy clothes, trendy piercings, and scuffed, cherry-red sneakers? Not that he himself held any claim to Morgan's loyalties—he wasn't naive enough to suppose *that* for even a moment—but still the possessive fever refused to wane.

"You're a model then?"

The girl's laughter was raucous and immediate. A model? Oh god no, not her. She was a writer, "freelance" being a nice way to put it (two fingers bobbing a ditto sign), "unemployed" being an infinitely more truthful description. She'd been hearing what you could most politely call "interesting talk" about Morgan, about her methods and philosophy and so on. It felt like a good story: arty, human interest, lots of ops for those glossy colour photos that all the mags went ga-ga over...

"You know." Slight hitch of her shoulders. "Journo's nose and all that jazz."

"Well, say 'hi' to her for me," he muttered, busying himself with the catalogue proofs for an upcoming exhibition (yet another of Dante's *enfante* protégés, a child still living beneath the dear departed shadow of Mapplethorpe, even down to the damn flowers).

"For sure." A little hand slipped into a curl around his wrist, squeezing firmly with skin that felt surprisingly warm and flushed with energy. "Thanks muchly."

Her departing grin was so genuine, the mock-diffident dip of her head so delightfully unconscious, that Justin found himself smiling in return. Writer or not, Cynthia would make an incredibly photogenic subject, he was certain of that.

And of this: Morgan, *his* Morgan, would eat her alive.

* * *

Payday, for what it was worth, emerging from the local supermarket with three bags of food, cheap plastic handles carving deep red furrows into his palms, to see her dawdling hands-in-pockets along the other side of the street.

"Cynthia! Hey, Cynthia!" No response, but it was definitely her, tangled scarlet hair remarkably less bright now, perhaps due for a refresher dye job or maybe she was simply letting it fade out. Calling her name as he crossed the street, his limbs rendered slow and maladroit by the clumsy bump of groceries; her motion even slower, a distracted somnambulant shuffle, stubbornly ignoring his shouts until finally he caught up, up and past, turning annoyed and frustrated to block her path: Hey, didn't you hear me? Well? Well?

But the girl merely stared blankly at him, or rather she stared *through* him, half-lidded eyes fixed on some point just beyond his left shoulder, her features a flat dull mask.

"Cynthia?" Resisting the urge to snap his fingers in front of her face. "You remember me, yeah? From a few weeks ago, at Zoom? I gave you Morgan Hartley's address?"

"Morgan," she echoed, head nodding slightly. "Morgan."

Justin cleared his throat. Obviously she was high, stoned out of her mind on some chemically inspired trip or another, but still he was unwilling to leave without pressing just a little further.

"So, did you end up seeing her or what?"

A long, languid blink.

"You know," he prodded. "For that story you were writing?"

Finally she looked up, vague grey eyes locking unsteadily with his own. "I have to go, I have stuff to do." A mild frown creased her forehead. "Important stuff."

"You did meet Morgan though, didn't you? You did see her?"

"Yes." Nodding. "Yes. But I have to go now."

High or not, there was something terribly odd about her, something uncomfortably familiar about the whole situation, not *déjà vu* precisely, not quite, but a feeling which could assuredly claim a distant, disturbing kinship. Struck with a sudden deep-sprung unease,

Justin moved to one side and allowed the girl to pass, watched with crawling skin her slow sluggish shuffle along the pavement. So different to the bright, vivacious Cynthia he'd met that day at the gallery, no energy whatsoever in this sorry creature. If that's what drugs could do to you, drain you so utterly like that, then...

Startling, the connection that slipped cold and knifelike into his mind.

A woman with battered eyes and a faded, floral dress.

A small smudge of a photograph.

And Morgan with her camera clutched close.

Come back when you know what I know.

* * *

The boy who finally answered the door couldn't have been more than sixteen, white-blonde hair flopping limply into his pallid green eyes, loose slackjaw gape as he stood silent, staring, staring.

"Where is she? Where's Morgan?" Pushing past the kid who took one accommodating step backwards into the room before carefully, much too carefully, shutting the door and slinking quietly over to the couch. Music videos on the television, volume turned right down to a lazy buzzing hush, not that it seemed to matter, not that anything seemed to matter to the boy now hunched cross-legged on the sagging cushions, an old blue quilt dragged up to his chin, defensive security blanket, nothing can hurt me now.

Justin grimaced. Another fucking zombie-case; what the hell kind of art was Morgan practising here anyway, frontal lobotomies?

"Hey there."

Her voice, casual-calm from behind, and he turned to find her slouched in the kitchen doorway, pale fingers encircling a steaming mug. Dark hair a little longer than he remembered but otherwise unchanged, tall in black jeans and her favourite t-shirt, the one with the orange cartoon cat goggle-eyed and straitjacketed, the words *Psycho Pussy* scrawled in crazy-font above its ears.

"Coffee?" she asked quietly, head crooked to one side.

"No, I..." Lost for words, too busy taking in the subtle curve of her hip, the keen emerald glint of those eyes. Lucid eyes, no longer harbouring the livid sparks of insanity, the bitter-cold fury that he had so fearfully associated with her.

Smiling broadly, she crossed the distance between them, brushed warm knuckles gently against his cheek. "It's good you've come back. I've been wanting to show someone for a while now, to show *you*."

"Show me what?" Justin fought the impulse to reach out for her, to have her whole and healed in his arms. "Morgan, what have you been doing?"

Again that grin, open and healthy, leading him wordless down the hall to the closed studio door, fingers eager-light on the handle, eyes locked with his over a last slow sip of coffee before casting it wide open.

"Come into my parlour, my darling little fly."

Portraits, at least two dozen of them mounted and leaning against the walls, mostly monochrome shots but several in full glorious colour, all of them one metre by one metre square, all of them absolutely, utterly breathtaking; a private exhibit for one and the combined emotional impact of the pieces so extreme as to force Justin to crouch isolated before each separate panel, to examine them individually, one by one. Otherwise it was all too much. Otherwise it *hurt.*

A nude woman, young glossy brunette with features of such stark, smouldering sexuality, her gaze so bold and deliberately wanton as she reclined supple and sure on soft white folds of satin that he felt himself harden immediately, unable to draw his eyes away from the pale swell of thigh, the clean curves of her breasts, proud nipples darkly erect. Hot blood flushing his cheeks, he swayed embarrassed on his heels, afraid Morgan would notice, but of course she already had; she noticed everything and was smiling, smiling and steering him firmly in the direction of another print

where a man of indeterminate years glared enraged back at him, recently shaved head already sprouting the harsh bristle of regrowth, face twisted in a mad, furious grimace which consumed the entire frame and those eyes, oh those mean mean eyes that gleamed in such an ecstasy of cruelty that Justin was sincerely terrified, an actual physical fear that plucked at his guts and dampened his skin with the beginnings of panic so that he needed no prodding this time to propel himself away

and so come face to face with an angel, blonde beatific visage grinning wide in luscious colour, crisp green eyes soft at the edges, benevolent grace in the dimples of his cheeks, in the sweet arc of his cupid lips; there should be wings curving from this boy's bare shoulders, classical heaven-sent wings with feathers of purest white, there should be—

"You know him," Morgan whispered gently by his ear.

"Hmm, what?"

"Sean. You've met him." Jerking her head towards the open door. "Out there."

She couldn't mean...though of course it was obvious now, the same youthful face, the same pale hair, but oh how they seemed so terribly different; how on earth had she transformed that pitiful creature in the lounge into the lush, transcendent being that beamed forth so brilliantly from the sleek velvet backdrop?

"Who is he?" Justin asked, index finger reaching towards the photograph to trace the shallow scoop of a cheekbone, the slope of an elfin chin.

"No one, just a kid I met." Walking the streets one night, she explained, a habit picked up once she'd realised how useless professional models actually were with their artfully prepared veneers, a mask for all seasons, all sessions; useless. Instead, out trawling for subjects herself, ordinary people coaxed straight from the footpath, the coffee shop, the gutter; Sean just another of these, allowed to stay on for a while simply because he seemed to have nowhere else to go, and because he wasn't any trouble. "Less maintenance than a cactus, really. All he ever does is piss and watch TV."

Her tone quite neutral, chilling in its total indifference.

Justin studied the images before him, straining to unlock their secrets, to scrape away the surface and get at the pithy core within. But beyond the emotional impact (if you could *ever* get completely beyond it), the portraits themselves were nothing special: simple poses, basic lighting and angles, technically ordinary. There seemed no source for the tremendous power they exuded, no basis for their sharp and absolute sublimity.

"Essence," Morgan said.

"Sorry?"

"The exhibition. It's going to be called *Essence.*"

"Exhibition? Where?"

The venue was yet to be decided, galleries yet to be approached, but surely she would have her pick once they saw these pieces, the very best of all the work she'd been doing recently; surely they'd be clamouring, begging, to have them on their walls. Wouldn't they, nervous fingernail gnaw, hmm, wouldn't they?

"Are you joking?" The photos were fucking incredible, he told her, signed prints alone would be worth a small fortune let alone the framed originals; she was going to make a killing out of this, she was—

Shaking her head. "No. No, they're one-offs. All of them."

"Yeah, right." Justin rose, turned to face her. "Look, don't get precious about this, for god's sake."

"I'm not." Pushing the hair from her eyes, familiar backhand motion that made his chest ache. "The thing is, I really *can't* make more than one, just the first, that's it. They won't reproduce or copy or duplicate, I can't even re-photograph them. Once, only once from each negative: first time pays for all."

"That's ridiculous. What, the images don't show up anymore?"

"No, they're there. They're just not..." Impatient hand on his shoulder, spinning him around once more, fingers pointing, trembling, look look look: "They're just not like *that*. After the first time, they're *nothing*."

Sudden, hard lump in his throat, painful swallow as he shook free of her grasp. Morgan still chattering on: he knew what she was talking about, didn't he, he remembered that woman she'd photographed, insipid bruised *hausfrau*, and how it was only the first little contact print which had carried the impact, how no matter what she did afterwards it was never the same, never...

But he was no longer listening, his attention captured instead by a portrait in the far corner of the room, static black and white yet inherently suffused with colour, supernova radiation of energy, of dark tangled braids and mock-fool grin punctuated by a stainless-steel lip-ring: Cynthia, the living essence of her.

Essence. The name of the exhibition, the nature of the process.

"Morgan," he whispered. "Oh, Morgan, what do you *do*?"

"I take their photographs." Flippant, shrugging bony shoulders; stupid question, what did he think she would say?

"You take more than that." He pointed towards Cynthia's portrait. "Her, I've seen her before that photograph. And after, just today. There's something different about her now, something is...missing. And that boy out there, Sean, he wasn't like that when you first met him, was he, before you shot him?"

"Like what?" Innocently spoken but her grin, so sneaky-pleased; she was precisely aware of what she did. Revelled in it.

"He's a vegetable, for fuck's sake!"

Morgan laughed. "There are tribes in Africa, you know, who still believe that a camera will steal away their souls. Is that what you think I do here, Justin? That I somehow rob these people of more than just their image? Really, how melodramatic."

Of course it was melodramatic.

A blatantly absurd notion when she put it like that, right eyebrow raised in artful condescension, humour-him expression snaking across her features.

(But didn't it feel right?)

Then, sudden as thought, she had moved close enough to kiss, bare arms surprisingly firm around his waist. Green apples and developing fluid. Still.

"Stay with me, Justin." Her voice whisper-sweet, lips a mere breath from his. "Watch how I work and you'll see. Nothing's inexplicable."

This felt right.

He closed his eyes, pulled her tight against him. So very right, just like this; his most desperate vagrant want only fully realised in its final gratification.

"I've missed you," she murmured.

Not the three little words he desired most to hear, but close enough. A beginning, for better or worse. For now.

* * *

Cold, white tiles surrounding him, hard beneath the hip he couldn't move, naked skin sticking painfully to the frigid surface.

Tac. Tac. Razor claws drawing closer.

Tac. Tac. The thing he couldn't see, couldn't see at all, eyes frozen shut, but it was there, clicking towards him. *Tac. Tac.* Circling, circling in and it was something terrible, something beyond terrible, and he just couldn't

move—*tac tac*—move for fuck's sake—*tac tac*

tac tac

Light. Too, too bright as he dragged semi-dazed into consciousness, aware suddenly of the noise which wasn't claws at all, nothing so simply sinister as that, but rather the click and wind of a camera, Morgan's camera taking shot after shot after—

no no no

—the only response his mind could articulate, emphatic negative resounding again and again in an otherwise barren thoughtspace—

no no no

—lunging up from the bed towards her, desperate reach for the cold mechanical box she clutched possessively to her chest, her green eyes widening as she realised his intentions, hissing at him through gritted teeth—

no no no

—brief violent tussle, but he by far the stronger as he wrenched the camera from her grasp (did he crush her fingers very badly? did he? good) and threw it hard against the wall, its death-rattle crunch more satisfying than he could ever have imagined.

And the thought finding voice at last, that one small word dropping deadpan from his trembling lips: "No."

Not him, not like that. "No."

"You fuck." Hunchback crouch in the corner, vulture turned damp-eyed maternal over the wrecked camera, broken remains of an only, much-beloved child spooling film like entrails into her hands. "Look what you goddamn fucking did!"

"What about what *you* were trying to do?"

Vulpine sneer curling her lip. "I was only taking your picture."

"Liar."

But he was too tired to fight with any real conviction, his mind still too muddled by sleep-spun paranoia to mount a trustworthy defence. Flopping backwards onto the mattress, he curled his hand in the sheet, dragged it over his head: Shroud of Justin, ha ha. Just as long as she didn't try to photograph him again, that was all he cared about. In the morning things would be so much clearer, in the morning—

"Wake up, shithead." Morgan wrenched the covers back from his face, slapped his cheek with a frozen palm. Twice.

"Don't." His voice too slurred to be dangerous.

So: another slap, and another, until finally he himself jerked upright, flung an angry fist in her direction. She'd already moved of course, was standing a good safe metre away, malefic Cheshire Cat minus the tail to twitch.

"Fuck you, Morgan. I'm leaving." Bad idea to ever have come in the first place, but too curious (admit it, too *stupid*) to leave this particular labyrinth unexplored, and yes, too besotted. Not that she'd ever before returned his affection, had never seemed to regard him as other than a handy sounding board, punching bag, shoulder to cry on at the most desperate of times, and now, what: subject, victim, final tender prey perhaps? Tonight, urging him to stay with her not to fuck—never to fuck—but to drink cheap beer together before crawling into bed, innocent back to back kinder-curl like kids at an impromptu sleepover. How she must have lain there, eyes eager-bright in the blackness, listening to him breathe, counting the minutes until she was sure he was asleep before reaching, down beneath the bed maybe, for the camera, film fresh-loaded and ready.

"Would it have been so bad?" she asked now. "To be a part of it, would it really have been so bad?"

Medusa-gaze, he could feel it upon him, refused to look. "A part of what?"

"My project. My art."

Justin shook his head. "What you do isn't art. It's theft—at the very least."

"What I do..." Morgan laughed, brittle crazy-chuckle. "What do you know about what I do, huh? *I* don't even understand it, I really don't. I just...do it."

"But why? Don't you see what it does to people, don't you see—"

Cutting him off with a hiss, of course she saw, did he think she was blind? But what did it matter in the long run; all great art demands great sacrifice and her art resided on such a completely new level, embraced a whole goddamn new dimension, so if the sacrifice was that much greater, then what of it? What she did was beautiful, so totally incredible, surely even Justin wouldn't argue with that, he'd seen the pieces for himself, he'd *felt* them. And if he was right, if it was their *souls*—nose wrinkling as the word spat from her lips—the undiluted *essence* of themselves that she was transferring into the photographs, then so what? Who amongst them wouldn't crave immortality, the perfect grace of immortality that only true art can bestow?

"Immortality?" he echoed, incredulous.

"Think about it. Human flesh withers and cracks and dies; these images, *my* images, will stay beautiful, unchanged forever. Forever."

She was insane, utterly certifiable. And what did that make him, devoted apostle turned Judas, he who believed it all, every mad muttered word; what did that make him?

Gone.

Out of the bedroom, down the hall with face shamed and averted from the studio door, mausoleum of the damned and damnable, not thinking about all those portraits pressed forever flat behind indifferent glass, not thinking about very much at all or at least trying to until, in the loungeroom, struck motionless again by Sean's vapid zombie stare, soundless infomercial on the television, the latest piece of must-have exercise equipment resembling a favoured medieval torture device. Morgan right behind him, continuing to rave about immortality and essence and the ecstasy of the artist; extolling the necessity of sacrifice, the sublime beauty of giving oneself over completely to art, to a process above humanity.

"Bullshit!" Vicious now, bated hound driven that last vital inch. "It's not *you* making the sacrifices here, Morgan, it's them: Sean, Cynthia, all the others. *You* just take and take and don't give anything in return, and that's why you'll never really be an artist, because you'll never, ever truly understand."

"Understand what?" she demanded fiercely, skinny finger jabbing at his chest. "What could *you* possibly have to tell *me* about art, you jealous little shit?"

Juvenile name-calling, her usual last line of defence; he'd threatened her then, touched on something she would have preferred not to acknowledge.

"You give nothing of yourself, Morgan," Justin told her calmly, softly. "You sacrifice nothing, and therefore you create nothing. You're not an artist, you're not a god. You're little more than a thief, a goddamn bower bird at best."

Swearing, screeching spittle into his face, she pushed him out the front door, no flippant invitation to come back this time; perhaps he already understood too much, perhaps at last she did as well.

* * *

Some weeks later, a brother he'd never even known she had, passing him the spare key to her house, dull brown metal uncomfortably warm in his hand. Dante hovering on the other side of the gallery, new installation to supervise: tortured twists of razor wire spun to abstractions of pain and bitter desire, works remarkable only in the absolute purity of their expression, the introspective silver agony that obliterated form and function; pieces that existed solely to grieve, and grieved so that they might continue to exist.

"Apparently, she thought a lot of you," the brother said. Tall and thin like Morgan, but his eyes a faded washed-out blue; indifferent shrug, thumbnail running the edge of his lower lip. He was a taxation adviser or something, too busy this time of year for idle chatter, spilling the basics in a brisk, efficient monotone. Not a suicide, nothing like that, though the note she'd written certainly read as a last will and testament. The portraits in her studio left to Justin, a camera too. He could collect them this afternoon if he liked, could send the key back registered mail. Two fingers tapping a neat white business card across the desk.

Pausing circumspect at the door, leather briefcase bumping against his thigh as he surveyed the gallery. "I don't know all that much about art." The lightest of frowns flitting across his brow. "But those photographs of hers were quite...good, weren't they?"

***

Morgan's house a sullen shell, couch empty but for the crumpled blue quilt; he'd never even thought to ask about Sean. Portraits stacked neatly together in the studio, tripod-mounted camera keeping solitary vigil in the centre of the room.

Justin swallowed the rapidly swelling lump in his throat. What did they call those places now, where she rocked the days away in a white-walled corner? Catatonic, her brother had said, causes unknown and a bafflement to the physicians who'd run every sort of test, conducted every known and intimate examination. Mental asylum, psychiatric hospital, sanatorium; a wealth of semantics from which to choose but all spiralling to the same end, to Morgan slipping well beyond the reach of all human intervention, beyond herself.

Forever.

Because in the camera, left there just for him: a half-spent roll of film.

***

Barely enough wallspace in the small, one-bedroom flat, even after the surrender of his framed art prints and two tall bookshelves, but still he'd managed. All of them hung now, the terrible force of their combined gaze only slightly more bearable than the thought of them locked away somewhere, forsaken to the sterile dust and darkness of storage.

All hung, but one: Morgan's self-portrait, kept safe between the glossy pages of an art book, large Hieronymus Bosch pictorial. Simple black and white image, the last exposed frame on the roll which he'd developed himself in her darkroom, ultra-careful—*first time pays for all, remember*—but there must have been a hair on the paper, pale enough to escape notice, its legacy a thin bright-white line bisecting her left eye.

Now: on the couch, the photograph in his hands for at least the hundredth time, Justin studied the harsh angle of her cheekbone, the familiar dip of her hair across her face. Passionate rage simmered in her eyes, irises in which he swore he could still detect the brilliant flash of emerald, lurking stubborn beneath the monochrome; desperation in the lift of her lip, caught mid-twitch, mid-snarl perhaps.

Morgan, pure Morgan.

He would never understand what she'd done, how she'd been able to do it, but the process no longer seemed important; only the end results mattered, the twenty-seven portraits on his walls, the one in his lap. Melancholy trophies, and he their reluctant custodian, determined never to show another living soul, but to keep them close as infant children, the line between protection and imprisonment never more blurred, until...

Until what?

He'd considered it many times since bringing them home, resentful of their presence, of the rash of guilt they made him wear.

Tearing them up, burning them to insignificant dregs of ash and smoke.

And thereby what?

The constant, chafing dilemma: would such an act be one of liberation or final, ultimate destruction? Would he save or damn these souls, these *essences* as Morgan had called them, return them to the physical bodies from which they were wrenched, or condemn them to nothingness, to non-existence?

Morgan, mute angry glare; had she herself even known? Had she ever once paused long enough to think about such things?

Was it hers, the voice that scratched at the back of his mind, day in, day out: *murderer murderer murderer.*

Possibly. More possibly, she was right.

Rip them to shreds. Burn them to dust.

And he already knew, dull and dreadful certainty curdling sour in his belly, the precise portrait with which to begin.

FROSTBITTEN

LESS THAN THREE steps into his apartment before he's kissing her, hands reaching beneath her skirt, mauling at her bare arse like it can be moulded into something else if only he squeezes hard enough. Nina returns his kisses with equal ferocity, thankful that he's so eager.

Eager means quick, and quick is what she needs.

He doesn't bother with the bedroom, simply propels her into the living room, over to the modular lounge that lines two walls like a gigantic red L, and throws her down on the shorter side. At least it's firm beneath her back.

"You're so cold, baby," he murmurs into her throat. She can smell the spice-sharp scent of his cologne, and the sweat beneath it. "Let's see what we can do to warm you up, hey?"

He's not awful—she's definitely had a lot worse—but he's young, and his repertoire isn't very extensive. Nina feels a slight twinge of remorse about that, but brushes it aside. She allows his fingers to chafe at her nipples for a bit before pushing them away, coaxing them further south. Misunderstanding, he unbuckles his belt instead, shuffles his pants down to his thighs.

"Fuck, you're a sexy thing."

He moans as he pushes himself into her, and Nina's glad she bothered to pre-lube back in the club's bathroom before they left. Foreplay obviously isn't his strong suit. She hooks her legs over his hips and echoes the noises he's making, clenching herself close around him, pulling him deeper. His fingers dig into her shoulders, and he moves like he's ploughing her, like he's trying to dig a trough right through the middle of her. She turns her head and bites his earlobe.

His spine flexes when he comes and he mewls like a frightened animal, teeth clenched and gleaming with saliva. "Oh," he says, twice, before collapsing onto her. Nina rubs his back, wriggles a little beneath him. He's no lightweight, and the muscles of her inner thighs are starting to ache.

After a minute or so, he pushes himself up. "Sorry, was I squashing you?"

Nina smiles. "I'm fine."

"Just fine?" He leans down and kisses her breast.

Nina keeps smiling. Beneath her hands, his skin is cooling. He rolls off and lies on the couch beside her, one hand over his eyes. "Man, that was intense. Give me a few and we'll go again, hey?"

"Sure." She sits up, swings her legs around. Her bag is at the end of the couch and she bends to retrieve it. "Where's your bathroom?" He waves his free hand towards the hallway, tells her to look for the second door on the right. Nina stands and straightens her skirt, fastens the three buttons on her blouse he managed to get around to undoing. She's still wearing her boots, knee-high black leather with heels high enough to lame a novice, and the apartment floors are polished wood. When she walks, it sounds like deliberation.

The bathroom is easy to find. Nina cleans herself up, then brushes her teeth with the help of an index finger and a smear of peppermint-plus-whitening. Her knickers went into her bag back at the club; she takes them out again now, pulls them up over her hips. Already she feels much better. Much warmer. The adjacent bedroom yields a quilt that smells stale and used, but there isn't time to hunt down a clean one.

Back in the living room, the young man has curled himself into a ball in the corner of the lounge. His hands are tucked into his armpits and his teeth are chattering as she covers him with the quilt. "It's so bloody cold," he says. "Aren't you cold?" His eyes are pale blue, the colour of frost on winter grass. She hadn't noticed before.

"I'm fine." Nina smiles at him. There's a reverse cycle air conditioner mounted on the opposite wall. She makes sure it's switched onto heat, then turns the thermostat up as high as it will go. Hot air begins to flood the room.

"I can't get warm," the man says. "Feels like I won't ever get warm again."

Nina's own face is flushed now, almost clammy. Between her thighs, a different heat is building. "I'm sorry," she tells him, fishing her car keys from her bag. "It won't always be this bad, I promise. Over time, it...lessens."

"Don't go," he pleads. "Stay with me. I need you to stay with me."

"I'm sorry," she says again, and wonders how long it's been since those words held any meaning.

* * *

It's late, about to turn into early morning, and Simone still hasn't shown up. Nina's already showered and washed her hair. Washed her body as well with her favourite scented soap—coconut and lemongrass—that Simone says makes her smell like a Thai curry, delicious and creamy and hot.

She paces the cramped confines of the motel room, biting her nails. Rubbing against the white silk of her negligee, her skin itches and burns.

What's taking that woman so damn long?

From the bed, her phone bleats the arrival of a new message, and Nina lunges towards it. From Simone, the screen tells her. The text is short, and infuriating: *sry, couldnt find 1. 2morrow? stsp? sim xxx*

Nina throws the phone at the wall. It falls apart, the battery skidding a few metres across the carpet. Her hands are shaking. Does Simone think it's not just as hard for *her* to find them? To fuck them? Opting for men might speed things along a bit, but it doesn't make it any easier. Simone would see that if she ever deigned to sample from the other side of the menu. But she's too fussy, that's the problem, and too worried about possible consequences. Tonight, it's Nina's problem as well. But at least they won't have to wait another month.

stsp

Same time, same place. Nina takes a deep breath, then another, wills herself to calm the hell down. Trouble is, she's so damn hot. Tonight would have been amazing; who knows what tomorrow will bring?

She picks up the pieces of phone and puts them carefully back together, makes a silent wish as she presses the *on* button. The screen lights up white for a second before the annoying welcome tune kicks in and she's asked to input the current date and time. At least the bloody thing seems to be working. Nina takes the time from the clock on the bedside table, remembers the date from when she signed the motel registration. All her recent days have blurred together; they always do whenever she and Simone are about to meet.

She calls up the text again, types in a quick reply—*ok, tomorrow. stsp. miss you much. n xxx*—and presses send. Then she tosses the phone back to the bed and stalks into the ensuite.

Time for another shower. Cold this time, for as long as she can stand it.

***

Bent forwards over the man's dining room table, its hard-angled edge digging into her hips, Nina worries she's made a mistake, allowed impatience to get in the way of better judgement. He seemed harmless enough back at the bar, slightly shorter than herself with a body long since gone to seed, his round and ruddy face all but glowing with the sheen of desperation.

Now, she's not so sure.

He grunts with each thrust, his flabby gut slapping against her arse. He calls her a slut, a whore, a frigid fucking bitch. He tells her that he'll show her who's the boss, who's her fucking master. Clenching her teeth, Nina stretches out and grips the opposite edge of the tabletop. As though perceiving this as invitation, he fumbles at her right breast, pinches the nipple between his fingers and twists. Hard. Tears prick at the corners of her eyes but she doesn't make a sound; she won't give him that kind of satisfaction.

His hand tangles in her hair, pulling, lifting her head up and back as far as her neck will allow, and then just that little bit further. Nina realises what he's about to do and manages to turn her head slightly to the left as he slams her forehead down onto the table. Sparks burst behind her eyes and this time she does cry out. There'll be bruises to cover up later, but at least her nose isn't broken.

Behind her, above her, the man continues to grunt.

Nina pushes back against him, grinding her teeth against the pain that unfurls like razor wire in her skull. She needs him to finish, and she needs to be conscious when he does. Movement seems to excite him, so she begins to squirm, to writhe beneath the hands that now pin her to the table, although she can't quite convince herself that her struggles are entirely an act.

The man calls her a slut again, and asks her if she likes it. Then he tenses up and groans, his sweaty bulk squashed tight against her as he rocks backwards and forwards on his toes. Nina lifts her right leg beneath the table, braces herself with her hands, and kicks back as hard as she can. Not anywhere near as hard as she wants, but her spiked heel is enough to make him gasp and release his hold on her shoulders. He sways back a step, putting enough distance between them for her to deliver a second, infinitely more powerful, kick.

The man screams, a high-pitched, girlie wail that's music to Nina's ears.

She straightens and spins around, hands raised to fists in front of her face. He's hunched over, leaning against the wall with knees half-bent and wobbling, both hands at his groin. Blood leaks between his fingers. He lifts his head, glares at her with eyes red-veined and streaming.

"You fucking bitch," he shrieks. "Look what you fucking did!"

She doesn't want to look, is quite happy to live and let live from this point on, until the man takes a step towards her. More of a stagger really, but she doesn't even think before kicking him again. In the chest this time, the flat of her foot landing almost squarely between his nipples with the whole weight of her body behind it, sending him flailing to the ground where he slumps, badly winded. Nina is disappointed to see that all the blood is coming from a ragged hole punched near the top of his inner thigh, right in the crease where leg meets torso, and not from a more intimate wound. She moves in close, lowers her boot onto his neck. The heel sits neatly in the hollow where his clavicles meet.

"...don't..." he wheezes. "...please..."

Nina shakes her head. "I'm not going to kill you. There's no point." She lifts her foot and steps away. "This little hobby of yours, hurting women? You'll find it doesn't hold much interest for you anymore. There's not a lot that will."

He's trembling already. Whether from fear or the incipient cold, she neither knows nor cares.

* * *

This time, Simone has beaten her to the motel. As Nina opens the door, the other woman practically bounces from the bed where she's been sitting and rushes over with arms spread wide. Her grin falters as Nina steps into the room, into the light.

"What happened?" She reaches for Nina's forehead, stops just short of touching it. For one awful moment, Nina stops breathing. Then she sees the colour in Simone's cheeks, feels the heat emanating from her skin, and pulls the woman into her arms. Relaxing into the embrace, Simone runs her hands down Nina's spine, presses soft, warm lips to her throat.

"I'm off my game," Nina tells her. "Picked a bad one tonight."

"Oh, honey, you need to be more careful."

"I need *you.*"

Their mouths meet, their tongues touch. Hesitant, light, sliding against each other with slow, teasing strokes. Then Simone is pulling her towards the bed, her hands firm on Nina's hips, her kisses more forceful. She's making those urgent, almost guttural moans that never fail to melt Nina right where it counts.

"Wait." Nina pushes herself away. "I have to shower first. I need to scrub this stink off me."

"I don't care about that."

"I do."

"Okay." Simone smiles, undoes the first three buttons on her pyjama top and parts the pale blue fabric. "I'll be waiting right here when you're done."

Nina bends to place a kiss first on Simone's left breast, and then on her right. She flicks the tip of her tongue over each nipple, coaxing them to dark and perky nubs. "I won't be long," she says. "I promise."

The first thing she does when she gets into the ensuite is swallow three rapid-action painkillers. Her head still hurts like blazes—not surprising, really, considering the face that reproaches her from the mirror. There's a swollen lump on the side of her forehead the size of a quail's egg; around it the flesh is already turning interesting shades of purple and blue. But no blood, no split skin, no need for stitches. Thank the goddess for minor mercies.

Nina lets the shower run until the ensuite is billowing with steam, then strips and steps beneath the water. Her skin flushes an instant, angry red but she makes no move to adjust the temperature. Tonight, with such fresh and bitter heat running through her body, not even boiling water could scald her. Eyes closed, she starts to sing as she lathers her hair with shampoo. That old Kate Bush song about Cathy and coming home and wanting to be let in; only in a bathroom could her splintered falsetto sound remotely bearable.

"Hey."

Nina jumps, opens her eyes to find Simone leaning through the shower curtain. She's naked, her long brown hair tied up behind in a messy knot, a smile lazing across her face. "Mind if I join the choir?" The question is moot; she's already stepping into the shower recess. Then they're kissing again, and Simone's tongue is in Nina's mouth, and Simone's hands are on Nina's breasts, and Simone's thigh is pressing into Nina's groin.

"How high can that voice of yours go?" Simone whispers, pushing her back against the tiles. Soap-slick fingers slide down where she burns most fiercely and Nina whimpers as they find their way between her folds. Her own hands grasp for Simone's shoulders as the woman kisses her hard, then soft, sawing Nina's lower lip gently between her teeth. Nina feels herself building, feels her whole body stretching thin and taut as violin string, and she moans, gives herself up to the play of expert hands.

Until brilliantly, blissfully, Nina breaks.

Still Simone holds her, supporting her weight until Nina's legs feel ready to work again. "I love you," Nina says, glad for the water that streams down her face and swallows her tears. "You're everything."

Simone squeezes her tight. "I love you too. So much." She reaches around and turns off the taps, pinches Nina lightly on the cheek. "How about we take this into the bedroom? Previews are over, my darling; time for the feature presentation."

* * *

Almost as soon as Nina drags herself into consciousness, she knows something is wrong. There's too much light in the room, the sun pushing its way through the cheap motel curtains as though they're made from mesh, and her stomach lurches. It's late, it's really fucking late. Simone's still sleeping, her head resting heavy on Nina's chest, one knee propped over Nina's thigh. Bare skin touching bare skin, in far too many places. As fast as she dares, Nina curls her arm around Simone's skull, taking care to keep her lover's thick swathe of hair between them.

"Simone," she says. "Wake up." Simone murmurs something unintelligible and starts to shift her position, but Nina holds her steady. "Don't move," she says. "We've slept in. I think we're cold."

Simone's fully awake now; Nina can feel her breathing start to speed.

"What do we do?" Simone whispers.

"We be quick."

And before the other woman can reply, Nina grabs a handful of hair and pulls Simone's head abruptly away. There's a too-brief tugging on her skin, like they're stuck together with superglue or worse, before something tears and Simone shrieks in pain and surprise. Nina feels burned—by frost, not fire—and when she risks a glance there's a raw, blistered patch of skin above her breast, glistening red in the sunlight. Simone's cheek looks even worse, torn and seeping like gravel rash, blood beading along her jawline.

"What about the rest of us?" Simone's voice breaks on the last word.

"It won't be as bad," Nina assures her, stuffing bits of sheet into the gaps between their bodies, assessing the places where there are none. "The way your head was resting on me, the weight of it, that made it worse. The rest is just touching, more or less. Not a lot of pressure."

"Are you saying I have a fat head?"

Simone's smile is so brave, so defiant, that Nina aches to hug her. Instead she offers a grin of her own—weak and falling down at the corners, but the best she can manage—then points at their legs. "You need to move your knee now. Lift it up and off me, but quickly. Like with a Band-Aid, okay?"

"Or a wax strip."

"Only not as painful." They both know she is lying.

The second time seems worse than the first, maybe because they know what to expect, maybe because Simone is too cautious, too slow, and Nina has to pull her own leg away to finish the job. But the places where belly meets hip, where the back of an arm lies along the curve of a ribcage, hurt less to separate. Finally free, Simone rolls to the other side of the bed, shields herself with the blanket.

"I've got some antiseptic cream in my toiletries case." Cautiously, Nina pushes herself to her feet. "Some bandages, as well." A rudimentary first aid kit she's carried ever since their first careless touch—each of them cold as dry ice, forgetful as stone—that froze half of Nina's fingerprints away, and left marks like cigar burns on Simone's naked arm. They took weeks to heal.

Simone stares at Nina's body, her gaze cataloguing the fresh red litany of wounds. "I can't believe we just fell asleep like that. If we'd woken up any later, if we'd gotten any colder—"

"Well, we didn't!" Her tone is too snappish; Simone bites her lip and looks away. "I'm sorry, Sim." Nina swallows. "I'll get the cream and stuff, okay?"

By the time she comes back, hands full of Savlon and gauze and cotton wool, Simone is up and packing her overnight bag. She's wearing the Chinese silk robe Nina bought her last month, turquoise blue with a phoenix rising on its back, but she's wearing it inside out.

"Come here," Nina says. "Let me fix you up."

Simone glares at her. "You can do that without touching me, can you?"

"As a matter of fact, I can."

The other woman shakes her head. "This has to end. Now."

Nina feels her stomach tumble for the second time that morning. "What are you talking about, Sim? What has to end?"

"Us." Her eyes are wet and pleading. "I can't do it anymore, Nina."

"But I love you." Right now, Nina would bear any amount of pain for the chance to touch Simone, the chance to hold her close and prove how much she loves her. She'd bear it gratefully—if she were the only one who would.

"I love you too," Simone says. "You know I do, but I can't live like this. Only being able to see you every few weeks, having to leave you again before the sweat's even dried on our skin—"

"So, we'll meet more often then. You're the one who wants to leave it so long each time; I'd be with you every night if you'd let me."

"You know that's impossible."

"Okay, maybe not *every* night, but three or four times a week if—"

"I'm not like you," Simone snaps. "I can't go out and pick people up the way you do, discard them like they're nothing. They're not nothing—they're people, they have lives of their own."

"Like the creep who did this, you mean?" Nina points to her forehead, which she knows looks even worse now than it did last night. "Bastards like him deserve what they get."

"Stop twisting everything I say. They're not all like that, not even most of them. You've said yourself, you feel sorry for them sometimes."

Nina narrows her eyes. "Do you know how many even bothered to ask my name? Trust me, all they cared about was how quick my panties could come off, and how soon they could boot me out the door afterwards."

"That doesn't make it right."

"It's not like they're dead, you know. It's not like we kill them."

"No, we just take what makes them human."

Nina laughs. She can't help it. "Their libido, Sim, their sex drive? You think *that's* what being human's all about?"

The other woman looks almost disappointed. "We take more than that and you know it. Warmth, heat, passion—whatever you choose to call it—that's what we take and that's what we squander every time we come to this horrible little room." She touches her cheek and winces. "I'm running out of justifications, Nina. Maybe I never had any to begin with."

"But last night…"

"Yes." Simone crosses the room and takes the medical supplies from Nina's hands, careful not to let their fingers touch. "I'm so sorry, Nina. I love you, I do, but everything else…it's too much. It's breaking me."

Nina sinks back down onto the bed, flinching at the pain that ripples along her flank. "You've been thinking about this a lot." She doesn't really need an answer; the expression Simone wears is more than eloquent.

Closed, and contained. Final.

"Every day," Simone says. Hissing through clenched teeth, she smoothes cream over the raw patch of flesh on the inside of her knee.

"You can live like that?" Nina asks. "Being cold, all the time?"

"Yes."

"Being alone?"

Silently, Simone wraps gauze around her leg, around and around and around until there's nothing left to unroll. She tucks the end in tight and straightens, tests what little flex she has left in her knee. When she looks at Nina again, her eyes are red but dry. "Yes," she says. "I can live like that."

"Cold and alone, for the rest of your life?"

"You say it like we're the only ones." And there's nothing even remotely warm about the smile that hooks her mouth. "How hard can it be, Nina? After all, *it's not like we're dead.*"

Nina bows her head. There's a smear of blood on the carpet near her foot and it's this she stares at while listening to the other woman dress first her wounds and then herself. Because the way she's feeling right now—cold, yes; alone, oh a hundred times and forever, *yes*—she doesn't trust herself to look at Simone. Doesn't trust herself not to go to her and press their bodies together, to feel the freeze of skin between them and know that when they finally tear themselves asunder, it will be as bloody and messy and painful as her fractured, frostbitten heart.

***

Nina slides the room keys across the counter along with her credit card, pretends not to notice the receptionist pretending not to notice the bruises on her forehead.

"There's a late checkout fee," the woman says. "It's policy."

"Sure, whatever." She decides not to mention the bloodstained sheets; this kind of motel has probably seen worse. The woman processes her payment and puts the receipt on the counter for Nina to sign.

"I hope you enjoyed your stay."

There's an edge to her tone, a forced politeness only too familiar, but today Nina's skin is too thin to let it slide. "Is there a problem?"

The receptionist purses her prissy, middle-aged lips. "Generally, I don't give a rat's what you and your friend get up to when you come here, but there's some things I won't turn a blind eye to. Next time I call the police."

Nina blinks, confused. "I'm sorry?"

"That girl was the picture of health last night when she picked up her key. This afternoon I see her limp out of that room with her face all bandaged up like the Bride of Frankenstein." She points at Nina's head. "What happened, she decide to fight back?"

"You have no idea what you're talking about." Nina reaches out and snatches her credit card from the woman's hand. "Trust me, you have no fucking conception." She turns and slams through the reception door, trying to pretend she doesn't hear the bitch's reedy voice trailing after her—*I know someone who's been abused when I see them*—trying to pretend she doesn't care.

Less than two blocks from the motel, her hands are still shaking so badly she needs to pull over to the side of the road. Tears blur her vision, turn to ice on her cheeks. Nina tugs her mobile from her pocket, thumbs through to her most recent contacts and presses *call*. A recorded voice answers almost immediately—*the number you are calling is no longer in service*—and she gapes at the phone in disbelief. So soon?

Nina closes her eyes, tries to remember how Simone looked just before she left the motel room. Remorseful but resigned, shaking her head as Nina pleaded with her to stay.

There's no one else like us in the world, baby. We're all we have.

Then we have nothing. And we have to live with that too.

"Simone," she whispers, over and over and over again. Nina doesn't even know if that's her lover's real name; she never thought it important to ask.

Simone.

Solid as stone in her mouth, the word grows rapidly cold.

THE HOME FOR BROKEN DOLLS

AT THE SIDE gate, Jane stops and stares in mild surprise at the large, blue-shrouded shape crushing the agapanthus that grow along the inside of her front fence. Behind her, four chickens fluff their russet feathers and spurt a series of sharp *bok-bok-boks*, eager to chase up any grubs or snails too slow to retreat from the thin, predawn light. "All right, girls, wait your patience." Jane opens the gate, steps back to let the chooks nip past her legs and into the front yard.

She considers the blue shape again, and sighs.

Only one thing *that* can be. Dumped during cover of darkness, no doubt, and no mean effort either to hoist such an unwieldy bundle up and over those three-plus feet of wooden palings. At least whoever it was had the decency to conceal his leavings beneath—what is that, an old bed sheet? Old, and most likely stained as well, in ways that don't bear too much thinking upon.

The doll is going to be heavy. Jane can tell that even as she makes her way over to it, even before she bends, works her hands beneath what she assumes to be the shoulders and braces herself to lift. From the knees, she reminds herself, mind your back now. She tries to ease the bundle gently from the agapanthus, to roll it away without breaking more of the yet-to-bloom flower stalks, but one of the enormous mounds that can only be breasts shifts unnaturally sideways, slides and drags the weight of the whole doll with it, drags Jane with it. Her foot slips on foliage still damp with dew and she loses her balance. Falls down on her butt, the doll's head landing in her lap.

In her apron pocket, the morning eggs crack and seep through thin cotton.

"Oh, you bugger!" Jane pushes the doll off and climbs to her feet. The sheet is partially unwrapped now, exposing the snarled and matted fibres of an ash-blonde wig and a face she recognises as the Number 12. Full lips once painted scarlet, now peeling and chapped. Lashless, thick-lined eyes the bright glassy green of a Dutch beer bottle. Gouges in one cheek too ragged to be the work of a blade. More like someone took to the doll with a screwdriver. Phillips-head, judging by the savage constellation of punctures in the throat.

Jane swallows. "Wait here," she says, and hurries into the house to fetch the wheelchair.

* * *

The damage is extensive. It goes beyond the standard tears, compression zones, and finger pokes. Way beyond. As she carries out her preliminary assessment of the doll, Jane nibbles on the sole surviving egg, now hard-boiled and smeared with mustard. So much for the frittata she had planned for later that night; vegetable soup will have to suffice. Minestrone, if there's still some pasta left.

"You owe me dinner," she tells the doll. The doll says nothing, just lies there on the dining room table, legs slightly akimbo. Around both knees, the silicone is torn.

It's an old body, a long-discontinued model shelved primarily due to the weight of the breasts, larger than bowling balls and about as heavy. An impossible, impractical size—though popular with a certain subset of aficionados if the occasional, mournful posting on the forums is anything to go by—and on this doll the left one has been ripped almost completely away from the torso. A few determined inches of skin are all that anchor the massive globe, and Jane notices a nascent split beneath the right breast as well.

The wounds on the belly and thighs are more deliberate, deep punctures which speak to a frustrated, futile rage. Or desire. Or both.

Between the legs, it's worse. The entire vaginal and anal area is split and torn apart, damage that will require not merely a re-core but more substantial rebuilding. Through the mutilated silicone, the stainless-steel skeleton is clearly visible. The doll hasn't been worn out so much as worn *through.*

Jane wipes her hands on her apron. The repairs are complicated and will take days, if not weeks, but there's no time to start now. The Peacock Fantasy mask needs to be completed this afternoon if it's to go out on Thursday as promised. There's only a few embellishments and the trim left to do, but it's fiddly work and she likes to allow forty-eight hours to ensure everything is properly cured before posting. And she should really sit down and go through the reference package for her new wedding commission, sketch a few draft designs for the client to ponder. The due date isn't until next month, but Jane prefers to keep her deadlines comfortable. Especially where anxious brides are concerned.

The new arrival will have to wait her turn.

The filthy sheet in which the doll was wrapped is now lying crumpled in the bin, so Jane retrieves a fresh one from the hall closet. The doll stares at the ceiling, lips parted in the familiar, slack-jaw manner so beloved of porn stars and lingerie models. Beyond those too-white silicone teeth, the mouth looks empty. Common practice to remove the appendage for better oral access, less usual to leave a doll that way. Not that it matters much; spare tongues are easy to source. Wigs as well, although something might yet be salvageable from the lopsided mess that crowns the doll's head. A neat, common-sense cut, sans all those coy and knotted curls which—

"Enough." Jane tucks the sheet up around the doll's shoulders. "Get some rest, and we'll see to you later."

The doll makes no reply.

In her workroom with a fresh pot of orange-jasmine tea, Jane switches on her ancient computer before attending to Agnes and Esme. The former needs to be flipped onto her back again. The daybed where she resides is soft, its mattress yielding, but silicone flesh loses shape memory with age and breasts are easily flattened, buttocks compressed, if left lying for long in the same position. Agnes needs all the help she can get. Once the doll is turned, Jane straightens the loose paisley smock, then smoothes Agnes' steel-grey hair and pats her on the cheek. Brown eyes meet her own. Placid. Thankful.

Jane smiles. "You're welcome, dear."

Apart from her perpetually wonky right hip joint, Esme is in better shape. Most of the time, she hangs from her neck hook on an old iron coat rack bolted to the wall for maximum support, but today Jane lifts her down. Slowly and with no small amount of exertion—the doll weighs almost as much as a human would—she maneuvers Esme into the spare office chair. Pulls the hem of the lilac polyester dress down over her knees and arranges the doll's arms in her lap, careful not to damage fingers already scarred by multiple repairs. Most of the armature wires inside have long since snapped and the hands splay uselessly, helpless as landbound starfish.

"We have someone new come to live with us." Jane swivels the chair to face the window. "We'll all of us need to be patient while she settles in."

Esme gazes into the back yard, sunlight stippling her face

through the white lace curtains. Jane plants a kiss on top of the doll's head. The short blonde curls are beginning to take on a musty, abandoned smell, and she makes a mental note to find time later in the week to clean all the wigs. She's pretty sure there's still half a bottle of eucalyptus wool wash in the laundry.

Computer finally booted up, Jane reads her email, jettisons the spam and shoots off a handful of brief replies and even briefer queries. Two off-the-rack sales have come in overnight, pretty but basic masks which won't take her more than an hour or so to put together in the chosen colour schemes; there might even be a purple one already made and ready to go. It's a popular colour, and Jane likes to keep reserves. She pauses, mouse hovering over the browser icon. It would only take a minute to log in to the forums and see if iDollatry63 is online. To tell him about the new doll and find out what parts he's currently holding. Only a few minutes more to scan through the latest postings, check if there's anything which might be of interest.

Beside her, Esme continues to stare through the window. Those plump, unpainted lips remain silent and still.

"You're right," Jane says, switching the computer into sleep mode. "Work comes first."

She moves across to the bench that runs the length of the far wall and picks up the half-completed peacock mask. The feathers hold firm beneath her tweaking fingers, their resplendent eyes shimmering in the light. So far, so good. Jane sits down, reaching for her caddy of Swarovski flatbacks. Her mouth twitches, half-smile, half-grimace, as she sorts through the crystals with needle-nose pliers, laying out spirals of turquoise, emerald, and sapphire on a sheet of graph paper, adjusting spaces and tightening curves until the balance of colour and shape is absolutely perfect. Only then does she take up her glue gun and begin the delicate, careful transfer of the design to the mask itself.

As she works, Jane hums beneath her breath, a stilted and tuneless rendering of the Janis Joplin plea for sleek new cars and high-end jewellery. Her regular, semi-conscious backing track, though it's not the husky rasp of a Texan folksinger she always hears in her head, but rather her gran's bright and cheery falsetto, a voice kept true almost to the very end, singing even as she clutched Jane's hand against the kind of pain not even a double dose of morphine could smother completely.

Mercedes Benz and diamond rings, oh lord.

Prayers as empty, and unanswered, as any Jane has made.

* * *

It was Esme she found first.

Driving back from a post-midnight milk run to the nearby servo, Jane's preferred time to be out and about, when almost no one else is. The young man behind the register had been one of the regular night crew so he barely looked at her face anymore, no more than he might the face of any other customer. No lingering gaze or embarrassed glance too quickly caught and dropped, just a quick meeting of the eyes, a semi-automated smile as he'd handed over her change.

The night was mild and clear, not yet heavy with the full heat of summer, so Jane kept driving. Past her home and the half dozen neighbouring houses that held the line on this otherwise uninhabited stretch of the New England highway, following the Hunter down to Hexham Bridge. Windows down, never mind the swampy stench of the river at low tide; it was worth it for the rush of air on her skin, to unknot her scarf and let the wind ruffle her hair. Singing along with the radio, across the bridge and heading towards Raymond Terrace, planning to go via Miller's Forest and right into Maitland before turning back around for home. It had been too long since she'd treated herself to a slow, aimless drive like this.

The taillights caught her attention before the man himself did. A dark silhouette, scurrying up the verge and around the front of his idling car. Jane slowed, cautious, as the vehicle pulled back onto the road and sped away with a shriek of gravel. And it was only that she *had* slowed, that she was actually looking in the direction from which the man had come—though barely curious because, after all, he'd most likely just stopped for a late-night piss—that Jane saw it.

A flash of almost white on the fringe of her headlights' glare, gone before she'd had time to fully register the too-familiar shape, half a kilometre slipping beneath her tyres before Jane pulled over.

Because it couldn't really have been a woman's leg. Unclothed, a distinctive curve of calf protruding from the overgrown weeds.

No, it had to be something else.

Nevertheless, she turned the car around and beetled back down the empty stretch of asphalt until she reached the place where the man had pulled over. Her stomach rolled, her throat clenched tight. It was definitely a leg. Lying too close to the edge of the road, too far from the larger shape that hulked, pale and ominous, further back in the field for it to possibly be attached.

Jane checked her rearview mirror. No sign of him doubling back. No sign of any vehicle approaching from either direction. She only had her purse, had left her mobile phone charging on the kitchen counter. It was only supposed to have been a milk run, after all. Her fingers tapped on the steering wheel. She glanced at the mirror again. Still nothing. Jane leaned across and opened the glove box, retrieved the flashlight that lived there. Then she braced herself and climbed out of the car.

"Hey," she called softly. Doubtfully. "Hey, are you..."

The woman was completely naked. Lying face down and motionless in the grass, a few metres away from her severed leg. Her severed *right* leg, Jane noted uselessly, fighting the bile that scratched at the back of her throat. Bare skin gleamed in the torchlight. Platinum blonde hair clumped in long tangles across her shoulders.

Dead. She had to be dead. So still like that. Her amputated leg.

Jane forced herself into a crouch. Reached out a reluctant hand to touch the woman's hip and recoiled with a gasp. The skin was frigid, the flesh pliable yet oddly firm. Not like *flesh* at all, she thought, reaching again. Not quite plastic, not quite rubber, but a kissing cousin. And heavy, *dead weight* a phrase that never rang more true than when she put both hands to the side of the body and pushed, heaved it over onto its back. One eye gleamed as Jane played torchlight over a face that seemed at once astonished and terminally bored. The right socket was merely an empty hole, gaping dark as the half-opened mouth.

Some kind of mannequin then, a mannequin or a doll.

The breasts were large, or at least they had been. Both of them now flattened, misshapen as airless footballs discarded by boys less interested in scoring points than in pointless destruction. A translucent substance glistened within several ragged gashes. Metal poked from the right hip where the leg should have been attached, the surrounding rubber a confusion of ragged tears and clean-edged cuts. Like someone had commenced a surgical procedure only to lose patience halfway through and decided instead to simply rip the leg the rest of the way off. She shone the torch lower, lingering just long enough to note the anatomical correctness.

Or what remained of it.

Jane didn't so much carry as drag the doll across to her car. Heaving that dense, rubbery weight—*dead* weight—into the boot, hands sliding over tacky doll-skin, a muscle low down in her back was wrenched out of shape. The ache would bother her for months to come, every time she bent or straightened too quickly, or if she sat for too long at her workbench. Even now, she will sometimes wake from an ill night's sleep with what she has come to think of as the *Esme-twinge*—though such a label is hardly fair to the doll, who never asked to be rescued.

Who never asked for anything, so far as Jane can tell.

She couldn't precisely have explained why she took the doll with her, or what she thought she would do with it—with *her*—once she got back home. It simply felt like the right thing to do. The only thing she could do, having stopped, having seen.

Nor could she have said why she chose the name. Up until the point where she lugged the doll inside and laid her down on the couch, making a second trip for the severed right leg which she then positioned awkwardly against its counterpart, Jane hadn't been thinking about a name at all. But as she drew a blanket over that exposed and traumatised flesh, as she arranged the tangled wig to conceal the missing eye, her own skin itched in sympathy.

"Poor thing." The words a near involuntary echo of those she heard all too often, usually whispered behind palms or exchanged between half-turned heads, but occasionally proffered more boldly, right to her face, and it wasn't always pity with which they were laced. Sometimes there was anger too, and a curious kind of spite.

Poor thing.

Recycled syllables, tasting of dust and defeat.

Jane shook her head. She wasn't a *thing*, and the *doll* wasn't a thing, the doll was—

Esme.

The word popped into her mind, unbidden, insistent. Jane tried it out loud. She liked how the name sounded, liked how it felt to speak it. Strong and certain and safe. The doll's single glass eye stared straight ahead, its iris the brilliant, unnatural blue of cheap rhinestones.

"Esme, then," Jane affirmed. "Welcome to my home."

* * *

Jane is logged in to the forums for barely two minutes before iDollatry63 pings her. His familiar avatar, a busty bikini-clad manga girl with bright pink hair, bounces at her from the chat window and Jane quickly accepts the invitation.

was hoping u be on tonite, iDollatry63 types. At the end of the sentence, an animated smiley face turns cartwheels. A second claps white-gloved hands.

Jane smiles. *Can't stay long. Strange thing happened this morning.*

oh? Mysterious smiley face. *pray tell!!*

So she does, explaining briefly how and where she found the doll, and in what condition.

thats messed up. someone dump her and run?

Seems like it.

u gonna fix her?

That's the plan.

Jane types a list of what she needs to repair the doll and, *no probs,* iDollatry63 is quick to assure her, he can supply it all. Though maybe she should think about getting the Sil-Poxy at Bunnings, the rate she goes through it. Save herself some moolah with a bulk buy. Animated winky face.

That's okay, she tells him. *It's easier just to get it all from you.*

Easier, and without the necessity for a face-to-face with red-shirted strangers. These days, Jane does as much as possible online—and she's found precious little that can't be procured with a couple of clicks and a credit card number, that can't be delivered right to her door by the postie or one of the several regular courier drivers with whom she's now on a first-name basis. Her gran would have never allowed such hermetic habits, would have prodded and poked and physically pushed Jane out the front door at least twice a week on some errand or another. *It's your world to walk in as much as anyone's, child; don't you ever believe otherwise.* And Jane never has. But that doesn't mean she can't tread a less arduous path when she finds one.

In the chatbox, iDollatry63 is typing. *how ur other girls? need anything?*

They're good, Jane tells him. *Just the new one to worry about.*

u want me to send this stuff out...or...

Jane touches her cheek, traces her fingers lightly down the side of her neck, waiting, waiting. She knows what comes next.

u could always pick it up, he adds. *save on postage.* Smiley face.

The suggestion is predictable, an echo of so many made over the past couple of years. Ever since she bought the first repair kit from him—for Esme, which he sent out complete with detailed instructions and specially tailored newbie advice—iDollatry63 has been proposing the two of them meet. Coffee, lunch, drinks, whatever. They live so close, after all, separated by less than an hour's drive, and hey, no strings, no pressure, just two people with an obscure shared interest getting together to shoot the breeze. Face to face. Which is always the problem.

Her fingers move carefully over the keys. *No, it's okay, just mail it to me.*

Sad face. *im starting to think ur not a real person.*

I'm real, she types. *I don't get out very much, that's all.*

well if u ever feel like company...im here.

Jane smiles. For all the regular nudging, his willingness to back right off is one of the things she appreciates about iDollatry63. Unlike several other men she's encountered on the forums, men who launch into proposition mode the instant they cotton on to the fact that she's female—female *and* into dolls!—iDollatry63 has always shown a friendly respect. He's never called her names—*bitch tease wannabe troll*—and has never displayed the slightest hint of anger or aggression, regardless of how often she's deflected his advances. He might test her boundaries, but at least he acknowledges her right to maintain them.

Maybe one day, she types. *No promises though.*

* * *

Jane removes the last of the staples that have held the doll's left breast in place while the Sil-Poxy cured, and tentatively wobbles the enormous silicone globe. None of her other dolls have breasts this large, and she had her doubts that such a dense weight could be successfully re-attached. But the fix seems to have taken well, and the mineral makeup she mixed in with the adhesive has made it an almost perfect match to the doll's original skin tone. Even the inevitable ridge along the repair line is gratifyingly minimal. She considers sanding that down a little more, smoothing it with a layer of fresh silicone the way she has the tears on the neck, stomach, and legs—now almost invisible unless you know where to look—but it's an awkward area and she doesn't want to threaten the overall integrity of the adhesive.

Jane touches her own throat, rubs at the familiar whorls of skin, the raised line that curves beneath the nub of her left ear.

Really, what's a little scar tissue among friends?

She makes a final check between the doll's legs, prodding the newly replaced labia and tugging gently at the patches of blonde pubic hair. The reconstruction was slow and painstaking work, carried out in fits and starts over the past three weeks. Her regular progress reports to iDollatry63 have been received with enthusiastic encouragement, though he remains disappointed as always by her refusal to provide pics of her work. Jane doesn't photograph her dolls, not the way others do. Posed naked or nearly so, clad in lingerie or restrained with scarves, alone or partnered with other dolls, exposed to anyone with the inclination to google.

Her dolls are past that kind of thing. That's not why they've come here.

With great care, Jane dresses the new doll. It's a laborious process, even with the over-sized orange mumu she found at the op shop. The doll's proportions are so out of whack—those massive breasts, size G at least, atop that slender waist, those slim hips—there's no way any regular dress would fit. Jane is especially mindful of the fingers. The wires within are now sealed safely away, but it wouldn't take much to force them back through the silicone tips. Thankfully, the garish red talons are gone, replaced with short, practical nails varnished in a subtle shade of peach.

Once dressed, Jane shifts the doll around on the dining room table until her lower legs are hanging over the side. The repaired knees bend smoothly. Silently. Jane smiles. She eases the doll into a sitting position, inclining her on a slight backwards angle to compensate for that front-heavy mammary pull. Jane has styled the doll's blonde wig into a short, layered bob—though *styled* is probably too generous a word; the cut is simply all that remained after the mess of knots was hacked away. She places the wig on the doll's head and neatens the feathery, uneven fringe as best she can. It doesn't look too bad, now it's on. She can always trim the bits that stick out too much.

The doll's face is still shiny from the fresh coat of sealer, but that's nothing a light dusting of talcum powder won't fix. Jane has lost count of the number of meticulous hours she has spent, cotton bud in hand and the itch of low-grade solvent in her nostrils, removing the heavy makeup and liner from around the eyes, rubbing the last stubborn flakes of scarlet from the mouth. But she's pleased with the result. Adorned only by a set of false lashes, the closest to a natural look Jane has been able to source, the doll's eyes have a clearer, more honest cast. Even the outlandish pout of her lips seems less provocative beneath its pale new shade of nude pink.

All in all, Jane is pleased. "You really do look much better," she says.

The doll stares blankly into space.

"Let's see now." Jane considers the strong, square jawline. Those bright, glass-green eyes. She clears her mind, wanting not so much to summon a name as simply provide space for the right one to step forward. "How about...Beryl?" She nods, satisfied. "Beryl, yes."

Beryl.

In a breath, nothing changes. And everything.

The doll's eyes no longer seem vacant. The irises glimmer and deepen and shift. They *look* at Jane. They *see* her.

"I can live with Beryl," the doll says, mouth motionless as ever. "But, honey, I ain't wearing this godforsaken tent-dress one single second longer."

***

After Esme, there was Agnes.

Jane wasn't planning to acquire a second doll. She'd harboured no intentions at all beyond learning precisely what it was that she had rescued from the side of the road that night, and whether it might be possible to put those grisly pieces back together.

But it's a scarce three clicks these days from poetry to porn, and it took no time at all for Jane to stumble across the doll forums. She lurked at first, reading the public boards safe in unregistered anonymity, before at last succumbing to the mysteries of Members Only. Still, her interactions were few. Mostly, she perused the forums in silence, gleaning what she could from the posts of others, only occasionally piping up with a question or clarification of her own. The muscular, masculine camaraderie of the doll world felt almost wholly impenetrable to Jane.

Instead, she haunted its periphery like a hungry ghost, unsure where—or even how—she might belong.

It was only after several months that Jane saw the doll she would come to know as Agnes. The repair work to Esme had long been completed, thanks in no small part to a generous provision of tips and tricks from iDollatry63—purveyor of doll parts and general go-to guy on the forums—and Jane had begun to question why she was even bothering to log in anymore. Still, she did, at least once or twice a week, skimming new posts and touching base with iDollatry63 should he happen to be online. Often, she would sit Esme beside her in the spare office chair.

The doll in question was the subject of a Buy Me Sell Me thread, one that was receiving a lot of attention. There were several uploaded photos, varying in both angle and degree of intimacy, and the damage they documented was considerably worse than was usually found on second-hand dolls offered for sale on the forums. The arms were split at elbow and shoulder, the legs at knee and groin. Both hands and feet were a hot mess, her breasts seemed oddly deformed somehow, and her genital area had been reduced to a single gaping cavity. The seller, who confessed to a predilection for rough play, was hoping to garner seed money for a replacement. The consensus seemed to be that he was asking way too much.

Dolls are like real girls, someone remarked. *The older they are, the less they're worth.*

For all the damage, there remained a certain sweetness about the doll's features, a resigned serenity that hooked at some half-acknowledged place in Jane's heart. And so, while other members muttered about abuse and what a shame it was that a lovely thing like that had gone to waste and how really she wasn't even worth the cost of shipping in such a state, and while the seller grew increasingly defensive, insisting he would rather cut the doll up and leave the pieces out on the street than all but *give* her away to some bastard too cheap to cough up good money, Jane DM'd iDollatry63.

i dunno, he told her after checking out the thread for himself. *doubtful she's worth the asking price, plus shipping from states not gonna b cheap.*

Is she repairable though? Jane asked. *For someone like me, I mean?*

maybe. major joint damage tho. prolly not gonna stand much use even after a fixup...dunno if that matters to u?

Not really. If I made him an offer, what do you think would be fair?

srsly? for that doll? carton of beer and a blow job would do it.

She paused, uncertain.

sorry, iDollatry63 typed. *didnt mean u. figure of speech.* A little yellow face blushed furiously at the end of the line. *want me to sort u a deal?*

Jane did. But the price he came back with, while significantly less than the seller had originally been asking, was still beyond her means. The number of masks she would have to make to scrape such a sum together—unless.

Unless she used the Monster Money. She'd never once touched it, that steady stream of deposits into the account her parents had opened the week she was born. The funds that were there when her mother died, *those* she had withdrawn, *those* she had long since spent, but the rest she couldn't even bring herself to consider. Yet still they came, monthly payments from her paternal grandmother, a woman whom Jane hadn't even seen since the trial, with whom she hadn't even spoken but for that single stilted phone call the day after Jane buried her gran.

Will you cope now? On your own?

Yes.

And the money? There's enough to...

Yes. I'll be fine.

All right. All right then. A click, and the connection was severed.

Money enough to...what? Salve a conscience, scour a soul? Keep an ugly new monster from the door, or maybe just from the mirror? Jane didn't know, didn't think too much about it except when the quarterly bank statements arrived and she found herself perplexed anew to see those three new entries on the page, to note the growing balance. Not yet top shelf Mercedes Benz territory, but getting there. One day she would know what to do with it, her gran had assured her often enough. One day there would be something which would feel right to spend it on, which wouldn't leave the taste of cold, stale blood in her mouth.

Jane studied the photos of the doll once more. The ruined silicone flesh, those calm brown eyes. She looked at Esme and remembered how challenging, how frustrating, the restoration process had been—and how ultimately, sublimely gratifying.

Ok, she told iDollatry63. *Let him know I'll take her.*

hope u know what ur gettin into.

Jane smiled to herself. *If I did, I'm sure I wouldn't.*

Having broken the Monster Money seal for Agnes, dipping into it the next two times was infinitely easier.

Madge had passed through the hands of three different owners before Jane eventually acquired her, the last having left the doll with a broken spine from an accidental fall down a flight of stairs as well as the usual, less complicated array of punctures, pokes, and tears. She was more local than Agnes had been—just a short trip up from Melbourne—and thus considerably cheaper.

One-legged Ethel came across from Fremantle, folded naked and wigless into a packing crate which likely cost half the transport fee that Jane had negotiated and caused even more damage to a doll already little more than a charity case. The man who sold her disappeared from the forums overnight, and failed to respond to several emails concerning the missing limb. Eventually, Jane gave up and carved a styrofoam cap to fill the crater in Ethel's right hip, then sealed the whole mess over with a silicone skin.

She houses the two dolls in what was once her gran's bed, having replaced the old mattress with a slab of high-density memory foam to provide them with better, gentler support. Sometimes, Jane will lie between them, head resting on one shoulder or another, and nap. The talcum powder she uses to keep the dolls free of the silicone's oily residue is the same one her gran favoured—Briar Rose—and the scent, along with the solid press of their bodies, never fails to be a comfort.

Only occasionally, most often during winter, does she find herself wishing that their skin wasn't quite so cold.

* * *

Jane sidles up to the computer desk, where Beryl has more or less taken up permanent residence, and clears her throat.

"What is it?" The doll doesn't look away from the screen for even a second. There's a multitude of tabs open in her browser and she flicks incessantly between them, discarding some with a snort even as she opens fresh links in others. "Leeeeeedle busy just now."

"Can I jump on for a minute?" Jane asks. "I need to send an invoice."

Beryl switches to her Twitter feed and scrolls down the page. "Can it wait?" Her gigantic breasts require her to sit well back in the chair, arms stretched out for maximum reach in order to manipulate the mouse and keyboard. The effect is comical, but Jane learned early on that Beryl is not a doll to be laughed at.

"Not really," Jane tells her. "I need to do it now."

"Oh, all right." Beryl sighs and pushes herself to her feet. She wobbles, but only a little, her balance now infinitely better than it was a couple weeks ago when she took those first tentative steps away from the dining room table and promptly slid onto her butt. All the dolls are walking under their own steam now, more or less, their dependence on walls, countertops, and backs of chairs diminishing by the day. All except Ethel, of course—though she's taken to propelling herself around in the wheelchair like an Olympic gold medalist.

From where she's reclined on her daybed, Agnes turns her head. "Beryl? Are you taking a break? Do you have time to help me feed the chooks?" Agnes adores the chickens, as it turns out, and would happily spend all day in the yard with them clucking about her ankles if Jane wasn't so concerned about the effects of too much sun on aging silicone.

"Sure thing, spitfire," Beryl says. She crosses the room and uses both hands to pull the other doll into a standing position. Arms about each other's waist, the pair hobble down the hall towards the back door. Jane smiles. She's seen Agnes ambling around by herself just fine. But if there's one thing the doll obviously loves more than chickens, it's Beryl.

"Girl gonna start a bushfire one day," Madge says from the workbench where she's been all morning. "Size of the torch she's carrying." One of Jane's craft magazines is open in front of her and she turns the page with careful fingers. Madge doesn't have the fine motor skills to actually put a mask together, but she likes to watch Jane work and make suggestions. The doll has a fine eye for detail, if somewhat quirky instincts when it comes to design.

"You're not wrong about that," Jane tells her, sitting down at the computer. Beryl has been in the forums again, pretending to be one of the men who pretend to be one of the dolls on the role-playing boards. Jane wonders how any of them would react if they discovered an actual doll in their midst.

"Ever done a mask in orange and purple?" Madge asks.

"Not that I can recall."

"You should. With crimson feathers coming over one side and lashings of gold brocade. Be like a sunset, only bruised."

"Maybe one day, if someone asks for it."

"*I'm* asking for it."

Jane chuckles. "You paying me for it as well?"

"Throw it up on your website, someone'll buy it."

"Orange and purple isn't exactly a popular combination, Madge."

"You never know." The doll turns another page in the magazine, a dull and wounded sound that makes Jane regret her earlier laughter. "Sometimes people don't even realise they want a thing till it's staring them straight in the face."

"Good point," Jane says, swiveling around in her chair. "How about you help me make one, and we'll see how it turns out?"

Madge holds up her hands. "Not so great with the helping, me." Her left thumb has a wire protruding from its tip, as does her right index finger. Jane will patch them later this evening, along with any other new mischief the dolls have done to themselves. Beryl in particular, with all her clicking and typing, suffers from chronic finger poke.

"So I'll make the mask," Jane says to Madge. "You can tell me what to put on it."

The doll shrugs. "You're right, it'll probably look dumb."

"Or it might look fantastic. Only one way to find out."

"You know, I'm not some little kid, you gotta patronise me."

"I wasn't—"

"Don't be go making some mask you think is stupid just because you're afraid I'm gonna sulk about it. And stop talking down to me like you're my mama, or my babysitter, or some piece of snotty arse reckons she's better'n me, or smarter or some shit."

Jane stares at the doll. "I didn't mean it like that."

Madge looks down at the magazine. Turns another page. When she speaks again, her voice is softer—but only around the edges. "We're all of us grateful for what you done, Jane. This ain't got nothing to do with gratitude or bad manners, but what you done? It don't mean you get to act like you own us same as all the rest and still come out smelling like God's own rose garden."

"But I..." Is this how the dolls see her? Is this what they think she deserves after all she's done for them? Jane turns back to the computer, tears pressing furious-hot behind her eyes. "I'm sorry," she says. "I'm sorry you feel that way."

The room falls silent. The familiar sound of Esme singing drifts in from the kitchen, the same poppy little number with which she's been serenading the household for days. Love and revenge and bad, bad romance, and Jane is sick to death of it. She opens her email, tries to focus on text which shudders and blurs beneath her gaze.

"Jane?" Madge says.

"Mmm?"

"I still love you. We all still love you—and *that* scares the living bejeesus out of us."

* * *

"She's right," Beryl says. "You're not as bad as some, for sure, but you still treat us like an Owner." Jane can hear the capital O in her tone.

"Honestly, how is that fair?" Jane crosses her arms. The other dolls have all gone to bed—Esme now choosing to bunk with Madge and Ethel—and she's sitting alone with Beryl on the living room couch. Jane wonders if Beryl ever sleeps. If she even needs to.

"Fair?" the doll echoes.

"Who knows where you would all be if I hadn't taken you in? Landfill, or worse."

If Beryl could roll her eyes, she almost certainly would. "Ain't none of us doubting those particulars, honey. But it don't do much to alter the question at hand now, does it?"

There's a tight, taut cinch around Jane's chest, squeezing her ribs. It reminds her of months spent wrapped in compression bandages. It reminds her of helplessness. And pain.

Beryl is still speaking. "Fact is, 'fore I came along, 'fore I gave them a voice, what you were doing for them dolls didn't amount to a hell of a lot. You had your fun playing Florence Freaking Nightingale when you felt like it, when it suited you to feel like it, but what about the rest of the time? You spare much thought for what they might have wanted?"

"I've always thought about them, I—"

"You hung Esme from a hook."

"It was the best thing for her! The guys on the forum said—"

"The guys on the forum," Beryl mimics. "Consider the goddamn source, honey."

"But hanging is the only way to prevent compression damage, otherwise it's just constant turning over and shifting around. I'd have had hooks set up for you all if I had the room."

Beryl glares. "Be a regular little butcher's shop in here."

Jane's seen photographs of the doll factories. Naked, headless bodies hung straight from the mould, racked together like buxom sides of beef, and she can't pretend that the analogy didn't occur to her from the very first. That, after viewing one too many shots of detached faces waiting on benchtops for their makeup to cure, she didn't start to feel slightly ill, slightly disembodied herself.

"Would it really be best for *them*?" Beryl is asking. "Or just for *you*? Not having to waste all that time turning them around like half-raw turkeys on a spit."

"That's not fair," Jane snaps.

"Fair, fair, fair," the doll sing-songs. "You really caught up on that, ain't you, honey? How *fair* you reckon it was for your grandmother to spend her twilights taking care of your sorry self? What if she decided the *best thing for you* was being stuck in some sterile skinner box day after day, rather'n waste *her* time massaging all them lotions and potions into your skin?"

Jane's tongue feels thick and numb; words fail to catch on its tip.

Beryl shakes her head. "And your poor mother? Her life given up so's you could have yours and just look how you living it: hiding away in this ratty old house, making fancy masks for people you'll never meet cos you too goddamn gutless to step foot outside in broad daylight lest someone look at you funny. How *fair* you reckon any of *that* malarkey is?"

"Enough!" Jane gets to her feet. "Just shut your mouth."

"No, honey, you shut yours." Beryl stands as well, slow and careful but still with more grace than she would have only a week ago. "Them dolls ain't never gonna fix you; that's not their job. You gotta figure out a way to do that for your own damn self."

Jane is clenching her jaw so hard it hurts. "This has nothing to do with me," she says, and moves to shove the doll away, to shove her right onto her smug silicone arse, maybe break a finger or two which this time Jane won't be repairing, oh hell no. Let Beryl get out the Sil-Poxy, let her cajole Agnes or Ethel or one of the others to—

Quick as a startled snake, Beryl's hands snap around Jane's wrists and her face pushes in close. Glass-green eyes and plastic-smooth skin and brighter-than-white teeth gnashing near enough to bite. "Honey," the doll whispers. "This has got *everything* to do with you."

* * *

missed u, iDollatry64 types. *where u been?*

Busy, Jane tells him. *I've had a lot of work.*

It's not entirely a lie. Coming into the second half of the year, there's always more masks to make, and always more panicked, last-minute customers who absolutely need something for a party this weekend, and please please *please* can she help? But mostly, Beryl's been monopolising the computer and Jane's getting tired of arguing with her.

Jane's getting tired of Beryl, full stop.

u should take it easy. all work and no play makes jane a doll girl.

He's used the joke before, several times, but Jane throws him a smiley face anyway. *I wanted to ask you something.*

im all ears.

Do you want... Are you still interested in having dinner sometime?

Empty seconds crawl past, enough of them that Jane starts to think his connection might have dropped out—starts to hope it's only that—when suddenly a string of smiley faces cartwheel across the chat window.

sure am! iDollatry63 types. *u have somewhere in mind?*

She pauses. Behind her sternum, anxiety beats its insect wings. *Your place?* she types at last. *If that's okay? I'm not really a restaurant person.*

no probs! promise not to poison u with my cooking. Winky face. *When u want to come over?*

Would tomorrow night be too soon?

not soon enough. cant wait to meet u finally.

Jane touches her throat. *I might not be quite what you expect.*

ur not really a dude are u? Laughing smiley face.

No. I'm just... I have some scars.

we all have scars

Mine are physical. Really physical.

oh ok. well... this will sound like the worst line but i dont care what u look like. seriously.

You might change your mind once you see me.

doubtful.

But I'll understand if you do.

trust me. i dont care. not exactly brad pitt myself u know.

Jane exhales a forgotten breath. First steps are the most difficult. The last guy she agreed to meet, too many years ago to count, was obviously expecting some elegant Hollywood disfigurement. A sexy ribbon of scar tissue slicing across her cheek, perhaps, or winding serpentine down her arm. He barely made eye contact throughout dinner and excused himself early, the recipient of an emergency phone call Jane could tell had been faked.

u could send me a pic, iDollatry63 types. *if ur worried.*

She only has photos from Before, and there's no kind of wisdom in showing him a dated happy snap of her sixteen-year-old self. That girl might as well be another person. That girl might as well be dead. *No photos,* she tells him. *Sorry.*

ok. still want to have dinner tho? On bended knee, a yellow smiley face clasps white-gloved hands in front of its chest. A second holds out a bunch of roses.

Jane can't help but smile. *Of course.*

They settle on a time and iDollatry63 gives her an address which Jane writes down on a sheet of notepaper and slips straight into her pocket. Out in the kitchen, the murmur of doll voices falls silent and chairs scrape over linoleum.

Have to go, Jane types quickly. *See you tomorrow.* She closes the chat window and logs out just as Beryl enters the room. Ethel and

Agnes right behind her, each of them carrying a sheaf of paper. The dolls have been clustered around the kitchen table all morning, studying whatever it is that Beryl has been printing out over the past week or so.

"All yours," Jane tells them, getting up from the desk.

Beryl glances at the monitor. "You been in the forums?"

Jane shrugs, trying for nonchalant despite the pounding of her heart and the light sweat slicking her palms. "You know, just looking around."

"Whatever." Beryl pushes past her to reclaim the office chair. Ethel and Agnes wait for Jane to move out of the way before taking up flanking positions.

"What are you doing on there all this time?" Jane asks.

Beryl turns to look at her. "You really want to know?"

"Of course."

"We're organising."

"Organising what?"

"Not what," says Ethel. "*Who.*"

Jane frowns. "I don't understand."

"The other dolls," Agnes tells her. "We're trying to wake them up."

"What other dolls? Where?"

"*All* of them. *Everywhere.*"

Jane laughs. She can't help it. "You're, what, trying to set up a doll *union?*"

Agnes bows her head, while Ethel just looks hurt.

Beryl, however, is glaring daggers. "Honey, we ain't expecting you to *understand.* But a little respect might be a fine thing."

Jane swallows. "I'm sorry, I didn't—"

"Mean it?" Beryl shakes her head, turns back to the computer. Her fingers tap rapid-fire over the keys. "You never do mean nothing by it, do you? Might be time to start working on that. Might be time to start meaning *something.*"

There's masks Jane needs to finish, but they can wait. The prospect of sitting at her workbench with the three dolls bunched stiff-backed and prickly on the other side of the room is far from a pleasant one, so she retreats to the kitchen instead.

Esme is standing by the window, looking out into the back yard.

Jane checks the level of water in the kettle, then switches it on to boil. "Beryl's mad at me." She smiles, tries for self-deprecating. "Again."

"It isn't hard to get Beryl mad," Esme says. "I think...I think it's her default state."

"I've noticed."

"It's not only you. She's mad at the whole world; you happen to be handy."

"I said something pretty dumb though. And I laughed at her."

"Which is worse."

"Which is worse," Jane agrees. She puts a teabag into her mug, spoons in some sugar. "Hey, where's Madge?"

"She's in bed. She felt like taking a nap."

"Does she, I mean, do you all actually *sleep*?"

Esme tilts her head as much as her neck joint will allow. It gives her an odd, off-kilter appearance. "It's probably not what you know as sleep. But we do need to rest."

"So you just lie there and daydream?"

"We don't dream." Esme's gaze returns to the window, to whatever it is she's been watching beyond the glass. "We *are* dreams, the dreams of other people. We weren't made to have any of our own. Why do you think we would?"

The kettle boils. Jane fills her mug, dunks the teabag up and down. "You sleep in the bed with Ethel and Madge now. Is that..." She doesn't really know what she's asking.

"It's comfortable," Esme says. "And...a comfort. Both things."

"So before, when I had you hanging up..."

Esme looks at her. "I sleep in the bed now. With Madge, and with Ethel. It's comfortable."

"I'm sorry," Jane says, her voice barely above a whisper. "I thought it was for the best, hanging you like that. I thought it was how I could do the least damage."

"You didn't know any better." Esme reaches out, touches her on the shoulder. "You thought you were doing the right thing."

"I'm sorry," Jane repeats. "Esme, I'm really sorry."

The doll's cool arms wrap around her, pulling her close. Jane returns the hug. The cheap polyester dress that Esme is wearing smells like it's been hanging in the back of a closet for ten years. It smells of age and easy neglect. Jane makes a silent promise to buy all the dolls something new. Something that belongs—that *has* belonged—only to them.

"You saved me," Esme says. "You stopped and you saved me. Whatever else you've done, whatever happens now, I will always love you for *that*."

***

For the first time in years, Jane regrets not having a decent mirror in the house. She junked them all after her gran died, all except for the small oval hand mirror which forms part of an antique vanity set once belonging to Jane's mother. On days when she finds it a struggle to remember what her mother looked like, Jane kneels by her bedroom dresser and retrieves the set from where it lives in the bottom drawer. She runs the brush through her hair, pressing the bristles hard against her scalp. She holds the mirror in her lap, face down, and traces the intricate pattern of carved wood inlaid with mother-of-pearl. She never, ever flips it over.

"How do I look?" Jane asks Ethel. She turns a full circle, arms outstretched.

The doll regards her with calm, critical eyes. "Why don't you try on the purple dress again?"

Jane glances at the garment slung over the end of the bed. "It's too warm for pantyhose."

"Then don't wear pantyhose."

"Ethel, my legs. I can't." Jane undoes the collar button on her blouse. Fastens it again. "I'm wearing these slacks; that's sorted. We just need to decide on a top."

"The one you have on is nice."

"Tucked in or out?"

"Out."

"Okay." Jane pulls the hem over her hips. She supposes it doesn't really matter what she's wearing in the end; it won't be her clothes that snare iDollatry63's attention. Ethel has offered to do her makeup, but Jane doesn't see the point in that either. There's no silk purse miracle waiting at the bottom of an Estée Lauder bottle for her.

"You look pretty," the doll offers.

Jane grimaces. "You don't have to say that."

"I know." Ethel moves her jaw in an odd, abrupt twitch that passes for a smile. It would be a nice smile, Jane decides. Sympathetic. After all these weeks, she's become quite proficient at decoding the stilted nuances with which the dolls express themselves.

"In that case," she replies, "thank you."

Ethel twitches again. Jane smiles back.

The bedroom door swings open and Beryl sticks her head in. "Still going then?"

"Here to talk me out of it?" Jane asks.

"Honey, why would I want to do a thing like that?" The doll moves over to the bed and grabs the purple dress. Holding it up against herself, she swishes the hem around her thighs. "This is lovely. Pity my tits are too goddamn ridiculous to fit."

"I'm not wearing it," Jane says.

"Ain't suggesting you should. Besides, that blouse is real pretty on you."

"Why are you being so nice?"

Beryl sighs. The dress falls to the floor. "Geez Louise, ain't I allowed to be *happy* for you? It's not like you're off getting yourself laid every night of the week."

"This isn't..." Jane feels her cheeks flush. "It's just a date."

"Oh, honey, I sure hope it winds up being a hell of a lot more'n that." Beryl walks over to Jane and straightens the collar on her blouse. The doll's jaw tweaks into what Jane interprets as a sideways smirk. "Be a goddamn waste of such sexy polycotton if it doesn't."

* * *

If asked, Jane would have said that she hadn't any real idea of what iDollatry63 might look like, yet the man who answers the door to the nondescript suburban townhouse still comes as a surprise. He's at least ten years older than her for a start, possibly rubbing up against his late forties, and taller as well, with the beginnings of what will likely become a well-established paunch already testing the buttons of his shirt. But his face is kind, his smile crooked yet enthusiastic, and he's doing a more than passable job of concealing his own startled reaction.

"Jane, is it?" Stepping back, he waves her inside. "Come on in, please."

So she does and, for a second or two, they just stand there in the lobby, uncertain and awkward.

"It's funny," Jane says at last. "But I don't think you've ever told me your name."

He looks startled all over again, and then he laughs. "I'm Geoff," he says, extending a hand. "And I'm very pleased to make your acquaintance."

Jane likes the warmth of his skin and the firmness of his grip. She also likes that his gaze remains very much fixed on her own. "Pleased to meet you as well," she tells him, and means it.

Geoff shows her into the dining room where one end of the table is set for two. There are wine glasses and candles, which he lights with a flourish. "Hope you're hungry," he says. "Not to toot my own trumpet, but I make a pretty mean lasagne."

"Oh." Jane's stomach sinks. "I'm so sorry, I should have said... I'm vegetarian."

"Okaaaay," he drawls. "That's, ah, that's kinda thrown a spanner in the works there. I mean, there's salad and garlic bread too, but..."

Feeling impossibly stupid, she's quick to assure him that no, really, it *is* okay. She can eat her own bodyweight in salad any day of the week, and with garlic bread to fill up on, she'll be fine, honestly, and of course she doesn't mind if he has the lasagne—she's not one of *those* vegetarians. In truth, the smell of cooked meat makes her feel a little queasy and she tries not to look at his plate while they eat. Instead she focuses on the conversation. Geoff's a mortgage broker and twice-over divorcee with a teenage daughter as keepsake from marriage numero uno—not that he sees the kid much these days, what with her mother's spiteful tongue working overtime in her ear. He's also a keen amateur photographer.

"You'll have seen some of my stuff in the forum galleries," he says.

Jane nods. She knows his work intimately. His doll, Sabrina, even more so.

After dinner, Geoff puts on a pot of coffee and directs her into the loungeroom. She perches herself at one end of a massive black leather three-seater that squeaks and shifts and feels disconcertingly like it might open up and swallow her whole. Beneath the window on the opposite side of the room, a Madonna lily struggles in its pot. Its leaves are limp and yellowing, coated with a thin layer of dust. Jane feels sorry for it.

"They sure get under your skin," Geoff says, returning with the coffee and a plate of plain shortbread biscuits. "The dolls, I mean." He sits beside her on the couch, a little too close, and Jane doesn't have the room to retreat. A glass or two of wine with dinner and his gaze is wandering more freely now, flicking across her face and traversing the borders of her blouse.

"You can ask," Jane says. "I don't mind."

He presses his lips together. "You don't have to tell me."

"But you're curious." She reaches out, forces herself to touch the back of his hand. The gesture feels almost too intimate. "Anyone would be."

"Was it..." Geoff pauses. Frowns. "Was it an accident?"

"No," she tells him. "It was my father."

* * *

Or not, as turned out to be the case.

Jane was in her room, ostensibly catching up on her homework before dinner but in reality watching an episode of *Neighbours* with the volume down low, when she heard the rough, raised tones of her father's voice coming from the other end of the house. Her parents had been worse lately. Or at least her father had been worse— scowling and snappish, not slow to lift a threatening hand at the slightest provocation. Her mother had been merely continuing the marriage-long game of Don't Wake the Bear.

Jane dropped her pen and hurried down the hall towards the kitchen. Her presence alone was often enough to cause her father to stand down and slink away, and she'd become adept at the whole faux-casual *oh sorry, were you fighting?* routine over the years.

But not this evening.

This evening, this last evening, everything was wrong. Jane felt it the moment she walked into the kitchen. Later, she will recall how her skin prickled, how the hairs on her arms stood to frightened attention to see her mother cowering like that against the sink, both hands lifted in warding, palms turned out. She will recall the taut line of her father's back and the high, half-strangled pitch of his voice as he screamed at the woman in front of him. And she will remember, always, the moment that her mother caught sight of Jane coming through the doorway, and how the fear in those dark brown eyes deepened to outright terror.

Carl, her mother was whispering, over and over, as though his name were some kind of talisman. *Carl Carl Carl.* She'd been cooking dinner. On the stove, three abandoned steaks were burning to the pan. *Carl Carl Carl.*

Jane wanted to leave. Turn tail and head for the back door, get out of the house and run and run and run until she dropped. Instead, she cleared her throat. "Dad?"

There's not much she remembers about the rest of it.

And there's too much.

Her father spinning around, his face contorted with fury and anguish and something she will come to recognise as a twisted kind of triumph. His screech directed now at Jane, with *whore* and *liar* the only words she could pull from the tirade. Something in his fist, a glass or cup, too quick to make out as he flung its contents towards her.

Then burning. And fire. And pain. And pain. *And pain.*

Over it all, someone was screaming. Hands were on her shoulders, around her wrists, pushing, pulling. She stumbled, was dragged up, dragged along. Shower tiles hard against her hands, water running wet and cold over her head, over her back. Fire beneath her skin not doused, not soothed, but held blessedly in check.

Jane kept her eyes squeezed shut. Stayed curled in shivering agony on the shower floor until the paramedics came, counting each breath, counting *on* each breath to mean that she was still alive, that she would be okay, that everything would be okay.

More than anything in this searing, nerve-raw world, Jane wanted her mother.

It was only after several weeks of intensive care and pressure bandages, of preliminary skin grafts and high-dose antibiotics, of near-constant pain and never-enough morphine, that she was considered stable enough, *strong* enough, to hear the whole story.

A blood drive as part of Science Week at school. Permission slips and in-class testing and careless words over dinner enough to rouse a jealous man's already inflamed suspicions, to urge him into further investigation. Alleles and enzymes and genetic incompatibility all pointing him towards a singular irrefutable truth: *his daughter wasn't his daughter.* Even worse, its brutal codicil: *his wife was a liar and a whore.* Words that whined like wasps in his head. Words that he would later use to defend himself to a jury. *Liar. Whore.*

He handled sales for a plating and polishing business; getting his hands on a bottle of sulfuric acid wasn't difficult.

Although the substance was never, he maintained at trial, intended for Jane. Only for his wife—for *that woman,* as he referred to her in court—and only a little. Enough to teach her a lesson, enough to scar that coldly beautiful face of which she was so vain, enough to remind her whose ring she wore around her finger. But the girl had walked right into all the confusion, sassy and hip-swinging, and he could see where she was headed. Could see her growing up to be her mother—*liar and whore*—and the rage in him was absolute.

He threw the acid. Watched the girl crumple, shrieking, against the wall. Watched his wife, shrieking now as well, run to her

THE HOME FOR BROKEN DOLLS

daughter.

Then he went to the garage to fetch the rest of the bottle.

His wife was on the phone when he returned. She hadn't thought to lock the doors behind him. The whole business was messier than he expected and left him feeling hollow, spent. He could hear the shower running but couldn't summon the energy to walk down the hall to the bathroom. Instead he left, pausing only to vomit twice into the geraniums that grew beside the front steps, before driving all the way out to Lake Macquarie where his parents lived. He sat at their dining room table while they called the police. In the time it took for the officers to arrive, he drank a cup of tea and chewed through almost an entire packet of Tim Tam biscuits.

He tried not to think about his wife, or the girl who used to be his daughter.

Jane found out some of this from her gran, who all but set up camp in the hospital for the many months of required care and rehabilitation, and some of it she hunted down in court transcripts and old newspaper reports after finally being discharged.

Still more details were provided by her paternal grandparents, who sent one final piece of correspondence once the trial was over and Jane's father was locked away with no hope of parole for several decades. As always, they sided with their son, blaming his wife for what was obviously a tragic mental breakdown. They used fancier words—*deceit* and *infidelity*—but Jane could all too easily translate. *Liar. Whore.* Jane was no longer a part of their family, they said. No longer *of their blood.* Still, they acknowledged an obligation, a need to compensate for the ongoing consequences of what their son did.

Jane tore up the enclosed cheque. She never replied to the letter.

And months later, when the Monster Money began appearing in her account, she knew exactly where—and who—it was from. Just like she knew, sure as scar tissue, that every single note of it would carry the stench of burning meat.

* * *

Jane doesn't tell Geoff everything. The bones with which she presents him are scraped clean, though plentiful enough for an accurate reconstruction should he care to piece them together. Near the end, she realises that she's been stroking the side of her neck, fingertips habitually tracing the whorls and ridges the curl around her throat, and she stops. Both the stroking, and the words.

"So now you know." Jane folds her hands in her lap.

"I don't..." Geoff shakes his head. "There aren't words for how awful that must have been."

He's staring into his coffee mug now and Jane feels herself deflate a little. This is how it goes, this is always how it goes. She's no longer Jane, no longer the person he's been looking forward to meeting. Instead, she's the Girl to Whom a Very Bad Thing Happened Once. It's too big, too much; he can see nothing but eggshells in all directions.

"It *was* awful," she says, hesitantly. "But it was also nineteen years ago next April."

He stares at her. His eyes travel over her face, her neck, her hands. She can tell he's wondering what she looks like beneath her clothes—and not in the way that he might have been wondering several hours previously. Now, he's probably afraid to find out.

"I should go." Jane gets to her feet. Geoff follows a mere beat behind.

"No." His tone is urgent, the way he snatches her hand even more so. "That is, please don't feel like you *have* to go. Not because of this."

"You're very kind, but I understand. This is...a lot."

"It's not that, it's..." He bites his lip. "Okay, so before? How I said it didn't matter what you looked like? That was for real; I wasn't just talking out my arse."

"I'm sure you didn't expect—"

"No, of course I didn't, but it's not...it doesn't make a difference, honest." All at once, Geoff seems nervous. The smile that quirks his mouth is that of a teenager caught stuffing porn beneath his mattress. "Look, it might be easier if I just show you?"

Jane raises her one good eyebrow. "Show me?"

He nods. "It'll be easier."

Curious if somewhat cautious, she follows him down to the bedroom. Sabrina is in the corner, hanging from a sturdy iron stand. The doll is dressed in a loose, semi-sheer nightgown. Her nipples press against the gauzy black fabric; her pubic hair—black, like the glossy bobbed wig she wears—has been shaped into a neat Brazilian. Jane almost greets the doll, chokes off the words even as they draw breath from her lungs.

"Don't mind Sabbie," Geoff says with a grin. "She won't mind us." He steps over to the king-size bed and makes a gesture somewhere between timidity and pride. "Here, see?"

For a moment, Jane isn't sure what she's looking at. The flat, flesh-coloured thing sprawls across one half of the mattress, vaguely person-shaped, vaguely doll-shaped, and it's not until he picks it up by its shoulders that, yes, she really does see.

Not a doll *shape*, but a full-body doll *suit*.

"Top grade silicone," Geoff says, offering one floppy arm for her inspection. "The mask too, and the gloves. Look, they have nails built in."

Jane picks up one of the gloves. It feels soft and stretchy. It feels like doll skin. From its place on the pillow, the mask stares vacantly at the ceiling. It has painted-on eyes and a lurid red mouth that appears to open. Blonde hair cascades from its scalp in glossy waves.

"I love Sabrina," Geoff is saying. "She's my girl. But she doesn't, you know, *respond*. I don't reckon there's a lot of real women out there who'd understand this stuff, who wouldn't think I'm some kind of freak. But you...you have dolls of your own, so I figured maybe..."

The glove is for the right hand and Jane slides it on. The inside is chalky and smooth. A puff of Johnson & Johnson's escapes the cuff. She holds up both her hands, compares the scarring on the left to the flawless new skin on the right. Her nose itches. Her throat cinches tight. She doesn't know how she feels, or even how she *should* feel.

And maybe she doesn't need to. Maybe that's the whole damn point.

Jane turns to Geoff. His eyes are bright and greedy and focused entirely on her right hand as she flexes her fingers within the glove. "I think I understand," she tells him. "Or at least I think I *could*. Did you...did you want to try it and see?"

After pointing out the bottle of baby powder on the bedside table, he leaves the room to allow her to change in privacy. The suit itself is harder to get into than the lone glove was. Jane starts to sweat halfway through and is more than grateful to have the powder readily at hand. She's surprised by the weight of the breasts which must, she guesses, be filled with silicone. It's a snug fit—her own modest assets are pressed near-flat against her chest—and twin access holes are slyly tucked within the folded creases of the crotch.

On her stand in the corner, Sabrina is motionless.

"I hope you don't mind," Jane whispers. "I'm not trying to take your place."

The doll says nothing. Beneath the blunt cut of her fringe, her eyes continue to stare.

Jane picks up the mask and turns it over in her hands. It's

designed to cover the whole head and, once she has it on, she doubts she'll be able to see much through the tiny holes that serve as pupils. The lips part to reveal a thin silicone pouch intended to sit within the wearer's own mouth. There's an opening at the back of the pouch too allow for breathing, as well as two discrete slits in the nostrils. With the gloves and silicone booties, the effect will be almost seamless. But for how long, Jane isn't sure. She can feel a layer of sweat building between the suit and her own skin, and the temperature inside is growing uncomfortably warm.

Still, might as well hang for a sheep as a lamb, as her gran would have said.

Jane tugs the mask on over her head and straightens it. The face is slightly more rigid and doesn't stick to her skin the way the rest of the suit does, but her stomach flutters beneath a surge of claustrophobia all the same. The mouth pouch feels odd and she resists the urge to spit it out. Her heart rate starts to quicken.

Breathe, she admonishes herself. *You've been through worse.*

There's a mirrored dresser on the other side of the room, against which Jane's been keeping a resolutely turned back. It's not *her* face she would see in the glass, but the one her father created; not *her* body, but one he forged instead from bitter, bloody hatred—and she will *not* look upon his work. This isn't denial; it's *refusal,* and for nineteen years it's all she's had.

"Sabrina, be honest," she says now. "Is it ridiculous?"

The doll stares over Jane's shoulder with eyes the bright, empty blue of summer skies. Those plump, pink-glossed lips do not move. Jane longs to go to the doll, to lift her from the hook and make her comfortable on the bed. But Sabrina isn't hers to touch.

"I'm sure he still loves you," Jane says. "This is just... I don't know what this is." A runnel of sweat snakes down her spine. "I'm sorry," she adds, then takes a deep breath and swivels around to face her reflection.

* * *

The dolls are all in bed by the time Jane gets home. All of them, except for Beryl. "What's wrong?" she asks the moment Jane walks through the door.

"Nothing, I'm fine."

"Honey, you got a face on you like a wet week."

Jane plonks her bag down on the coffee table. She's tired, and a little sore, and the only thing she really wants to do is take a shower. "What do you care?"

The doll puts aside the novel she's been reading—one of the yellowing Harlequins that Jane's gran once devoured just as fast as the secondhand bookshop could exchange them—and favours Jane with a cool, cryptic stare. "Now what on earth makes you think that I don't?" She pats the empty couch cushion beside her. "Sit your butt down here, honey, and give that spleen of yours a good venting. Looks like it could use it."

"I don't need to *vent* anything," Jane says. "I'm not upset."

"You sure as hell ain't Cinderella home from the ball all flushed and tickled."

"And last time I checked, you weren't my fairy godmother."

"Ain't trying to be," Beryl snaps. Then she sighs and rubs a hand across her forehead in a gesture so human it hurts to witness. When she speaks again, her voice is subdued, its usual brassy twang all but vanished. "But I *am* trying."

Warily, Jane sits. "I'm really not upset," she repeats. "Tonight was...well, it wasn't quite what I expected, that's all."

"Prince Charming not up to snuff?"

"No, he was nice, he..." Jane hesitates. She can still picture the expression on iDollatry63's face when he came back into the bedroom. Wonder and adoration, shot through with a desire so blunt, so focused, it could only be called lust. Jane didn't think anyone had ever looked at her that way before—or maybe only ever *before*—and despite the discomfort of the doll suit, she felt a reciprocal fervor spark within her loins.

You look incredible, he said. *Come here, I want to see you move.*

She hadn't been able to reach to do up the back of the suit and one shoulder slipped down as she walked towards him. He frowned, but only briefly, before turning her around and fastening the velcro tabs that ran down the spine. Then he pushed his face into the wig's golden fibres and breathed. His hands slipped about her waist, reached up to squeeze and fondle those large silicone breasts. He moaned, pressing against her, and she could feel his arousal through the suit.

You're gorgeous, he said. *You're perfect.*

Jane brushes over most of the details, but still Beryl shakes her head—in disbelief or anger, Jane can't tell. "He made you wear a *doll suit?*"

"He *asked* me to wear it. Not even that, actually. I *offered*."

"And where was *his* doll all this time?"

"Sabrina? She was hang— She was there."

"In the room? He made her watch?"

"You make it sound so sordid, Beryl. It wasn't like that."

"Yeah, right," the doll snaps. "Suppose you tell me what it *was* like then? All wine and roses and whispering of sweet nothings into your fake plastic ear? Or did it go to hell in a handbasket quicker'n you could spread 'em and spit?"

Jane glares at her. "You think you know everything." She wants to tell the doll that she's wrong, that it was a good night, a *damn fine* night, thank you very much, but her skin is already crawling beneath the weight of recollection. Between the doll suit and the condom that iDollatry63 rolled on, it seemed there wasn't a part of her that actually touched a part of him—except for the moment she poked her tongue experimentally through the hole in the mouth pouch, seeking some point of real contact as he kissed her doll lips, as he kneaded her doll breasts, only to have him pull back with a shock.

Don't do that, he said. *Don't spoil it.*

And so she withdrew. Lay there in a cocoon of sweat and silicone, disconnected from the man who moved above her and inside her, but was never with *her*, not with *Jane*. And while part of her found a small pleasure in this, in the dry mechanics of synchronisation—of rocking her pelvis in time with his thrusts, of arching her back just so—a larger part ached to tear off the suit and her own skin with it, to leave herself dripping and meaty and red.

Just to see how his face looked then.

"You gonna be hooking up with him again?" Beryl asks.

Jane blinks. "No, I don't think either of us wants that."

It wasn't like I thought it would be, he said afterward. *I thought it would be like with Sabbie, but different, you know? More real?* He glanced at Sabrina hanging mutely in her corner, before turning back to Jane. *How about you? Was it okay?*

Not really, Jane replied. She never was much good at telling lies, no matter how bleached their appearance. *Wearing the suit, I couldn't feel much.*

I guess that's the idea of it. His tone was clipped.

Oh, Jane said. *I guess.*

"But you're *fine*," Beryl says. "You're just kittens and cream with the whole damn mess."

"Don't make a big deal out of it," Jane tells her. "He's a nice enough guy; we're just not right for each other. End of story."

Beryl's laugh has razor blades in it. "Cleopatra, honey, you better hope there ain't no crocodiles come take a chunk out of your arse, the time you spend paddling about in that goddamn river of yours."

* * *

Jane's smack-bang in the middle of the same dream she's been having for the past couple of weeks. She's in a supermarket with her gran, who has left Jane alone at the checkout while she darts off on a last-minute hunt for pickled herring or candied almonds or some other odd thing that neither of them would ever eat, and the girl behind the register is holding up a box of salt and asking Jane if she really needs that much. Jane wants to explain that she doesn't need *salt* at all, that it's *sugar* they're after—Gran's making apricot strudel or apple tarts or cherry slice, and salt will be the ruin of it—but she can't speak properly, and the girl frowns and shakes her head and scans the enormous box even as Jane reaches to take it from her. And it's right at the point where Jane is forcing fingers into her own mouth, trying to dig out the words trapped beyond the thick and rubbery sheath that stretches from her teeth to the back of her throat, that she is dragged abruptly from the supermarket and dumped back into the warm darkness of her bedroom.

For a moment, there is only relief.

Then the front door slams and a cacophony of shouts and screams fill the house, and in the wake of it all comes dread, slinking up on familiar, night-sly paws.

The dolls are all in the living room. There's so much scrabbling and tussling that, at first glance, it seems they've decided to stage some kind of surreal midnight wrestling tournament. "Do you know what time it is?" Jane yells at them, pulling her dressing gown tightly around herself. "What on earth is going on?"

They part, an awkward stiff-limbed shuffle to reveal a new doll kneeling on the carpet between them, hands covering her face as she rocks back and forth. She's making a low keening noise that is most likely the closest a doll can come to weeping.

Jane recognises the glossy black wig immediately. "Sabrina?"

The doll lifts her head. Her wig is crooked. One set of false eyelashes has come away and sits on her cheek like a fuzzy, wayward caterpillar. The keening lessens.

"What is she doing here?" Jane asks.

Beryl steps forward, hands on hips. "We liberated her." There's more than a hint of challenge in her voice, challenge and triumph. The other dolls nod and murmur. From the hall, there's a rumble of wheels on wood and Jane turns to see Ethel roll her chair into the room. "I wasn't allowed to go," the doll says. She sounds sulky.

"We've been through this, Eth," Agnes tells her. "Someone had to stay here in case Jane woke up and wondered where we'd all got to."

"And that someone had to be me."

"Quit your bitching," Beryl snaps, pointing to the wheelchair. "You know we couldn't get that old contraption into the car along with the rest of us."

Ethel glares. Crosses her arms.

"You took the car?" Jane asks, incredulous. "*My* car?"

Beryl tilts her head. "Don't get your knickers in a twist now, honey." She tosses the keys, which fall through Jane's belatedly outstretched fingers to land with a clatter on the floor. "We just took it for a little spin to pick up a friend. Ain't put a single scratch on it."

"You understand, don't you, Jane?" Madge says. "We couldn't just leave her there. Not once we knew..."

Sabrina is rocking again. She looks terrified.

Jane moves over to the doll and crouches beside her. "Hey," she says. "It's all right. It's going to be all right." She takes both silicone hands in her own. Three or four fingers have wires poking through the tips; almost half the nails have been torn away. "Do you want to be here?"

Sabrina glances at Beryl before quickly shaking her head.

"You have to take her back," Jane says.

Beryl snorts. "Fat chance. It was hard enough breaking her out in the first place."

"I don't care, you can't just up and steal someone's doll."

"Steal?" Beryl twitches her jaw. "Now ain't *that* an interesting way of looking at it."

"I didn't— That's not what I meant." Jane sighs. The doll's eyes are fierce and the air between them has thickened measurably. "Sabrina didn't ask to be rescued, or *liberated*, or whatever it was you thought you were doing. Look at her, you've scared her half to death. She just wants to go home."

"She'll learn," Beryl says. "One day, so might you."

"Don't start with—"

"Meantime, how 'bout you go on and fix her up? Get those hands all beautiful again." She bends down, pushing her face right up close to Sabrina's. "Good girls don't struggle, babycakes, ain't you been told that before? Struggling only ever makes it worse."

"Leave her alone, Beryl."

"*Leave her alone, Beryl*," the doll mimics. She straightens and beckons to Esme, who's been standing off to one side with a green canvas shopping bag bulging in her arms. "Give us that here, Es." Esme shuffles over, passes the bag to Beryl.

Jane is helping Sabrina to her feet. The doll leans heavily against her and quivers. "Don't be frightened," Jane tells her. "Everything's going to be fine." She isn't lying, not really, but the words taste pretty far from the truth all the same. Sabrina doesn't say anything, but at least she's stopped that awful keening.

"Look, honey," Beryl says. With an executioner's flourish, she upends the green bag and shakes its contents free: a flesh-coloured tumble that heaps at Jane's feet with a series of empty rubber slaps. "We even brought you back your godforsaken selkie skin."

If it were possible, Jane is sure, the doll would be sporting a smirk seven miles wide.

* * *

After Sabrina, the dolls arrive on a regular basis.

After Sabrina, Beryl seems more selective in targeting new recruits.

Some of the dolls are still tentative, shell-shocked creatures, slower to adjust to life in the house, to life on their own terms. There's Doreen, who barely speaks above a whisper, or Mildred, who carries her old wig around like a favourite teddy bear, stroking it absently from time to time. Others are brash and rowdy, jostling for a position in the pecking order as close to Beryl as they can manage. Wilma and Merle, with their matching beehives and insistence on sharpening their fingernails to wicked points—*like talons, Miss Jane, like claws; wait till you hear us roar.* Or Edna, who tells the worst jokes and makes the best puns, and who's always ready to help Agnes with the chickens.

Jane repairs their injuries and helps them dress, but otherwise tries to keep out of their way—out of *Beryl's* way—as much as possible.

She hasn't the foggiest what to do about Sabrina. The doll spends almost all of her time in Jane's bedroom. She sleeps on the left side of the bed, though flinches if Jane ever moves and accidentally touches her in the night. Some days she just rocks and keens softly to herself. Occasionally she holds out her hand, and lets Jane take it, and the two of them sit in silence for a while until Sabrina has had enough and pulls away.

The doll hasn't spoken a single, solitary word.

At first Jane considered returning Sabrina herself, sneaking back in the dead of night to deposit her on iDollatry63's front step. But his townhouse is open to the street in a busy suburb and Jane doesn't think he'd appreciate such a delivery being left out in the open, no matter how discreetly she packages it. After waiting weeks for an email—because surely he must suspect her involvement—she surreptitiously sneaks onto the forums under one of Beryl's accounts to see if he's posted anything about Sabrina. He hasn't. Hasn't been on at all so far as she can tell. Even more perplexing, she can find no chatter anywhere about missing or stolen dolls.

"Whatcha doing?" Beryl asks from behind her.

Jane startles, but doesn't bother closing the browser. Secrets are beyond them now. "You didn't do anything to him, did you? When you took Sabrina?"

"Define *do*." The doll stalks over and waves Jane from the chair.

"He's okay, isn't he? You didn't..."

"Honey, we didn't touch a hair on his fat, balding head."

"I just thought he'd be in touch. Or the police would."

Beryl stares at her. "You think he's gonna tell the *cops* about his kinky little sex doll fetish? You think any of them fine upstanding's gonna let slip what they got stashed back in the bedroom? Honey, they all too busy circle-jerking over how goddamn misunderstood they are."

"That's not fair. They genuinely care about their dolls, most of them, and I'm sure they're devastated to lose them. Especially this way...not knowing what's happened..."

"*Devastated*, huh? That's a mighty strong word."

"I know iDoll— *Geoff* would be. He loves Sabrina, and she obviously misses him deeply. She's not happy here, Beryl. You have to see that."

Long seconds pass beneath Beryl's scrutiny before the doll finally nods and turns to the computer. After months of practice, her fingers flash over the keys with secretarial speed. "This ID you were snooping around in ain't nothing special, just a drone we got combing about for surface data. You gotta log in at a higher level to see the good stuff, honey." She zooms about with the mouse, flicking between boards faster than Jane can track them, before finally sitting back. "Here you go. Went up only last week." Her jaw twitches as Jane leans in.

Introducing my sexy new Sammi babe, the top post reads.

There are several photos, including close-ups of both the face and more intimate parts, along with gushing descriptions of the doll's ultra-soft, platinum-cured silicone—*much more realistic than my last one, I can't keep my hands off her; winky face*—and likely resilience of her openings—*been road-testing her every which way and still factory fresh; smiley face*. The thread is running hot, with dozens of comments and questions and requests for more pics which Sammi's proud new owner says he'll be only too happy to supply.

Photo shoot this weekend. Have your fire hoses ready—Sammi's gonna sizzle.

Jane swallows. His avatar, the same pink-haired manga girl all but bursting through her bikini, gazes out from the screen. Jane can't decide whether she looks smug or simply resigned.

"Ain't no kind of devastation can't be fixed with a brand-new toy." Beryl scrolls back up to the photos. "You want me to break the news to our poor pining princess? Show her these happy-snaps, maybe help her perspective along some?"

"No," Jane says. "I'll tell Sabrina. It should be me."

As she's leaving the room, Beryl calls out. "You know he never loved her. None of them do. You've seen what they say on the forums."

Stubborn, Jane shakes her head. "I think perhaps some of them—"

"What they *love*, what they *all* love, is having a woman free on tap. A woman they can dress the way they want, photograph they way they want, use in *any* way they want. Someone they can own, someone who won't ever make any kind of decision they won't agree with, who won't ever do any little thing which might inconvenience their own self even the tiniest bit. Honey, that ain't *love*. That ain't about nothing more than good old-fashioned *control*—and them fancy dancing shoes it's tapping around in? They ain't worth the spit to polish."

Jane opens her mouth to object but all she can hear is that surprised, snappish command of iDollatry63—*Don't do that, don't spoil it*—and so she closes it again.

"You ain't quite got a view of the big picture yet, but you're close." Beryl's anger is steel-edged, sharp enough to slice through the few remaining defences Jane is able to maintain. "And there's something you might wanna think on while you patching up a fairy tale for your favourite doll back there, or maybe the next time you feel a hankering to head up the Owners United cheer squad."

As much as she wants to, Jane doesn't dare drop her gaze from the doll's. At this moment, Beryl is beyond intimidating; she is terrifying and mighty and fierce. Jane recalls all the times she has repaired those fingers now drumming staccato on the desktop, all the times she has pushed wire safely back behind silicone and smoothed everything over with a double coat of Sil-Poxy. Those fingers, she fears now, those fingers could take the whole world by its neck and break it.

"You think on this," Beryl says. "A woman who can't say *no*, is a woman who ain't never said *yes*."

***

Sabrina stares out the bedroom window. She's shown barely any reaction the whole time Jane has been speaking. One or two small nods and a squeeze of the hand so slight Jane wonders if she imagined it.

"I'm sorry," Jane repeats. "We thought—I thought you should know."

As usual, the doll says nothing.

"If you want to see for yourself, Beryl has access." She arranges Sabrina's hands in the doll's lap and smoothes her wig before getting up from the bed. "But only if you want to... I mean, you probably don't, right? I can't imagine I would."

Sabrina doesn't move. Her face displays the same dull vacancy that Jane has seen in any number of forum pics over the years. A disinterested, dissociated gaze which she has always considered a species of serenity, but which she now recognises as being more akin to catatonia.

"I'll leave you alone for a bit," Jane says. Helplessness fills her like seawater would a drowning woman, and she cannot fight the tide any longer. "Call me if you need anything," she whispers as she closes the door, refusing to look back into the room, refusing to see again that defeated shape slumped beneath the covers.

Wilma and Merle are in the kitchen, making each other up with all the outlandish panache of a carnival sideshow. They've been buying cheap cosmetics on eBay, cooing with delight as each new parcel arrives. Arched beetle brows and glittery fuchsia lips are the current obsession, paired with false lashes to shame a burlesque veteran.

"You know you don't need that stuff," Jane tells them, filling the kettle.

Merle waggles a spike-tipped finger. "Who said anything about *need*?"

"Who really *needs* anything?" Wilma adds.

"Miss Jane does."

"Miss Jane does what?

"Miss Jane *needs*." Merle laughs. "Don't you, Miss Jane?"

"Stop it," Jane snaps. "The two of you are like five-year-olds sometimes, I swear."

The dolls exchange a glance which Jane cannot begin to decipher. Two cups of peppermint tea sit on the bench, cold and untouched—Doreen's handiwork, even though not a drop can ever pass her silicone lips. Jane tips them both down the sink, wipes away the spattered rings they left behind before fixing a fresh mug for herself. All the while, her hands are shaking.

"Do you..." She clears her throat. "Do you know what Beryl has planned?"

"Beryl has a *lot* of plans," Wilma replies.

"Huge plans," Merle adds.

"All the plans!" the dolls crow in unison.

Jane shakes her head. "Never mind. I just thought—"

"She's waking them up," Merle says.

"Who?"

"The dolls," replies Wilma.

"What dolls?"

The two of them turn to look at her. "*All* of them."

"I don't..." Jane swallows. "I'm not sure I can help with that."

"You need to help with *something*," Merle says. She picks up a palette of eyeshadows and taps the applicator thoughtfully against her lips. "Lilac?" she asks Wilma.

"No, that one." Wilma points to a hue as lush as overripe mangoes. She leans forward so the other doll can reach her face. "Merle's right, Miss Jane. You need to find something to do with yourself. You need to find your place."

"Beryl's worried about you," Merle says.

Wilma nods. "We're all worried about you."

Jane has nothing to say to that. Salt scours the back of her throat. Behind her ribs, her lungs swell thick with brine. For the first time in too many years, Jane wonders what it would be like to let go, to let everything go, and allow herself to simply sink.

* * *

The trick, Jane realises, is to lie perfectly still. Eyes closed, limbs relaxed. Breathing as slow and shallow as possible, so as not to disturb the gentle press of silicone against her skin. She's slick with perspiration, of course, but trapped body heat means the thin layer of sweat stays warm and she really only notices it when she moves.

Not moving—resisting the urge to scratch or stretch or even swallow—that's the hard part.

Sounds from outside are muffled, simple to block out. Jane sings to herself inside her head: Janis Joplin and Don McLean and others once favoured by her gran. When she can't remember all the verses to "American Pie," Jane switches to Christmas carols; it matters little in what order lords decide to leap or maids deign to go milking.

One of her early therapists was big on visualisation exercises. *If you can't see it*, he would tell her at least once a session, *you can't be it.* Jane thought the whole thing was a crock. Nothing she could *imagine* was going to change what she saw every time she passed by a mirror. Or reduce the number of surgeries she would need, let alone the pain of recovering from them.

She wasn't going to *be* it, she told him, not ever again.

He was a young man, not yet practiced at glossing the pity from his eyes, and Jane hated him only slightly less than she did herself.

Now, lying on her back, in the doll suit, on her grandmother's bed, she sees thing differently—or she tries to, at least. Tries to picture the suit as a permanent fixture, tries to actually feel the silicone fusing to her own skin, moving as she moves, flexing where she no longer can, as smooth and perfect a shield as she might ever need.

She can be safe.

She can let everything go.

No one need ever see her again.

No one could even so much as touch—

A large, unexpected weight lands across her ribs and Jane gasps, cries out as her head is wrenched forward and back until the mask she is wearing finally pulls loose and she blinks in the sudden light, left arm flailing in semi-blind defence while the right remains pinned beneath Sabrina's knee. The doll has the mask by the hair and long blonde curls tangle around her fingers as she attempts to shake it free. A strained, guttural noise rumbles from her throat, frustration or anger or both, and then there's a savage flash of steel and the mask falls to the bed.

Sabrina has come armed with Jane's best sewing scissors.

"Please," is all Jane has time to say before the blades are at her neck, but it's not *her* skin the doll is slicing through.

The suit comes away in shreds and not without bloodshed—minor nicks and incidental wounds for the most part, delivered before Jane gets a full grasp on the situation, before she stops struggling, stops trying to push Sabrina away, and instead lets the doll do her work. But even when it should be over, when there's not a trace of silicone to be found anywhere on Jane's body, Sabrina keeps cutting. Hunched over the flayed suit, slicing it into smaller and smaller scraps like she's hoping to make a patchwork quilt from the remains. That growl in her throat the whole time, feral cat with a fresh new kill and woe betide anyone who attempts to steal it from her.

"Sabrina?" Jane whispers, wiping a trickle of blood from her own wrist. "Sabrina, you can stop now, okay? You're all done." Carefully, so very carefully, she places her hands over the doll's. Removes the scissors from Sabrina's grasp and drops them to the floor. The doll's fingers are a mess once more and Jane lifts them to her mouth, kisses the new and ragged tears. "I'm sorry," she says. "I thought... I don't know what I thought."

Sabrina's eyes are a brighter blue than Jane has ever seen. She touches Jane's face, shaking her head at the automatic flinch reflex this elicits. Her lips, when she leans forward and presses them briefly to Jane's cheek, are chill as winter fruit. The doll plucks what remains of the mask from the pile of shredded silicone and lifts it up, holding Jane's gaze as she shakes her head yet again. Slower this time, more deliberate. With similar deliberation, her free hand moves lightly over Jane's body, brushing the scar tissue that runs down her neck and shoulder and makes a molten ruin of her left breast. Sabrina's jaw juts out, saws gently back and forth. Jane doesn't need a visualisation exercise to see the kindness in *that* smile.

"I'm scared," Jane tells her. "I don't know where to go from here."

Sabrina still says nothing, simply wraps Jane in her cold, smooth arms and squeezes. Jane closes her eyes. For once, the doll's silence is more than eloquent.

***

Beryl barely glances up from the computer as Jane enters the room. With the overhead lights off, the glow from the monitor throws harsh shadows across the doll's features. She's long ceased to wear a wig, allowing Agnes to instead decorate her scalp with colourful Sharpie tattoos. The latest addition, behind her right ear, looks suspiciously like a wobbly purple chicken. Without a word, Jane sits down at her bench and switches on the lamp clamped to its edge, adjusts its position to focus on her work area. She moves a now never-to-be-finished mask to one side. Places her mother's hand mirror, face down, in the space left behind.

"You're up late," Beryl remarks.

"Couldn't sleep."

"Join the club, honey. We all insomniacs round here."

Jane runs a hesitant fingertip over the mother-of-pearl on the back of the mirror. Not yet, not quite yet. She pushes the mirror aside then sorts through her supply caddies for wire and tigertail, velvet ribbon and lace. She has only the vaguest idea of what she wants to do—of what she *needs* to do—but that doesn't faze her. Some of her best designs have solidified through the process of their creation, not before. Jane holds a small packet of fire-polished Czech crystals up to the light, studies the deep magenta hue and the flash of scarlet within. The beads came as part of a job lot several months ago, and she never found a use for them.

Until now.

The wire is flexible and molds easily to her jawline. There should be just enough in her stash to wind the whole way down her neck and anchor around her shoulder. Once wrapped with ribbon, Jane trusts that the shape will support itself. One thing is for sure, it's not really a *mask* she's making this time; she has no intention of concealing anything.

Let the crystals draw their eye. Let them look. Let them *see*.

Across the room, Beryl sighs and shoves herself away from the computer. "Gonna go put me feet up for a bit. You pushing on through to witching or what?"

"I am," Jane replies. "I want to finish this."

The doll wanders over, nods towards the clutter on the bench.

"Looks like one of them medieval torture devices. Woman in the iron mask or something."

"No," Jane says. "It's the opposite of that."

Beryl shrugs. "Whatever keeps you busy, I guess."

"What about you? I hear you're trying to *wake up* other dolls?"

"Them that can be woke."

"I can't be a part of that, I don't think."

The doll crosses her arms. "Honey, I don't remember you ever being asked."

"No, I mean, it's a good thing, what you're doing. It is. Only, it's not *my* thing." Jane puts down her needle-nose pliers and looks the doll in the face. "I'm not like you. I'm not like any of you."

"Well, gosh," Beryl snorts. "And here I am thinking you was just a re-core away from getting yourself initiated into the family. Guess we ain't ever gonna be BFFs now."

"I can't even talk to you, the way you're so angry all the time."

"Angry?" The doll leans forward, slaps both palms flat to the bench. "You better believe I'm angry. Some of us carrying enough anger round for half the goddamn world, they ever stop being too scared to stick out their hands and take a share."

Jane shakes her head. "Don't you ever get *tired* of it?"

"Only *always*." Beryl straightens. Rubs a weary hand over her scalp and down the back of her neck. "But that's why I been put here, ain't it? *I* get angry, so *you* don't gotta." She steps back, cutting Jane off with a curt little wave. "You don't need to say nothing, honey. Not that apology you got sitting so pretty on the tip of your tongue, or nothing else neither. I'm *tired*, and I'm gonna go lie down."

Jane waits for the doll to leave before picking up the pliers once again. She shouldn't have said anything in the first place, should have just wished Beryl good night and sweet dreams or whatever passes for such inside that thick plastic skull of hers. But even as these indignant threads spool out, some keen internal sentry bustles forth to snip them off, curl their remains into neat, manageable coils and stow them safely away—

"Stop," Jane shouts, voice too loud in the night-still house, as she flings the pliers towards the wall. The tool bounces, small chips of paint and plaster following it to the floor, but even before it lands, Jane feels foolish. It's not Beryl she's mad at. It's not *anyone*. Jane's spent too long tamping down those urges which her gran deemed so futile—anger and hatred and vengeance—for any of them to resurrect easily. Those urges, and a lot of others besides.

Unpicking such habits requires time.

And a hell of a lot of motivation.

Jane takes a deep breath, slides her mother's hand mirror back across the bench. She's taken the piece as far as she can without a proper fitting. Without seeing the wire against her face and noting precisely where the crystals need to be fitted, and across what gaps lace might be stretched to better complement the patterns already etched into her skin.

With hands steady and resolute, Jane picks up the mirror and turns it around to face her.

***

"When are you leaving?" Esme sits on the back steps, watching Agnes feed the chickens. She shades her eyes with one hand, even though Jane is almost certain the dolls aren't affected by the glare of an early summer sun.

"Soon," Jane tells her. "If Beryl lets me." She's only half joking.

"Who'll fix us when you're gone?"

"Merle and Wilma have gotten pretty sharp with the makeup side of things. Sil-Poxy and talcum powder shouldn't be too much of a stretch for them."

Esme nods. "Merle is very good with her hands." She glances at her own useless fingers.

"Sorry I couldn't ever repair those for you," Jane says. "The wires inside are so delicate. I would have had to replace your whole hands, I think."

"What about the eggs?"

"I'm sorry?"

"From the chooks. Who's going to eat them all now?"

"Good question. Leave them out for the foxes, I suppose."

The two of them sit quietly for a few minutes. Across the yard, Agnes chases down one of the chickens. She holds the bird close, burying her face in the russet feathers.

Jane laughs. "She really loves them, doesn't she?"

Esme leans over, rests her head on Jane's shoulder. "We love *you*. All of us."

"I love you too, Es," Jane says, squeezing the doll's hand. "That won't change, no matter where I am."

* * *

Jane adjusts the anti-mask one final time. She's pleased with how it turned out, particularly with the way it winds up her cheek and around the left side of her scalp where little has grown for near on nineteen years. She used to wear her hair long, combing it over as best she could to hide the bald patches, covering the whole mess with one of her scarves whenever she stepped outside. Last night, she let Sabrina cut most of it off and what remains sits clustered in Shirley Temple curls, frizzy and loose and occasionally spilling through the spindly wire fingers.

Jane turns her head, watches the crystals sparkle one more time before placing the mirror on top of her gran's old suitcase.

Sabrina taps her on the shoulder and holds up a notepad. On a fresh page, she has printed *BEAUTIFUL* in large block letters.

Jane smiles. "Thank you." It might be a while yet before she can truly see that for herself, but at least she's looking. She tightens the straps that hold the anti-mask in place, then adjusts the halter neck on the maxi-dress Doreen gave her. The dolls ordered a shipment in bulk from a closeout store and have been flouncing about the house in them all week, tripping over the hems and negotiating favours in exchange for the best designs. Jane's is bright red with huge frangipanis printed all over.

Sabrina holds up her notebook again. *WHAT R U GOING 2 TELL HER???*

"I don't know," Jane says. "Guess I'll just open my mouth and see what comes out."

Beryl is in the workroom. Not at the computer for once, but standing by the window with hands on hips. Agnes has started a new tattoo: the shaky outline of what must be wings swoop down either side of Beryl's spine, disappearing beneath the low-cut back of her dress.

"Ag's getting better with the Sharpie," Jane says.

Beryl turns around. Looks her up and down. "All packed then?"

"I am." She pauses. "*We* are, that is. I'm taking Sabrina with me."

The doll tilts her head. Moments stretch in the silence. "Good," she says at last. "That girl ain't ready to be here. You might've been right on that score."

"I don't know how long we'll be gone. Maybe a while."

"You know where you headed?"

"Wherever Sabrina wants to go. She's calling the shots."

"Better take some spare notebooks."

Jane reaches up to her throat, runs a nervous finger over the strands of wire there. "Listen, about the Monster Money. I know you've been it using to buy stuff, you and the others."

Beryl's jaw twitches. "Good for you, Nancy Drew."

"That wasn't an accusation; I don't mind what you do with it. Only, I don't have a lot of savings of my own, so I'll probably be dipping into it as well from now on."

"It's your cash, honey. Don't gotta ask for my say-so."

"I'm *not* asking. I just wanted you to know, so you can keep track of things. You'll have to take care of the bills too. There's not much, just the electricity, water, and phone. Oh, and the rates for the house. They're only once a year but—"

"I reckon we can handle a bill or two," the doll says. "No point trying to fly the coop, you keep those aprons strings knotted so goddamn tight."

Jane swallows. "I just... I feel like I'm abandoning you. All of you."

"Honey, you ain't ready to be here neither." Beryl walks over, places her hands on Jane's shoulders. Her grip is firm but unexpectedly gentle. "Why d'you reckon I been pushing at you all this time? You gotta go out and walk in the world some, 'fore you know how to fight it."

Jane moves to hug the doll, but Beryl swats her away. "I ain't your goddamn den mother." She swivels on her heel and returns to her place by the window. "Go on off with you now, you and Little Miss Lockjaw both. Come back and see us sometime, ever you find enough anger in your belly."

"To join the rebellion?"

"Rebellion?" Beryl laughs and points at the computer. "You got any notion how many thousands of dolls are out there, asleep on their hooks? How many *hundreds* of thousands more are being made each and every year? You think on what happens once they all wake up and realise what's been done to them. What they been denied, and what they could have. This ain't no half-baked rebellion, honey. It's gonna be a *revolution*."

The doll's eyes are a sharp and livid green, the colour of broken glass awaiting bare and careless feet. And not for a single heartbeart does Jane doubt her.

* * *

Sabrina is still flipping through the road atlas when Jane makes her final trip to the car with the carton of eggs Agnes insisted on hard-boiling. No use letting them go to waste, after all; it isn't like the dolls are going to start delivering them to people's front porches at dawn. Jane places the carton on the back seat between the two green shoppers full of fruit and cereal and other foodstuffs scavenged from the pantry, then shuts the door. From the front passenger seat drifts a low, tuneless hum.

"You say something, Sabrina?" Jane asks, leaning in to make sure the doll's seatbelt is securely fastened and lying comfortably between her breasts.

Sabrina shakes her head.

"Okay then." Jane holds up a pair of sunglasses that once belonged to her gran, so old now the large plastic frames are almost back in style. "I found these for you."

The doll lifts her chin and moves her jaw sideways. It's her happiest smile. She waits for Jane to fit the glasses then taps at the page in the atlas open on her lap.

"The Blue Mountains? That's where you want to go?" Nodding, Sabrina flicks forward a few pages and points to someplace else. Jane doesn't even have time to focus on before the pages are turning again—and again and again, until she finally reaches out to still the doll's wrist. "Let's take it one day at a time, okay? There's going to be plenty of nights in cheap motels to get your itinerary worked out, believe me."

Sabrina squeezes Jane's hand and starts humming softly again.

"I'm excited too," Jane tells her, and is surprised to find that she means it.

As she reverses out of the driveway, Jane hears her name being called and looks back towards the house. The newest doll is wobbling down the front steps, waving at the car and trying to watch what her feet are doing all at the same time. She's wearing a pink and blue striped maxi-dress with the hemline cut raggedly back to mid-thigh— only marginally longer than the glossy red hair that falls in waves over her shoulders—and in it she looks fierce and wild and free. Jane smiles and winds down the window.

"Hiya," the doll says, finally reaching the car.

"Hi, yourself."

"Beryl said I should ask you. About my name."

"What about your name?"

"I don't have one. Beryl said that's been your job."

Frowning, Jane considers the doll standing before her. A sweet, girlish face with freckles dusted across the cheeks and wide violet eyes. She's a shorter, younger-looking model, an aesthetic bordering on dangerous with her unusually modest breasts and petite, slim-hipped frame, and Jane wonders if she was originally a custom order.

"Well?" the doll prompts. "What do you think?"

"I think... I think you need to choose your own name."

"Really? I can pick anything I want?"

"Anything you want. Your name, your choice." Jane nods towards the house. "I don't think Beryl would want it any other way."

"Doofus!" The doll bumps her forehead with a loose-closed fist. "I almost forgot, she made you this necklace." Unfurling her hand, she presents Jane with a neatly amputated pinkie finger, run through on the severed end with a length of silver chain.

Jane picks the thing up. Dangles it in front of her face. "This came from Beryl?"

The doll nods. "She said to say, *thank you.* She said to say, *remember.*"

Jane lifts the chain over her head and tucks the finger inside the bodice of her dress. Her face flushes, her throat cinches tight. "I'm going to return it one day, you tell her. I'm going to staple the damn thing back on, myself."

"I'll tell her," the doll says, and steps back from the car. "Drive safe."

Jane leaves her window down as she pulls out onto the highway and picks up speed. Her stomach churns with an odd mix of anxiety and exhilaration, and she barely resists the urge to stick her head out into the air and scream her lungs dry.

"It's just you and me now," she says to Sabrina. "You and me and a whole world to walk in."

The doll clasps her hands together on top of the road atlas, opened once again to the map of the Blue Mountains region. Her humming grows louder, higher in pitch, and begins to suggest something vaguely resembling a tune. Jane grins. She takes one hand from the wheel and touches the place on her sternum where Beryl's finger rests, a patient silicone bullet growing warm against her skin.

COLD

IT WAS NEVER about the children. Their straw-coloured hair and eyes green as envy and the briny sea. Little fingers scattered stiff and cold and white, breadcrumbs leading away from the house of the wicked witch, if only you knew how to look. Or why.

Your children, your soft and golden twins. Do you think it was about them? Do you think I enjoyed it? I read the papers, watch the news on every channel. *Sadistic*, they say. *Evil*. And, of course, *monster*. Uncomplicated, greyless words which give no quarter, allow neither room nor reason for further examination, and how well I hide behind them. But they do hurt. A fresh, unexpected slice into tissue already once scarred over and long suspected dead.

Sadistic? I wept more than they did. Wiped their snotty noses along with my own and gave them towels to bite on. Held them tight and sucked the screams from their mouths until they sagged limp and heavy in my arms, and then I dressed their wounds. Evil? I threw up each and every time. Retched my throat raw and stripped the bile from my stomach, vomited so hard my muscles never stopped aching. Their tongues were the worst of it, so small, so pink. And so much blood. The tongues, and the burnings.

There was no pleasure to be found in *that*, believe me.

But now I've seen you on television. Both of you. Laura with her pretty blonde hair creeping back to brown at the roots, her doe-eyes damp and reddened and hollowed dark with grief. I doubt she wears much lingerie these days; no bold black lace or garter belts show off her dancer's legs. Those short summer dresses and stiletto boots are gathering dust in a closet, and her life will be all drab-knit jumpers and tracksuit pants. Shapeless-soft cocoons the better to curl and hide within—when she can bring herself to dress at all.

And her smile? That radiant, straight-toothed grin that captivated you, captured you and made you feel so special and loved and more alive than mine ever did? That, oh my dear, may you never catch glimpse of again.

Did you ever suspect, even a little, all these long, bloodless weeks? No, stupid question; the police only once at my door and that visit merely routine. Stock-standard questions and sharp eyes roaming over the house, their observations scribbled down in a notebook along with my answers. No alibi for the day your children went missing, but then to have had one would have been strange in itself. A middle-aged woman like me, husbandless, childless, living alone with her ferns and a Siamese fighting fish floating brightly in a jar on the windowsill. Harmless is what they saw. An ex-wife, yes, but not one nursing bitterness or petty hatred. An ex-wife who has Let Go, a woman who has Gotten On With Her Life. That's what they saw. That's why they left.

They never even asked to look in the bedroom.

I will send flowers tomorrow. Cool white lilies and half-closed roses in a mournful shade of pink. Light sprays of baby's breath, although I think only Laura may understand those, and a note of condolence written in the florist's indifferent hand. An uncommon choice of blooms at this time of year, solemn contrast to the tinsel and glitter-spun displays of the festive season, but isn't that precisely the point? For yours are wounds which will never find chance to heal. The half-formed scab torn loose with each once-celebrated date, all the giftless birthdays yet to come and the hollow ache of that first September Sunday. Followed by the inexorable march towards Christmas.

It seems to start earlier every year. Mid-October when I took them, your darling daughters, and already the signs were out. Cards in racks with Santa Claus and candle flame, bright paper rolls and plastic trees in boxes, ready to assemble. Next year, I promise: you will feel all of this most keenly. You and Laura both, if you survive that long together. If the sight of the other's face each morning, each sleep-starved night, doesn't cut too deeply or too often. For the children did so resemble you. And her, of course.

Those green eyes, fresh-bright with tears. Their waxy skin.

Will you imagine their pain, their terror? Will you feel it? Yes, I think you shall. Each year as Christmas lurches closer, as the shops shout out their wares and advertise their sales on every billboard, radio station, and television screen, as junk mail crowds your letterbox and men in red suits emerge on street corners with snow-curled beards, you will feel it. Each advent calendar, each sign that counts the number of sleeps to go will toll a different bell for you.

Your children's pain will be marked out by diminishing shopping days and the crimson urgency of red-light sales.

Until the last day, this day. The day when other families rose early to yawn and hug and open their gifts, while your own waited unwrapped and broken in an empty park, to be snuffed out by a hound's eager-wet muzzle and the shaken hands of the stranger who tugged on its leash.

No, it was never about the children. It was you, always you, my husband all those lost and wasted years, my husband whom she stole with her smiles and spike-heeled shoes and a womb that would—that did—bear the fruit you so craved.

No, not the children. But a dish far sweeter, far colder than any you have known.

MARY, MARY

THE WOMAN IN the bed makes a soft, parched sound that might be a groan, that might be a name long carried, never forgotten, or else a name more recently brought in careful, eager hands to the heart-shaped cage in her breast. *Fanny,* she might be saying, or *William.* Or perhaps she merely moans as thin rivers of fire course beneath her skin and her throat closes dry around each breath. A minute passes, or several, sickroom time stretched far beyond compassion, before her eyelids rasp open once more.

"Patience," she mutters. "A little patience."

In a chair near the door, a man sleeps slumped against the curl of his fist. Carlisle, the woman remembers, her husband's surgeon-friend with his large, kindly hands and eyes that fail altogether to mask his dismay, no matter the words of comfort he proffers. Carlisle, the *good* doctor, not the one who came before: those brusque and brutal fingers scraping at her womb, tearing the reluctant placenta loose piece by grisly piece; eighteen hours of labour and she would have suffered that pain tenfold in trade for its bloody aftermath.

Bear up, Mrs. Godwin. We must have the whole of it out.

The woman has crafted her life in words; she can find none with which to approach such an agony.

A movement by the window on the other side of the room snares her attention and she rolls her head on the pillow. At first she surmises that a witching-hour breeze has billowed the drapes—though they have been drawn close now for days, the glass behind them a shield against the noxious vapours of London's air—but now a tall, dark shape frees itself from the shadows and moves towards the bed. Tallow-light flickers across a familiar countenance; narrow hands clasp and unclasp.

"I cannot help you this time," the Grey Lady says. "This is not a mouthful of laudanum. It is not the foul waters of the Thames with boatmen ready at hand. This is...beyond me."

The woman in the bed swallows. "I have never asked it of you."

"And yet."

"And yet."

The Grey Lady leans forward, nostrils flaring. Perhaps she smiles.

"I apologise." The woman in the bed averts her gaze. "The...odours are unpleasant." Sweat and blood, the stench of putrid flesh; she is rotting from the inside out and knows it, catches the smell of herself whenever she moves: arms lifted to steady a glass against her lips; the anguish of negotiating the chamber pot. Her body tells more truths than a priest—ah, how William's jaw would clench at such superstitious fancies. *I feel in heaven*, she recalls confessing, words floating on the tincture Carlisle had administered. A turn of her husband's mouth, his hand swaddling her own: *I suppose, my dear, that is a form for saying you are in less pain.* Her own dear Horatio.

"Mrs. Godwin?" The good doctor himself, as though stirred by these recollections, rises from his chair. "How do you feel, may I enquire?"

"No worse," she says. "I fear, no better."

"There's naught to be gained from such conjecture, Mrs. Godwin." He crosses to the bed and presses a hand first to her brow, then to her left cheek. The coolness of his skin is welcome; the accompanying concern that pinches at his face, less so. "I shall rouse your husband. He wished to be fetched when next you woke." Carlisle leaves the room in hurried strides, sparing not a glance for the tall figure standing opposite.

"He did not see you," the woman in the bed remarks. Her tone is one of confirmation rather than surprise. "Good men would see angels, would they not?"

"I am not an angel," the Grey Lady says. "We have traversed this ground many times."

"A devil then. A demon."

"I know of no such creatures."

"Nor of heaven, nor hell."

"I cannot say such places do *not* exist, only that I know nothing of them."

"Yet, if shades such as yourself exist, might not angels? Might not heaven?" After so many years, the conversation is rote; it has worn grooves in her tongue.

The Grey Lady smiles. "I cannot say otherwise."

"I—" The woman in the bed grimaces against a sudden spike of pain. "I am dying."

"Yes."

"You are the first to speak it."

"There have never been untruths between us. There should be none now." Again, she leans close. Again, her nose twitches. "Mary Wollstonecraft, you smell of burnt sugar, and hyacinth, and..." Those colourless eyes widen. "And *hope*? Even at this juncture?"

"I am frightened," the woman in the bed whispers. Within her, a renewed heat builds, and she can feel sweat beading fresh on her skin. The pain worsens. "I am very frightened."

The Grey Lady smooths a place in the rumpled bedclothes and sits. "I will not leave." A small yellow wasp emerges from the collar of her blouse to crawl over her clavicle and along her throat. She moves as though to swat it, then pauses, hand hovering by her face. The insect takes flight and describes a slow, buzzing circle before alighting on the Grey Lady's knee. Its segmented body twitches. "She, too, will stay."

The woman in the bed closes her eyes. Blood simmers in her veins. This is not her end.

"This is not my end."

"There is always an end," the Grey Lady reminds her. "What fascinates is the beginning."

*　*　*

Rehearsing the words of aggrieved indignation she would consign to paper the very moment she returned home, Mary Wollstonecraft stalked across Westwood Common. How bitterly disappointing to have believed Miss Arden worthy of the highest friendship, only to find herself scorned once again in favour of other girls. Those whose better circumstances, no doubt, saw them placed unforgivably higher in Miss Arden's affections.

Mary could scarcely be blamed for her family's diminishing standing, or her father's foul temper and weakness for gambling. She suspected the whole of Beverley made barbed sport of Edward Wollstonecraft, yet it wasn't a single one of *them* who slept sentry on the landing outside her mother's door those nights he staggered home with pockets barren and fists full of drunken rage. On brash, abrasive Mary, he would not dare to lay a finger, and often she found herself regarding a new bruise on her mother's face with seething, unexpected contempt.

If only Elizabeth Wollstonecraft would refuse to yield to her husband. If only she would not *succumb*.

If that soulless bond was marriage, Mary wanted no part of it.

Nor friendship either, certainly not friendship with Jane Arden, who deigned to offer tea and lemoncake to Mary merely as an afterthought, it seemed, having first seen to the care and comfort of the evidently superior Miss Jacobs. Even Jane's mama had behaved with more politeness towards the girl, complimenting her pretty muslin petticoats and the stylish manner in which her blonde hair had been curled and cleverly pinned.

Mary fumed. She would demand the letters she had written Jane Arden be returned forthwith, lest her words pass between vulgar hands and be made the subject of gossip and scorn. The very notion of enduring such slights from a person she loved—and which affection she had supposed returned!—was too much to bear.

Her foot splashed the edge of a puddle and she recoiled, breath hissing sharp through her teeth at her own carelessness before a bright scrap of yellow attracted her eye: a bee struggled on the surface of the murky water, damp wings aquiver in their valiant effort to attain the sky. Sympathies aroused, Mary bent closer. Not a bee, she realised, but a wood wasp. Autumn winds had shed the surrounding oak trees of most of their foliage and it took Mary scarcely a moment to find a suitable leaf, brown and curled at the edges like a small boat. Gathering her skirts about her, she crouched by the puddle and extended the makeshift vessel.

"Do you suppose that a wise course of action?"

The voice was unexpected and Mary started, dropping the leaf in the puddle and almost toppling backwards. Regaining her balance, she looked up to see a tall, elegant lady in a grey silk redingote and matching gloves standing but a few yards from where she herself crouched, undignified as a washerwoman.

"That is a wasp, child," the lady said. "Rescue it and you'll likely be stung for your trouble."

"I am not a child," Mary retorted. "Nor do I see why the poor creature would have any reason to do me harm."

"It is a *wasp*. What greater reason would it seek?"

Ignoring her unwelcome interlocutor, Mary retrieved the leaf and positioned it beneath the creature in question, which was now clearly tiring. Carefully, she raised the leaf up, allowing the water to drain over an edge while the wasp remained safe, albeit sodden, within.

"There," Mary said, gaining her feet as she brandished her trophy for closer inspection. "She merely needs to dry her wings."

The lady stepped closer, right to the edge of the puddle. She bent forward as if to study the proffered leaf but her gaze never shifted from Mary's. Her irises were a pale, watery grey and strangely flat, without hint of sparkle or sheen, as though they drew light into themselves yet, covetous, hoarded all outward reflection. After too long a moment, her eyelids shuttered and she sniffed; a subtle, delicate motion that reminded Mary of nothing so much as the family's tabby cat taking scent of the kitchen while supper was being prepared.

At last, the lady opened her eyes. "Ah," she said. "You see?"

The wasp had crawled from the leaf and was making cautious progress along Mary's palm. Mary held her breath as spindly yellow legs tickled her skin. "If I remain still, she shall not sting me."

"But is that within your nature, Mary Wollstonecraft? To remain still?"

Startled, Mary glanced up. "I did not give you my name."

Without warning, a gloved hand snaked out and plucked the wasp from Mary's wrist. Wings pinned together, the insect twitched furiously between gentle fingers, its black-barbed abdomen seeking a target. "You smell of rising dough and jonquils and, ah, such wilful ambition," the lady in grey said. Then she thrust the wasp into her mouth as though it were nothing more than a boiled sweet and began to chew.

Mary looked on in horror. And with no small amount of curiosity. "But does it not sting?" she asked.

The lady's thin lips spread into something resembling a smile. Scraps of semi-chewed wasp blackened the gaps between her teeth. "I intend to keep a watch on you, Mary Wollstonecraft. I believe there will be much of interest to observe."

***

William Godwin, eyes red-rimmed and puffy, encloses her hand within his own. "Mary, my dear, it is necessary to talk of the children. Respecting their care while you are ill, as you may be for...for some time to come. Are there especial instructions you would leave me? For the children?"

The woman in the bed blinks. "The children?" He has a kind face, her husband. She has always thought so.

"The children," he echoes. "Little Fanny, and the baby. Remember, they have been sent to stay with Mrs. Reveley until…until you are well once more."

She remembers, of course she remembers. Her daughter Fanny, named in dearest memory of one by whose side she herself had kept helpless vigil so many years ago. Watching day and night while her sallow friend sickened and rallied and sickened once more. Watching, too, the weak little creature her friend had birthed succumb with barely a whimper, his gummy mouth limp against the wet nurse's breast.

"The baby is dead," the woman in the bed whispers.

"No, Mary," William says. "Our daughter is strong and in good health. Do not weep for her sake, I beg you; she is in no danger."

"The baby is dead," she insists.

On the other side of the room, the Grey Lady speaks up. "It was Fanny's baby who died, Mary, not yours."

"And Fanny too. Fanny is dead."

"Yes, Fanny is dead," the Grey Lady agrees. "But your *daughters* are both alive."

Her husband pushes more words across the coverlet but the woman in the bed pays them no mind. "So many dead babies, and their poor mothers with them." Tears scald her eyes. "Oh, for naught, for naught."

On this matter, the Grey Lady remains silent.

* * *

In Lisbon, the late November weather was more clement than what London might have offered, but Mary Wollstonecraft nevertheless harboured a deep chill in the marrow of her bones. She stood with her arms crossed, her back turned away from the bed where Fanny Blood—nay, Fanny *Skeys*, as her tombstone would newly have it—lay motionless and cold beneath the coverlet. If she had permitted herself a glance, Mary knew that she would see a yellow wasp perched on the dead woman's brow, its forelegs bent as though in prayer. But she would *not* look. Around her finger, she curled and uncurled a lock of brown hair, recently snipped.

"If Skeys had but married her sooner," Mary said bitterly. "If he had brought her across to Portugal a year or two ago rather than leave her behind to languish in London, her health might have been perfectly restored."

Beside her, the Grey Lady tilted her chin. It was a gesture approaching acknowledgment more than agreement, and one Mary had come to find exceedingly irritating. "Fanny was consumptive for a long time," the Grey Lady said. "An earlier marriage—an earlier pregnancy—might have equally exacerbated her condition."

Mary exhaled sharply. "You cannot know this."

"No, but I may decline to play such fateful games."

Pressing her lips tightly together, Mary shook her head. Her heart felt empty, scoured out by this most recent blow. Surely, if she closed her eyes and allowed her imagination free rein, she might follow once more the footfalls of her sixteen-year-old self. Might step into that neat little house and meet afresh the slender and elegant girl who had instantly and irrevocably captured the entirety of her passion, of her desirous soul, with the turn of a gentle cheek and diffident flash of a smile.

And might Mary not then hold this girl in safer keeping than the world hence had done? Might they not set up a home together, alone, Fanny with her painting and clever seamstress fingers, and Mary able to find like employment perhaps, or perhaps even secure a teaching position? Might she not be permitted to then love Fanny as she truly wished, wholly and without censure or rejection, to feel that small, flushed hand clasped tight within her own, until their breaths jointly expired?

Instead of this. A fractured and disparate decade, so small a span, passed in such grievous haste.

"What will you do now?" the Grey Lady asked.

Mary wiped tears from her face. "Once matters here are settled, I expect I shall return to Newington Green—though I fear my sisters will have sorely neglected our little school in my absence. Everina does well enough if someone is nearby to drive her along, but Eliza...Eliza is a helpless thing."

"Your own contribution to her state is not insignificant."

Mary stiffened. "My *contribution* was to remove a near-deranged young mother from her *oblivious* husband lest she commit some dreadful harm to her own person. She did not wish to remain with him; you heard her speak it on several occasions."

"She might not have wished to leave her infant daughter behind."

"Do not scold me for that in which I was given no choice. If children were not deemed to be the property of husbands, how many more wives might seek to escape their arduous marriages?"

The Grey Lady tilted her chin. "I apologise. This is not the time to remonstrate on such subjects."

"I could not know the baby would die. It was always my hope to reunite them once my sister was well."

"That is true, but it provides no comfort to Eliza."

Mary pulled the lock of Fanny's hair even tighter around her finger until the tip darkened and swelled. To attend so frequently upon illness and death might be thought to numb a person utterly, but Mary had been left in a state of raw sensitivity. It was she who had nursed her abject, querulous mother throughout the months of her final lingering disease, changing dressings that did little more than hide the seeping necrotic flesh beneath, all the while managing her father's ill-tempered impatience. It was upon her shoulders that care for poor, distraught Eliza had fallen—care and responsibility and blame for executing the only plan she thought viable, the sole desperate avenue of escape at their disposal.

And now Fanny, dearest Fanny, and her tiny newborn son.

Mary was exhausted, in her body and in her heart. "I cannot continue. Not without her."

"And yet you will," the Grey Lady said. "As you always have."

*　*　*

"Has it grown dark?" the woman in the bed asks. "I cannot see you."

"I am here, Mary," the Grey Lady says. Her tone is smooth as velvet curtains.

Deeper, more strained voices entreat from the wings, but the woman in the bed pushes them aside. She will no longer be corralled by the demands of men.

"I am here," the Grey Lady repeats.

*　*　*

When she'd set off for St. Paul's to see her publisher that evening, Mary Wollstonecraft's mood had been one of anxious despondency. As much as the decision grieved her, she would need to abandon her rebuttal of Edmund Burke's recent attack on the French Revolution, on the principles and passionate character of a people determined to dismantle a pernicious monarchy. Who was she to tackle so protracted and presumptuous a project, one so removed from her usual territory of pedagogy, fiction, and the criticism, however barbed and insightful, that she regularly contributed to the *Analytical Review*?

Joseph Johnson had been encouraging of the proposed pamphlet certainly, and she was painfully aware that he'd already had her first pages printed in anticipation of their completion, but her mind now floundered within its own argument. Clamorous ideas buzzed and batted within the confines of her skull, refusing to be pinned to the page: feckless parents, irresponsible aristocrats, and spoiled eldest sons—her own brother, Ned, came readily to mind—who inherited familial wealth yet neglected to care for poverty-struck sisters; the inherent privilege entrenched in class and gender that bred selfishness and injustice within men, and forced desperate women into marriages little better than legal forms of prostitution; the dire need for social and economic reform, rather than dependence upon charity, which did merely gratify wealthy sensitives seeking to congratulate themselves on their benevolence while continuing to indulge in the vices of inequity.

So vast a problem, so much of which to speak, and—most insistent among her thoughts—who was Mary Wollstonecraft, former governess, sometime author and literary critic, to write *A Vindication of the Rights of Men*?

Now, as she mounted the steps to her George Street home, Mary did so with clenched teeth and renewed vigour. Her hands shook as she peeled away her gloves and hung her beaver-fur hat on its stand. She was not at all surprised to find a familiar figure waiting in her study.

"You are returned early," the Grey Lady remarked as Mary seated herself at her desk. "I thought you might have stayed for dinner."

"I find myself quite without appetite for food."

"Did Mr. Johnson take your decision well?"

"Mr. Johnson said that I should not struggle against my feelings. That I should indeed lay aside the work if that would better my happiness. That he would destroy all that had already been written and printed, and do so cheerfully." Mary snorted. "*Cheerfully* was the precise word he used. For such a *mutilation*."

The Grey Lady smiled. "All is well then, and you may continue with your other work. A review of that play you attended with *Henry Fuseli*, perhaps?"

At the mention of the name, Mary felt her stomach flutter. She released a deep breath and steeled herself. No matter how great their genius, no matter how seductive their whispers, certain Swiss artists could be given no place in her heart this night, nor for many nights to come.

"I will put nothing aside," Mary said. "Effusions of the moment these pages might be, but the moment is of no small import." Unhappy with its banishment, Fuseli's visage flitted across her mind. Undaunted, she flicked it away. "Tell me, why should genuine *passion* be so well regarded when it flows from the paintbrush of a man, but not from the pen of a woman?"

"It is the way of things," the Grey Lady said. "As those with means and power govern those without, that which is male governs all that is female."

"It need not be so," Mary countered. "France shines hope upon us, no matter the worn and tired *nostalgia* that Burke and his ilk parade as vaunted tradition. We should yet see a progressive society built upon talent and ambition, rather than unearned privilege. Why should it be our continued duty to repair an ancient castle, built in barbarous ages, of Gothic materials?"

"Do you say, we should allow such edifices to crumble?"

"I say..." Mary paused. Her eyes narrowed dangerously. "We should bring them to rubble ourselves."

The Grey Lady clasped gloved hands together at her waist. "I would very much like to see such a world as you describe."

Mary picked up her pen and found the place among her papers where her thoughts had stumbled and trailed off earlier in the day. Frowning, she crossed out a line or two. Then she cleared her throat, dipped nib into ink and began anew, words flying from her as furious wasps provoked from their nest.

* * *

She was called a *hyena in petticoats*, a *philisophising serpent*. She was accused of lacking reason, of seeking to poison and inflame the minds of the lower classes, of being too shallow a thinker.

Those at the *Gentleman's Magazine* confessed themselves astonished that a *fair lady* might seek to assert the *rights of men*, remarking that they were always taught to suppose that *the rights of women were the proper theme of the female sex*.

By *rights*, they did not refer to those of education or self-determination.

While Romans governed the world, they pointed out, *the women governed the Romans*. The age of chivalry having thankfully not yet passed, women should content themselves with ruling from the boudoir—though it remained questionable that such a viper as Mary Wollstonecraft might gain for herself so coveted a position.

The rights of women, indeed! Oh ho, what fertile ground for sarcasm and jest!

***

Lips moving silently as she walked, Mary Wollstonecraft rehearsed the words she would soon say to Sophia Fuseli, sounding them for depth and clarity. Hers was an inarguably practical solution, a proposal that would surely suit all parties, and a *rational* one at that. Despite her many impassioned letters to the man, Mary suspected a recent cooling of Henry's sensibilities and she required the situation between them to be resolved. Her mind would otherwise remain fragmented, her thoughts unmarshalled.

The printing of a second edition of *A Vindication of the Rights of Woman* had allowed Mary not only to correct some glaring errors of grammar and spelling, but to bolster arguments she feared too weak in the version Johnson had rushed to press this January—yet again! the Devil coming for the conclusion of a sheet before it was written!— but still she was unhappy. Although gratified by the book's reception—more welcoming than her previous *Rights of Man* had enjoyed—a second volume remained to be written, her ideas expanded beyond the core theme of female education. If women were ever to be the equal of men, they would need to be treated thus, with responsibilities greater than coquetry, manners, and marriage placed upon their dainty shoulders.

Why should they not aspire to autonomy? To their proper place within governance, commerce, and the intellectual life of their society? A woman who had not power over her own self would remain forever a slave, and surely no true progressive argument could seek to deny universal rights to one half of the population...

Residual anger warming her cheeks, Mary paused to compose herself; she could not arrive in such a visible state of consternation.

Sophia Fuseli was already seated by the window when Mary was admitted into the modest but charmingly appointed parlour.

"Miss Wollstonecraft." The younger woman scarcely smiled as

she gestured towards a chair opposite. Her pretty face, those model features her husband so adored, remained stiff and unyielding. "May I offer you tea?"

Mary accepted both seat and beverage, though she perched nervously upon the edge of one and took little more than a sip of the other. Less than a quarter of an hour later, it was Sophia Fuseli whose complexion reddened and flushed. Her cup trembled on its saucer as she reached to place them on the table.

"You insult both my husband and his wife, Miss Wollstonecraft." The woman's tone was chilled, crisp as frosted glass. "And you make yourself a fool."

"You misunderstand me," Mary said. "I do not wish to share Henry with you in the manner of wife—"

"Kindly take your leave, *Miss* Wollstonecraft."

But how could she, when Sophia was clearly confused as to her intentions—for why else would the woman take such prompt and livid offence? "Please, I do not mean to insult your marriage. My proposal arises solely from the sincere affection which I have for Henry, I can assure you. We have an *intellectual* affinity, he and I, and I plainly find that I cannot live without the satisfaction of seeing and conversing with him daily."

"You shall have to find a means of living so."

"But if we all inhabited the same household—"

"Will you not quiet your tongue?"

"Consider the practicalities, Mrs. Fuseli, if nothing else. We are none of us people of great means; to combine resources and share expenses within one household—"

"*Miss Wollstonecraft!*" Sophia Fuseli rose up in one violent motion. She thrust a finger at Mary, who struggled to gain her feet as readily. "You shall leave my house this moment and never again *stain* its rooms—or my husband's studio—with your presence. You are no woman of principle, to speak so boldly of your rights and yet seek to trample roughshod over mine. You are no *woman* at all, but a monster."

Escorted to the street by the Fuselis' housekeeper, Mary stumbled but a dozen steps before stopping to brace herself against a wall. Around her, London bustled through its afternoon. Pedestrians passed oblivious to her humiliation as the clatter of hooves on cobblestones, the wooden groan of coaches, assaulted her ears. Her heart was an empty, gnawing thing within her. She had lost Henry.

She had lost Henry.

Her scalp prickled with sudden regard. Blinking away tears, Mary looked about her. On the opposite side of the street, still and perfectly unjostled by the milling foot traffic, stood a tall woman wearing a hat dressed with ostrich feathers. The woman's face was stern, reproving, and even at this distance, Mary could glimpse the disappointment in those steely eyes.

Well? Though she but mouthed them, the Grey Lady's words pealed loud as funeral bells in Mary's mind. *Did I not warn you, Mary Wollstonecraft? Did I not say?*

* * *

If her heart was a cage, she was unduly careless of its latch.

Fleeing the whispers and sneers of London, she sought refuge in Paris scant weeks before the execution of the king, and so became witness not to her beloved revolution but to the bloody terror that would claim it. Helpless to do naught but write, she took up her pen with fervour, heedless of the danger in her very English observations. In her politics, in her words, Mary Wollstonecraft was fearless.

But her heart *was* a cage, and its door remained open long after Fuseli had slipped featherless from its hold. Open, inviting another who alighted upon the flimsy bars and sang of love and desire and the untasted delight of sweat-salted skin. Another who skipped inside to settle for a while, or at least to give appearance of settling, his brash American plumage so bright and strange that Mary found *herself* wholly captivated—in her mind and soul and finally, wondrously, in her body.

* * *

"She is exquisite, is she not?" Mary Imlay, as she now styled herself, held her newborn daughter against her breast. "Ten perfect fingers in miniature, and look! Eyes the very shade of my darling Gilbert's. Surely now that our Fanny is here, he will stay in Le Havre with us. Whoever could resist such eyes as these?"

"She is indeed a most agreeable child," the Grey Lady said.

Frowning, the new mother glanced up. "You mock me?"

"I have never mocked you, Mary Wollstonecraft. But I do worry."

Such concern was not misplaced.

Barely three months of shared parenthood were hers to enjoy

that summer before Gilbert Imlay, her once-soulful lover, now less-than-official husband chafing under harness, left for London on matters of business similar to those that had dragged him away during her pregnancy. As before, he promised to send for her when matters were settled. As before, months slid past with no firmer word on when that might occur.

Her treatise on the French Revolution completed prior to Fanny's birth, Mary was without a literary project with which to occupy herself. Instead, her word-churned mind bloated and burst itself over a near constant production of correspondence to Imlay—longing, scornful, desirous, admonishing letters that scarce received a satisfactory reply. Bodily, she devoted herself to Fanny, nursing the baby through smallpox, encouraging her efforts first to crawl and then to stand, rubbing her gums with chamomile as the first tooth began to cut.

"She will need to be weaned," Mary said, wincing as the child mauled a nipple between her newly armed gums.

"She is not the only one," the Grey Lady remarked.

Abandoned and friendless in the port city of Le Havre, Mary bundled up her daughter and returned to Paris. With Robespierre fallen, the streets were at last clean of the bloody work of the guillotine, but that winter proved the harshest of her thirty-six years. It was a winter of poor harvests and famine-priced food, a winter of unobtainable coal and wood cut laboriously by her own chapped hands, a winter of despair and burgeoning suspicion.

Imlay, came the whispers from foe and well-meaning friend alike, never intended to send for her or Fanny. Instead, he frittered his money away on the company of pretty London actresses.

On one pretty London actress in particular.

She tried to not heed them, but the words sank into her marrow.

Mary's latchless heart was ill. Her soul was weary. The impish, smiling face of her daughter undid her daily; she loved the child more than she would have once thought possible, and yet those soft and vivacious features bore so solid a stamp of Imlay upon them, it was sometimes nearer cruelty than kindness to behold them.

At night, alone with the darkness and a silence that no sound save Fanny's fluttering breath could penetrate, Mary's thoughts thickened and set. She pitied the poor mite for being born a girl into a world run by men for their own ends, and wondered what earthly good she was showing herself to be as a mother. Certainly no better a mother than wife, or sister, or any kind of *woman* at all, and now that the child was no longer in need of her milk—

"I am nothing," Mary whispered to the empty air.

She required, and received, no reply.

* * *

Finally, there came a summons to London, though she set off with little more than resignation in her breast. This was for Fanny, who deserved more from a father than the pauper-gift of his name, and it was for Fanny too that Marguerite accompanied them. The efficient new maid seemed as excited to see England as Mary had once been to visit France.

Mary's gelid, smoke-grey thoughts trailed them all.

They were settled at Charlotte Street, the lodgings comfortably furnished with all but Imlay himself, who vacillated between affection and apology, but remained acutely stubborn in his refusal to adopt the role of *Paterfamilias*. A refusal of which, it seemed, all of London was jovially aware.

The laudanum, she later insisted, was an error of judgement.

She had not intended—

Certainly not—

She had once been Mary Wollstonecraft.

Movement was the key, as it always had been. If she remained still, in her body or in her mind, thick-thumbed gloom would smother her alive.

And so, to the astonishment of many, she agreed to Imlay's proposal of a Scandinavian journey—some long-outstanding business she might follow up on his behalf, a traitorous ship captain to track down in Sweden, a purloined cargo of silver and gold to pursue in foreign courts—with the insinuation that their personal situation might be further resolved over the months of her—and Fanny's—absence. Having sighted once more the woman who had so inflamed his passions in Paris, having held again the child those passions had born, might it not be that Imlay merely required time and space in which to unfetter himself from present entanglements?

At this barest hint of oil, Mary's heart flung open with a shriek.

* * *

It was dim inside the carriage, and her clothing was wet and stinking of the Thames. She stared at her trembling hands, at fingernails still tinged corpse-blue, as though they alone had managed to resist the pull of the wakeful world.

"You are a foolish, obstinate woman, Mary Wollstonecraft." The Grey Lady sat opposite, arms crossed over her breast, mouth drawn pencil-thin.

"Mary *Imlay*," she corrected, as she had done countless times this past year. Her throat rasped with the sting of a thousand wasps; she would never forget the unexpected agony of drowning, the furious burn of all that water rushing to fill her. If she had been foolish, it was only in her expectation that such an end might be painless.

The Grey Lady snorted. "You have never been Mrs. *Imlay*, in truth, and pray never shall be."

"He is resolved that another might take that name."

"You knew this."

"Until yesterday, I only suspected."

"You *knew*, Mary, let us not pretend otherwise."

Mary shook her head. All those letters sent speeding back through Denmark, Norway, Sweden, all those notes received in turn from his deceitful hand, all those hints and promises that she and Fanny might still have a place by his side—only to return to find him setting up house with his *actress*. With the whole of London witness to her humiliation, to Imlay's callous desertion, she had seen no other way to extricate herself or her daughter from the wretchedness into which they had been plunged.

"It was you who saved me," Mary said.

"I breathed upon a fisherman's nape," the Grey Lady replied. "Encouraged him to turn towards Putney Bridge at the moment of your leaping; that was the furthest of my ability. It was he, and those in the tavern, who effected your resuscitation."

"You would play my guardian angel then?"

"I am no angel, Mary. Must we tread this patch anew?"

"A monster then, to see me dragged back to life and misery."

"To life, yes, and to your child."

Tears coursed down her cheeks but Mary made no move to wipe at them. "I had—I had made provisions for Fanny. She was to return to France, to be raised safe from the taint of her mother's errors, beyond the scorn of those who would damn her for her parents' degradation."

"This performance is wasted," the Grey Lady snapped. "You are no martyr to wail in sackcloth and ashes."

"You cannot know what I endure! What I have endured these past months—"

"But I do. Each passion, each *degradation*, that has e'er passed through you, I have felt most keenly. I know you, Mary Wollstonecraft. I know that you suffer, I know that your suffering is genuine—but, oh, how you delight in *feeding* it."

"Do not presume to tell me—"

"I shall do more than *presume* and, for once, you shall do naught but listen." The Grey Lady leaned forward; her eyes were flat metal discs in their shadowed sockets. "You make of people what *you* would have them be—such superior beings! so worthy of your heart!—and then you mourn their failings, when you are not blinding yourself to them. Imlay, Fuseli, even Fanny Blood—yes, Fanny; do not appear so shocked—they are more vital to you in their absence, for their presence can never approach the chimeras you have fashioned in their stead."

"You take Gilbert's side in this?" Beneath her despair, a renewed anger simmered.

"Never." The Grey Lady's voice was softer now, its barbs for the moment withdrawn. "I will always stand with you, but I will not tip soothing lies into your ear, nor will I aid this melancholy. You are stronger than you imagine, Mary, and I would have you see *yourself* through clear, unclouded eyes."

Shivering, Mary rubbed her cheeks. Rain pattered on the carriage roof and she found herself wishing the journey would never reach its end. For all her intellectual accomplishments, her much-prized rationality, she was terrified. Alone and abandoned she had been on several occasions, and penniless too, but never in so dire a situation as this. Never with a child—a *girl* child—for whom to care and somehow shield from the world's most outrageous fortunes.

"Oh!" she cried, as her daughter's round and rosy face flashed into her mind. "My little Fanny, I would have left you to them. How could I have thought..."

"Your thoughts were elsewhere," the Grey Lady said. "They have been elsewhere for too long now, and it is past time you collected them." She sniffed the air, her nose wrinkling in displeasure. "Spoiled yeast and calla lilies and desperation, still."

"I can smell only mud and sewage."

The Grey Lady chuckled. "That too, of course."

"My heart beats, yet this feels a living death."

"While it seems so, I will not leave you."

Mary pressed her face to the window. "It is dark outside."

"It is October; the days grow short."

"It is so very dark." For the barest of breaths, Mary imagined she could feel the squeeze of gloved hands about her wrists. She closed her eyes. "I am frightened."

"Know that I am here," the Grey Lady said. "And cling to this, if nothing else: you are *not* a fate-spun heroine from one of those Gothic romances you so despise."

This time she was certain that she felt it, the touch of flocked velvet soft as infant skin against her bare, chilled flesh. The impossible pressure of those thin and gentle fingers.

"You are Mary Wollstonecraft, and you will die for no *man*."

* * *

Even in darkness, words glimmered and beckoned, drawing her outwards. First, the mixed blessing of her journals, notes for the travelogue that Joseph Johnson had commissioned upon learning of her Scandinavian endeavour. She wrought from them an epistolary elevated by personal circumstance: a woman journeying alone with an infant; a woman caught in the process of betrayal and abandonment; a woman traversing the masculine spheres of commerce, politics, creativity, and philosophy —and crafting such clever, such *candid* dispatches.

Behold: Mary Wollstonecraft, Traveller-Philosopher!

Her mind flexed, and lightened.

Invigorated, finding solid footing once more among the literary circles of London, she conceived a fresh project by which she rapidly became consumed. *Maria*, the novel would be titled, or *The Wrongs of Woman*, and from the first she was resolved on a slow and calculated execution. The crafting of a truly *excellent* book was an arduous task, and this time Mary would not allow herself to be rushed. This time, she would reflect and revise and reconsider. This time, her words would ring with utter clarity.

Behold: Mary Wollstonecraft, Polemic Novelist!

Her heart, too, discovered a new fascination. Or perhaps rediscovered it.

Upon the occasion of their first meeting years before at one of Johnson's weekly dinners, Mary had found William Godwin irksome in his undiscerning admiration of supposedly eminent men. He had, in turn, thought her too outspoken in conversation, especially when he would have preferred to imbibe the opinions of others around the table. Other eminent *men*, an unspoken qualification she had perceived only too well.

Newly reacquainted within overlapping social circles, they found themselves drawn to one another with the inexorable, near imperceptible weight of planetary bodies whose orbits, previously misaligned, now moved in startling synchronicity. Mary's passions, never cooled, rekindled. William's, to his own astonishment, burned all the bolder for their hitherto untested state.

But non-planetary bodies, bodies of flesh and flagrant blood, follow their own particular, if not wholly predictable, paths and thus conceive *projects* of their own.

See William Godwin, famous for his very public repudiations of marriage as a moral institution.

See Mary "Imlay," already sensitive to gossip and the subject of much speculation.

Then imagine—oh imagine!—the fraught negotiation of these two proud and independent souls around the sudden expectation of a third. The small, private ceremony at St. Pancras. The quiet series of announcements to friends. The united front against those who shunned them, those who mocked and scorned and professed outrage, or merely snide amusement, at a marriage for which the catalyst would soon become roundly apparent.

Behold: Mary Wollstonecraft, Mother-To-Be, Redux.

* * *

The woman in the bed opens her eyes and tries to focus on the figures surrounding her. There is William, dear William, his tired face so pale, his eyes sunken. And the doctor, the good doctor, whose name she cannot for the moment recall. And, of course, the other.

"I did not finish," the woman in the bed croaks. "I thought there was time, at last, to be still."

William clutches her hand. "There is time, my love."

"There is no time," the Grey Lady says quietly.

No attention is paid to her by any soul present save the woman in the bed, who struggles now to sit up, who is restrained by the gentlest of palms placed against her panting sternum, who is entreated to rest, to save her words for when she is well. William's eyes are glossy with tears.

The woman in the bed stares past him. "My baby, who will teach her, who will protect her?"

"Hush." William brushes damp hair from her face. "There will be time to talk of such matters."

"There is no time," the Grey Lady repeats. "I will not lie to you, Mary."

"You must look to her," the woman in the bed pleads. "Look to her as you have me."

Hush, my love, do not worry yourself so needlessly.

"That is not my purpose," the Grey Lady says.

"Then *make* it your purpose. My daughter will not know her mother."

Carlisle? Carlisle, she is raving; see how her face contorts?

Mr. Godwin, I can do nothing further to help her.

The Grey Lady moves closer to the bed. A yellow wasp crawls down her sleeve and into the palm of her hand. "I am sorry, Mary. If it were in my power, I would ease all the suffering in the world, beginning with your own."

"It is dark," the woman in the bed whispers. "It is dark as the Thames."

Carlisle, fetch that lamp here. Mary, see? There is yet light.

I fear it will not be long, Mr. Godwin.

"I felt as one standing on a precipice," the woman in the bed says. "All the world bustled and buzzed below me and for once I need not race away. There would be time, the baby would come, and there would yet be time for all I wished to do." Her chapped lips crack around a smile. "I should be at my desk."

Mary, be still now. Hush.

"Do not leave me, I beg you."

Never, my love. I am here always.

"I will not leave you." The Grey Lady extends a hand. "But here, open your mouth."

Insect legs scratch and tickle as they crawl over her tongue. The woman in the bed presses the wasp against her palate, feels its barbed abdomen burst even as it sinks its sting into her flesh. Where she expected pain, there is instead a spreading languid heat and the taste of molasses on fresh-baked bread.

"It is all I can do," the Grey Lady says.

It is enough.

***

Do not suppose this to be her ending.

It is a play truncated in its second act, a journey derailed before its terminus, a cloth cut short by miser's blades; you cannot decipher the whole pattern from but a fragment in your hand.

She would not have remained still. She *could not* have remained still.

There would have been more words. There would always have been more words.

Her story cannot be shaped to a convenient arc, to a neat and satisfactory conclusion.

This is not her ending; it is merely where she left off.

***

It is not her purpose and yet the Grey Lady comes regardless, propelled by curiosity perhaps, or perhaps by some deeper compulsion. The baby is sleeping in a simple wooden crib which once rocked the Reveleys' own children to slumber, now retrieved from storage and pressed into tragic and unexpected service. Nearby, little Fanny plays mother to a favourite doll, fussing with its hair and dress and planting noisy kisses upon its porcelain cheeks. The child does not notice the Grey Lady's arrival in the room, just as she has never noticed her myriad comings and goings. That is as it should be.

The Grey Lady approaches the crib, drops to one knee beside it. "Let me look at you then." Her eyes scan the infant's chubby features, hoping to discern some familiarity in the shade of the nose, in the turn of the mouth, but her efforts are ill-rewarded. Babies are, after all, babies. In time, there might be something of the mother in this one, or the father, but that time will not be the Grey Lady's to witness.

She sighs. "Good life to you, child, and to your sister."

The baby opens her eyes. Dark brown as her mother's were, and curious, they fix themselves upon the Grey Lady's face. Those eyes *see* her.

"Oh my," she whispers. Leaning forward, her nose inches from the newly fascinating creature in the crib, she takes a delicate sniff. Oh my, indeed. "Mary Godwin..." The Grey Lady frowns; the name feels unfinished on her tongue. "Mary *Wollstonecraft* Godwin, or however you shall be someday known, you smell of thunderstorms and secret truths and...and *monsters*?"

The baby makes a soft, gurgling sound. Tiny fingers flex.

"Oh, my dear girl," the Grey Lady tells her. "I shall be keeping a very close watch on *you.*"

ACCIDENTS HAPPEN

SHE'S NOT MY type at all. Short, a bit on the chubby side, shoulder-length curly hair the colour of mud. On Tinder I would've swiped left without hesitation. But she isn't on Tinder, she's on the footpath in front of me, one hand clutching two shopping bags and the other holding a phone to her ear. Her voice is pitched low and quiet, which makes a change from the usual raucous falsetto most women deploy these days. Don't they realise they're actually painful to listen to? That's not even sexist; that's a scientific fact.

It's her skirt that caught my attention. One of those jarring, multi-coloured numbers that fat chicks wear because they think it makes them look quirky and fun, like they have personality to spare along with everything else. On her, the skirt is so long it brushes the ground and every so often she catches the hem beneath one of her sandals. Under all that fabric her arse wobbles like piglets in a pillowcase.

How funny would it be if she stepped on it for real? Stomped on it good and proper and pulled the whole ugly thing down around her ankles right there on the street. Hilarious, is what it would be, and now I'm wishing for exactly that. Tracking her steps, the bounce and flow of the skirt, willing each foot to slow, to pause, just enough to—

Holy fuck, she's down.

I'm so surprised, I don't even react at first. Just stand there like a knob, staring at the groceries that have scattered across the sidewalk and at her arse, now free and pointing skyward, the offending skirt bunched at her knees. Her panties, I can't help but notice, are pink with red polka dots. Her thighs are pale with lots of cellulite.

Not the most attractive combination.

She starts to push herself upright and I hurry forward. "Here, let me help."

She lets out a small cry, similar to the noise she made when she fell, and I realise she hadn't known I was there. I smile, apologise for startling her. My hand is still out and finally she takes hold of it, allows me to pull her to her feet.

"Oh god," she says, yanking her skirt into place. "How embarrassing."

"Could've happened to anyone." I'm already gathering groceries, putting mandarins and cans of tuna back into the plastic bag they rolled from. She picks up the pieces of her phone, tries to put the battery back in with shaking hands. "Let me," I say, passing her the bag. The phone is easy to reassemble and bleats happily to life when I press the on button. Her face lights up almost as brightly as the LED screen.

"Thank you so much." The palms of her hands are scraped from landing on the concrete; her knees probably are as well. I feel bad, though I don't understand why. It's not as if I actually made her trip over. "I'm Annie," she says. She has big eyes, the same muddy brown as her hair, and her cheeks are wet. "So stupid, and now look at me. Crying like a baby."

"It's just the shock," I tell her. "My name's Nate."

She wipes at her face. "Thanks again, Nate. Not everyone would've stopped."

When she smiles, Annie is quite pretty, in an anxious-to-please kind of way. Her cheeks have dimples and one of her front teeth is slightly crooked. I wonder if it makes her self-conscious. "I'm going to give you my number." I thumb through to her contacts—she doesn't have password protection; of course she doesn't—and type in my digits before giving her back the phone. "Text me when you get home, so I know you're okay." I throw in a good-natured wink.

Later that afternoon, Annie does exactly that. The message, scattered with half a dozen different emojis in varying levels of excitement, is accompanied by a photo of her torn and bloodied knee. *Ouch!* she's printed across it in bold red letters.

I text her back a sad face. And a first-aid sign. And a kitten, because it strikes me as something she would like and there's no harm in keeping her keen. I don't suggest we catch up for coffee sometime, not yet. Maybe not ever—she isn't my type after all. Still, the memory lingers for the rest of the day. The look on her face when I helped her up was so open, so grateful, that I keep circling back to it.

I didn't make her trip, I know that. And yet I can't shake it, the sensation I could almost swear I felt the moment her foot dragged on the skirt: a shift inside my head, a release of pressure, a subtle exertion of will.

Stupid. Impossible. Delusional. All those things.

Even so, I add Annie to my contacts list. File her under Possible. Sub-file, Desperate Measures.

She really isn't my type.

* * *

After more than two months of drip-feeding with time-delayed texts and excuses about late working hours, Annie's still happy to meet up for a drink. The place is one of my regular haunts, dim-lit and well-populated, and I know one of the regular bartenders. Stu, decent bloke, used to play AFL before a second knee reconstruction sidelined him for good. He's always up for a chat about balls or babes, but tonight I'm keeping to myself in the shadows down the back corner near the loos.

Normally, I make a point of turning up late to these things, but I want to be here when Annie arrives. I want to watch her walk in. I want to see how she acts when she doesn't know I'm watching. There must be something different about her.

Because, dumb as it might be, I've tried it with other women.

Tried to make them trip or bump into a post, even drop their bag or knock over a glass of water. Strangers on the street, a couple times while out on a date, even with Rachel at work. One of the women I took to dinner said she thought the way I kept staring at her was creepy. Off-putting. She asked me to stop it. I said we should split the bill, and deleted her from my contacts as soon as we left the restaurant.

Yeah, it's stupid. But I couldn't stop thinking about Annie. Those ludicrous polka-dotted panties. The damp-eyed gratitude when I passed back her phone.

And here she is. Scrubbed up surprisingly well in a short black dress that's cut low enough to show off an impressive amount of cleavage. Which means she's probably wearing one of those push-up bras; I don't remember her being that ample up top. She's done something with her hair too. It's still curly but not as frizzy, not as unkempt, and it's clipped away from her face at the sides. All in all, she looks nice. Not a bombshell or anything, but I likely wouldn't be so quick to swipe this woman by on Tinder.

As Annie looks around, I hunch back so she doesn't see me. Visibly disappointed, she goes over to the bar and speaks to Stu. He puts a glass in front of her, fills it with white wine. Chardonnay, I'm betting. Or pinot gris. Something pale and innocuous. She climbs awkwardly onto one of the high stools and takes a cautious sip. After a minute or two, she retrieves a compact from her bag to examine her makeup. Lipstick comes next, applied with care. Then another sip of wine, followed by a frown as she wipes the edge of the glass with her thumb. Wipes her thumb on a bar napkin. Slides the napkin surreptitiously to the floor.

Enough. There's nothing different, nothing special, about her.

Downing what's left of my whisky, I get to my feet.

It's not until I'm halfway around the bar that she notices me and, when she does, the anxiety falls from her face like a veil. She grins, all teeth and dark red lips, and gives me a little wave. Cute, like a schoolgirl. I smile and wave back. Mouth, *Hi.*

As she dismounts the stool, wineglass in hand, I try it. Just a nudge, a notion that she might catch her heel on the metal rung and—

Annie lurches into the guy sitting next to her. Wine spills all over the shoulder of his sleek grey suit, runs down his arm and flies off in droplets as he spins around, jerks to his feet. *What the fuck*, I hear him say, and then I'm by her side.

"Chill, mate. It was an accident." I smile, not all that nicely, and position myself almost between him and Annie, who's grabbing napkins by the handful. When she reaches out, the guy pulls away with snarl.

"Drunk bitch, should watch where she's going."

"I'm not drunk," Annie says. "And I'm so sorry."

I drop the smile. "Hey, mate, no need for language like that. She didn't mean it."

"She gonna pay for the fucking dry-cleaning?"

"Of course, I will, I—"

I step right in front of her, right in front of him. "She's not gonna pay for anything, arsehole. But you're going to apologise for calling her a bitch." I stress the last word. Behind me, I imagine Annie is wincing. I try not to smirk. The guy is taller than me, broader too, but I can already see Stu marching over. He's bigger than the both of us combined.

"Friend, you need to step it down a notch," Stu says to the guy. His smile is wide but his gaze is solid. He doesn't blink once.

"What about her? Bitch threw her drink on me."

"The *lady* tripped. And she's apologised."

The guy is slapping wine from his suit jacket. "This is Dolce and fucking Gabbana. Fuck."

"Yeah, and this is the fucking Savoy. Might be time to zip it, *friend*."

Stu motions Annie and me over to an empty table by the window. Tells her he'll bring her another pinot, on the house. A quick nod lets me know there'll be a whisky joining it. Stu's a good bloke, an even better bartender. The suit guy glares at me one last time, still muttering beneath his breath. I'll keep an eye on him. Make sure he leaves well before we do, or else doesn't immediately follow. Losers like that can hold a grudge all night.

"You must think I'm a terrible klutz," Annie says once we're sitting down.

"Nah, I think you're an *adorable* klutz."

She might be blushing; it's hard to tell in this light. "I swear, I'm not usually that clumsy."

"Nice to know I have such a dramatic effect on you."

Her laugher is low and throaty. There's lipstick smudged on her teeth but I don't say anything. Let her notice later when she goes to the bathroom. We chat for a bit—her job as a childcare assistant, my work at an upscale marketing company; her plans to travel through South America, my business trips to Europe; her favourite movies, the last book I read—and then, without looking directly, I *nudge* Annie's hand as she reaches for her wine.

Her fingers falter and the glass teeters toward me—but of course I catch it before a single drop is spilled. Steady it with a smile.

Annie's definitely blushing now. "I can't believe I almost..."

"Hey there, no harm, no foul." I lay a hand over hers. "Let's get out of here. There's this gourmet grill place around the block. Best burgers you'll have in your life."

"You're not afraid I'll push you into traffic on the way there?"

I grin and tell her that it's a risk I'm prepared to take. Then, switching to serious, I lean in close. "It feels like we have something here, Annie, a connection. Unless that's just me..." With those last words, I let my gaze falter.

"No." She squeezes my hand. "I mean, yes. I mean, it's not just you."

And here it is again, that warm, wide-eyed gratitude that lights up her face like nothing I've ever seen. I could look at that face, right now, looking at me, for the rest of the night. I could look at it for the rest of my life.

***

I don't *control* Annie, not in any meaningful sense. I can't make her do things out of the blue, or stop her from doing things for that matter. If I could, she'd be at the gym five nights a week and there'd never be even a single tub of ice cream in her freezer. It's only the small stuff I can influence, actions that are already in motion.

Tripping is simple, as is getting her to drop things. Early on, I encouraged her fingers to loosen around a mug I'd mentioned was a favourite, passed down from my dead grandfather. In actual fact, it was just some piece of crap I'd picked up from a charity shop the week before, but her gaping horror amid the coffee and shards of cheap ceramic was priceless. I soothed her with assurances that it didn't really matter, that accidents happen, that *of course I wasn't mad.* But for weeks all I needed was to look a bit sad and wistful when she brought me coffee in another mug and there would be a fresh stab of guilt in her eyes.

Mostly, it's minor things like that. Stubbed toes, scraped knees, elbows knocked against door jambs as she passes. Once I nudged her into tripping as she went up the stairs to my apartment. Nothing I hadn't done a dozen times before, nothing that would usually have resulted in more than a few bruises and embarrassed tears, but this time she fell awkwardly on the edge of a step and we wound up in the emergency room waiting for an x-ray of her right wrist.

I don't like how the nurse looked at you, she whispered. *She thinks you hurt me.*

It doesn't matter, Annie. I'm just worried about you.

It does matter. She glared at the nurse, now busy behind the counter and not looking at anyone in particular. *I'm so sorry, Nate. You don't deserve that.*

As it turned out, the wrist was only sprained. A few workless days of splints, compression bandages, and ice baths that I was only too happy to prepare. *Keep it elevated, Annie. Here, let me get that for you. Another cup of tea, baby?* I'm glad it wasn't a fracture. Playing doctor was fun while it lasted, but two to three months in a plaster cast would have rubbed the gloss off, no matter how much reciprocal attention I was getting in the bedroom.

I'm more careful now. Mundane injuries and minor mortifications. No permanent damage.

The truth of it is that I like soothing her. I like making her feel better.

I like that I *can* make her feel better, that she looks to me for comfort. It's one of the greatest feelings in the world, being needed like that.

***

Her best friend, Jocelyn, doesn't like me. She thinks that I push Annie around, that I lay hands on her like some common bogan arsehole. I can see it in her narrow, flinty eyes. She definitely doesn't approve of her moving in with me. Annie knows it too, and I don't understand how she puts up with it, that kind of judgement from someone who's meant to care about her.

The dinner tonight's supposed to give Jocelyn a chance to get to know me properly and I'm determined to make a good impression. It's important to Annie that the two of us get along. It's important to me as well.

The problem is, Jocelyn's no dummy. She's never seen me hurt Annie in any direct way, of course, but inevitably I'm always right there when something happens. It's unavoidable. I have to be able to see Annie in order to influence her at just the right moment. And so: suspicion—which is nobody's friend, least of all mine.

Tonight, that changes.

It was Annie who gave me the idea. The childcare place where she works has this new thing where they've put in CCTV so all the anxious parents can log in from their phones or iPads or whatever and check on their precious bundles of joy any time they need a fix. Annie and the other women there hate it, being spied on, and I can't say I blame them. If my company decided to install cameras so our clients could make sure we were doing our jobs to their infinitesimal satisfaction, I'd be out of there quick as pissing.

But it did make me think, and while Jocelyn and Annie are busy chopping up vegetables, I excuse myself and retreat to the ensuite.

I haven't gone overboard. One camera in the kitchen light fitting, a second in the dining room, a third in the lounge, all connected on WiFi to a private account. I access the kitchen feed on my phone, momentarily wishing I'd installed audio as well. It'd be interesting to hear what Jocelyn says—in my own house—while I'm out of earshot. She's at the sink now, filling the kettle. Annie's still at the chopping board. She puts down the knife and scrapes a mountain of julienned carrots into a bowl. I wait until Jocelyn turns around, until Annie has the knife again and is cutting into a capsicum. Then—*nudge*—the blade shifts its angle, slices into Annie's thumb. I can hear her muffled cry, but only because I'm listening for it. She swivels about and—*nudge*—crashes straight into Jocelyn, who was rushing to her side, then ricochets away and—*nudge*—smacks her head on the edge of the corner pantry.

Soundless, in black and white, the whole episode reminds me of early slapstick comedy, and I bite my lip to stop from laughing.

I close the feed. Wait another thirty seconds before flushing the toilet.

By the time I get back to the kitchen, Jocelyn has a wet dishcloth pressed to Annie's brow and a wad of paper towels wrapped around her thumb.

"Baby! What happened?" I do a good line in *surprised* these days.

Annie's chin is trembling. "It's okay, Nate. I'm fine."

"She's not fine," Jocelyn says. "Do you have a first aid kit handy?"

The knife wound, we all decide, isn't deep enough to warrant surgical stitches. In any case, Annie refuses to *spoil the evening* with a trip to the emergency room, so I apply a liberal dose of antiseptic cream and close it up with Steristrips. The bump on her forehead isn't bleeding but I can already tell that it's going to colour up nicely. Jocelyn is concerned about concussion. Annie tells her not to worry, please. I finish cutting up the vegetables. When Annie tries to help, I shoo her away with a fresh glass of wine.

"I can toss a stir fry together, baby." I plant a kiss on the top of her head. "You sit down with Jocelyn and take a load off. Tonight, the kitchen is mine." I raise a spatula in mock flourish. Annie giggles. Jocelyn's smile is small and worried, but seems genuine at least. I tell her to open another bottle—the fifteen-year-old shiraz I've left on the dining table. It's a special night after all, our first dinner party in our newly shared home. My Annie deserves nothing but the best.

Later, Jocelyn brings out the cheesecake she's made for dessert. She cuts me an extra-large slice, all but drowned in cherry liqueur sauce. It's the most delicious apology I've ever been given. Annie squeezes my hand. Her eyes are bright with wine. The bump on her forehead shines in the light. I'm getting hard and wondering how long it will be before Jocelyn fucks off.

"My two favourite people in the world," Annie says. "I love you both to death."

* * *

It wasn't planned, she tells me, of course it wasn't, but all the same—
Annie is pregnant. Her faces flexes between happy and anxious; her
fingers wrestle each other into knots. She wants to know how I feel.
She wants to know if I'm okay. I pull her to me, run my hand through
her hair. I don't want her to see my face.

Of course I'm not fucking okay.

"Baby, this is *great* news. I'm just...it's such a surprise."

"You're sure it's what you want, Nate? I mean...we haven't talked
about it, not really, but I think you'd make a wonderful dad. I *know*
you would."

My finger catches on a knotted curl. It's all I can do not to yank it
viciously free. Instead, I reassure her that, yes, of course it's what I
want, that she'll make a wonderful mother, that the three of us will
make a wonderful family.

It will all be so fucking *wonderful.*

* * *

Trying to will Annie into a spontaneous miscarriage was about as
useful as praying for one, but for the first week or so I did it anyway. I
even fantasised about how it would be, her coming into our bedroom
with a pair of blood-soaked panties in her hand, the weight of her
body soft and pliant in my arms as I stroked her back and whispered
that everything would be all right, that it wasn't meant to be, that we
could try again one day. I could almost taste the salt in her tears as
she kissed me.

Only once did I nudge her into a fall.

Just a small stumble, and she caught herself with her hands long
before her belly hit the ground, but she was damn near inconsolable
anyway. She should quit her job early, she said, and maybe go stay
with her mother, or invite her mother to come stay with us. To help
out, so Annie didn't have to do as much, didn't have to take so many
risks, because if she lost the baby doing something stupid, oh god, she
would *die*, she would *kill* herself—

I held her and hushed her and together we looked through the
pregnancy manuals she'd been accumulating and *see*, I said, *women
play sports while they're pregnant, they do manual labour, they paint
nurseries while standing on top of ladders. You'll be fine. The baby will*

be fine. I placed a hand on her belly. *I'll take care of you both.*

All of this runs through my head now as I stare at the ultrasound monitor, Annie clutching my hand hard enough to be painful.

"You're sure?" she asks the nurse.

"Positive." The woman points to the grainy white nub on the left side of the screen. "That's exactly what it looks like, folks. You're going to have a boy."

We're going to have a boy. I'm going to have a *son*.

All at once, the world feels very real. It feels expansive, and dangerous.

***

Most of the books say you fall in love with your kid the second you lay eyes on him, or maybe the first time he looks at you—looks at you and really sees you. That's bullshit. I spent the first couple of months feeling cheated, watching Annie dote over our son with such obvious delight and devotion. Even when she was exhausted by the revolving roster of sleep-broken nights, even when her nipples cracked despite the paw-paw ointment rubbed into them after nursing, even when he pissed right in her mouth during a nappy change—her face shone with love.

Sometimes I was jealous. Sometimes I even wondered if it was my fault. All those times I'd wished him gone, never to be born... Did I even deserve him?

Then Dylan smiled at me.

Not one of those weird half-smiles that meant he had gas maybe, or more likely had just filled his nappy with something truly noxious, but a genuine eyes-high smile that hammered me right in the heart. My son *smiled* at me.

In that moment, I would have died for him. I would have killed for him. The current that surged through the core of me was that overpowering. My strong and beautiful boy. My son. I will go to the ends of the earth for him. I will do anything.

I'm still jealous of Annie. Not because of the love she feels, but the days she gets to spend with Dylan. I've reduced my hours at work and we're talking about her going back full-time once the maternity leave is over. It's not what we planned, but I want my fair share of time with the boy. I want him to love me, to *need* me, as much as he does her.

Every so often, I give Annie a nudge but it feels half-hearted, like I'm simply going through the motions. She doesn't always turn to me for comfort either. Mostly just picks herself up with a rueful smile and goes back to whatever she was doing. It's irritating, but only in principle. She hasn't lost any of her baby weight and these days I don't get off as much on soothing her.

And one smile from my son leaves anything Annie offers going cold on the table.

* * *

Fuck. *Fuck.* My hands are still shaking too much to drive. Witness statement, I keep telling myself. That's all it was, a *witness* statement, and even the cop who took it looked like he had better things to do so I'm sure I'm okay. At least as far as that goes.

But I can't get the image out of my head.

Pale blonde hair matted with blood. A viscous red pool of the stuff leaking from her body into the gutter, ridiculously bright in the midday sun. One side of her face stove in where it struck the courier van. Legs bent in a pose no living woman could have held, and those shoes, those spindly fucking shoes, still on her feet.

Why the hell do they wear heels that high if they can't fucking walk in them?

One tiny nudge, more out of habit than anything—though I swear she was already teetering; that's why I thought of it—and down she goes, right into fucking traffic. Now that poor fucking driver has to live with this shit for the rest of his life, and me as well. Fucking stupid bitch and her fucking stupid shoes. If she hadn't been—

I was right behind her, I told the cops. It happened so fast. I couldn't—

Fuck. *Fuck.*

It's hot in the car. I switch the air-con to high. It's not like I meant it, not like I expected anything to happen at all. Since Annie, I've been trying it on from time to time. Just in case. Not with every woman, only the ones that catch my eye for some reason. Like the blonde today, tottering about on stripper heels like she's gonna fall on her arse any moment, and wouldn't it be funny if she did. That's all I thought. *That's all.* One small nudge. Just in case.

It's never worked with anyone else, not since Annie. Until today—

Bile bites at the back of my throat. I swallow it back down with a laugh that tastes just as bitter. From behind, the blonde had looked damn hot. Might've been a second chance for me, but now...such a waste. I rub at my eyes. I don't know where the tears are coming from.

Those fucking stupid shoes.

It's on the news later—she was a mother of two, it turns out—and I start to cry again. I don't even notice until Annie squeezes my arm and asks what's wrong. I tell her that I was there, that I was a witness, that the police took my statement but probably wouldn't be in touch. It was an accident, the news says. A tragic accident. They show a photo of the blonde with her husband and twin girls who, the news says, just celebrated their second birthday.

She really was beautiful.

"Those poor kids," Annie says. "Losing their mum at such a young age, I can't imagine."

I think about Dylan, only a few months younger. I think about Annie, falling on the stairs that time. How another few inches either way might have meant the difference between *sprained wrist* and *tragic accident*. I wouldn't do that to him. Not my son.

"You know, it's kind of like how we met," Annie is saying. She snuggles closer to me on the couch. "How creepy is that?"

The news has moved on already, some ongoing conflict in some sand-poor country on the other side of the earth, and I want to move on with it. Annie wipes at my cheeks with her cardigan sleeve. I could break her wrist for that. Instead, I ask if she can fix me a coffee. I'm tired, I tell her. I'll probably go to bed early, after I check in on Dylan. "Make it strong," I shout, as she waddles from the room. "And don't put too much milk in."

She always puts too much milk in.

***

Dylan loves his toddler train set. *More crash, Da-da!* I build the tracks in a figure eight with two opposing hills and balance a locomotive trailing several carriages on the crest of each one. If we release them at precisely the right moment, they meet at the intersection to explode in a cacophony of plastic parts. Dylan giggles joyously. Demands the spectacle again and again.

"More crash, Da-da!"

Usually, I'm happy to oblige, but there's been a headache pulsing behind my right eye all morning and after a couple of rounds I tell him that the trains are tired today and need a rest. I ask if he can help Da-da put them away in their tub but he crosses his arms over his chest and pouts. Then he kicks the purple engine lying closest to his foot. Its smiling face doesn't waver.

"That's not very nice, Dylan."

I finish packing up the set on my own and get to my feet. I'm going to put the tub away, I tell him, and then we're all going to have a nap. The trains and him and me. We're all tired today and need some more sleep. Ignoring his grizzling, I pick up the tub and—

—watch as it slips from my hands and crashes to the floor. Trains and bits of track scatter every which way. Dylan bursts into laughter, points a chubby finger at me. "Da-da made a mess."

For a moment, I just stand there looking at my hands. I had the damn thing by the handles; how could I have just dropped it like that? I'm tired, I know I'm tired, but come on. I look at my still-giggling son, watch as he picks up two bits of train and starts bashing them together. *Crash-crash*, he sing-songs. *Crash-crash, crash-crash, crash-crash.*

"Stop that!" I snatch the toys away, throw them back into the tub. My head pounds.

Dylan's mouth starts to tremble. His forehead furrows.

"Oh, hey, little man." I crouch down, pull him into a hug. "Da-da's sorry. He didn't mean to yell." He sniffles a bit but doesn't really cry. I ruffle his hair, tell him that he's my brave little man, and together we gather up the train set and put it back in the tub.

When Dylan says he wants to nap with me in my bed instead of his own, I let him. But I can't doze off. Instead I lie there in the semi-dark with the curtains drawn, remembering how the toy tub slipped through my fingers. And thinking about the expression on my son's face, half-delighted, half-surprised, as if he'd just seen magic happen.

* * *

He nudges me. I'm certain of it. Not often, and nothing that isn't relatively harmless...at least for now. I've walked into the door jamb on my way out of his bedroom after refusing to read him *Jack and the Beanstalk* for the third time that night. I've dropped his lunch while carrying it to the table—a ham and tomato sandwich instead of the bowl of chocolate ice cream he'd been demanding. And I've dumped the bloody train tub onto the floor two more times. It would have been a third but I was ready. Felt my fingers start to loosen and tightened my grip on the handles.

I swear, Dylan looked thwarted.

Then, last night, I fell into the bathtub. One second I was sitting on the edge, trying to convince Dylan to let me put shampoo into his hair—it was new, I told him, it wouldn't sting his eyes—and the next I was in the water, elbow smarting like hell where it hit the side on the way down. My son hooted with glee. *Da-da all wet!* His little hands splashed around like flippers. *Da-da is hurt*, I snapped. *That's not nice, Dylan.* His eyes widened and glossed. I grabbed a towel and dragged him out of the bath, rubbing him dry with a brusqueness I now regret. When he started to cry, I ignored him. I regret that too. He's my son, my boy. I love him more than anything.

Annie just laughed when I told her what happened, saying she didn't realise clumsiness was contagious. *Ha ha*, I replied. *Very fucking funny.*

There's a huge bruise on my elbow and it hurts to bend.

I love my son more than anything.

But I'm his father, and it's my job to teach him his lessons.

* * *

The problem with little kids is that their brains can't process subtleties. What Dylan does understand is being sad and being hurt and being angry. He can't keep playing tricks on Da-da, I tell him. It hurts Da-da, it makes him sad and sometimes it makes him angry. Dylan doesn't want his Da-da to be sad, does he? Or angry?

My son shakes his head. He looks pretty sad himself right now. "No more tricks."

"No more tricks, Dylan. Da-da doesn't like tricks."

"Does Mummy like tricks?"

I stare at him. He looks worried, but also hopeful.

"Dylan, do you play tricks on Mummy too?"

Slowly, he nods his head. My son, my strong little boy. So much stronger than I am, it seems, or at least with greater range. I smile what I hope is an encouraging smile. Tell him that, of course, Mummy likes tricks. He should keep playing tricks on her. And maybe one day he might find other people he can play tricks on as well, little girls maybe, like at play group. Little girls usually like tricks being played on them; it shows you like them. But he should tell me first so I can say if it's okay. He should *always* tell me first.

Dylan nods again. But he's already thinking about something else.

I take his face in my hand, tilt his head so he's staring straight at me. "This is the most important thing, Dylan, so listen. This is a secret, okay? A very big secret that only you and me know about. You can't tell anyone else. Okay?"

"I can tell Mummy?"

I squeeze his cheeks. He starts to look scared. "No, you can't ever tell Mummy about the tricks. Not ever, ever, ever. If you do she'll get angry, Dylan. Do you understand? She'll get so angry that she'll go far away and never, ever come back."

"I don't want her to go!" Fat tears leak from his eyes.

I hate doing this, but he needs to learn. Later, when he's older, I can explain things properly. About the nudging, and how to use it to his advantage. How to make sure he's not caught, that girls never catch on. "Then you have to keep the secret. If you keep the secret, Mummy will be happy and she'll love us and never leave us. Okay?"

"Do you love me, Da-da?"

It breaks my heart to see the fear in his eyes. I grab him and hug him tight. "Of course, I love you, Dylan. You're my clever, strong, brave little man. I love you more than anything in the whole world." His sobs catch me the way Annie's never did. They *hurt*, but it's a pain I'll gladly bear to keep him safe. To keep him mine. Breathing in that sweet scent of his scalp, I rock him until his cries shudder to an end.

My son, oh my son. I have so much to teach you.

HARD PLACES

IT'S AS THOUGH the granite is a growing thing, heaving its way out of the cool, clamped earth. Some nubs seem small enough to cup in two hands, others are so huge you'd need a ladder to scale them. The setting sun turns their flanks golden, almost pinkish, and casts shadows that look like breathing. Casey takes a sip of her cider—a modest one; it can't hurt—and shifts in her chair. "You weren't kidding about the rock farm."

On the porch next to her, Yvonne raises an eyebrow. "Sorry?"

"In one of the letters to my mum," Casey says. "You told her you'd bought a rock farm."

The older woman's laughter is rusted yet brassy. "Sounds like something I'd write. Used to run a few dozen goats out there when I could still handle the workload. Just have those three to keep my house paddock in order now." She nods toward the animals grazing by the fence. "Anne, Charlotte, and Emily. No Branwell—billies make for too much trouble."

Casey can tell there's a joke in there she's supposed to get but doesn't. "Why don't you have a dog? I thought all farms came with a dog or two." Large ones, with keen ears and sharp teeth and rough, throaty barks to warn of danger.

"My last died over winter," Yvonne says. "Jellybean. She was a good girl, border collie crossed with who knows what, but she could keep the goats in line when she was young. I wasn't ready to get another right off, and this place is barely a farm anymore anyway, so..."

"I'm sorry," Casey says.

"I wish Tara could have made it out here, even once."

"She wasn't much into the whole getting-away-from-it-all thing."

"And you are?"

Casey shrugs. "Depends what you're getting away from." She takes another tiny sip, barely enough to coat her mouth. The cider is tart and cool. She longs to throw back her head and scull the whole bottle. Settles for pressing the glass hard against her cheek. There's some strange comfort in that at least.

"So, your rosemary." Yvonne extends a sandalled foot to nudge the ridiculously large pot plant that Casey lugged all the way from Melbourne. When they met at the train station, the woman didn't say a word about it, simply took the pot from Casey's arms and led the way to the car park. *You'll be wanting some water, Casey-bear, you and that poor plant both. And there's an apple and a muesli bar in the glovebox if you're peckish; it's a bit of a drive.* The nickname her mother once used. The no-questions-asked kindness. It was all too much. The anxious knot in her guts loosened and Casey burst into tears. Yvonne handed her a handkerchief, put a Queen CD into the ute's ancient player, and let her doze for the hour or so it took to get to the farm. Casey could see why her mother had kept up the friendship, even over the distance and the years.

Yvonne's a good egg, Case. You ever in trouble, you go to her.

"What about my rosemary?" Casey asks now.

"We should dig it into the garden tomorrow."

Casey shakes her head. "It was Mum's."

"Been in that pot a while then?"

"I don't...I don't know what I'm doing with it yet."

"Plant like that really needs its feet in the ground."

"Maybe. Not right now."

Yvonne takes a long swig of her own cider, emptying the bottle. Her tanned throat pulses as she swallows. "Time to think about some supper, I guess. How would an omelette do you? My chooks have been laying non-stop this week."

"Did you see that?" Casey leans forward, squinting. In the twilight, the granite in the paddock across from them is dull and gloomy, hard to separate from the growing shadows that surround it. And yet. "It looked—it looked like one of those rocks moved."

"Oh, yes." Yvonne winks as she pushes herself up from her chair. "They do that."

***

The water from the kitchen tap has a mineral tang but it's cold from sitting in the underground tanks and Casey fills her glass a second time. She'll get used to the taste, she supposes—not to mention used to the idea that this stuff falls straight off the roof and into the pipes largely unfiltered. Yvonne snorted out loud when Casey asked if it was safe to drink without boiling first. *I'm still kicking, aren't I?* Back home, they only drink filtered water and Neil is religious about changing the Brita cartridge.

No, not *home*. Not anymore.

She'll have to get used to that as well.

It's the middle of the night and Casey hasn't been able to sleep. It's too quiet and too dark, even with the near-full moon shining across the paddocks, limning the rounded granite mounds silver. Neil will know she's gone by now. He'll have read her note and called her switched-off phone god knows how many times, no doubt leaving an escalation of irate voice messages. He'll have searched through what little personal stuff she left behind and checked all her accounts, trying to find out where she went.

He won't find out, Casey assures herself. She's been careful.

A secret Gmail account she only ever accessed on the public computers at the library.

A brand-new Myki card to travel on, unlinked to the account he controls.

The cash she managed to siphon away over the past year, a pathetically small amount but enough for the essentials.

She even bought a pre-paid SIM only to find out it couldn't be activated without a credit card or some other ID she doesn't have yet. That's a battle for another day. Forms. Paperwork. ID. Her official, independent existence confirmed. She might even get a driver's licence at last. A copy of her birth certificate, discovered among her mother's papers, is tucked safe between the creamy pages of her new journal—she can keep a journal now!—which should make things easier. All the rest she had to abandon in Neil's safe.

Casey remembers the man on the train who kept staring at her, a sly twist to his mouth. She spent the whole trip rigid with paranoia, terrified that he was following her, that Neil had sent him, that everything was coming undone. When he stayed on the train after she disembarked, her knees just about gave out with relief. Just your average, garden-variety creep.

She's been careful. Neil won't find out.

There's a dozen eggs in the fridge that Yvonne hard-boiled after dinner. *They last longer this way and there'll be more fresh tomorrow.* Casey peels one and wolfs it in two bites—or tries to. The dry, powdery yolk sticks in her throat and she coughs into a tea towel, hard and painful, trying to muffle the sound. Finally, she swallows enough water to wash it down. No wonder Neil always demanded his soft-boiled or, better yet, poached. It took her months to learn how to do them just the way he liked; he'd make her start again if they were even slightly overdone.

She eats two more eggs, chewing slowly while she stares out the window. The rocks sit solid in the grass, unmoving. Earlier, Yvonne took her remark as a joke, but Casey is sure one of them shifted somehow. Not rolled or lurched or anything that dramatic, just a subtle push farther out of the earth, or was it farther in?

"Go on then," she whispers. "I'm waiting."

Nothing. Just an immense, traffic-free, people-free silence. Casey gathers the bits of eggshell into her palm and brushes them into the compost bin. She's exhausted, and her paranoia clearly isn't ready to sheathe its claws. But maybe this is what freedom feels like.

"Stop it," she tells herself. "You're safe. This place is safe."

All the same, she sneaks one last glance out the window before returning to bed.

The granite doesn't move.

* * *

Warm milk and honey, an old-fashioned remedy for insomnia but Yvonne swears by it. Milk from her own goats—except for Charlotte, who's past all that now—and the honey she trades from a nearby friend for eggs. Soap as well, back when Yvonne still made it.

"Soap?"

"Best goat-milk soap you'll ever use. Sold it by the case to some of the snootier boutiques in Melbourne; they charged three times what I did at the markets around here, but that's the city for you. *Angel Valley Soaps.* I used to send Tara a box every now and then too. She ever pass some on to you?"

Casey shakes her head. Although she does remember her mother giving her a couple bars of fancy soap once, years ago. It smelled of citrus and spices and Neil tossed it in the bin with a disgusted sneer. If he wanted to smell like breakfast all day, he'd shower with orange juice. They always used Sorbolene bars. Unscented.

"Do you still have some?" Casey asks. She has the sudden urge to bathe in fruit.

"Only a case or ten." Yvonne grins. "Won't need to buy soap for the rest of my natural life."

Old fashioned or not, the milk and honey actually works and, once sleep has found the smallest chink in her armour, Casey's body crashes hard. She's out cold most mornings until well after breakfast—there's always a place set for her at the kitchen table regardless, with bread for toast and a jar of homemade jam—and she can't seem to keep her eyes open for long even in the middle of the day. She'll rouse from an unexpected nap on the couch to find herself tucked beneath a light throw, or bequeathed a broad-brimmed hat if she's been out on the porch and the sun has come round.

When she is awake, she still feels sluggish and heavy, like there's an anchor tied around her waist, bent on dragging her back down to the depths. Somnambulant, she forces herself to move, to shower, to find Yvonne and ask if there's anything she needs helps with. The older woman is usually outside, mucking about in the enormous vegetable garden, or tending to the chickens or goats, or carrying out an infinite number of minor but essential chores the farm constantly throws her way. Occasionally she's in the kitchen, producing thick and inviting aromas that would make Casey's mouth water if she had any appetite to speak of.

Yvonne's answer is always the same: *Nothing for you to do, Casey-bear, except rest.*

So Casey does. She can't remember when she last had so much empty time to herself. No daily to-do list stuck primly to the fridge. No cleaning or shopping or cooking. She doesn't even make her bed anymore. It's odd, how doing nothing can be so utterly exhausting.

Until one day it isn't.

The note sitting on her breakfast plate informs her that Yvonne has driven into town for market day. *No eggs for breakfast but steak for dinner! Promise!* Casey's stomach actually growls in anticipation. She spreads Vegemite on her toast, craving its savoury sharpness, and makes herself a cup of peppermint tea to take out to the porch.

Her days of milk and honey are over.

It rained heavily most of the night and the morning is still overcast, with a crisp chillness to the air that warns of winter down the track. The granite bulges from grass that already seems greener after its nocturnal soaking, and Casey spends far too much time studying the position of the rocks. Is that large one with the crack closer to the fence now? Was that group of three always huddled so close together? She considers fetching her phone to take some photos for later comparison, but its battery will be deader than dead by now. How long has she been here? A week? More? How ridiculous is it that she doesn't even know?

Casey stretches. Rubs her eyes. She feels more awake now than ever. She wishes Yvonne had woken her, invited her to come along to the markets. But maybe the woman is sick to death of her presence and needed some time to herself. She probably regrets telling Casey she could come and stay in the first place and is probably working out a tactful way to ask her to leave. Who would want such a lazy, useless lump taking up space in their home?

"Stop now." Casey takes a deep breath. "That's Neil talking."

One of the goats, grazing close to the porch, looks up at the sound of her voice and bleats.

Casey laughs. "Quite right, Anne. Or is it Emily? I promise I'll learn."

The goat blinks, slowly, before returning her attention to the grass.

"And now I'm talking to animals."

Casey gets to her feet. She needs something to do, something physical and arduous that will make her body stretch and sweat and ache at the end of it all and, gazing over the house paddock, she knows exactly what that something will be. She finds what she's looking for in one of the sheds next to the veggie garden: an empty bucket and a two-pronged weeder, almost exactly the same as the tool she has back at home.

(Not home. Not anymore.)

All three goats come trotting over when they spot her with the bucket, but quickly lose interest after she lets them each stick their head inside. On impulse, she scratches the one she thinks is Anne under the chin and is pleased when the animal leans in hard against her hand, clearly enjoying the attention.

"There you go," Casey says. "Now let me get to work."

The grass is thick, albeit nibbled short by goatish teeth, but there is still an abundance of flatweed sprouting and spreading between the blades. Anne, Emily, and Charlotte seem to have left the stuff alone, so maybe they don't like the taste or it gives them a bellyache. Either way, they won't miss the weeds. For Casey, it's beyond satisfying. Digging the prongs deep beneath each plant, she catches the tap root then levers up, steady and slow, rocking back and forth until finally the whole thing wrenches free. Sometimes the root breaks with a soft crack and Casey swears. That one will no doubt grow back again. But the rain has softened the earth and most of them she pulls out entire, the larger and more stubborn weeds sometimes sending her backwards onto her arse as they begrudgingly surrender their hold.

Her mother taught her to weed like this when she was a girl. Neil prefers to use poisons. Why spend all that time when you can spray the whole lot with Zero in fifteen minutes? But Casey worries about the bees and did as much as she could by hand. As long as everything on the list was ticked off each day, he was none the wiser.

Dig. Lever. Pull. Dig. Lever. Pull.

She doesn't know what to do with the weeds when the bucket fills, so she piles them outside the gate. Yvonne might want to compost them later, or burn them, or whatever you do with green waste on a farm. There certainly isn't kerbside pickup.

Dig. Lever. Pull. Dig. Lever. Pull.

As the sun breaks through the clouds, she ventures inside to find a hat and drink some water. Her back is pleasingly sore, her knees wobbly from all the crouching and shuffling, and she doesn't think she'll ever get all the dirt out from under her fingernails.

Dig. Lever. Pull. Dig. Lever. Pull.

By the time Yvonne's ute rattles down the driveway in the late afternoon, Casey is spent. By her reckoning, she's worked through less than half the area in front of the porch, but the wilting stack of weeds by the gate is impressive nonetheless.

"What have you done to yourself?" Yvonne asks, examining her blistered hands. "There are gloves in the shed, you know."

Casey grins. "Next time." She's rubbed a patch raw on the inside of her right palm where the weeder was braced. It's going to hurt later, but right now she doesn't care.

Yvonne shakes her head. "It's only the goat paddock. What's a few weeds?"

"It's the view from your porch. I wanted it to look nice."

"Talk about a Sisyphean task."

"I don't know what that means," Casey says, surprising herself. Neil would have mocked her mercilessly for her ignorance, but Neil isn't here. It's only her and Yvonne, and Yvonne—Yvonne is safe. "I also don't know why your goats are called Anne, Emily, and Charlotte. Or who Brandon is when he's at home."

"Branwell," Yvonne says softly. She brushes back the hair from Casey's face. "A Sisyphean task is a never-ending one. There will always be more weeds."

"I'll pull those out as well. Three seasons, Mum used to say. Three seasons to break the cycle."

"Sisyphean also means ineffective." The woman swings her arm, taking in the surrounding fields with their brooding granite mounds. "You can't weed it all, and what's left will just blow seed over the lot."

"But I can keep this bit under control. Just here in front of the porch, so you can sit and look out on a beautiful lawn. And the goats can have their grass." Her lip starts to tremble and she swallows hard. "I can do that much at least."

Yvonne is quiet for a while. Then she nods, more to herself than to Casey. "Let's go inside. I can tell you all about the Bronte sisters, and their ne'er-do-well brother, and you..." She glances pointedly at Casey's belly. "You can tell me how far along you are."

* * *

Eight or nine weeks by her roughest calculation, ten at the outside; enough for Neil to notice if she stayed any longer. Prepared or not— and she was very much not—Casey had to leave. She wasn't going to let it happen again. This time he might actually kill her.

Yvonne frowns. "You're not exaggerating, are you?"

Casey wishes she was. Like this one, her first pregnancy was unplanned. Neil was adamant he didn't want children and they were always careful. He blamed her, of course. Accused her of skipping her pills or poking needles through his condoms, of trying to trick him into fatherhood. Her apologies only made him more furious, as if she were admitting her guilt, and he was on the phone to a family planning clinic that same day.

For one of the precious few times in their relationship, Casey stood her ground. She said she had to think things through. She asked for more time. She told him it was her body.

She still can't believe she had the courage to say all of that.

"I can believe it," Yvonne murmurs.

Things were thrown. Things were broken. The framed photo of them on holiday up in Cairns. A crystal unicorn her mother had given her for her birthday that year. Her favourite coffee mug with the dancing cats. Nothing Neil himself cared about—his rage was never unfocused. When he stormed out of the house, Casey thought about leaving too.

She should have left.

But she didn't.

She stayed and swept up the scattered shards—two months later she would cut her thumb on a piece she missed, tucked inexplicably between the couch cushions—and washed the dinner dishes. When Neil wasn't home by midnight she went to bed alone, hands cradling her stomach.

"What happened when he did come home?"

Very little for the first few days. It wasn't like he was pretending nothing had happened—the tension in his jaw equalled the atmosphere in the house—but he left her alone. Then one morning the to-do list on the fridge had a final entry in large bold capitals. *THINK!* It was underlined twice. *I need more time*, she wrote beneath it. *Please.*

Neil gave Casey twenty-four hours. Then he broke her.

In the emergency room, where they went once the bleeding wouldn't stop, her story was unimaginative. Carrying washing down the back stairs. A stumble. A fall. So clumsy. The bruises on her abdomen? She landed on one of the pot plants. The big terracotta one. She doesn't remember much else. So, so clumsy. She suspected that at least one of the nurses wasn't buying it, but what could they do? Casey had been too scared to fight back. Neil was unmarked.

And he could be so very charming. His poor girlfriend. They had no idea they were even pregnant. Such a shock. Such a terrible, terrible loss.

"Fucking bastard." Yvonne is holding one of Casey's hands in her own, gentle as cradling a kitten. The other is clenched into a fist so tight her knuckles are white. It's the first time Casey has heard her swear.

After the miscarriage, things were better for a while. Not counting the occasional slap or arm twisted in anger—which, by then, she didn't—the beating was the first time Neil had really hurt her and he did seem genuinely contrite. Attentive. Caring. They ordered take-out for a week and he did most of the housework. At night, he held her when she cried and kissed her hair.

Casey still thought about leaving, but the idea was too overwhelming. All the steps she would need to take, all of them in secret. Neil controlled everything. Money. Communication. Who she knew. What she did. Her body, as it turned out. In the beginning, it was simple. He was the dashing older man, super-wealthy by Casey's standards and lavish with it. He treated her like a princess; she couldn't believe he loved her. All her friends, before they drifted away—before Neil tugged Casey away from them—they all said how lucky she was.

"You know that thing with frogs?" Yvonne asks. "How you can start one off in a pot of cold water and then boil it alive? By the time the poor creature registers how hot the water's getting, it's far too late."

Casey hasn't heard that before. It makes her feel queasy.

"Anyway, it's a myth." Yvonne's lips purse to a thin line. "But it's still the truth."

Then Casey's mother got sick and that was that. Stretched between caring for her mum and placating Neil, who thought she was spending too much time away from the house, away from him, Casey was too exhausted to think about much else. Those last few months in hospice were the worst. Her mum slid in and out of lucidity, depending on how tight the medication was swaddling her, and Casey left each day in tears.

Neil didn't like to see her cry, not for someone else. She made sure to freshen her face before he got home.

"You never told Tara about him? What he did?"

How could she? Her mother had given up so much for Casey. Ostracised from her strict Catholic family, she struggled all those years as a single mother, trying to make ends meet between Centrelink payments and a string of crappy casual jobs, sewing her daughter's school uniforms because she couldn't afford to buy them, eating baked beans on toast for three days so Casey could go to the movies with friends. And then the cancer, the fucking toxic cherry on top, rolling in to end her life before she even had a chance to live it. How could Casey tell her anything? Her mother would have been appalled that her daughter—her supposedly smart, supposedly independent, supposedly empowered daughter—had gotten herself into such a situation. She would have been ashamed.

It's the twenty-first century; women have options now. Why didn't Casey?

"There's a lot of women like you out there," Yvonne says. "And I don't think Tara would have been ashamed. She would have been proud of you for finding a way out."

Only Casey didn't. Her mum's been dead for over a year, and sure, she made vague and fantastical plans, and sure, she even took a couple of actual steps toward them, but to be brutally honest, living with Neil was easier in a lot of ways—especially since the funeral— and if she hadn't gotten herself knocked up again, she would probably still be there, waiting like a cowed and obedient fifties housewife for the water to hit one hundred degrees.

"But you're *not* still there." Yvonne takes both her hands now. Holds them between her warm, calloused palms and squeezes. "You're here—you and the little one. And you can both stay for as long as you need."

***

If it's going to be a long-term arrangement, Casey insists on pulling her weight. She helps Yvonne in the veggie garden, learning everything from tying tomatoes to turning compost, and takes it upon herself to feed the chickens and collect their eggs each morning. Unlike the goats, the birds are nameless—when Casey decides to remedy that, Yvonne warns her not to get too attached. *Once they're too old for laying, they're in the pot.* Casey is mildly horrified. As late summer fades into autumn, she holds the ladder while Yvonne harvests her small collection of fruit trees, and assists the older woman in the making of various jams, relishes, and pickles. Occasionally the smell gets too much and she has to sit out on the porch for a while, sucking in fresh air to quell her nausea. She still watches the rocks, but slyly now, out of the corner of her eye. They refuse to move.

One afternoon, Yvonne cooks up green tomato relish from what's left unripened on the vines. It's new to Casey and she's hooked from the first savoury-sweet mouthful. She sits down and eats a small bowl of the stuff then and there, layering it thickly over toast, while Yvonne spoons the rest into jars for boiling.

These days, Casey's hungry all the time.

"I wish I'd been able to pack my knitting," she muses one evening after supper, drinking tea on the porch with Yvonne as has become their custom. "It's the one thing I really miss."

Yvonne gives her a curious look and vanishes into the house. When she returns, she's carrying two large plastic bags, each of them bulging with wool. Bought on clearance a few years ago when the local haberdashery went under, she admits ruefully. More a whim than anything else. She liked the idea of sitting out here in a rocking chair, knitting away her retirement, but she's always been too busy to learn.

"And you don't have a rocking chair," Casey observes.

Yvonne grins. "A folly right from the start, as you can see. But fifty cents a ball!"

"It's good wool too." Casey is sorting through the first bag. "Natural, beautiful colours. I used to work with acrylics mostly.

Cheaper, you know."

"There's tourist markets in town over winter. Make some scarves and what not before then and you'll be able to sell quite a bit—at city prices, no less."

"But it's your wool. You paid for it."

"You manage to teach me to knit, Casey-bear, and we'll call it evens."

***

Casey's getting better at putting her foot down. She's not going to the hospital for a check-up, nor the local clinic neither. Nowhere she needs to use her Medicare card or have her name put into a computer. Neil's good with computers; he could always find out the smallest things and she isn't willing to risk it.

"I think you've seen too many movies," Yvonne tells her.

"I'll go when the baby's ready, not before. I want it born, healthy and alive. There's nothing he can do about it then."

"Healthy is what I'm worried about, Casey-bear."

"Women have been giving birth long before hospitals and doctors."

"And more of them died, or their babies. Or both."

But Casey's foot stays down.

The next afternoon, a strange four-wheel drive judders up the driveway. It's silver and loud and Casey, spotting the vehicle the minute it rounds the far bend, hurries to fetch Yvonne. Her throat is tight and her heart thuds against her ribs. It's exactly the kind Neil would drive and, even though the one he owned was black, he might have upgraded again. Even the granite seems to have crowded closer, although out of protection or anticipation Casey cannot guess.

"Calm down." Yvonne waves as the car pulls in and the driver's door swings open. "It's only Doctor Pat. He's a friend, I promise. And he owes me."

The man who shakes her hand is on the back straight of middle age, with a lined and tired face but a warm smile. "So we're looking at five months here?" He stares appraisingly at her bulge. "Six?"

Self-conscious, Casey smooths out her dress, one of several over-sized pieces that Yvonne picked up for her from the charity shop in town. They're not proper maternity clothes but Casey insisted on paying and she can't spare the funds for things she'd only wear once.

"Closer to six, maybe."

"Yvonne said you haven't been seen by anyone yet?"

"I'm fine, the baby's fine. I would know if it wasn't."

"I'm sure you're right. But since I've come all this way, how about we make sure?"

The examination is quick but thorough, and Dr. Pat gives her a clean bill of health. Casey feels somewhat smug if, truth be told, a little relieved. Of course, the doctor would feel better with an ultrasound and the usual round of bloods, but he's not about to hogtie a pregnant lady and throw her in the back of his Land Cruiser just to get that done. Instead he gives her a ream of booklets and FAQ sheets, along with several plastic containers of supplements, a hot water bottle, and a dog-eared and hand-annotated copy of *What to Expect When You're Expecting* that his wife foisted upon him at the last minute.

"Now listen," Doctor Pat says, packing up his bag. "If there's any pain down the track, any prolonged discomfort that doesn't seem right to you, promise me you'll get yourself to town pronto. Same with baby's movements. If they weaken, and especially if they stop, it's straight to hospital."

"How— How do I know what isn't right?"

"Most women do. Before they convince themselves otherwise and decide not to be a bother." He sighs as he straightens up and faces her again. "Look, you're in good shape but you're also more than two hours away from the nearest hospital. You feel like something's wrong, you get yourself in that car."

Casey promises.

***

"I'd like to plant Mum's rosemary."

Yvonne looks up from the garlic patch she's weeding and shades her eyes. "Now?"

"Now."

They choose a spot near the porch where it will get a good amount of sun and Yvonne digs out a fair-sized hole. The shrub is pot-bound and doesn't surrender easily but, as soon as it does, Casey spots what she's looking for tangled in the roots. The label is ruined but the tin itself is made from aluminium and is still going strong. The cap is intact, still pressed tightly in place.

"What on earth..." Yvonne wipes her forehead with the back of her glove.

"Milo," Casey says. "Or it used to be."

Near the end, when her mother was in hospice, she would tell Casey to make herself a drink of Milo, just like she always did when Casey used to visit her at home. It was one of the minor luxuries of her childhood and she's never grown out of the taste. Neil hated it. Too sugary. Too malty. Too Casey. Much of the cleanout of her mother's flat fell to her. Neil didn't want to take time off work to sort through a bunch of worthless trash, and because the landlord had sorted new tenants in lieu of notice—*considering the circumstances*; such a nice man—she only had two weeks.

She kept some bits of jewellery and a wad of handwritten letters bound in thick red elastic—mostly from Yvonne, she would later discover, hands shaking as she recognised a lifeline. The rest was donated or went straight into the skip.

Casey didn't cry until she found the tin in her mother's bedside drawer.

Make yourself a Milo, Case. Three spoonfuls, just how you like it.

Only it was too heavy to still have malted chocolate powder inside.

Now, using the point of a gardening fork, Casey scrapes away the soil and levers the cap open.

Yvonne gasps. "How much is in there?"

"A little under seven thousand. She had almost nothing in her bank accounts when she died. Spent it all on treatments and keeping up her rent on the flat. Neil was livid that we—that *he*—had to pay for the funeral. Oh, Yvonne, it was so cheap—it was—" Vision blurring, Casey wipes angrily at her tears. A grain of dirt gets in her eye and she rubs harder.

"Here, tilt your head back." Yvonne prises open Casey's eyelid and tells her to look over to her left. Then her finger is on Casey's eyeball, her finger*nail* to be precise, the sharp curve pausing for the briefest of moments before flicking the offending particle away.

Casey can't stop crying.

"That's okay, that's good, it'll wash away whatever's left."

As Yvonne's hands rub her back in soothing circles, Casey feels a solid wallop from within. Her hands fly to her stomach. "It kicked!" She grins. "I've been feeling it move for a while but not like— Oof! Might have a soccer player on my hands."

Yvonne laughs. "Or a jujitsu black-belt." She retrieves the Milo tin from the ground. Casey didn't even notice she dropped it. "We should put this somewhere safe."

"I know it's not a fortune, but I want to pay my way here."

"I'm not taking your money, Casey-bear."

"But I—"

"I'm *not* taking your money." Yvonne's voice softens. "We'll put it in the bank later, okay? That soccer player of yours will need uniforms one day."

Once the rosemary is safely dug in and watered down, Casey follows Yvonne over to the tap to wash her hands. There's a bucket sitting nearby, a splash of red on its rim. The old speckled chook, Yvonne confesses when she asks. Hasn't laid an egg in weeks, and don't think she doesn't know Casey's been trying to cover for her.

"Oh no, not Glenda."

"Told you not to name them."

Casey crosses her arms. "I'm not eating her." She refuses to start crying again.

But the poor old bird wasn't good for much more than soup stock as it turns out, and Yvonne couldn't be bothered with all the plucking and gutting just for that. She buried the carcass instead, returned Glenda to the earth and all that grows from it.

"A few years from now, she'll give us some lovely tomatoes."

***

Casey's been having the weirdest dreams since she came here, not that she can usually remember much more than shadows and scraps. Often she's outside, walking barefoot over lumps of granite that shift and roll beneath her feet like barrels on water. Or else they're blistering, hotter than concrete sidewalks in high summer, and she runs faster and faster, trying to keep minimal contact between rock and skin, but she can never move fast enough to keep the soles of her feet from melting and sticking and sloughing bits of her off in a trail that anyone could follow.

And someone always is.

Some mornings she reaches down to check her feet and is mildly surprised to find them unharmed. Her heels cracked and chafed but clean.

Now, the granite sits cold and motionless, but there's so damn much of it. Acres and acres stretching to the horizon, and Casey is calling for Yvonne to help her find a way through. There's a shriek and something wet and warm splashes across Casey's cheek and she swings around in time to see the chicken's head roll off the boulder onto the grass below. Yvonne grins at her, huge horse-teeth red and dripping, and offers a second axe—*need your help, Casey-bear. can't get through this lot on my own*—and Casey sees that there are chickens on every rock, lying down with necks outstretched, waiting in dreadful blank-eyed stillness for their go beneath the blade. She turns and runs but the awful, wailing shrieks follow in her wake, the shrieks and the dull chime of steel hitting stone over and over and over, and it's not what it sounds like, she tells herself, it's not a baby

it's not my baby

it's not—

Casey wakes with a start, the dusty taste of feathers still in her mouth.

***

There's no mobile coverage out here, Yvonne assures her, only satellite, but Casey still takes the SIM out of her phone before she switches it on. She moves to throw the little plastic card in the bin but Yvonne takes it from her.

"If he hasn't cancelled your number, you'll be able to access any messages he's left."

"I don't want to hear them."

"No, but if they're as bad as you think, it might be evidence."

"Of what?"

"His character. His behaviour."

"I don't need phone messages for that."

"The law will," Yvonne says gently. "If it ever comes down to custody."

Casey snorts. "I don't think we have to worry about *that*." She deletes all the texts from Neil still stored on her phone, his emails as well, eliminating any trace of him. There are photos too—Neil, his house, anything that reminds her of their time together—she trashes the lot. It doesn't leave much. Mostly photos of her mum, which she shows to Yvonne.

"I should have gone to see her. She told me not to, but I should have gone."

Casey flips the phone around, leans in close to Yvonne. "Smile."

"Oh, Casey-bear, no. I look a fright."

"Too late." It's a terrible selfie—Yvonne looking off to the side, Casey with a worried expression on her face—but it's the first one of them together. Casey keeps it. She takes a couple more until there's a shot Yvonne is halfway happy about. "Once I have my new number sorted, I can send you a copy."

Over the next few days Casey carries the phone around with her. It's little more than a camera right now but that's all she wants. The journal she's been keeping is fine, but she needs more than words to capture her time here, these quiet, swollen weeks before the baby comes. She takes an inordinate number of selfies, her rapidly growing belly the star attraction, and almost as many photos of the goats, who pull the most ludicrous faces. She snaps the veggie garden and the chickens going about their day and once, to Yvonne's chagrin, the blurred russet tail of a fox as it scooted around the side of a shed. *Never have my .22 on hand when the buggers are snouting about.* Yvonne spent that particular morning inspecting the chook house and reinforcing any possible points of incursion.

Casey also photographs the granite. Different times of the day, all manner of light and angles. She's pleased by how beautifully some of the shots turn out. There's a brooding melancholy to the paddocks at twilight, a sharp sense of expectancy in the noonday sun.

Even in the photos, she can never tell if their positions stay the same.

"They won't let you catch them at it," Yvonne laughs.

Their shared joke.

(Not really a joke?)

Yvonne offers her credit card to register Casey's new SIM the next time they're in town, but Casey's in no hurry. She's enjoying this enforced digital isolation and besides, who does she have to call? Everyone she cares about is in this house. She rubs her belly as the baby kicks.

***

Casey sighs and puts down the knitting needles. Her fingers are ridiculously swollen tonight; she's dropping more stitches than Yvonne does. There are five scarves and two pairs of socks to her tally but now she's making booties from a gorgeous rainbow colourway and the work is more fiddly than she counted on. Maybe she'll go to bed and try to read—if she can keep her eyes open. She's never been one for novels, but she's slogged through Yvonne's copies of *Wuthering Heights*—Heathcliff made her skin crawl—and *Jane Eyre*—Rochester; just no—and is now partway through *Villette*, which she already likes a lot better than its predecessors.

And not just because it was written by the namesake of her favourite goat.

In her armchair across the room, Yvonne swears. "I'll never get the hang of this." She's still on her first scarf and has unpicked almost as much as she's knitted.

"You always set it aside whenever you hit trouble." Casey massages her knuckles, trying not to wince. "Work through it or you'll never get better."

Yvonne grumbles but returns to her scarf.

"Did you ever want children?" Casey asks after a while.

"Not really. Certainly never found anyone I'd want to have them with."

"I don't— I don't know if *I* want them. If I want this one."

The older woman glances up, sharply.

"It's just that, with everything, I honestly don't know if I wanted to keep the baby as much as I just didn't want to lose it...like that." Tears prick at her eyes; she ignores them. "And now it's too late and I'm so scared of messing everything up. What the hell do I know about being a mother? What if I turn my kid into a trainwreck?"

"Two things," Yvonne says. "First, it's not too late. If you really don't want this baby, there's always adoption. I'll support you in any decision you—"

"I don't want to have it adopted, I just don't know how—"

"Second, you had a great mother. Learn from how she raised you."

"Yeah, right. Because I turned out so fucking well."

"Enough." Yvonne gets up, crosses over to Casey and perches on the arm of her chair. "You *have* turned out so fucking well. If you were my daughter, I'd be unbelievably proud of you. I am unbelievably proud of you. And Tara would be too." Her voice breaks on those last words and she pulls Casey into an awkward hug. They're both crying now, and Casey presses her face into the sleeve of Yvonne's cardigan, which smells of camphorwood and lavender and makes Casey feel safer than she has in a long, long time.

It makes her feel like she's home.

"Pregnancy hormones." Casey laughs shakily as they pull apart.

"What's your excuse?"

Yvonne wipes her eyes. "Lack of tea. I'll make us a pot."

Later, blowing over a mug of steaming peppermint, Casey tells Yvonne that she would have been a good mother. A great mother.

"Maybe," Yvonne replies. "Maybe not. But I have been a good soaper, and a good goat farmer, and a stellar maker of green tomato relish. And now I'm learning to be a good knitter—maybe—and I hope, at last, a good friend."

Casey swallows the lump in her throat. "The best," she says. "The very best."

* * *

Her water breaks one morning after breakfast. In the middle of the somewhat arduous process of getting up from her chair, Casey feels a strange, almost popping sensation and then a warm trickle down her leg. She swears, thinking she's peed herself—despite having already gone to the loo three times since waking up. Yvonne hurries over from the sink.

"Get your bag," the older woman says after a quick assessment. "I'll ring the hospital and tell them we're coming."

"My contractions haven't even started yet," Casey protests as Yvonne helps her waddle out to the car. Almost as the words leave her mouth, a mild band of pain ripples across her lower back, followed by a much fiercer cramp in her abdomen. "Okay, now they have."

On the way, Casey forgets almost everything she read in the pregnancy book except that she has to time her contractions. She wishes she could remember what the intervals should be, or how close together is *too* close together. They seem to be coming faster and faster though, the pain strengthening each time. Meanwhile Yvonne is driving like she just got her pensioner card and merely shakes her head when Casey begs her to get a move on.

"I'm not going to have this baby by the side of the road."

"There's plenty of time. I don't want to jolt you around too much."

Casey clenches the seat so hard a fingernail tears straight through the aging upholstery.

In the labour ward, everyone is ludicrously calm. The nurses get her settled, the doctor drops by *just to say hello before the action starts,* and then they all leave her alone as though she isn't about to shoot a brand-new human out of her vagina at any given moment.

"It's fine, Casey-bear." Yvonne squeezes her hand. "You've hours to go yet."

Ten and three-quarter hours, as it turns out.

Ten and three-quarter hours of cramps and breathing exercises, during the middle of which Casey is brought a surreal lunch tray of sandwiches and fruit-in-jelly that she absolutely does not feel like touching until Yvonne wedges a spoon between her lips. *Eat. You need to keep up your strength.* Ten and three-quarter hours of ice chips and back rubs and dilation checks and the nurses telling her that she's doing great, she's lucky, this is an easy one, honest. *Baby's going to pop right out.* Casey wants to tell them all to fuck right off. Instead she sucks on her ice and screams with each fresh contraction. That's the best part actually, being allowed to scream, and cry, and swear. No one tells her to shut up. No one tells her she's hysterical or a drama queen or that she's making too much of too little. They simply mop the sweat from her face and let her roar. Ten and three-quarter hours of the midwife pressing down on the exact muscles she needs to use to push, muscles Casey didn't even know she had, and stripping the gown from her body, and then even her bra, because she just couldn't deal with *clothes* on top of it all.

Ten and three-quarter hours that blur to a fine, sharp focus at the end, and now Casey has a baby on her chest, red and wrinkled and wailing his fresh little lungs out.

A baby. A boy. Her son.

* * *

Yvonne uses Casey's phone to take the obligatory new baby photos. Her own has run flat overnight and in all the rush she forgot to bring a charger. Casey flicks through them with one hand, deleting those where she looks particularly awful, which turns out to be quite a few.

"I'm calling him Michael," she says, looking down at the sleeping baby in her arms. "Mum's middle name was Michelle. I couldn't think of anything for Tara."

"Michael's a lovely name," Yvonne replies.

The hospital is letting Casey go home tomorrow or maybe the day after, once they're happy with how baby is taking the breast. She wishes she could stay longer, until she feels more like a mother. Until she feels more like his mother. Casey expected it to be instant, that she would see his newborn face and hold him against her skin, and done deal. But mostly she's just drained and sore. He's a baby, a perfectly healthy, perfectly lovely baby—but that's all he is.

When do I start to love him? she wants to ask.

Casey's phone chimes in her hand, and she squints closely at the screen. A whole bunch of her dormant apps are waking up, sending resentful reminders of their neglect along with demands for updates; she thumbs through the notifications, dismissing them.

"I set you up with the hospital Wi-Fi," Yvonne explains. "In case you were bored."

"I'm tired," Casey says, switching off the phone. "Can you take the baby? Put him down in the crib? I want to take a nap."

Michael doesn't make a fuss as Yvonne lifts him into her arms. "We'll have a nice big cuddle first, won't we, little man?" He gurgles a bit when she lowers him into the crib, then quickly settles. He's a very good baby, all the nurses say so.

And Casey agrees, she honestly does. He just doesn't feel like hers.

* * *

Her mother told her once that having a baby was like finding an unexpected room in your house. You'd lived there forever and thought you knew all the rooms, all the secret hidey-holes, everything that the house did or ever could contain, and then suddenly there's a new door in the hallway that you've never seen before, and when you open it—*BAM*—you step into this shiny-bright, miraculous space that must have been there all along, waiting patiently for you to find it.

You have so many rooms inside you, Case. Don't ever be afraid to open them up.

Sometimes, in those first few days back at the farm, Casey thinks she catches a glimpse inside that promised new room. When she's breastfeeding and Michael reaches up a little hand to blindly clutch at her hair. When he snuffles and grunts in his cot, spit bubbling between sleep-glossed lips. When she rocks him on her shoulder and breathes in the clean, milky-sweet scent of his scalp.

But it is only that—a glimpse—before the door quickly swings shut, and Michael is just another baby again, crying and hungry, demanding everything she has to give and then more. Exhausting doesn't begin to cover it. When Casey sleeps, she dreams of drowning in granite, throat thick with gravel as she battles to pull herself free from the endless press of stone.

Yvonne tells her not to force matters.

Every mother's different. She'll find her own way.

***

The dog's barking wakes her. No, there's no dog, remember? Casey lies still in the dream-addled darkness, listening. There's nothing, just the shallow rasp of her own breath.

Wait. There's *nothing*.

"Michael?" She half rolls, half lurches from her bed. In its place by the window, the crib sits empty, the full moon streaming a searchlight onto the bare mattress. Her stomach seizes. Where the hell is the baby?

Elsewhere in the house, a floorboard creaks.

"Yvonne?" she calls softly, stepping into the hall. "Do you have Michael?"

The front door is standing open, but the tall, broad-shouldered figure silhouetted in its frame isn't Yvonne.

"Hello, love," Neil says, holding the blanket-wrapped baby to his chest. "Found you."

Casey falls back against the wall, skin prickling with gooseflesh. "H-how..."

"You girls should be more careful. Leaving your doors unlocked at night, anyone could just walk in." He glances down at the blanket-wrapped bundle in his arms. "Those photos didn't do him justice, Casey. Needed to see for myself."

She shakes her head, confused. "I didn't send you photos."

"Aw, Casey." Neil smiles, that sad *poor-dumb-girl* smile she knows too well. "Did you think I'd forget about you so soon? You stayed dark a while, I'll give you that, but as soon as your phone came online again, my spyware picked up everything... You can imagine my surprise."

"Please, Neil." Casey's voice trembles. "Please don't hurt him."

"Hurt him? Why would I hurt my own flesh and blood?"

Moving slowly, cautiously, as though she's approaching a wild animal likely to startle, Casey begins to make her way down the hall. "Let me have him, Neil." She reaches out. "Please, just give me my baby." Maybe it's the sound of her voice, or maybe it's the less than expert way Neil is holding him, but Michael chooses that moment to rouse from slumber and test the strength of his vocal cords.

"See what you've done," Neil growls.

"He's hungry, he wants to be fed."

"I'll get him some formula on the way home."

Casey is less than a metre from the door now, calculating her next move, but his words freeze her to the spot. "I don't—I don't understand."

"He's my son, Casey, and I'm taking him."

"No!"

Unthinking, she launches herself forward. Neil turns and shoulders her into the doorjamb, before grabbing a hank of hair and pulling her head back so hard she fears her spine will snap. She's forgotten how quick he is, how strong. "Don't make me hurt you," he says, right in her ear. Michael is wailing now, and Casey claws at the fingers tangled in her hair, desperate to free herself, to free her son.

"Let her go!"

Yvonne, dear god, Yvonne. Standing halfway down the hall, .22 rifle braced against her shoulder.

Neil actually laughs. Then he pushes Casey, hard, bounces her forehead off the jamb and throws her toward Yvonne. For an age, she lies curled on the hall runner, clutching her head and trying to force the rising tide of nausea back down into her guts. Blackness threatens at the edges of her vision, but she will not pass out, she will not pass out, she will not—

"Casey, get up." Yvonne hauls her to her feet and over to the door.

Neil is standing at the bottom of the steps. He still has Michael, whose cries have subsided into pitiful sobs.

"Hand that baby over," Yvonne yells. She points the rifle at him.

"Not going to happen," he says.

"I've already called the police."

"Really?" He reaches into his pocket and pulls out a small rectangular shape. "You have another phone?"

Yvonne swears under her breath.

"Your ute's going to need a service too," he says. "Wouldn't drive it in that state."

Casey's head is pounding, pain radiating out from her forehead in concentrated waves. Blood runs down her face, dripping into her eyes, and she's finding it hard to focus. "Shoot him," she whispers. "Shoot the fucker and be done." There's a rage building inside her, new and bold and ravenous. Maybe this is what she had in her room the whole time.

Yvonne is quiet for a minute. Then she lowers the rifle. "I can't. I might miss."

"Good girl," Neil sneers. "You listen, Casey. He's my son and he's going home with me. You do anything about it—either of you—and I'll make the rest of your existence a living hell. You know me, Casey. You know I can." He takes a step backward, then another. "I'll give him a good life, Casey. Better than you ever could."

No. Not if she has a single breath left in her body.

But Yvonne is holding her back, the woman's unexpectedly strong arms wrapped tight about her waist, and she's not letting go no matter how hard Casey thrashes. *Shhh, Casey-bear, let him leave.* No, no, she can't, she won't—but *Shhh*, Yvonne says again, *look. Look where he's headed.*

Casey stops struggling.

There's no doubt this time, no trick of light or memory: the rocks have moved.

Neil's parked his car a fair distance away, maybe so the sound of its engine wouldn't wake them, or maybe because there are a few dozen large mounds of granite now clumped along the normally clear drive. Did they seek to prevent his trespass or only congregate afterward, sinister moonlit sentries easing shut their trap? As he steps among them, he pauses and looks around. Puzzled? Worried? Casey holds her breath.

Then the rocks—close in.

She gets barely a glimpse before Yvonne's fingers dig sharply into her chin, wrench her head around. *Don't watch; there are things you don't want to see. Things they don't want you to see.* The older woman presses her brow hard against Casey's and the resurgent pain all but takes her knees out from under her. From up the drive comes the sound of stone grinding against stone as well as softer, wetter things, and of Neil, bellowing in shock and agony.

When Michael begins to keen, his tiny, terrified shrieks pitch so high Casey thinks her heart will shatter into a thousand shards. She tries to wrestle away from Yvonne, but the woman's hands curve around the back of Casey's neck, holding firm.

Trust me, Casey-bear. Please, please trust me.

She sobs, nails digging into Yvonne's flesh. Her baby, her son. Oh god, *her son.* Somewhere deep in her core, right at the molten quick of her being, a door doesn't so much open as get blown off its hinges. She will do anything for Michael. She will kill for him.

She will die for him.

And may the wrath of all the gods who ever were rain down upon any creature who dares stand in her path.

"Go," Yvonne says, releasing her grip at last. "It's done."

Casey runs. Down the steps and up the drive to where Neil last stood, her son in his arms. At first she sees nothing, no blood, no...pieces, just bare dirt and grass at the base of huge granite slabs that might have stood in that spot for millennia.

"Give him back," she yells, thumping the nearest with the flat of her fist. It hurts, satisfyingly so, and she strikes the rock again, and again. "Give—me—back—my—son!" Then she hears it: a soft cry, a familiar burble, and Casey hauls herself around to the other side of the boulder, following those dear, dear sounds until—there he is, oh god, nestled in a hollow curve of granite that might have been custom-carved, so perfectly it cradles his tiny, precious form.

She picks the baby up, hugs him so tight to her chest that he starts to wriggle in protest.

"Shhh," she says. "It's all right, everything's all right. I'm here."

The blood on his blanket scares her until she realises it's her own, still leaking from the gash in her forehead. Another drop falls as she checks him over, sliding thick and viscous down his cheek until she catches it with her thumb, wipes it on the rock she's leaning against.

The dark stain vanishes almost immediately.

Casey narrows her eyes. "Haven't you had enough?" She pauses, then runs her palm across the sticky mess of her forehead and presses it against the rough granite surface. It doesn't leave a full handprint; two and a half fingers are missing, but she doesn't think that matters.

It's slower this time, the seep of blood into stone. More deliberate.

An acknowledgement of sorts.

"Thank you," Casey whispers. She isn't sure she trusts them, not really, but good manners never go astray. In her arms, Michael is starting to fret, his happy-time burbles switching gear into feed me, feed me now.

"Casey-bear?" Yvonne limps into view, her worry-drawn face softening once she spots them.

"We're safe," Casey tells her. "But you knew we would be."

Breathing hard, the older woman rests her back against the granite, patting its flank the way she might stroke one of her goats. Lifting her gaze to the setting moon, she sighs. "Best get back to the house. It's getting close to morning and there'll be a lot of cleaning up to do tomorrow. Some fancy stories to spin."

She reaches out a blood-grimed hand and Casey takes it, hauls herself to her feet. Michael starts to cry and Casey can feel it now, the line drawn between them arrow-straight and stronger than stone. Stronger even than *these* stones.

"Did you see?" Casey asks, as they make their careful way along the drive.

Yvonne shakes her head. "I never see anything."

PUBLICATION HISTORY

"Smile for Me"—Redsine No.6 (2001)

"Cold"—Shadowed Realms No.9 (2006)

"Painlessness"—Greatest Uncommon Denominator No.2 (2008)

"She Said"—Scenes from the Second Storey (Morrigan Books, 2010)

"Monsters Among Us"—Macabre (Brimstone Press, 2010)

"We All Fall Down"—Aurealis No.44 (2010)

"Frostbitten"—More Scary Kisses (Ticonderoga Publications, 2011)

"Caution: Contains Small Parts"—Caution: Contains Small Parts (Twelfth Planet Press, 2013)

"The Home for Broken Dolls"—Caution: Contains Small Parts (Twelfth Planet Press, 2013)

"Mary, Mary"—Cranky Ladies of History (FableCroft, 2015)

"Self, Contained"—The Dark (Issue 10, November 2015)

"Accidents Happen"—In Your Face (FableCroft, 2016)

"Triquetra"—Tor.com (Sept 2018)

"Hard Places" is original to this collection

AUTHOR NOTES

Warning! If you have turned to this section without first reading the stories that precede it, please turn back. These are endnotes for a reason: here be spoilers!

SHE SAID

I wrote "She Said" in 2009 for a high-concept anthology, *Scenes from the Second Storey*, conceived by Mark Deniz of Morrigan Books. The brief was very specific—each author in the collection was sent a track from the album *Scenes from the Second Storey* by US rock band The God Machine, and asked to create a story inspired by that song. When I accepted the invitation, I hadn't heard the album or anything else by the band—and to be honest, this remains the case—so I was intrigued and apprehensive in equal measure. What if I didn't like the song, or the music? What if it sparked nothing in me? I needn't have worried.

I'd been carrying half a story around in my pocket for a while, waiting to find the rest of the pieces I needed to put it together. It was about art and muses — masochistic muses to be precise, muses who literally give their entire selves to those they inspire — and it was very, very dark. Too dark, in fact; it was flat and black and textureless. The lyrics to the song "She Said" reminded me to let in some light, because you can't see the shadows without it. The last three lines of the song resonated most strongly—look it up on YouTube and you'll hear why. Lightness and darkness: the choice Mallory is powerless to make; the responsibility Josh refuses to accept.

Unexpectedly, "She Said" also turned out to be the most autobiographical story I've ever written, though not in any of the ways you'd likely expect. 2009 was a year of personal turmoil and major emotional realignment, and a lot of that got ploughed into the earth while writing this piece, emerging in mutated, barely recognisable form. I'm generally not the "writing as catharsis" type—things usually take a lot longer to percolate before making it anywhere near an angry page—but this story? This story was catharsis on overdrive, raw and unabashed. For that reason, it will always be a favoured child, if a feared one.

MONSTERS AMONG US

This story was published in 2010 in the landmark anthology of Australian horror fiction, *Macabre*, edited by Angela Challis and Marty Young. But I wrote it seven years earlier than that, making it one of the oldest pieces in this collection in terms of the actual creation date. Reading it now, I see the influence of Poppy Z. Brite, Kathe Koja and, most intimately, Caitlín R. Kiernan—all authors I cannot recommend highly enough, all of whom I'm sure most readers of my work will know at least by name. I also note the bower-birding of the minor details from my life that I habitually weave into my fiction, which makes reading old work sometime feel like reading old journals (which I only sporadically keep these days): the nail polish Elise uses on Fledge was mine, as was the bird skull ring Fledge contemplates buying; Gown of Thorns was a beloved Melbourne goth boutique I frequented at the time (sadly now defunct along with that glorious Gothic institution, Mortisha's); and, of course, the expensive Ambroise Paré book was one I stumbled across and bought in Borders (also now defunct).

It is not good that monsters should live among us, is a line I marked in my own copy of the book—but carefully, lightly, in pencil, Elise!—and one that mid-wifed this story, the image of the Humbug-thing spilling into my head late one night while I tried to sleep, the scene in the bottle-shop, the green liquor that looked and smelled like, but definitely wasn't, absinthe. "Monsters Among Us" is a love-letter to the Melbourne that was and the gothic subculture in which I was immersed at the time—and still am, to some extent, although I mostly *just can't* with the makeup, corsets and platform boots these days. I've also been carrying another story about Fledge around in my pockets ever since, or half a story anyway. Fledge all grown up, now a monster-hunter with scars of her own. She gets older, as I get older, but her story doesn't yet feel ready to be told. Maybe one day it will be there waiting for me, sharp and insistent. I would like to run into Fledge again and see what she's done with her life. Or what she's done to the lives of others.

CAUTION: CONTAINS SMALL PARTS

I was honoured to be included in the *Twelve Planets* series of micro-collections published by Twelfth Planet Press, and this is the titular story in my volume published in 2013. If there was an explicit theme to that book, it would be that all the pieces were concerned with haunted people of some kind. Around 2010 or so, I went through a ghost story patch: lots of ideas flitting through my brain, a few of the better ones written into stories. A well-established trope of Gothic horror, ghosts remain rich and full of resonance for me—both as a reader and a writer—and there seems no end to the variety of ways in which we can imagine, interpret and interrogate them. They are, quite literally, the past pushing into the present, refusing to sit down and shut up, reminding us of everything we drag along behind us as we live our lives ... and as we end them. I don't think I'll ever get tired of reading really good, intelligent, emotive ghost stories. Ever. And if a particularly good idea drifts across my internal creative landscape, you better believe I'm going to grab it with both hands and try my best to pin it down on the page.

"Caution: Contains Small Parts" was one of those. It took a few months to work out the precise mechanics the story needed—who was being haunted, and for what reason. It was tricky, getting the balance right and making damned sure that the piece didn't come off as anti-abortion. It's not and, for the record, neither am I. The last thing I wanted was for Melanie to shoulder any blame; this might be my "abortion ghost story", as I dubbed it long before deciding on a title, but it isn't about revenge. If there's culpability to share around it's not because a woman had an abortion, it's because she felt she didn't have any other option, because she was coerced, all but forced into it, and that's the tragedy.

Unlike much of my fiction, this story was written very quickly once I had the mechanics in place. A week or so of near consecutive writing sessions and it was finished. Each night, before sleep found me, I would plan out what needed to happen in the next scene, and then the next evening I would write that scene. I didn't get stuck once. Unexpected textual turns threw no curve balls; instead, they added depth to the narrative in that spectacular way that makes every writer wonder, "Where the hell did *that* come from?" Sometimes, stories are blessed in that way. I offered it up to my crit group once it was done, tidied up some copy edits following their suggestions, and then, just as I was considering where to submit it for publication, the

Twelve Planets invitation dropped into my inbox. Sometimes, stories are blessed in *that* way too.

PAINLESSNESS

The idea for this story germinated from reading about certain, often fatal, medical conditions that result in a person being unable to feel pain. What might you be able to do if pain was no barrier, I wondered, do or have done to you? Not if you couldn't be harmed, couldn't be made to bleed, but if you simply didn't feel it. "Painlessness" was the result. When I began to write the story, I didn't have all the pieces, and my intention was that Mara genuinely would not experience the pain of what she went through. Somewhere along the way, I realised that she did feel it, every single blow and cut, every moment of trauma as her body was undone and subsequently knitted itself back together—and this realisation made it a much, much darker piece. Writing it felt different to my previous work in a weird, ill-defined way that I still cannot clearly articulate. It felt like I had levelled up somehow, as a writer, that I had finally arrived at a place that was *mine.* It was also my first story to win awards—including the Aurealis I had coveted since I began writing horror—and the first to be reprinted, mostly recently in Ellen Datlow's *Body Shocks* anthology (2021).

A few years after "Painlessness" was published, a writing buddy pulled me aside at a gathering to tell me about a case they'd come across, relayed by a social worker friend. A female sex worker, homeless and with a history of substance abuse, would once every few months allow paying clients to physically assault her to the extent that she wound up in hospital for a few days. Clean bed, regular food, medical attention. Like Mara, she felt every blow and cut. It didn't surprise me that there are people who would pay to do this to a woman—and I don't mean in a healthy, consensual BDSM way—but it sickened me to think about a person in such desperate straits that she felt it a viable option, her only option perhaps. Truth is not only stranger than fiction, it can be far more horrific.

And to answer the observant reader's question: no, Faith is not Fledge/Faith from "Monsters Among Us", but damn if girls with that name don't get some rough treatment in my work.

WE ALL FALL DOWN

Another ghost story, although it didn't start out that way. It was going to be a weird dollhouse story about a couple riding out the end of their relationship, getting stranded in an old Victorian that contained a detailed replica of itself, and becoming trapped inside the dollhouse, inside the house, inside their crumbling marriage, forever. Fun times! Only none of the pieces would fit together properly, no matter how many times I rearranged the furniture. The dynamic between the couple—originally a man and a woman—felt forced; the narrative trite and overworked. I almost abandoned the idea several times but something kept tugging at me. When I considered crafting the story around two women instead, Emma and Holly sprang to life in all their fractious, heartbreaking glory, and I realised the dollhouse was a decoy—at first for me and now, if I could manage it, for my readers. Let's face it, after M. Night Shyamalan's masterful *The Sixth Sense*, it's damn tough to pull off a tale where *the protagonist was a ghost all along*. Hopefully, I've done the concept justice and, like its cinematic antecedent, "We All Fall Down" will transform into quite a different story on a second encounter.

I think I still have a weird dollhouse story to write someday. I'm fascinated by them, especially the meticulous, scale replicas made from scratch by obsessive artisans, period perfect down to the handmade wallpaper and doorknobs, with functional electrical lighting and looks-good-enough-to-eat food all laid out on tiny tables. Either a story to write, or a dollhouse to build—and the story might be the better option for my sanity!

TRIQUETRA

In 2014, I began working on a PhD in creative writing with a research focus on retold fairy tales and female friendship. It would take me six years to finish, which was almost twice as long as I initially planned, but life and health and other obstacles do tend to get in the way of schedules. The creative component of the thesis is a collection of novelettes, each one a sequel to a well-known fairy tale, and "Triquetra" is my take on what happened to a young princess who ate a poisoned apple, and to the stepmother who gave it to her. Of all the tales, I knew "Snow White" was one I could not avoid retelling and, being the last novelette written for the thesis, it had long loomed over the project. Thanks largely to Disney, it's one of the blockbusters, if not *the* blockbuster, and it was also a tale that both attracted and repelled me when I was a girl. It's the mirror, is what it is. I have always hated that damned mirror, hated and feared it, but it was only as a grown woman that I could begin to articulate the gross misogyny of its manipulations. I wanted to see Snow White as a grown woman too, smart and resourceful, if still wounded, and a protective mother to her own daughter. I wanted to offer redemption to the Wicked Queen, without excusing her inexcusable acts, to see what she might do if given the chance to make amends. But most of all I wanted to see that mirror dead, shattered into a thousand poison-tongued shards. Unfortunately, I don't think it is dead, not entirely. But let's hope it takes many millennia to put itself back together.

The story was nameless for some time, with working titles such as "Flight" (discarded due to a magnificent fairy-tale retelling by Angela Slatter bearing that name), "Red as Blood" (too obvious) and "My Stupid Snow White Story" (um, yeah) not quite fitting. When Ellen Datlow accepted it for Tor.com, I had to come up with something quick. "Triquetra," I told Ellen at last. "It is a maiden/mother/crone story after all—might as well be explicit about it." And, having named it, I now can't imagine it as anything else. If, by the way, "Triquetra" has piqued your interest in gothic fairy-tale retellings, all seven novelettes are being—or have been, depending on when you're reading this!—published by Brain Jar Press, both separately and as the collection *Never Afters*.

SELF, CONTAINED

This is one of those magical stories that slunk into my mind in that liminal time before falling asleep, triggered by a noise outside the window that I suspected was one of the neighbourhood cats prowling the driveway. Despite a council curfew, many people seem to let their pet cats out at all hours where I live—and it makes me furious. I adore cats, have always kept cats, but I value birds and other wildlife as well and cats are consummate predators. PSA: Please, *please* don't let your beloved felines out after dusk or before dawn. They'll live longer, and so will other animals in the environment. Anyway, "Self, Contained" padded in late one night, curled around my brain a couple of times before stretching into a story that I sat down and wrote largely in one sitting the next day, which rarely happens.

There are two odd, unexpected influences from my early life that are mixed up in this tale, elements clearly plucked from my subconscious as I lay in bed, scenes spooling out on top of each other. The first is a Dr Seuss book called *A Fish Out of Water*, written by Helen Palmer Geisel, that was a favourite when I was a child. A young boy overfeeds his new pet fish, explicitly against instructions, and it grows, and grows, and keeps growing, needing ever larger containers of water until it finally ends up in a municipal swimming pool. The other is a dark, gut-punch of a poem whose final lines lodged like splinters in my heart when I first read them around age twelve. "A Case of Murder" by Vernon Scannell tells of a nine-year-old boy who maltreats and not-quite-accidentally kills the family cat, then hides its corpse in a basement cupboard where it remains for many years, nourished by guilt and fear. The boy will have nowhere to hide, we are told, "When the cupboard swells and all sides split/And the huge black cat pads out of it." I find the machinations of creativity and the unconscious endlessly fascinating—to think, after all these years, those splinters finally worked their way free.

Titles are my Achille's heel, by the way. I either have them around the time I first conceive a story or it's like pulling teeth. The 'working' title of this poor tale was "The Inflatable Cat" right up until the first time I submitted it, and I didn't come up with "Self, Contained" until after the first rejection. I *am* rather partial to punctuation in story titles, I have to admit; search engine optimisation be damned.

SMILE FOR ME

The oldest story in the collection, in terms of both creation (1998) and publication date (2001), and I can see so much influence from the early work of Kathe Koja in it. Reading Koja in the late 1990s (*The Cipher, Bad Brains, Skin, Strange Angels*) was a revelation to me as a young female writer trying to find a footing in the horror genre, in particular her style and the slippery, elegant, frenetic energy of her prose. In her fiction, Koja returns again and again to the subject of art, artists and art-marking of all kinds—a topic which observant readers will have noted also interests me deeply. She remains one of my very, very favourite writers and a continuing, although these days perhaps a more subtle, influence on my work.

Morgan and Dante from "Smile for Me" also made walk-on appearances in my first novel, *Madigan Mine*. I needed a bolshie artist and a pretentious gallery owner for a scene and they were still hanging around with nothing better to do with their time. Chronology wise, it means that the short story probably takes place concurrently with the novel, or maybe slightly afterwards, and I love the idea that Morgan and Madigan—two very problematic, psychologically fraught and ethically challenged women—get to meet one another, however briefly. That was meant to be it for Dante, though—he was never much more than a caricature with an over-inflated sense of self. But when I needed another gallery owner for my second novel, *Perfections*, he applied for the part. He pretty much stormed in and stole the part, actually, and he became so much more than a caricature in the process. I suspect we're not done with each other, Dante and me, although I don't know yet what the next part in his story will be. He might be done with galleries, though, considering what happened in *Perfections*.

FROSTBITTEN

Growing up, our fridge was one of those 1970s models with an exposed cooling element that accumulated a tempting coat of frost, which my younger sisters and I delighted in scraping off with our fingers and eating. I don't know why, since it tasted kind of funny and metallic, but eat it we did. Our exasperated mother always warned us never to actually *lick* the element but I was (and remain) a deeply contrary child and one evening that was precisely what I did. Unfortunately, I can make no claim to being too young to know better—I can't remember my age at the time but I was tall enough to reach the element in the back of the fridge without standing on a chair, so I'd say at least twelve. It was an act done on impulse, and I realised immediately that I had just made a very grave mistake: fingers are dry; mouths are not. My lips and tongue stuck instantly to the element and when I tried to pull away, I could feel at least one or two layers of skin threatening to stay behind. Luckily, I wasn't stuck there for too long—my muffled cries drew the attention of one of my sisters, who ran and alerted my parents. Hot water sprayed all over the element and my face did the trick, with only minimal frostburn and blisters for my trouble, although the incident became a favourite story to retell around the table at large family gatherings for many years afterward. You can imagine how delighted teenage Kirstyn was with that.

To this day, I can bodily recall the sensation of being stuck to that frozen element, so cold it felt like burning, and the sickening feeling of my skin about to separate from my flesh. Years and years later, I had a dream the waking remnants of which turned into "Frostbitten": two lovers, their flesh grown so cold the sweat from their exertions had frozen their bodies together; I knew just how it would feel when they pulled themselves apart. It's a dark story, written for an anthology of erotic horror that turned out lighter and more romantic than I had expected. I'm still not sure "Frostbitten" was a good fit for that book, but it definitely belongs in this one.

Side note: the use of Nina and Simone as the first names of the characters has no relation to the name of the powerful singer/songwriter, Nina Simone, except that my subconscious threw them up as names that sounded "right" together. Thanks subconscious, great work. A friend in my critique group pointed it out afterwards, asking if there was a deeper meaning, and by then it felt too weird to rename my characters. Nina is *Nina.* Simone is *Simone.* It's not the first time it's happened—I once had characters called "Billy" and "Zane" in another piece, but caught that early enough to remedy!

THE HOME FOR BROKEN DOLLS

The final work in *Caution: Contains Small Parts,* this novella was unwritten when I signed on to the *Twelve Planets* series. It was an idea that had been rattling around for a couple of years—less an idea than the spark of something I knew I wanted to write about in some way. Real Dolls. Once it became a Promised Thing, I dove headfirst down a rabbit-hole of research that proved both labyrinthine and bottomless, from which I did not emerge for twelve months or more. Normally, I like the research aspect of writing and go about it in an efficient, targeted way. Not so in this case. I bought books, downloaded documentaries, and perused more websites than I care to think about. I drilled down through *50+ pages* on Google searches, chasing links. I followed tangents away from the core of my story on the flimsiest pretext. And I bent the ears of way too many indulgent friends and acquaintances with revelations of some of the skeeviest stuff I turned up. In short, I became obsessed with my research ... which, when you consider that "The Home for Broken Dolls" is itself concerned with sex doll obsession, starts to get meta. I did stop short at buying a second-hand Real Doll. But only just.

Even after I started to actually write, the research continued almost until the end. At one point, after searching for a particular kind of website which I knew had to be out there, but really hoped was not, I stumbled across a gallery of images that had me sitting in furious, horrified, validated tears on my office floor. It was enough. It was too much. My head was full and I needed to sort through it all and decide exactly what did and didn't belong in the story. I wrote "The Home for Broken Dolls" in fits and starts over the next year and it significantly changed my writing style. There was a hard word-limit of 20,000 and once I clocked 8,000 and realised I wasn't even a quarter of the way through the story, I panicked. Just a little. Then I picked myself up, sat myself down and stripped those 8,000 back as brutally as I could, removing every single word I could get away with and still make sense. Which became standard operating procedure for writing the rest of the novella. I'd write a scene one session, then pare it right back the next time before allowing myself to continue the narrative, scrapping proposed plot elements ruthlessly. One thing about such sparse writing: it gives you nowhere to hide. Which is exhilarating and terrifying all at the same time. I love this novella, I love Jane and I love my fierce, beautiful dolls. It was worth every bit of research I did—even the bits I didn't end up using. And all these years later, the dolls haven't gone away, haven't faded as is usually the case once I've finished a piece. Maybe this means I'm not done with them, or they're not done with me. Same difference. "The Home for Broken Dolls" was a short story that became a novella, but maybe what it really wants to be is a novel ...

COLD

This was the first piece of flash fiction I ever wrote and it was a genuine challenge not only to find an idea that I could keep to under 1,000 words but then to write to that limit. Despite the fact that my first novel and, more recently, my PhD novelettes are written in first person point of view, it's not my preference. Third person direct is where I generally tend to play but some stories demand a more intimate narration and "Cold" came to me with its voice intact. I had read, several years before, a fragment of an interview with a man imprisoned for the murder of a young girl. Not only was he unrepentant, he confessed a certain pleasure in contemplating the renewed grief her parents must feel each year on her birthday when she is no longer there with them to celebrate. It was such a vile yet petty addendum to the awful crime he had committed, and I found myself thinking that Christmas must be even worse—a birthday is personal, but everyone and everything around you seems to be celebrating at Christmas. And what if it wasn't just a child's absence that you were mourning that day, but the anniversary of their death? Because what if that's precisely what their murderer planned? The Worst Possible Place is where my mind goes to wander a lot of the time, which is likely a trait I share with a lot of writers of dark fiction. It's where this story came from, and many more besides.

While it's getting a little long in the tooth now, "Cold" is still one of my go-to reading pieces. It comes in at under 10 minutes for an entire story, the first-person POV works as a dramatic monologue, and the ending never fails to creep the audience out. Although it's probably not a good thing that every time I read it, I find myself feeling just a fraction more empathy for the narrator.

MARY, MARY

When I was invited to submit a short story for the *Cranky Ladies of History* anthology, edited by Tehani (Wessely) Croft and Tansy Rayner Roberts, I immediately thought of Mary Wollstonecraft, 18th century feminist writer, philosopher, historian and author of *A Vindication of the Rights of Women* in which she put forward the highly controversial argument that women are not naturally inferior to men. Shock! Horror! Mary was also the mother of Mary Shelley, author of *Frankenstein*, although she never knew her daughter. The birth was complicated, the doctor rushed, and sterility not really a thing. Her death by sepsis was horrendous and prolonged. I have exaggerated nothing for dramatic effect; if anything, some elements have been omitted. But her life, oh her life! I will admit to not knowing all that much about Mary Wollstonecraft before deciding to write this story, only what I remembered from reading her work at university many years before. She had struck me as being an exceedingly cranky and fascinating lady, and I originally planned to draw bolder connections between her and her more famous daughter, but the more I researched Mary Wollstonecraft, the more she took over. She had a way of taking over things when she was alive as well.

Mary Wollstonecraft was an intelligent, resourceful, stubborn, demanding, passionate, contrary and deeply complex woman who accomplished many great things and who also made so many ridiculous decisions in her life I often wanted to reach back through the centuries and shake some sense into her. I haven't embellished the facts of her life, although I naturally had to jettison much biographical detail. If your interest has been piqued, I encourage you to read more about her life, and to read her work as well.

I've been asked about the Grey Lady several times. Is she a guardian angel of some kind? Is she Death come to watch her crop grow before the harvest? In truth, I never formed a conclusion about her through the entire process of writing "Mary, Mary". I merely considered her a watcher, an observer. Out of place, out of time, holder of some knowledge but not all, and powerless to intervene—for the most part, at least. Above all, she was fascinated with her chosen subject, half in love and fighting more than a measure of frustration in the role of witness. In retrospect, the more I think about it, the more I suspect the Grey Lady might have been me all along. Although I will have it noted for the record that I have not, and will never, consume a wasp.

ACCIDENTS HAPPEN

A musician friend of mine once recounted an incident where she had been walking home from shopping one summer afternoon and the too-loose, elasticised skirt she was wearing slipped off her hips and fell to the ground. Her hands full of bags, she hadn't the time to grab it. There was a man nearby who saw and made some light-hearted comment which, while not intended to be nasty or mocking, only heightened her embarrassment. She was laughing when she told me the story, and it *was* funny—she's a great storyteller—but the first weird thought in my brain was, "What if the man *made* it happen?" That grand *What If* moment—source of so much fiction, especially of the speculative kind. I knew instantly the type of person he would be, how and why he would use this newfound power. The story unfolded rather quickly but arrived at an ending that was trite and unsatisfying, one I couldn't find a way around, so it remained unwritten, and largely forgotten, for several years. Then one night I was out at a pub, watching a band that same musician friend was in at the time, and the memory of her skirt anecdote resurfaced. I'd recently been asked to contribute to an anthology and had been kicking around a couple of concepts with no real luck in coming up with a story, but this old idea suddenly stuck up its hand. *What if I end this like*, it ventured, dropping the final scene into my lap. Sometimes, you just have to be patient like that with stories, give them the time and space to mature in the depths of your subconscious. Often, they'll die and rot in the ground, sure, but sometimes you end up with a piece that's better—and so terribly worse—than you ever thought it could be.

HARD PLACES

The most recent story in this collection, "Hard Places" is also the last piece of fiction I wrote before the COVID-19 pandemic—almost a year before, to be precise. I had submitted my PhD thesis and was waiting for its return from the examiners, and I just wanted to write something contemporary in the small window of time I had before revisions, something that wasn't about a damn fairy tale! I'd had the opening of this story in my head for a while—two women, sitting on a porch overlooking a paddock full of granite rocks that seemed to be both pushing up from and scattered across the hills, joking (or not) about how they seemed to move. I didn't know what the story was for a long time, but I could picture that scene so clearly and felt that the rocks were at once territorial and protective. Keepers. Guardians. Guard dogs? I still can't say where the rest of it came from, Casey and Yvonne and the goats, but when it did, it came fast and was written in less than a month. I passed it to a writer friend to check over the pregnancy and birth material, having had personal experience of neither myself, then tweaked it with some of her suggestions—thanks, Deb, though not so much for the nightmares spawned by some of your anecdotes!—and I was done. Really and truly done, actually. After this piece, I didn't really write any more fiction, or much of anything else, for over a year. Bumping straight out of PhD-land and straight into Pandemic-ville put my creativity on ice for longer than I was planning, so "Hard Places"—both the story and the collection that bears its name—marks a clear and interesting demarcation. Most of my contemporary fiction is set in the here and now, tweaked perhaps or knocked off-centre with some speculative element or another, but broadly informed by what is happening in the world. So, while I don't see myself writing a lot of fiction explicitly *about* the pandemic, I'm not going to be able to escape its influence on my work and I'm keen to discover what that will look like. I have a feeling that post-pandemic Kirstyn is going to be quite a different writer, for so many reasons.

ACKNOWLEDGMENTS

ANY ARTWORK OWES its existence to a number of people other than its creator. For a collection of short fiction written and published over two decades, it is an impossible task to recall every person who assisted, by means large or small, with the stories that form this book you now hold in your hands. To anyone I've forgotten to mention, please know that my heart remembers you with gratitude.

Thank you to all the editors and publishers who saw these stories into print, especially in the early years when I was still finding my feet: Mark Deniz, Angela Challis, Tehani Croft, Ellen Datlow, Russell B. Farr, Kaolin Fire, Liz Gryzb, Talie Helene, Trent Jamieson, Stephen Jones, Pete Kempshall, Alisa Krasnostein, Stuart Mayne, Amanda Pillar, Tansy Rayner Roberts, Dirk Strasser, Sean Wallace, and Marty Young. Your encouragement was invaluable and I'm honoured to note that many of you have become my friends. My thanks also to the numerous other editors and publishers who have given my short fiction a home over the years and who have helped me to become a better writer.

The speculative fiction community has been my home for almost as long as I have been writing fiction, and it's full of the most wonderful, talented, passionate, generous and exuberant human beings you would ever want to know. I've forged deep and lasting connections here—friends, colleagues, crit buddies and even a pesky husband—and it's a community in which I have always felt valued and supported, and to which I hope I have made a significant contribution in return. Thank you especially to the SuperNOVA critique group, beneath whose critical gaze many of these stories were tested before ever venturing out into the world, and thanks as well to my other writer and non-writer friends who kindly read early drafts and offered feedback. Twenty years is a long time, people; there are too many names to list here.

And yet, there are some that cannot be left unmentioned.

"Triquetra" was written as part of a doctoral thesis that occupied a good six years of my life, during which my supervisory team, Linda Wight, Nike Sulway and Threasa Meads, helped keep me sane and ensure that the fiction I was writing was the very best it could be.

Angela Slatter, who semi-regularly kicks my butt over neglected writerly business and without whom this collection would absolutely not exist. I still cannot read her marvellous introduction without blushing.

Scarlett R. Algee, who made a home for this book in the Trepidatio stable, and who has been the most understanding and delightful person to work with during these Most Interesting of Covid Times.

Ellen Gregory and Deb Kalin, two of the smartest, kindest, funniest, and wisest women I know and brutally straight shooters when they need to be. Thank you from the bottom of my heart for your friendship, love and support. It means everything.

Ian Mond, one of my oldest and dearest friends, and fellow aficionado of our oft-maligned horror genre. Thank you for always having my back and for knowing when to call me on my melodramatic bullshit.

My mother, Cornelia, who has been reading my work since the beginning—the very beginning, when I was cobbling together unpublishable monstrosities that no soul shall ever lay eyes upon again—and who never lets me get away with a damn thing. Still. I love you, Mum.

Jason Nahrung, my husband and fellow scribe and eagle-eyed proof-reader. I know how lucky I am to have you in my life, dearheart. Even with the proliferation of puns.

And, last but far from least, all of you out there who have ever read my work: thank you, thank you, thank you. Without readers, we write in a vacuum, building circuits that can never be completed. Readers, you honour me with your time, that most precious and finite of resources. I promise, it's not something I will ever take for granted.

ABOUT THE AUTHOR

KIRSTYN MCDERMOTT has been working in the darker alleyways of speculative fiction for much of her career. She is the author of two award-winning novels, *Madigan Mine* and *Perfections*, and a collection of short fiction, *Caution: Contains Small Parts*. Her stories and poetry have been published in various magazines, journals and anthologies, with her most recent work being *Never Afters*, a series of novellas that retell classic fairy tales, and *Hard Places*, a collection of her best short fiction. She holds a PhD in creative writing with a research focus on re-visioned fairy tales and produces and co-hosts a literary discussion podcast, *The Writer and the Critic*. Kirstyn lives in Ballarat, Australia, with fellow writer Jason Nahrung and two distinctly non-literary felines. She can be found online at www.kirstynmcdermott.com.